Revealed Mercy

A Journey into the Tower of Trust

Eve M. Harrell

To Tony,

Every day is an adventure with you.
Thank you for choosing to journey with me.

I love you.

Table of Contents

Prologue

May 6
Baldersville, Georgia

Michael opened his eyes to darkness. "Oof," he muttered, holding his throbbing head as he shivered against the cold, damp floor. Memories danced with consciousness as he tried to remember how he ended up *here*. A deafening silence filled the room until he heard the distant sound of footsteps. He recognized the heavy thud of brown combat boots on concrete as they drew closer. Suddenly, the footsteps stopped feet from his aching body. The heavy metal door before him swung open, and bright light spilled through, attacking any semblance of hope he had for relief. Squinting, he looked up at the towering silhouette breaking the light's path in his cell.

"Get up," the man commanded, his voice a deep growl echoing in the small, confined space.

Blinking to adjust his gaze, Michael asked, "Who are you?"

"Don't concern yourself with trivial things, Bagman. The CO has summoned you. Don't make me tell you again. Get up."

As Michael attempted to stand, light illuminated what he hoped he would never see. Tales of this windowless room swirled through the compound. *"Never, ever find yourself in The Dark Room,"* people would say. *"You don't come out the same way you went in,"* others would claim. A sudden wave of nausea overwhelmed him as the grimy gray floor appeared to move.

Glancing at the concrete wall to his side, Michael trembled as he read the illuminated words, "I want to go home," written in a dull shade of red.

Tapping his watch, the agent said, "Come on, Bagman. The CO does not wait for anyone."

Reluctantly following the man, he immediately recognized the tattoo on the neck of the Agent-in-Place, or AIP, as he was called. Once upon a time, Michael longed for the respect this man received due to his station. Personally, he regretted the name "Bagman" given to him, even if it was all he had.

In the beginning, he was enthralled with the mission of the PKO. Finally, an organization deploying a real solution to the chaos in the world. Their idea of peace; however, meant strict obedience and complete loyalty. Michael never had a problem with obedience; a pecking order was required for anything to be accomplished, but the more he found himself obeying orders, the less he recognized himself. Incidentally, returning from one of these *obedient* missions with a boatload of stolen goods and a harrowing tale of *chaos* would cause Michael to ask the question, *is the solution promised by the PKO adding to the chaos they promise to solve?*

Catching a glimpse of his sister, Maddie, on the grounds of the PKO was the final straw. Assigned to San Bernardino, California, Michael only ventured to Georgia every few months. An impromptu delivery to Baldersville led him to see Rachel, Maddie's friend, working in the gardens. Suddenly, he had a bad feeling in the pit of his stomach, and moments later, his worst fears were confirmed when he saw his sister stand with weeds in her hands. *What have I done?* He mumbled to himself.

For months, memories of his last moment with Maddie haunted him. The Christmas gift she left on the hood of his car was carelessly thrown in the closet of his nondescript room. It only served as a reminder that he wasn't good enough for his family. He couldn't shake the look on her face when she quietly uttered, "Merry Christmas," in response to his annoyed glare after he stormed out of the house. Her haunted brown eyes lingered in his mind ever since and would ultimately be the catalyst to calling his dad. As he wondered what was in the small, wrapped package for the hundredth time, he didn't have much hope of opening the gift any time soon as he watched the determined gait of the armed agent before him.

Entering the chow hall, he felt threatened by impending doom as he glanced at the insignia mounted proudly on the block wall. The upside-down cross overlaid by a bolt of lightning was the pride and joy of the PeaceKeepers Organization. A man's success rested on receiving this badge of honor. Respect hinged on this tattoo, or so he used to believe.

"Well, hello, Bagman. You can have a seat there. The Case Officer will be with you shortly."

Michael recoiled under the cold glare of Carissa Blackwell. Nodding as he looked away, he knew better than to say a word. People tended to go missing when disrespecting her.

The foyer leading to the CO's office was opulent, much like the grounds. Each campus had perfectly tended grounds but humble accommodations for the workers. This was by design. The residents were to live humble lives, serving the PKO, even as those in a station above the Agent-In-Place lived luxuriously. This was another sign of success at the PKO.

"You may enter, Bagman." Carissa's eyes glinted as she smiled mockingly.

Michael suddenly felt self-conscious over his unkempt state. After being captured by the campus guards the night before, he had not had a shower or even a change of clothing. His stomach growled as he thought of the meal he had missed.

"Good morning, Bagman." The deep male voice reverberated around the large office. "Please, have a seat."

Michael's nerves screamed as the door closed behind him.

C HAPTER 1

Song of Summer

June 30
Wild Rock, Tennessee

Walking through Grammy's Garden, Maddie was grateful for the shade, which offered a welcome escape from the hot and sticky day. Stopping to pick tomatoes for supper, she chose the best one from the vine and took a bite. As the juice dripped down her chin, she laughed over the mess she was making. After placing a handful of tomatoes in her pocket, she checked the stake to confirm it was stable.

Grammy let Maddie and Matthew plant their own tomato plants shortly after they arrived in Wild Rock. Watching them grow was therapy for Maddie. Something about connecting with life seemed to heal her wounded heart.

"Hey, Maddie, check out what I found." The red-eyed insect looked weird in her brother's hand but seemingly harmless.

"It jumped right on 'em, it did." Grammy's face lit up over Matthew's find.

Maddie's wariness was obvious as she took a step back. "What is it?"

Matthew looked at Grammy and said, "Chickada?"

Grammy laughed at his attempt. "Why that'd be a "ci"-cada, Boy."

"Ci-cada. Hi, Mr. ci-cada," he said as he drew it closer.

"Hey, what's it doing?" Maddie's face reflected her concern over the insect's fascination with her brother's hand.

"It's okay, Mads, he won't bite. He's sucking on me, but only because he thinks I'm a tree."

"Why don'tcha put him on that tree over thar?" Grammy asked.

"Aw, man." Walking over to the tree, Matthew touched a limb and watched as the brown-winged insect jumped from his hand.

Grammy stopped suddenly and said, "Shh, listen."

Matthew and Maddie obeyed Grammy as she began looking into the trees.

"What are we listening for?" Matthew whispered.

"That song, Boy, listen."

Cupping his ear, Matthew whined, "But I don't hear a song."

"Wait, do you mean the crickets?" Maddie asked.

Grammy laughed, "They ain't no crickets, Maddie Ruth, those be cicadas."

"Wait, so that thing Matthew had in his hand makes that whirring sound?"

"Yes ma'am. We're expectin' a brood of 'em this year and the next, so we'll be hearin' a serenade all summer I 'spect. They're resurrectin' from the earth to bless us with the song a summer."

Taking the tomatoes out of her pocket, Maddie asked, "What do you mean?"

Grammy took the tomatoes from Maddie's hands and placed them in her bag as they walked toward the house. "This Cicada only comes out of the ground ever' seventeen years or so. And when they do, they remind us of Jesus' resurrection and the resurrection of all mankind."

"What do you mean, resurrection?" Maddie followed Grammy as Matthew stayed behind to monitor the movements of his new friend.

"Well, the Good Book says that one day Jesus'll return as

King over all the earth. Those who died because of their testimony of Jesus'll come to life and reign with 'em for a thousand years. After those thousand years, the rest of the dead'll resurrect. Those who followed Jesus in their lifetime will dwell with him forever."

"Oh wait, I read about that! Doesn't the Bible say that there will be no more crying or pain, that we'll be with God, and he'll dwell with us?"

"That's right, Girl. So, ya been readin' Revelation, have ya?"

"Well, not all of it. Sonya told us about a verse in Revelation and I read it."

"That thar is our inheritance, Maddie Ruth. It's important to read that book so we know what's comin', but more important ta know the hope that's ours."

"Max!" Matthew ran past them up the path when he saw Max jump out of Aunt Lisa's car.

"That dog'll be the death of me, Moma." The slam of the car door echoed Lisa's frustration.

Grammy's brow furrowed with concern as she touched her daughter's shoulder. "What'd he do now?"

"In the middle of his groomin', he decided to run after a squirrel. Took me an hour ta catch him and then another to give 'em a second bath."

Shaking her head, Grammy chuckled, "That boy ain't never learned that the squirrel done got the best of 'em."

"Well, he's clean now and Eva Mae is needin' her supper. Do y'all have everythin' ya need?"

"Yes, ma'am. Thank ya, Dorter. I appreciate ya and love ya dearly." You couldn't miss the love in Grammy's eyes as she looked at her intently and then hugged her tight.

Aunt Lisa took a deep breath and beamed from her mom's encouraging smile as she got back into her car. "Bye, Moma." Waving, she put the car in gear and drove away.

"Come on young'uns let's see about eatin' Sister's yummy 'maters."

Maddie considered asking Grammy about resurrection but a knock on the front door interrupted her thoughts.

"Hey, y'all, whatcha doin'?"

Running to the living room, Maddie squealed, "Rachel!" Opening the screen door, Maddie hugged her friend.

"Hey, Rach, check out the Tommy toes Maddie and I planted!" Grabbing Rachel's hand, Matthew led her toward the kitchen.

Laughing, Rachel looked at her friend with a quizzical expression and asked, "Don't you mean tom-a-toes?"

"Nah, Grammy said they're Tommy toes! Ya know, picked straight out of Tommy's toes." Matthew laughed as he grabbed the cherry tomato from the counter.

Maddie shook her head as she handed her friend a bag of seeds.

"Ohhhh, Tommy Toes," Rachel nodded and winked at Matthew. "Hey, do you think Tommy will miss 'em?"

The belly laugh that rumbled out of Matthew amused everyone in the kitchen as they watched him run after Max.

"Boy, don't ya give that 'mater ta Max!" Grammy called over her shoulder.

As the girls grabbed a knife and began cutting the little tomatoes, Max let out a protective bark after the screen door slammed.

"Now, Max, let Mr. Tom come on in. Don't pretend ya don't know 'em."

"Oh, he's fine, Grace. We're good friends, aren't we, Boy?" Tom bent down to pet Max behind his ears.

Hearing Grammy call Rachel's dad, Maddie's eyes widened in surprise. "Your dad is here?" She asked Rachel.

"Yes, he got in last night!" Rachel smiled at her friend. "Oh, and wait 'til you hear the story he has to tell." She whispered.

Maddie took a deep breath and grabbed a paper towel. "Mr. Tom, how's Dad?"

"He's fine, Maddie."

"And Michael?"

"Well, we don't quite know where he is yet, but your dad is on the trail."

She didn't realize she was holding her breath until it left her mouth with a big whoosh. "Thank you, God," she whispered under her breath. When Maddie arrived at Grammy's, she felt like she was in a protective bubble, but her dad and brother were never far from her thoughts.

"How's his leg, Tom? Is it healin' right?" Grammy was looking a bit pale herself.

Winking at his daughter, Tom answered, "Yes, ma'am, right as rain. I guess you'll want to hear the story."

"That'd be nice, but do ya mind if we lay out supper and say a blessin'? You're welcome to sup with us a'course." Grammy pulled out the plates from the cabinet and laid them on the table.

"Thank you. How can I help?"

"Could 'ya grab the casserole out of the oven?"

"Yes, ma'am, you've got it." Grabbing an oven mitt, Tom grabbed the hot dish and placed it on the counter. "Wow, this smells great!"

"Grammy, what are we eating tonight?" Pulling napkins and forks from the cabinet, Matthew began setting the table.

"Roast Chicken with zucchini casserole, sliced 'maters, and blackberry cobbler fer dessert."

"Yum!" Maddie elbowed her friend over the news of her favorite dessert. "Can we have ice cream?"

Matthew wrinkled his nose. "Do I have to eat the yuk-kini?"

"Boy, where'd ya get that from? You ain't never had anythin' yuk in this house."

"Well, let's just say it's not to my likin'."

Grammy snickered, "Boy, ya got spirit, ya do. Jes' try it. I put a pound a cheese in it jes' for you. And, yes, Maddie, ever' one who eats their "zu"cchini can have ice cream." While speaking to Maddie, Grammy winked at Matthew.

"Wow, a whole pound?" Matthew dug out a serving spoonful of casserole just to pull the strings of cheese loose.

"Mind yore manners, Boy, we got comp'ny."

"Yes, ma'am." Giving the spoon to Maddie, Matthew picked up his fork and ate a chunk of the cheese layer off the top.

Raising her brow in disapproval, Grammy said, "Matthew, can ya say the blessin' fer us?"

His attention focused on the cheese, Matthew moved to fold his hands as he prayed, "God, we thank you for today. Thank you for the Cicada and for Tommy's toes. We are grateful for this cheese and for the ice cream that we get to eat tonight. God, please bless Mr. Tom and Rachel, Grammy, and Maddie. Oh, and please bless Max. In Jesus' Name, Amen."

"That was a fine prayer, Matthew. A fine prayer, indeed. Now, let's eat."

Rachel and Maddie giggled as Max snuck under their feet. Matthew took that as an opportunity to sneak a couple pieces of zucchini under the table.

Ignoring the exchange between her dog and grandson, Grammy asked, "So, Tom, how's my boy?"

"He's healing up nicely, Grace. The doctor stitched him up and he's been running laps ever since."

"That's mighty good. And Jacque?"

"She's doing better. Olivia has been checking in on her and says that she is smiling again."

"Mr. Tom, will Momma be able to come for my birthday?" Maddie's stomach was a bit unsettled as she considered having a birthday without all her family around her.

"I'll see if we can make that happen, Maddie." Tom winked at Rachel. Turning to Grammy, he said, "Grace, I must thank you for connecting us with Joe and his team. They were instrumental in helping us get into the compound."

"My pleasure, a'course. Joe an' George go way back."

"Maddie, we didn't want to worry you at the time, but we thought we'd lost your dad for a moment. After seeing Michael surrounded, your dad attempted to distract the guards so we could rush in and grab your brother. Spooked, one of the guards took a shot. We were waiting for his signal when we saw him fall like a log. Suddenly, the lights went on and an army of guards came running toward us. Joe's boys moved like lightning to pick your dad up. You should've seen them sling him over their shoulders like a sack of potatoes. They were so agile; you would've thought he was a boy. When we got back to the church, David was offering them a job."

"Yeah, those boys were a might feisty and never could back down from a challenge," Grammy chuckled.

Before taking a bite of casserole, Tom asked, "How did George know Joe?"

Grammy smiled as she reminisced, "Shortly after George left the Navy, he and Joe met on a construction job an' grew to be best buds. When Joe met Peggy, she led him to the Lord, and he was called into ministry. Not long after, the Lord called 'em ta lead a church in South Georgia."

"Well, he's quite a guy. And those men of his are top-notch. I'd love to see them train my Seals," Tom said.

Grammy laughed. "Now that, I'd like ta see."

Night sounds comforted Maddie as she stepped out of the shower. Thinking about the cicada and the serenade Grammy spoke of earlier in the day, she wondered about other insects and animals that made up the whirling symphony. *I'm going to have to ask Emma what she thinks about writing a song* from the cicada's song. Smiling as she stepped into the hallway, she suddenly stopped as sobs interlaced with broken prayers reached her ears from the direction of Grammy's room.

Maddie had never heard Grammy pray like this. Quietly opening her door wider, she watched as her dear Gram fell on her face, weeping. The fear Maddie had fought for so long began to rise as she heard her Grammy desperately ask for help on behalf of Maddie's dad and brother. She said nothing was impossible for God, and he was their refuge. She asked God to send his angels to guard and protect them. *Is she afraid?*

Maddie wondered. Grammy said when she was afraid, she prayed, but this prayer sounded different from what Maddie was used to. Instead of begging God, she seemed to be speaking promises. Was this what a prayer of surrender looked like?

May 6
BALDERSVILLE, GEORGIA

"Good morning, CO, Sir." Michael was nervous but figured this was a good time to show some courage.

"You may call me CO Larkin."

"Yes, Sir, CO Larkin."

"May I get you a drink, Michael?"

Surprised over the use of his first name, he looked up at the CO and nodded. "Coffee would be great."

"How long have you been here?"

Uncertain how to answer the question, Michael figured the truth would be the best option: "About a week."

"Hmm, and you've served at San Bernardino for fourteen months. Would that be correct?"

"Yes sir, CO."

"CO Larkin."

"Yes, CO Larkin."

"You serve as a Bagman?"

"Yes, CO Larkin."

"As I understand, you haven't fulfilled any independent missions?"

"That is correct. I'm in training."

Handing Michael a cup of coffee, the CO said, "If you are in training, why did they send you to Georgia by yourself for a week?"

"My mom is in the hospital." Michael's hand shook as he peered into the swirling black liquid.

Distracted by something outside of the office window, the

CO responded, "Oh, that's too bad."

Looking intently at the back of the CO, Michael waited for the other shoe to drop. The repercussions for being found on the grounds after eleven were great. If the CO knew that he had helped his dad rescue his sister and her friends, he could say goodbye to future missions and possibly his life.

"Oh, what to do with you, Mr. Bennett?"

"Sir?"

"So, you were visiting your mom in the hospital?" Turning, he peered over his glasses at Michael.

Concerned by the doubt evident in the CO's voice, he answered, "Yes, CO Larkin."

"If you were here to visit your mom, then why were you on campus after eleven?" Looking at the stack of papers on his desk, he continued, "I don't see any missions set for May fifth?"

Michael didn't think that far ahead. He wished he had gone over this part of the plan with his dad. Thinking up a quick reason he hoped would stick, he said, "Well, CO Larkin, I had to deliver a package to Mac in the kitchen."

"A package, hm? What sort of package?"

Michael hoped the items found on his person hadn't been squandered as he answered, "Ms. Carissa loves the homemade salsa our chef in San Bernardino makes. I had some in my bag last night, but the guards took my bag before tying me to the tree." Thankful he'd thought to bring the salsa with him, he prayed the CO would buy his partial lie.

"That was unfortunate, wasn't it? But you do understand that when the campus is under attack, everyone who fails to be orderly becomes a suspect?"

"Of course, CO Larkin. I understand."

"You don't mind if I check your bag?"

"Not at all, Sir. I'm sure Mac would understand if you gave Ms. Carissa the salsa?" Everyone knew how the CO felt about Carissa.

The CO's face lit up with the suggestion. "Well, I think that would be excellent." Turning back to the window, he asked again, "So, what shall we do with you, Mr. Bennett?"

"Sir, I am expected in San Bernardino for a mission at the first of the week." Heartburn began to rise in his chest as he took another sip of the coffee. Deciding it wasn't worth it, he set the cup down.

"Hmm, well, if your story checks out, we will send you back to San Bernardino, with an escort, of course. The events of last evening concern Mr. Baldur, and he wants to be sure you are fully protected." Looking down his nose at Michael, he asked, "Do we have an understanding?"

"Yes, CO Larkin, I understand completely."

Buzzing to the front office, the CO said, "Carissa, please have Mr. Bennett's bag brought to me." Looking up at Michael, he said, "You may go."

Michael walked out of the office on eggshells. He expected an execution after last night's events, but apparently, he was able to talk his way out of this one. Perhaps he had some of his dad's tactical expertise after all.

CHAPTER 2

Introductions

July 1
Wild Rock, Tennessee

Bursting with a secret, Maddie couldn't keep a smile off her face. Since her return to Wild Rock, she and Grammy were making plans for her birthday. When Grammy asked how she would like to celebrate, Maddie didn't hesitate, a pic'n 'n grin'n. She wanted her Fam to experience the absolute freedom to be had under God's stars. This same freedom could be found anywhere, but there was just something about Wild Rock and her people that made Maddie feel closer to God. *Could it be the mountains?* She wondered. All she knew was that it was imperative that Grammy keep the party details under wraps so she could surprise her friends. It would probably be best if Matthew didn't know either. He would certainly spill the beans if he knew the details.

While Maddie was over the moon about her birthday plans, she had another secret. Rachel loved gospel music, and when Maddie mentioned meeting with Ms. Lorna, Rachel jumped out of her skin. Today, she would have the opportunity to meet Ms. Lorna herself.

Maddie loved surprises. There was such joy to be had in recognizing little blessings and that joy seemed to multiply when others recognized them as well. Once upon a time, she would be so anxious over moments like this, worrying if it would be good enough or if her friend would even respond as she'd hoped. But today was different. She knew that Rachel would find joy in this surprise, and she couldn't wait to see her face.

"How do I look?" A nervous glance came over Rachel's face as she sought confirmation from her friend.

"I think you look beautiful," Matthew's head peeked into the room for just a moment as he ran after Max.

"Matthew, privacy, please!" Maddie laughed at her brother as he slammed the door behind him. "Do you think he waits outside just to find a reason to butt into our conversations?"

"Na. Personally, I think God uses people at the perfect moment who are willing to be used by him." Rachel straightened the front of her dress for the hundredth time.

Brushing her hair, Maddie looked at her friend through the mirror. "What do you mean?"

"Well, God knows that I'm nervous about today. He also knows that you will tell me exactly what I want to hear, so he uses another who's ready and willing to be his mouthpiece. God does it all the time."

"Wait, you're nervous?" Not knowing what to make of this news, Maddie sat in a nearby chair and looked at her friend.

Sitting on the edge of the bed, Rachel said. "Yeah, wouldn't you be? Meeting a whole bunch of people that you don't know?"

"Sure, but I never thought you'd be nervous. What else makes you nervous?"

"Honestly? Not knowing the future."

"But don't you have faith?" Cocking her head to the side, Maddie wondered how she could have missed this about her friend.

"Of course, I still worry about things I can't control. I am human, ya know." Wiggling her eyebrows, Rachel attempted a smile.

"So, what do you do?"

Opening her hands before her, Rachel asked, "Well,

remember the rocks?"

"Yeah."

"I take the nervous and anxious thoughts, and I lay them down, sometimes daily." Rachel's hands turned as she watched the invisible rocks fall to the floor.

Maddie suddenly remembered the rhythm Rachel taught when she was frustrated that she couldn't fix her mom. A little embarrassed that she had to be reminded, Maddie asked, "Well, do we need to do that now?"

"Can we?"

Getting on her knees, Maddie exclaimed, "Of course! Do you want me to pray?"

"I would love that."

"Okay, let's do it. But Rach, I'm not sure I'll know what to say." It was Maddie's turn to be nervous.

"Just close your eyes and listen to the voice inside." Rachel joined her friend on the floor.

With her eyes closed, Maddie prayed.

> *God, we thank you for today. Thank you for my friend who's spending my whole birthday month with me! I'm so happy she is here. Lord, I pray that you will surround her today. We lay down any nervous and anxious thoughts at your feet and ask for your strength. And Father, please remind my BFF that she is loved, and because of that, Wild Rock will love her too. In Jesus' Name, Amen.*

"Amen. Thank you, Maddie." With tears in her eyes, Rachel hugged her friend.

Scrunching her face, Maddie asked, "Did I do it right?"

"It was perfect."

The ride to church seemed to take forever. Matthew entertained everyone with his latest cicada escapade as baby

Eva Mae played peek-a-boo with Rachel. All the while, Maddie rehearsed how she would introduce her friend to Ms. Lorna. *Hi, Ms. Lorna. Meet my best friend, Rachel. Tada, Rachel, meet your childhood icon, Lorna Kyle.*

"Earth to Maddie, where'd ya go?" Rachel and Eva Mae both played peek-a-boo with Maddie to grab her attention.

"Huh? Oh, nowhere, I was just thinking," Maddie answered as they drove up to the Church.

"Say hi to Ms. Bonnie for me, Girls. I gotta run. I'm leadin' Sundy School for my ladies this mornin'." The car door closed behind Grammy as she walked toward the sanctuary.

"I gotta run, too. Billy's bringing his new boomerang to church this morning." Matthew ran off in a flash toward the reception hall.

"Aunt Lisa, do you need help with Eva Mae?"

"No ma'am, thank ya kindly. We'll be jes' fine, won't we, Girl?" Eva Mae giggled as Aunt Lisa tickled her.

With Bible and journal in hand, Maddie and Rachel made their way to the Sunday School Hall. Deep in conversation about the campus's layout, Maddie almost didn't see Jacob until it was too late.

"Hellooooooo, I feel a little déjà vu comin' on. Maddie, who's yer friend?" Shooting the proverbial head nod the girl's way, Jacob then smiled for the benefit of his friends as if to say, "How you doin'?"

Trying to cover her embarrassment with a sly smile, she said, "Jacob, Rachel, Rachel, Jacob—and friends."

"Ohhhh, this is the guy?" Rachel placed her arm on her friend's shoulder and pretended to size Jacob up.

Looking at her friend, Maddie laughed, "He's harmless." Turning toward Jacob and his friends, she asked, "Hey, you never introduced me to your friends."

"This is Rory, and this crazy ginger is Jared."

Jared playfully punched Jacob while Rory tipped an invisible hat as he looked intently at Rachel.

Rachel blushed and looked away.

Seeing her friend's embarrassment, Maddie quickly deflected, "It's nice to meet you, Jared, and Rory. Do y'all play the banjo too?"

"Ya know it, just a bunch 'a pickers." Grabbing his belt, Jared did a little jig.

Placing his hands in his pocket, Rory stepped back shyly and said, "I play the fiddle, too."

"What's a fiddle?" Maddie asked.

Placing both hands in the air, he closed his eyes and pretended to play. "Ya know, a violin." Rory seemed to get lost in the action.

"Oh yeah, I remember. Were you the one playing with Ms. Lorna last year?" *Oops, there goes the surprise*, Maddie thought, a little disappointed she let the name slip out.

Looking at Maddie, Rachel's eyes gleamed when she brought up Ms. Lorna.

Running his hand through his dark blonde hair, Rory said, "Nah, that's my Pap. He's been playin' a might longer 'n me."

"That's cool. Maybe Rachel can hear y'all play while she's here." Maddie nodded at her best friend. She would love the music of the Tennessee mountains; of that, she had no doubt.

"How long will ya be in Wild Rock?" If Rory's green eyes were laser beams, Rachel would be a puddle.

Finding her voice, Rachel answered, "The month of July."

Rory's intense look turned into a big smile as he answered, "Well, I might be seein' you 'round then."

Rachel just grinned, unsure of what to say next, which had never been something that happened to her. She always had something to say.

Noticing her friend's awkward silence, Maddie smiled at the group, "Well, we gotta get going, but we'll see you guys later."

Walking away, Rachel let out a big sigh, "Okay that was weird."

"I know, right? These Wild Rock boys are really weird." Maddie laughed.

As they walked into Ms. Bonnie's classroom, Maddie immediately noticed Amy Jayne sitting in the back corner. She looked sad and disconnected.

"Hi, Amy." This was the first time Maddie saw her new friend since she'd returned to Tennessee.

"Hey." The downcast look on her face made it clear she wanted to be left alone.

"This is my friend, Rachel."

Amy's quick smile disappeared as quickly as it appeared. "Good ta meet ya."

Rachel's eyebrows raised in compassion as she looked at her friend then smiled warmly as she looked at the girl sitting in the chair. "Hi, Amy."

"If ya don't mind, I'd like to be alone." Crossing her arms, Amy looked toward the wall.

"Oh, sure thing." Placing her hand on Amy's shoulder, Maddie replied, "If you need somebody to talk to, we're here for you."

A moment passed before Amy looked at the girls and said, "Thanks, but I'm good."

"Good mornin', Ladies. Maddie, who's your friend?"

"Hi, Ms. Bonnie. This is Rachel. She's visiting from Atlanta."

"Hey, Rachel. We're so glad you're visitin' with us. Have a seat. Oh, and Ladies, let's circle up today, shall we?" Grabbing a red chair, Ms. Bonnie walked over to Amy Jayne's seat and smiled. Amy looked a bit uncomfortable but turned her seat toward the group."

"Thank ya, Girls. I wantcha' ta open yer Bibles to Psalm 46. There are ten of ya, let's go 'round the room, and each of ya read a verse."

Amy Jayne began with verse one. Maddie could tell something was wrong with her even as she read. Last year, when Maddie was invited to the dance around the fire, it was Amy Jayne who invited her into their circle. Now, it was as if she didn't want anything to do with anyone, and that had her a little worried.

Going around the circle, each girl read a verse. Maddie read.

"He says,
'Be still, and know that I am God;
I will be exalted among the nations,
I will be exalted in the earth.'"

Ms. Bonnie finished with verse eleven.

"The Lord Almighty is with us;
the God of Jacob is our fortress."

"Who can tell me what questions we ask when we read God's word?" Ms. Bonnie asked.

A girl across from Maddie answered, "We ask what the word says about God, who wrote the scripture, who is the scripture written to, and how I apply it in my life?"

"Very good, Esther. So, who wants to tell us what this scripture says about God?"

Raising her hand nervously, Rachel answered, "God is with us, no matter what we face."

"That's right, Rachel. Is there a specific verse that sticks out to you?"

"Yes ma'am, 'Be still, and know that I am God.'"

Sitting back with her hands clasped, Ms. Bonnie said, "Tell me 'bout it."

"Well, being still is hard for me, but I try to sit with him every day."

"Tell me what sittin' with God looks like."

"I read my Bible and journal. And I pray, of course."

"Anyone else? What does being still look like to you, Girls?"

"I like ta sit on the dock at Sycamore Lake."

"That's good, Esther. Does God reveal himself when you're sittin' on the dock?"

"Well, I guess. It's peaceful."

"God's word says that his eternal power and divine nature are clearly seen. How does Sycamore Lake show us God's nature?"

Amy Jayne responded, "It was created by God."

Ms. Bonnie smiled at Amy Jayne, "That's right. Everythin' God created reveals its Creator. So, Rachel, when you read his word, and Esther, when you sit on the dock, you both are witnessin' somethin' God created. What do ya think about God when yer in his creation?"

Everyone was quiet as they pondered the question.

After a moment, a girl Maddie didn't know lifted her hand, "He gives me strength?" She asked.

"That's right. Somethin' to be grateful for, ain't it?"

"Yes ma'am."

"Esther, when yer sittin' on the dock and ya see the water ripplin' or the trees swayin', tell me how Psalm forty-six can be seen."

Reading the book before her, Esther said, "When I'm sittin' thar with my feet in the water, I see the trees larger 'n life. This verse ten says to know that he is God, he'll be exalted among the nations. When I see those trees, I know he's thar."

"What does exalt mean, Ms. Bonnie?"

"Well Amy Jayne, that's a good question. The way I understand it, exalted means high or lifted up. In this case, he can be seen by ever'one."

Ms. Bonnie shared how God reveals himself so we can see him and then meets us where we are in our struggles. "Girls, strugglin' builds strength. Never forget it. Be still and know that he is God, and r'member he is with ya, all the days of yer life, if ya let him. Now, 'afore I let you'ns go, I leave ya with two words- awe and wonder. Find out what those two words mean in context with this week's scripture and be ready to talk about it next week. Y'all have a good week!"

"That was awesome!" Rachel was filled with excitement as she and Maddie walked down the hall.

"I know right? Every time, I learn something new." Maddie shared in her friend's excitement.

"So, from all that," twirling her hand around in a circle, Rachel asked, "what did you learn?"

"Well, that part we read in Psalm forty-six about God burning the shields, what was that all about? Did that have anything to do with the shield of faith?"

"I dunno. Let's research it later."

Suddenly, Maddie's excitement turned to sorrow as she remembered the upside-down-cross with a lightning bolt covering it. *God, where is Mike? Is he safe?*

Recognizing the change in her friend, Rachel asked, "Hey, You, where'd you go?"

"I was just thinking about Mike. I wish he could be here."

"Yeah . . ."

"Rach, do you think he's okay? You don't think he got into trouble because of us, do you?"

"Honestly, I don't know. I hope not. Are you worried?"

A deep frown settled on her face as she answered, "Yeah."

"Look at me." Rachel grabbed her friend's hand. "Remember, when you're thinking things like this, you've got to give them to God, right?"

"Yeah, I guess. Mr. C, my counselor, says that worry doesn't help anything. I just . . ."

"Let's pray about it, okay?"

"Okay."

Rachel led her friend in a quick prayer. Maddie opened her eyes and took a deep breath.

"Better?"

Maddie smiled at her friend, "Yes, thank you. I don't understand why I get down so quickly."

"Your feelings are real, Maddie, but they're also yours to control, or they will control you."

"You're right, thank you."

"Always."

Maddie stopped her friend before they walked into the sanctuary. "Hey Rach, before we go in there. . ."

"Yeah?"

"I have a surprise for you."

Rachel was giddy with anticipation.

"Ms. Lorna is playing the piano today."

"Wait, I get to meet THE Lorna Kyle?!?"

"Yep!"

"Oh, my goodness, oh my goodness, oh my goodness! Do I look okay?" Rachel smoothed her dress as she looked at her friend.

"You look beautiful." Maddie smiled as she opened the double doors.

ATLANTA, GEORGIA

David awoke to the buzzing of his phone on the side table. "Hello?"

"Mr. Bennett, please hold for Mr. Baldur."

Suddenly wide awake, David wondered if he had heard the woman correctly.

"Good morning, Mr. Bennett. I hope we did not disturb your sleep."

The heavily accented voice gave David chills. "Who is this?"

"Lucien Baldur, at your service."

"Why should I believe you?"

"As I understand, you and I have a common goal. You are looking for your son, Michael Bennett, are you not?"

CHAPTER 3

A Mighty Deliverer

The tapping of Rachel's foot distracted Maddie as she listened to the sermon. Looking up at her friend, she couldn't help but smile at the starry-eyed gaze pointed toward Ms. Lorna. Maddie had never seen her friend so nervous, but nervous she was.

As the service ended with the punctual "amen," Maddie stood and stretched, offering her hand to her friend.

Frozen in place, Rachel said, "What do I do?"

Grammy, sitting on the opposite side of Maddie, said, "Girl, yer more nervous than a cat in a room full of rockin' chairs. What's eatin' ya up?"

"Grammy, Ms. Lorna is one of Rachel's favorite gospel singers. She's a little nervous."

"Heavens to Betsy, well, if that don't beat all! Ya know, Rachel Girl, Lorna Kyle puts her britches on one leg at a time, jes' like the rest of us. Come on, let's go say hey."

Maddie gently nodded to encourage her friend to move forward from her frozen state.

"Lorna Kyle, don't you look mighty fine on this Sundy."

Ms. Lorna turned with a big smile for her spunky friend. Playing up to Grammy's dramatic greeting, she responded, "Well, if it ain't Grace Bennett. Yer a bit feisty this Sundy mornin'." Winking at her friend, she turned to Rachel and took her hand, "And who might you be?"

Wanting to fill the quiet, Maddie answered, "This is my best friend, Rachel, Ms. Lorna. She's a big fan of yours."

Patting her hand, she asked, "Ah, is she now? And what is yer favorite song, Ms. Rachel?"

"Um, uh." Rachel looked up at the ceiling as she tried to remember. Suddenly, her eyes grew big as she said, "Mighty Deliverer!"

"Well, I'd say that's one of my favorites, too. There's a story behind it, ya know."

Rachel gasped. "Really?" Looking at her friend and Grammy, she asked, "Can we hear it?"

Grammy answered, "I'd say we've got time. I got a hankerin' for some chicken and dumplin's. Join us, Lorna?"

"I'd be honored. May I have yer arm, Rachel?"

"Yes ma'am!"

"Grammy, can we have banana pudding?" With his lip stuck out a mile, Matthew made his pleading face as he followed behind.

"Boy, you keep eatin' that banana puddin', and yer gonna be a puddin'!"

"Well, you know what they say: 'You are what you eat!'" Matthew cackled as he ran up to hold the door open for the ladies.

"Pastor Ron, that was a mighty fine lesson today."

"Why, thank ya, Ms. Grace. I see ya brought comp'ny. Who might you be?"

"My name is Rachel Monroe, Pastor Ron."

"Hey there, Rachel Monroe. I 'spect yer from Atlanta, same as our Maddie here?"

"Yes, sir."

"Well, enjoy our little Wild Rock, ya here?"

"I sure will, thank you."

As they walked toward the car, Rachel turned to Maddie, "It's so cool that Pastor Ron greets you after church. Does he speak to everybody?"

"Yup, every week."

Winking at Rachel, Grammy said, "Our Pastor Ron is a shepherd, that he is!"

The restaurant was filled with the Sunday Church crowd. Maddie sat quietly, amused, as she listened to Rachel and Ms. Lorna chat.

"Hey, Ms. Grace, good to see ya this fine Sunday."

"Well, hey, Suzanne. How's yer baby doin'?"

"Oh, Ms. Grace, Jeremiah has an ear infection. He sure could use some of yer prayers."

"Well, I'll be, let's lift 'im up right now, shall we?"

After grabbing Suzanne's hand, Grammy encouraged everyone to bow their heads as she prayed for baby Jeremiah.

Maddie noticed Suzanne wiping away a tear before taking their order.

After Suzanne walked toward the kitchen, Rachel asked, "Grammy, do you pray for every waitress?"

"Why a'course. The Good Book commands us ta pray fer one another. It's a gift the Father gives us. Ya know, I think Ms. Lorna has somethin' ta say 'bout prayer. Don't ya?" Winking at her friend, Grammy smiled.

"So, ya said yer favorite song was Mighty Deliverer. Did I hear ya right, Rachel?"

"Yes, ma'am."

"Do ya know what it's about?"

"Can I cheat a little?" Pulling out her phone, Rachel searched for the song lyrics.

Ms. Lorna laughed as she clapped her chest dramatically. "Be still, my heart. I thought she knew ever' word."

Grammy shook her head and whispered to Rachel. "Give that one an inch, and she'll take a mile."

Rachel read the lyrics quietly and then looked up at Ms. Lorna. "Did this really happen?"

"Well, kinda. Ms. Grace here, she's the ole man a'course."

Grammy snorted as she laughed at her friend's comment.

"Did our Maddie here tell ya 'bout my bout with self-destruction?"

"She said you almost died, and Grammy took care of you."

"I did, physically and spiritually. Ms. Grace here introduced me to Jesus, who saved me and gave me a peace that transcends all understandin'. I had to share the gift he gave, and so I wrote a song from David's words in the Psalms."

"What does this line mean? 'Praise oh Lord my Rock who trained my hands for war?'"

"What do ya hear in those words?"

"I guess that David trusts the God who trained him."

"That's right, Rachel. Yer a mighty smart young woman. How old are ya?"

"I just turned seventeen."

"Well, yer wise beyond yer years. David, a man after God's heart, trusted God to be with 'im. Grammy here trusted God to be with her, and I trusted God to be with me. And the story continues."

"Can I be a man after God's heart?" Holding his glass, Matthew nervously crinkled his eyebrows together, waiting for her answer.

"Well, here ya go." The food looked so good. Maddie's stomach growled even as she curiously awaited the answer to her brother's question.

After everyone began eating, Ms. Lorna looked at Matthew. "Matthew, tell me 'bout yer boomerang. I hear you've taken a likin' to Mr. Tom and that business of his."

"Oh yes, it's so much fun! Mr. Tom is teaching me everything he knows. By the end of the summer, he promised we'd make a house full of boomerangs."

Ms. Lorna chuckled as Matthew spread his hands wide, describing how he created his new toy. "How long would ya say it takes fer ya to make one?"

"Hm…" Placing his index finger on his cheek and his thumb under his chin, Matthew looked up as he considered his answer. "I'd say eight hours, give or take a couple, 'cause Mr. Tom likes to joke around, ya know."

"Yeah, I know all about Mr. Tom." Ms. Lorna winked at Grammy. "Would ya say that you give yer heart into doin' a good job?"

"If I don't, the boomerang won't swoosh right." Mimicking the throw, Matthew almost hit Maddie's fork.

"Matthew!"

"Oops, sorry."

"That's right, Matthew, ya give yer all so the boomerang'll work jes' like it's s'posed to. King David gave his all knowin' his God was always there fer him and would never leave him. In ever' battle David faced; his God was with him. He knew that it was God alone who would save his people. The rocks he used to take the giant out, well, they were tools jes' like yer boomerang. And in the hand 'a God, they were mighty powerful. He knew it, trusted him, and operated on this truth ever' day of his life. That's how David was a man after God's own heart and how we too should be men and women after God's own heart."

"Ohhh." Matthew nodded his head as he popped a spoonful of mac and cheese into his mouth.

Looking at her hands, Maddie wondered what tools God would give her.

"Ms. Lorna, would you say that yer a woman after God's own heart?" Aunt Lisa asked as she handed Eva Mae a chicken nugget.

Taking a deep breath as she laid down her fork, she answered, "I hope so, Lisa. When I stand before the Lord, I pray that ever' word I spoke, ever' song I sang, ever' heart I pointed to Jesus will glorify him." Ms. Lorna's voice sounded shaky as her eyes watered. "I want ever' ounce of joy he gave me to boomerang back to him, for he delivered me mightily from the fire. Life wouldn't be worth much without my Deliverer." Ms. Lorna scooped up a piece of chicken as she winked at Matthew.

On a humid Monday morning, Maddie and Rachel sat quietly on Grammy's back porch. Maddie smiled as she saw Ms. Carolina Wren flit around in the bird feeders. Rachel read her Bible and wrote in her journal as she did every morning. Maddie had hers open to the scripture Rachel read yesterday.

"Hey, Rach, can I ask you a question?"

Placing her pen down, Rachel propped her chin on folded hands and said, "Shoot."

"I was reading the scripture you read yesterday, Psalm 144, right?"

"That sounds right. Read it to me?"

Reading through the chapter, Maddie said, "'Blessed is the people of whom this is true; blessed is the people whose God is the Lord.' Doesn't it sound like this is a war?"

Closing her journal, Rachel looked intently at her friend. "Yes, it is."

"Remember at the PKO when you said everyone was walking around like zombies, just existing?"

Rachel looked toward the mountains and sighed, "Yeah, it was so sad."

"Do you think we are walking into a war? Is that what the end times are all about?"

"The end times are the end of an era of sin and death, but more importantly the return of Jesus. He is the One who will set the captives free and put sin and death away for eternity. What you just read, is his promise. He will deliver us, rescue us, and provide for us. But, yes, there will be a battle. Remember what Sonya shared about the armor of God in Ephesians six?"

Turning to the scripture in her Bible, Maddie read, "For our struggle is not against flesh and blood, but against the rulers, against the authorities, against the powers of this dark world and against the spiritual forces of evil in the Heavenly realms."

"That's it, the battle is now. The war goes on around us. It's a war of good vs evil. But Maddie, this promise in Psalm 144 means that Jesus won the war! He calls us to join him in that victory."

"Don't get me wrong, I'm thankful for what I learned about myself at the PKO, but honestly, I just want the nightmare to end. Rach, what if it's only the beginning?" Fear crossed Maddie's face momentarily as she looked at her friend in horror.

Rachel placed her hand on her friend's and looked at her with sadness in her eyes, "Yes, the beginning of the end of sin and death. Maddie, my dad always told me that every battle is costly, and every soldier must make a choice if he or she is willing to sacrifice for the goal. Our goal is Jesus, who already paid our sacrifice so we would be set free from sin and death, so we choose to follow him into battle knowing that he will deliver us."

Maddie looked at her hands. Her PKO battle scars, as Rachel called them, reminded her of what God had done. Picking up her Bible, Maddie re-read, "'Praise be to the Lord my Rock, who trains my hands for war, my fingers for battle.' I remember when the thorns from the roses cut into my hands. I was so angry that day that I refused to wear gloves, remember?"

"I remember you came to dinner a bloody mess! I thought Jade would have your head that day."

Maddie smiled, "Oh yeah, I forgot about that. I miss Jade."

"Yeah, me too. But she'll be here for your birthday." Rachel's eyes brightened at the thought.

"I know, I can't wait. I remember feeling so hopeless. I knew Dad would rescue us, but I didn't know how."

"Did you feel the thorns when you were pulling them out?"

"Ya know, I don't even remember."

"Maddie, what if God used those thorns to remind you that he was with you through the pain, protecting you? And now, you have a battle scar that will always remind you. What is the next verse again?"

"'He is my loving God and my fortress, my stronghold, and my deliverer, my shield, in whom I take refuge, who subdues peoples under me.'"

"Hey, remember how Sonya challenged us to memorize scripture and speak truth to negative thoughts?" Rachel stood up and began chanting the rap Jade created, "SECH! Suffering, endurance, character, hope. . ."

The girls rapped for a hot minute as Matthew ran out the back door. "What are y'all saying?"

Laughing hilariously, Maddie and Rachel collapsed in a heap on the deck.

ATLANTA, GEORGIA

"Mr. Bennett?"

David cleared his throat. "What do you know about Michael?"

"Oh, I know a great deal about you and your family. We have much to discuss, Mr. Bennett, or shall I call you David?"

"How did you get this number?"

"As I said, we have much to discuss. Let's meet, shall we? Join me at the King and Queen building on July fifth. I will have my assistant text you the details."

As the line went dead, David attempted to gather his scattered thoughts. How did Lucien Baldur get his number? What did he know about his family?

Typing a number into his phone, David waited for the familiar voice of his friend, Mordecai Aronoff.

"David, my friend, shalom! How are you?"

"A bit shaken up, currently. Do you have a moment to talk?"

"Certainly. Let me go to my office." After a few moments, Mordecai continued, "Okay, how can I help?"

"You will never guess who just called me."

"Well, I do hope you will tell me. I was never good at guessing games."

David wasn't feeling the humor. "Lucien Baldur."

"Hm, he is known to be a man who is very direct."

"Mordy, how would Lucien Baldur get my information?"

"He is very well connected, David."

"He says he knows about Michael."

"Well, we have learned that he owns the property where your son works, my friend. I expect he knows a great deal. What did he want?" Mordecai's curious tone was unmistakable.

"He wants to meet."

"Are you going to meet with him?"

Trying not to offend his friend, David pounded the desk before him as he attempted to control his rising anger. "Do I have a choice? I need to find out where Michael is."

Mordecai paused, then quietly responded, "David, we've been friends for a long time, and we've weathered many storms together. I can only imagine how hard this is for you, my friend. The thought of losing either of my boys would gut me. Please know that I am an ally and I need you to hear me on this. You need to go in with a plan. This man is not one to trifle with. Please remember what I said when we discussed BALDR Industries and their newly acquired properties. If he is the antichrist, he has an agenda."

David took a deep breath and closed his eyes. He still wasn't convinced his friend wasn't just supporting a conspiracy theory. However, after being completely shut down in his investigation with the FBI, he had to consider that something was happening. "Of course, thank you. Can you please send me what you know about him?"

"Yes, straight away. David, this man is crafty. He is the master at twisting your words against you."

"I understand, thank you."

"Is there an appointment set?"

"Yes, July fifth."

With concern, Mordecai replied, "My prayers go with you, my friend. Shalom, shalom."

CHAPTER 4

A Matter of Trust

"Time to skedaddle!" Grammy called out as she turned off the light switch.

Dragging his bookbag across the floor, Matthew made his way to the front door. "How long will we be gone again?" He asked.

"Rachel, did you pack a curling iron?" Maddie yelled.

"Yeah, I've got one."

Opening the screen door, Aunt Lisa yelled, "I've got a car runnin' with a sleepin' toddler. If we're gonna go, let's get."

Grammy had a surprise trip in store for Maddie, Matthew, and Rachel. All they knew was they were to pack for four days. Maddie was so excited she couldn't stand it!

"Did ya pack yer swimsuits?" Grammy asked.

"Wait, we're going swimming?" Matthew jumped for joy.

Grammy gave her favorite grandson "the look" as she said, "Now, I tole ya to pack for summer. Run an fetch 'em."

After a formal salute, Matthew ran toward the back of the house. "Yes ma'am," he shouted.

"Hey, what do I look like, yer maids?" Aunt Lisa shook her head as she grabbed the dropped bags.

"Here, let me help." Grammy picked up a bag and walked down the stairs with her daughter. "Is Richie gonna be alright without ya for a couple days?"

"Oh yeah, he's so happy to have his crew over for fireworks

on the fourth. He won't miss us at'all."

"He don't mind feedin' Max, does he?"

"Naw, Momma. You know he and Max are best friends."

Grammy snorted as she mumbled, "More like frenemies."

"So, Grammy, where are we going?" Matthew asked for the hundredth time as he ran outside, stuffing his swim trunks in his backpack.

Placing her hand on her hip, Grammy looked at her daughter. "I reckon we're goin' way down yonder. That 'bout right Lisa?"

Lisa pointed toward the road as she answered, "Yes ma'am, we're aimin' for over thar."

Maddie and Rachel laughed as Matthew rolled his eyes.

"Alright, Lisa, we'd better git on if we're gonna make it a'fore supper."

Maddie had a revelation. Whispering into her brother's ear, she watched as his eyes got round as saucers.

"Are we going to the beach?" He asked.

Grammy laughed as she answered, "Let's jes' say we got a little surprise planned for you'ns."

"But what's the surprise?" Matthew groaned.

"If I tole ya it wouldn't be a surprise, now, would it?"

Maddie had to laugh at Grammy's attempt to keep the surprise secret. As the travelers neared the ocean, she teased Matthew with questions about where they were. She would open the window and say, "Oooh, Doggie, smell that air!" Matthew responded with guesses that included an endless litany of fast-food restaurants. His excitement was finally rewarded; however, when they drove up to Cape Henry.

After passing through the security gate, they drove up to a lighthouse, where they climbed what seemed to Matthew to be at least a thousand stairs. *Dad would love this,* Maddie thought to herself.

As they reached the top, Maddie and her family stood in

awe of the ocean that seemed to never end. Confused to find only glass windows and stairs, Maddie looked for the "light."

Matthew must've read his sister's mind as he asked, "Where's the light?"

Aunt Lisa pointed to the white and black lighthouse in front of them. "This one's fer vis'tors. That one thar is currently used to guide ships."

"I wonder how far the light goes?" Matthew asked.

"Nineteen miles," Aunt Lisa answered.

Matthew's eyes widened as he tried to calculate the distance. "How far is that?" Matthew asked.

"That's 'bout as far as Grammy's house to the bottom of Wild Rock Mountain."

"Whoa, that's far!"

As Matthew chatted with Aunt Lisa about the mechanics of the lighthouse, Maddie and Rachel watched the powerful waves crash into the beach before them. Pondering the vastness and fury of the ocean, Maddie wondered, *how many ships have traveled through this bay?*

"Isn't it crazy that one light can guide ships into shore?" Rachel asked.

When it was time to leave, Aunt Lisa drew them together to take a picture and then led them out. Maddie was relieved that the descent down was much easier than the climb.

After exiting the lighthouse, the girls and Matthew ran to meet Grammy who was holding Eva Mae. Matthew chattered on and on about all he learned at the top of the enormous lighthouse.

Their visit to Cape Henry ended at a granite cross in a small garden. Grammy told a story of the first settlers who arrived on Cape Henry and made a covenant with God on behalf of the nation. Afterward, Grammy led them in a prayer she called a petition. As they brought the covenant before the Lord, she thanked him for honoring it and blessing our land.

The girls were exhilarated as Aunt Lisa drove out of the security gate. Amazed at the covenant of 1607 that Grammy told them about, Rachel asked, "Why have I never heard about it in school?"

A sudden slam on the brakes interrupted their conversation, leading them to peer out the window. Traffic was stopped. A crowd of people stood on either side of the street. It appeared to Maddie that hundreds were holding up signs as they yelled, "NO ORDER NO PEACE." She had heard this message before. Worried, she wondered, *were these people from the PKO?*

Rachel grabbed her hand and shook her head. "Not today," she mouthed.

Maddie was conflicted about Rachel's instructions. She wanted to tell Grammy who these people might be, but at the same time, she wanted to obey her friend.

Aunt Lisa was visibly shaken when someone tried to run out in front of their car.

Grammy looked at her daughter with calm. "It's okay, jes' go slow."

Working their way through the people, Aunt Lisa breathed a sigh of relief as they made it to the other side.

"Ya did good, Dorter," Grammy said as she patted her arm.

Stunned over the harrowing moment, everyone sat quietly as they traveled. Thankfully, it wasn't long before they pulled into the complex where they would be staying.

Maddie couldn't believe this place was all theirs for four whole days! According to Grammy, a couple from church had a free condo in Virginia Beach for the week and asked if they would like to use it. She jumped on the chance, of course.

As they investigated their temporary digs, Rachel and Maddie were delighted to be assigned a room of their own, while Grammy, Aunt Lisa, and Baby Eva Mae called dibs on the other. That left the living room, which Matthew was happy to take, considering he could have the TV all to himself.

Soft hues of red, pink, and gold colored the early morning sky as Maddie and Rachel sat on the balcony. Maddie still couldn't believe she was here!

Rachel, ever the morning person, encouraged her friend to get up early to witness the beautiful sunrise. As Maddie listened to the waves crash in, she re-read the scripture Ms. Lorna shared from Psalm 144.

Rachel was quite impressed with Ms. Lorna's testimony. It got Maddie thinking: *where do I fit in your story, God?* Looking at her hands, she thought about Rachel's revelation that God would use her battle scars to remind her he was with her. She was riddled with doubt. *What can God really do with somebody like me?* She wondered. *David was a king; I'm just a girl.*

After writing verses one and two in her journal, Maddie prayed,

> July 4
> Father,
>   I want to be a woman after your own heart. Show me what you want me to do. Train these scarred hands, Lord. In Jesus' Name, Amen.

"Hey Rach?"

"Yeah."

"Do you trust God?"

Placing her pen on the table, Rachel smiled at her friend. "Yes."

"So, you trust him with everything?"

"Yeah, why?"

"I was thinking about how Ms. Lorna said we had to trust God to be a woman after his heart. I've asked him to grow my faith, but I'm not sure I trust him with everything."

"Do you want to be a woman after his heart?"

"I do."

"Daddy told me once that a relationship with God starts by seeking him."

"That's it?"

"Hey, remember when Eva Mae started walking?"

"Yeah."

"Who did she walk to?"

"Aunt Lisa."

"That's right. And she didn't walk right away. Didn't she fall a couple of times?"

Maddie giggled as she thought about Eva Mae's toddling.

"Daddy said that a relationship with God begins with belief and grows by taking one step at a time toward him—just like Eva Mae. And if we fall, he is there to help us get back up. This builds our trust."

"So, faith and trust aren't the same thing?"

Walking out on the patio, Grammy asked, "Are you Girls 'bout done? Once yer brother gets up, we gotta get."

"Yes ma'am. Hey Grammy, are faith and trust the same?"

"Why, that's a good question." Grabbing the back of a spindly chair, she asked, "Do ya have faith that this chair'll hold me?"

The chair was a little rickety. Maddie looked at Rachel and wondered if this was a trick question. "Uh…"

"Looking at the chair, I can have faith that it'll hold me, but trust is when I sit down." Grammy sat down and grabbed the table when the chair began to wobble.

"Oh, so trust is following through with faith?" Rachel asked.

"That's right as rain, Girl. Now, if that be all, finish yer breakfast and let yer ole Grammy here get Brother up so we can go swimmin'."

"Wow, check it out. Where does it end?" Matthew ran down the sand as he kicked the surf.

Watching a sandpiper make its way down the beach, Maddie connected with the awe in her brother's voice as she wondered the same thing.

"Isn't it amazing?" Rachel asked.

"Yeah. Have you been here before?"

"It's been a long time. Dad's busy season is summertime, so we typically don't get to go to the ocean."

As Aunt Lisa and the girls set up camp on the beach, Matthew ran into the surf. Maddie and Rachel sat down to enjoy the view.

"Ya know, Ms. Bonnie asked us to think about awe and wonder, do you think she knew we were going to the beach?" Maddie asked Rachel.

Gazing at the horizon, Rachel smiled and said, "This view is gonna give us a lot to write about, isn't it?"

Running up to his family, Matthew asked, "Hey Maddie, do you think there are three people on the other side of the ocean looking at the ocean and wondering if there are three people on the other side looking at the ocean?" A perplexed look came over Matthew as he asked this very serious question.

"Absolutely." Maddie chuckled. This seemed to satisfy her brother as he ran back into the surf.

"Is it okay if we walk down the beach?" Maddie asked Grammy.

"Shore, y'all go on ahead. We'll be here when ya get back."

As they walked down the beach, Maddie recalled the verse from their lesson, *be still and know that I am God.* "It's hard not to believe in God when you look at this view."

"I know, right? Imagine how big the ocean is, and it still isn't greater than God's love for us."

Maddie thought about that for a moment. "People talk about finding peace at the ocean, do you think God is here?"

"God is everywhere, Maddie."

"I know, but do you think there is more of him here?"

"I think we connect with him here because we are reminded that the ocean is wide and deep yet mysterious and dangerous. To be still and know that he is God is to know that he is greater even than this ocean."

"That's deep."

"Yeah, just like the ocean."

As they laughed at the analogy, the girls went to look for

Matthew.

Looking at her friend, she said, "Hey, the first one back to the blanket gets the float!"

The race was on!

Rachel's long legs determined the winner of the race as she made it to the float first. Out of breath, Maddie came in a close second.

Grabbing the float, the girls made their way to Matthew. Shielding the sun from her eyes with her hand, Maddie looked out to find her brother, but he was nowhere to be found.

"Grammy, have you seen Matthew?"

"He was right thar," Grammy said as she stood up. "Where'd that boy go?" She asked worriedly.

Maddie breathed a sigh of relief as she saw the familiar curly redhead pop up out of the water, happy to show off the prize in his hand. "Don't do that to me, Matthew," she said under her breath.

"That boy's gonna be the death 'o me," Grammy muttered after sitting back down.

Wading through the waves, Maddie made a beeline for her brother with Rachel not far behind. Maddie found the undertow of the waves to be quite strong.

"Hey Maddie, look what I found!" Matthew showed off his new seashell.

"That's pretty, where'd you find it?"

"It was on the sand, all the way at the bottom. Would you like me to get you one?"

Before Maddie could reply, Matthew dove under the water.

Suddenly, she realized just how big the ocean really was and how very far they had waded. A tide that appeared so powerful from the lighthouse seemed downright furious in front of her. *It won't take much to go under,* she thought to herself.

A cry from behind her confirmed her fears, "Help!" Matthew yelled.

Turning to find her brother, a wave crashed over her. Stunned for a split second as she tried to catch her breath, she suddenly shot to the top. A moment of panic set in as she realized she couldn't see him. It was then that she heard his voice once more, "Help, Maddie!"

As soon as Maddie ventured to make it to her brother, another wave hit her. She didn't know what to do. She could feel the panic rising inside of her, her heart racing at the thought of not saving her brother. *I MUST find him!* She screamed inside her head. Frantically swimming against the current, a sudden, small voice said, "Stay calm. Don't fight it. Just float."

Feeling the small hand of her brother grab her arm, she yelled, "Matthew!" as she pulled him close to her.

The fight had left Matthew exhausted, as he collapsed on her. While her brother was heavy, Maddie felt a supernatural strength within her to hold both herself and her brother up on top of the waves. Waving her hand for help, she figured staying put would be better than trying to swim to shore. Thankfully, the waves stopped their overwhelming pull so Maddie and Matthew could float as they waited. A few moments passed before two lifeguards came and helped them wade into shore.

Rachel and Lisa came running as soon as they made it to shore. After checking Matthew for a pulse and signs of breathing, one of the lifeguards laid him on his side, encouraging him to cough up any seawater.

Maddie felt anxiety grab her tightly as the lifeguard hovered over her brother; thankfully, he didn't drown. Distressed, she couldn't help but remember when he almost died in the hospital. Not again! She thought.

After a few moments, Matthew looked at his sister and gave a thumbs-up. "I'm good, Mads!" he said in a hoarse voice.

Maddie shook her head and knelt beside her brother, "You scared me to death, Matthew!"

"No, I didn't. You're still alive!" He corrected softly as he sat up beside her.

"Are you Matthew's mom?" The lifeguard asked Aunt Lisa.

"I'm his aunt, and this is his Grammy."

The lifeguard smiled warmly and said, "Matthew is okay,

but you must watch him for forty-eight hours. If he experiences fatigue, behavioral changes, cough, chest tightness, or shortness of breath, call 911.”

“Yes, sir, thank you so much.”

Kneeling, he tousled Matthew's hair as he said, “You gave us quite a scare, little man. Next time you wade out, bring somebody with you, okay?”

Embarrassed, Matthew looked up at the lifeguard as he said, “Yes, sir, thank you.”

After the day's excitement, Grammy decided to keep everyone close as they celebrated Independence Day with their neighbors on the beach. Sporting the red, white, and blue flag given to him by the lifeguard, Matthew marched around them as if nothing had happened.

Maddie was learning not to hold on to things, and today was no exception. After the lifeguard left them, Grammy thanked God that everyone was okay and prayed his promises over them both. Holding her hands out in front of her, Maddie laid her fear in her hands and slowly rotated them to drop it at the cross, repeating Grammy's prayer that God's mercies would never end. She was surprised at how quickly her heart calmed after the crisis.

Suddenly distracted by the sunset, Maddie said to her friend, “Wow, look at that.” Afraid to close her eyes, she watched as the sun met the water; the sky exploding into a burst of color. As the sun was swallowed up by the ocean's vastness, it seemed to leave behind its fiery mark as if to say, ‘I will return.’

“Yeah, it's quite powerful. Have you ever considered that God paints a brand-new picture for us every night?” The wonder on Rachel's face was unmistakable.

“Yeah.”

“Hey Maddie, do you know what you did today?” Rachel asked.

Looking at her friend, curiously, she shook her head.

"In the moment you listened to that voice, you trusted God. You're becoming a woman after his heart."

The exploding fireworks surprised everyone who suddenly looked up at the display. Maddie thought back to the moment when the voice told her to stay calm. Before now, she had no free moment to think about where the voice came from. Somehow, she knew it was God who helped her in that moment. Looking up into the night sky, she was grateful for his help.

As the fireworks show ended, Maddie looked at the sleeping figures of Matthew, Eva Mae, and Rachel. A wave of gratitude overcame her as she realized the people she loved were safe. They endured a great deal in the last year; today, they are alive and well. A nagging reminder of the protestors carrying signs at Cape Henry attempted to distract her from her gratitude, but she wouldn't think about that now. Instead, she looked up and said, "God, thank you for helping us today."

"It's time ta gather our things. Maddie, can ya wake them three, and let's get on up to our room? We've had a long day."

"But a blessed day, Grammy."

Maddie couldn't miss the smile on Grammy's face as she worked to get everyone up.

ATLANTA, GEORGIA

Atlanta Humidity hit David like a pile of bricks, causing him to quickly regret the dark blue suit when he walked out of his front door. Jacque spent fifteen minutes preening over how handsome he was, tightening the dark blue tie multiple times as they stood on the front steps.

Driving into the parking deck, he proceeded to park the Tahoe. Eight forty-five, he had fifteen minutes. With his hands glued to the steering wheel, he closed his eyes and pondered the coming meeting. As much information as he had gleaned over the last year, he knew Lucien Baldur better than perhaps he knew himself. But Lucien didn't know that, or did he?

When Maddie went missing, David was on autopilot. He had been in dangerous situations before, and he knew what to do. Now with Michael's disappearance, David was angry. Why were his superiors shunning him? Whenever he spoke about his family's situation, they gave some flippant reason why they refused to open a case against this guy. Even his mentor, Admiral Rick Osborne considered the conversation moot. David smelled a rat.

As the elevator doors opened to the reception area of the thirty-fourth floor, David was unsurprised to see the opulence before him. A bohemian chandelier was the centerpiece of the room. If David had to guess, the piece cost more than his yearly salary.

A very beautiful woman sat at a single desk. Standing, she smiled at him warmly and said, "Good morning, Mr. Bennett. May I get you a coffee?"

"No ma'am, I have a meeting with Lucien Baldur."

"Yes, of course, right this way."

As he followed the woman, David took a mental picture of his surroundings. Lucien Baldur appeared to be a minimalist, but everything looked very expensive.

"Mr. Bennett, come in, come in. Please have a seat. Thank you, Zoe. You may leave now."

The man David had studied was wealthy and suave. He had seen him on TV, but to see Lucien in person was to realize that he had youth on his side, which surprised him. As the two men sized one another up, Lucien placed his fingers together and peered at the man across from him.

"So, Mr. Bennett. Am I what you expected?"

Snapped out of his thoughts, David put on his best poker face and said, "Actually, no, I expected someone older."

The room suddenly felt cold when Lucien laughed. It was a laugh that made David's skin crawl. But the moment was gone as Lucien's face transformed into the suave debonaire gentleman everyone perceived.

David was not dealing with just anyone. Only one other time had he peered into the face of evil, and he was beginning to believe that this was no comparison.

"Let's get down to business, shall we? There is the matter of your son, Michael."

"Yes, where is he?" David had to cool his anger even as his nostrils flared.

"My, my, did I just see the face of passion, Mr. Bennett?"

"I'm not sure what game you're playing here, *Mr. Baldur,* but I want you to tell me where my son is NOW."

"Of course, but first, I have a request." Lucien stood up, filled a small glass and took a sip.

David could see the calculating glance he threw his way before he gazed out the window.

"What is that?" David asked.

"You have access to information that I need. I have your son. Give me what I need, and I'll give you your son. It's the perfect business transaction."

"What information?" David asked.

"Oh, come now, *Commander Bennett,* I know of your relationship with Mordecai Oronoff. The intel I have slipped his way has been very lucrative for you. Has it not? Now, you owe me. Mr. Oronoff is sitting on information that will save the world. That is where you come in. You glean this intel from your friend and give it to me, and Michael is yours. Then you will be a hero to history as you partner with me to save the world."

CHAPTER 5

Sweet Sixteen

July 15
Wild Rock, Tennessee

The morning was hot and humid, but Maddie didn't care. Her Fam was coming in today and she was on cloud nine! Grateful as she was for the time she had with Rachel, she couldn't be more excited to see the rest of her girls, Jade, Katelyn, and Emma.

"Hey Grammy." Skipping up to the counter, Maddie plopped a kiss on her Gram's cheek.

"Good Mornin', Love. How'd ya sleep?"

Standing with her hands on her hips and a sly smile on her face, Maddie said, "Finer 'n frog hair."

Cackling, Grammy replied, "Girl, ya never cease ta surprise yer ole Grammy here."

"Guess what?"

Looking at her through the corner of her eye, Grammy asked, "What's that?"

"You don't know?"

Throwing up her hands, an exasperated Grammy said, "Now, how should I know anythin' yer not tellin' me?"

"Tomorrow's my birthday!"

"Well, I'll be, ya don't say." Perplexed, Grammy looked at

the ceiling.

"Grammy!"

After taking her granddaughter's face in her hands, her gram said, "Maddie Ruth, there ain't nothin' I'd rather do than celebrate yer turnin' sixteen."

Maddie smiled as she hugged her Grammy tight.

Turning back to the French toast before her, Grammy asked, "So, what time can we 'spect yer friends?"

"Jade's mom is bringing them around lunchtime. Is that okay?"

"Well, that'd be righter 'n rain." Grammy rubbed a pinch of sugar on her granddaughter's nose. "Go get yer brother up, will ya? Breakfast is jes 'bout done."

Walking to the back of the house, Maddie opened her brother's door and saw him sitting up in bed reading.

"What'cha readin'?"

"Maddie, did you know that Davy Crockett was born down yonder?"

"Down where?"

"You know, over thar."

Shaking her head, she laughed at her brother's imitation of their Grammy. "Matthew, be specific."

"Grammy said he was born about an hour from here in a town called Limestone. Can we go see his house, Maddie?"

"I guess, but you've gotta ask Grammy."

"Hey, did you know he ran away when he was only thirteen? That's only two years older than me!"

"Well, don't be getting any ideas, little Bro. Oh, by the way, Grammy wants us to come for breakfast."

"Breakfast!" Hopping out of bed, Matthew ran past his sister and made a beeline for the kitchen.

Shaking her head, Maddie walked past their shared bedroom where she overheard Rachel on the phone.

"I'm sorry, Kate, no I won't say anything. You're coming though, right? Okay, good. She'll love it. Can't wait to see you guys! It's been way too long."

Continuing down the hallway, Maddie wondered what that was about. She didn't want to betray her confidence, but she was very curious about her friend's conversation. *God, what should I do? Should I say something?* Deciding to let it go for now, she called for her friend to come for breakfast.

As she walked into the kitchen, she caught sight of Matthew standing on the bench making a deal with Grammy about something.

"Shhh, why a'course, Boy. What'd ya think it was?" Grammy quickly grabbed something from the counter to show Matthew as she looked at her granddaughter through the corner of her eye.

Maddie was starting to think something fishy was going on. "So, what's for breakfast, Matthew?"

"Grammy made us French Toast!"

"Yummy, I was wondering what the powdered sugar was for. Did you make that yummy blueberry jam too?"

"Ya mean compote, don't ya? It wouldna be the same without it, now, would it?"

In preparation for the big day, Rachel, Maddie, and Matthew were helping Grammy pick vegetables from her garden. As she plucked tomatoes from her special plant, Maddie thought back to her fifteenth birthday. If you had told her she would be getting her hands dirty as she picked tomatoes from her very own plant, she would have laughed at you. But here she was.

Bending down to pick up a few that dropped from the vine, she jumped up as she heard Rachel yell, "They're here!"

Grabbing the bucket of tomatoes, Maddie ran toward the front drive. "Hey!" Maddie yelled as Matthew ran past her with Max not far behind. *No fair that Max can run faster than me!*

Out of breath, Maddie set her bucket down to welcome her friends.

"Wowza, who'd of thought Grammy lived so high up!

Check out that mountain!" Kaitlyn looked up and down as she got out of the car.

"Hi, Ms. Alisha. Kaitlyn!" Maddie grabbed her friend.

"Girl, I don't know what y'all been doin' up here, but this is amazing!" Jade joined her friend in looking up as she exited from the back seat.

Maddie grabbed Kaitlyn and Jade's hands and jumped up and down for joy.

Rachel had one arm around Emma as they walked from the back of the car.

"Emma!" Maddie ran to say hello to her musical friend.

"I need a minute, Mads." Emma looked pale and held out an arm to keep her distance.

"What's wrong?" Maddie asked, concerned.

"She's a little car sick, bleh." Gagging, Jade teased her friend as Maddie helped her to a chair.

"I'll be okay. Thank you, Maddie." Emma smiled weakly.

"Come on Girls, let's get your bags inside." Jade's mom, encouraged.

Alisha Jackson was tall and beautiful with a long steady gait. Maddie loved listening to her tell stories of her work in the hospital. As an OB/GYN, she loved bringing life into the world and sharing the stories of each one.

Picking up a bag, Maddie asked, "Ms. Alisha, any new baby stories?"

"Well, I did deliver a beautiful set of triplets over the weekend." Ms. Alisha looked back at her as she walked up the stairs with two bags.

"That would be three babies." Jade said satirically.

"Three babies! In the belly?" Matthew pulled up his shirt and looked at his stomach. "I can't even fit three hamburgers in my belly!"

The screen door slammed behind her as she said, "You'd be amazed at what God can do, Matthew."

Maddie picked up the last of the bags as she thought about Ms. Alisha's reply. After their spring retreat, Jade came home so excited to have said yes to Jesus. She encouraged her mom to go to Church, where she too decided to follow Jesus. All the girls were so happy to see them both filled with joy after everything they had gone through.

After the girl's rescue, Ms. Alisha would tell them stories of how Jesus would comfort her through the witness of miraculous new life. God gave me a vision of his hand in every birth. *"This was proof to me that he had each of you in his perfect hand."* She would say. It was so amazing to Maddie that Ms. Alisha was able to be so close to God as she delivered babies. *I wonder if I could do that,* she pondered.

Suddenly, Maddie stopped as she clutched her chest. Closing her eyes, she remembered the smell of the musty hood over her head. Hearing Rachel's voice in her head to breathe, she slowly began speaking Yah-weh, as she attempted to slow her breathing. After about five breaths, she opened her eyes to the loving concern of her Grammy.

"You alright, Love?"

Maddie noticed her gram's hand on her arm. When did Grammy come outside? She wondered. "Yes ma'am, I'm okay."

"What'cha thinkin'?"

"I don't know, all of a sudden, I was back in that van with the hood, the shag carpet, the fear." Placing her head on her grandmother's shoulder, she wept quietly.

"Look at me, Maddie Ruth."

Maddie looked up.

"It's okay to weep. R'member, the Lord holds a bottle jes fer yer tears. Ya gotta let it out."

"I know. I thought I was okay. I haven't thought about it in weeks. I don't understand why . . ."

"Well, I 'spect it's cause yer friends are here. Have y'all talked 'bout yer experiences?"

Maddie looked toward the trees. "No ma'am. Jade and Kaitlyn don't want to talk about it."

Nodding her head, Grammy said, "Yeah, I 'spect so. It may be time, don't ya think? Let's pray on it. The Lord still has some healin' for youin's."

"Hey, Maddie, are you coming? The girls are in the back oohing and aahing over Grammy's garden." Rachel called out the open screen door.

"Are ya good?" Grammy comforted her as she caressed her shoulder.

Maddie nodded as she breathed a slow breath of relief. "Yes, ma'am. I'm good."

"Come on, let's show yer friends the Lord's bounty!"

Later that night, the girls were lying on the back deck looking up at the night sky.

"Check out those stars." Kaitlyn said in awe.

"I know, right. I had no idea Tennessee had more stars than Georgia." Jade looked up as she nudged her friend.

Kaitlyn laughed as she smacked Jade's shoulder. "You know they don't, silly. There just aren't any lights to take away from the stars."

"Is that why we can see more stars here, Kate? I always wondered." Maddie said as she looked up.

"Yup, light pollution is a star killer." Kaitlyn replied.

Putting her hands in the air in the shape of a diamond, Jade asked, "Hey, does this remind you guys of Woodlands?"

In a faint reply, Rachel said, "Yeah. . ."

"I miss Woodlands. Do you think we'll ever go back?" Maddie asked.

"We made a promise, of course we'll go back." Emma said emphatically.

"Gosh, it seems ages ago. Can you believe only five months have passed?" Rachel asked.

The quiet was thicker than butter as each girl sat in her thoughts. Maddie felt it was time to address the elephant in the room.

"Girls, can we talk about the PKO?" Maddie asked.

Kaitlyn immediately stood up and said, "Nope, nope, nope."

Maddie sat up and grabbed the edge of her friend's shirt, "Kate, I know this is hard, but we need to talk about what we went through. Rachel and I saw something when we went to the beach."

Shaking her head, Kaitlyn said angrily, "Not gonna do it."

"If not now, when?" Rachel asked.

"Not now, not ever!" Kaitlyn ran into the house and slammed the back door.

Jade let out a big exhale. "She's struggling, y'all."

"I know, we all are." Maddie said.

"What did y'all see?" Jade asked.

"There were a whole bunch of people with signs yelling, NO ORDER, NO PEACE." Maddie answered.

Emma turned white as Jade sat in shock. Taking a deep breath, Jade closed her eyes and said, "She's having nightmares."

"Jade, you weren't supposed to say anything." Rachel cried.

"Hey, we're all gonna be sleeping in the same room tonight, you're probably gonna know it by morning."

"What kind of nightmares?" Emma asked.

"I've heard her yell, 'let me go.' But all she'll tell me is that she dreams of running through the fields and never finding her way out."

"We can't let her suffer like this." Emma said sadly.

Rachel grabbed Emma and Maddie's hands and said, "She's gotta do it, Ladies. Remember what Sonya says, we must choose to let go."

"Can we pray for her?" Maddie asked.

Sitting up, Rachel said, "Of course. Why don't you start?"

Maddie felt great compassion for her friend. As she prayed, she saw herself sitting in front of Jesus with her head bowed. Rachel taught her to see herself in the throne room of God, recognizing His sovereignty and His grace. Maddie didn't know what Jesus looked like, but she would get a picture in her head and focus on what she knew about him. He was sovereign, kind, loving, and just. He heard our prayers and knew them even before we asked. Knowing these things gave Maddie a confidence she never had before. She just knew God heard her prayers even if she didn't hear his voice. And what always followed her prayer was a simple peace. After she finished, each girl lifted her own cry to Heaven. Rachel finished with a simple "In Jesus' Name, Amen."

Attempting to change the mood, Jade stood up, grabbed a couple of hands, and said, "Come on Girls, let's go find the party master and start planning this party tomorrow night."

"Oh yeah, tomorrow's my birthday!" Maddie jumped up, suddenly excited for the next twenty-four hours.

The morning of Maddie's birthday was sunny and bright. As Ms. Carolina Wren loudly serenaded her outside her window, she thought, *where have you been, Ms. Carolina?*

Everyone but Rachel slept soundly on the two beds in the room. Rachel, ever the early riser, was up with the sun spending time with Jesus.

Grabbing two cups of coffee, Maddie walked out on the back deck to sit with her friend quietly.

Placing her pen down, Rachel looked up and smiled as she mouthed, "Thank you."

"How'd you sleep?" Rachel asked.

"Okay, I guess. Jade kept elbowing me."

Rachel laughed. "She does that. Watch her, she'll have you on the floor before you know it."

Shaking her head, Maddie said, "It's nice to have everyone here."

"Yeah, it is."

Suddenly, hands covered Maddie's eyes as she heard Rachel giggle. Her heart pounding, she asked, "Who is that?"

Hearing a loud clang directly in front of her, the hands fell off her eyes as a chorus of Happy Birthdays arose like a symphony around the table.

Looking down, she smiled as she saw a handmade sculpture of her very own Ms. Carolina Wren.

"You guys. Who did this?" Maddie could feel tears crowding the corners of her eyes.

Rachel looked down at her friend as she replied, "Emma formed and fired the clay. Kaitlyn carved it."

"See the eyelashes, that was me." Kaitlyn smiled.

"I painted it." Jade said proudly.

"Look at the bottom," Rachel encouraged her friend.

Maddie picked up the delicate clay bird and looked at the inscription underneath, *"The Lord is with you, Mighty Warrior."*

"Wow, did you do this Rachel? How did you write it so perfectly?"

"With a little fire and a lot of grit." The wink sent Maddie into giggles as she remembered Matthew's messy lesson on grit.

"Thank you all so much! I love it!" Standing up, she gave each of her girls a hug.

"So, what is the plan for today?" Kaitlyn asked.

Rachel's wink said it all. Maddie's sweet sixteen would be the bomb!

It had been a long time since David had been to his adolescent home. Guilty reminders of his deep desire to leave this place left him in a sour mood. Jacque's mood didn't seem to be much different as she sat beside him.

David and his sister Lisa were complete opposites. While she loved their childhood home, he wanted to be anywhere but here. Growing up with a military dad taught him discipline, but not much love. He loved his dad but could only connect with him when seeking after hard things. The only time David received a hug from his proud dad was when he announced that he would be joining the Navy after graduating from college. Unfortunately, this moment was one in a million.

"Do you think Maddie will be surprised?" Jacque asked

nervously.

"Mom told me she has no idea we're coming. When I talked to her last week, she seemed a little disappointed when I told her I was on a mission."

Jacque looked out of the car window in silence.

Driving up to the house, David was surprised at the number of vehicles surrounding the white house. *Does Mom know what she's getting herself into?* He thought to himself.

"Dad! Mom!" Matthew ran down the front stairs with Grammy's Basset hound, Max, in tow.

"Hey Sport." David gave his son a high five.

"Hey Mom, how are you feeling?" Matthew asked a bit timidly.

"Today is a good day, Son. Give me a hug, I've missed hearing your tennis shoes running across the house." Jacque said.

"Where is Maddie?" David asked as he grabbed their bags from the back of the Tahoe.

"She's in the back with Grammy and the girls. They're decorating for the party."

"Well, don't tell her we're here yet. Let your mom get settled and then we'll come around to the back."

"Okey dokey!" Matthew went running toward the back.

Walking into the house, Jacque turned to David and said, "It's been a long time, hasn't it, David?"

"I was just thinking the same thing. A birthday party is better than a wake."

"Do you miss your dad?" Jacque asked.

"Yes, now, and again. Honestly, it's been his voice that has helped me in the last year."

"I'm sorry, David."

Sitting down on the couch next to his wife, David moved the hair out of her face, "About what, Love?"

"I know this has all been so hard for you. You've had to carry my burden while you valiantly looked for Maddie, and now Mike. I truly don't know what I would have done without you."

David pulled his wife close to him. "I love you Jacque, you know that don't you?"

Jacque nodded as she looked up with tear-filled eyes.

"I know that I haven't been the best husband to you." David went quiet as he gently touched Jacque's cheek with his own. "I wish I . . ."

"No, don't do that." Jacque said as she pulled back. "None of this is your fault, do you hear me? We are here, together, celebrating our daughter's sixteenth birthday. That is what matters, right?"

"Yes, how are you feeling?"

"I'm okay, truly." A smile lifted as she looked toward the back of the house. "I'm looking forward to seeing my daughter."

"I thought I heard y'all in here. David, ma boy, come give yer ole Momma a hug!"

"Hi Mom."

"Jacque, it's good ta see ya, Dorter."

"Hi Mom, thank you for all you've done for the kids. You've been such a blessing to us all."

Grabbing both of their hands, Grammy said, "We're family, I wouldna have it diff'rent."

"Does Maddie know we are coming?"

"Naw, ever'body's kept a tight lid on this 'un. She's gonna be so 'excited!'

Suddenly, the back door slammed as the kitchen filled with the joy of loud female voices.

"No, I don't think that would be a good . . . Dad! Mom!" Maddie dropped what she was carrying and ran into the living room to greet her parents.

"Hello, Ruthie."

"Maddie, your hair is beautiful. It's getting so long!" Jacque said.

Overcome with emotion, Maddie grabbed her parents into a big hug. "But, Dad, I thought you were on a mission."

"Well, I decided to play hookie for a couple of days."

"Yay! Oh, thank you Guys. Did Grammy tell you what we're doing tonight?"

"Something about a bonfire?"

"No, a pick'n 'n grin'n, Dad, get it right." Matthew interjected.

David laughed as he felt the peace of having most of his family in one room. "Well, there you go."

CHAPTER 6

Life is a Dream

Elated as she hung the last of the bulbs for the bonfire, she thought, *How I would love to hold a party like this at home!* Sitting down to look at the finished product, she was delighted at the soft white light emanating from the perfectly round bulbs.

Rachel sat down admiring Maddie's work. "Wow, look at that! Looks great, BFF."

"Thanks, I was just thinking how awesome this would look in our back yard."

"Do you miss home?"

"A little. Can you believe it's been a whole year since we celebrated last?"

"Wow, a whole year. Weird how birthdays work like that." Rachel laughed.

Leaning over to bump her friend, Maddie said, "You know what I mean. A lot has happened in a year."

"And yet, here we sit."

"Yeah."

Catching a glimpse of Maddie's parents walking through the garden, Rachel asked, "Are you glad your parents were able to come?"

Maddie's eyes gleamed, "Yes, did you know about it?"
Rachel smiled.

"How could you keep a secret like that from me?"

"What, and miss this face?"

"Momma looks good, doesn't she?" Maddie asked.

"She does."

"I wonder how she'll like the party. You know how she likes everything to be shiny and perfect."

Aghast at the thought, Rachel asked, "Who says it won't be shiny and perfect?"

Maddie shrugged. "It just won't be, you know. . ."

"Her way?" Rachel asked.

With a haunted look, Maddie paused before agreeing, "Yeah."

"Maddie, just because it isn't the way she would do it doesn't mean she won't like it. Give her a chance. This is your birthday. Don't worry about what she'll think; it's what you think that counts."

"You're right. It is quite perfect, isn't it?" Maddie asked, suddenly giddy.

Admiring the lights as they surrounded the fire pit, Rachel answered, "It's getting there, and once we finish hanging these decorations it will be quite perfect. So, let's get to it before the girls get back."

Grammy sent Jade and the girls on a mission for the makings for S'mores. Maddie couldn't think of a better birthday dessert.

"So, who else is coming?" Rachel asked inquisitively.

"A couple of people from Grammy's Church."

"Jacob?" Rachel asked as she glanced at her friend from the corner of her eye.

Maddie chuckled. "Are you asking about Jacob or Rory?"

Rachel turned to hide her flushed face. "Jacob, of course. Do you still like him?"

"I don't know. When he's alone, he seems nice. But when he's around his friends, well, it's just awkward." Maddie shrugged her shoulders.

"I see that. You know what he's doing, don't you?"

Looking at Rachel as she lit a candle, she asked, "What?"

"You know how a peacock shows off his feathers when he's interested in a female?"

Maddie almost dropped the candle as she laughed at the visual. "Are you calling Jacob a peacock?"

"I'm just saying, guys show off for girls when they're with their friends. Let's test the theory. Tonight, when he's with his friends, look at him for an extra couple of seconds and see how they act. I'll bet you a dollar he likes you and they give him a hard time about it."

"You've got a bet," Maddie said as she sealed it with a fist bump.

"Looks good Ladies, looks mighty good," Grammy said as she walked toward the house with Maddie's parents.

"Grammy, is everyone in the band coming?"

"You know it! Only the best for ma girl!"

Maddie did a little dance and said, "I can't wait for y'all to see this. Rachel, it's the bomb!"

"I've played in a couple of pic'n n' grin'n's." David said.

Maddie couldn't believe her ears. "Wait, what? No way!"

"I did grow up here, Ruthie."

"Oh yeah."

David smiled as he looked at Jacque and said, "I even played for your mom a time or two."

The look on Jacque's face was one of longing and butterflies. Preparing to share her parents' level of cringe worthiness, she thought better of it when she realized what her dad was saying. "Wait, but what instrument do you play?"

"I think we'll keep that a surprise for now, you'll find out tonight."

Maddie exchanged excited glances with her friend. *Tonight was going to be awesome!*

Nerves began to set in as Maddie got ready with the girls. What if they don't like my Wild Rock friends? An immediate frown of concern flashed across her face as she glanced at herself in the mirror. Forcing a smile for Emma, she finished brushing her hair.

"Can I braid it?" Emma asked.

"Sure."

As Emma began parting her hair, Matthew walked into the room with a flower, "Happy Birthday, Maddie."

"Oh Matthew, it's beautiful!"

"I picked it just for you. And I combed my hair, too. Does it look okay?"

Smiling at her brother's perfectly combed curls and nervous grin, Maddie said, "You look very handsome, Brother. But why so extra?"

"You only turn sixteen once." Matthew blushed as he ran out of the room.

A quartet of "awes" surrounded Maddie as Emma put the finishing touches on her hair.

Pulling little curling tendrils loose, Emma asked, "What do you think? Isn't she beautiful, Girls?"

The reflection in the mirror quite surprised Maddie. Remembering her mom's compliment, she examined her pale clear complexion while pulling the thick braid forward and running her fingers down the plaited strands. Always pulling her hair back in a ponytail, she wasn't one to spend a lot of time on her looks, but today she almost glowed.

Preoccupied with admiration for Emma's work, Maddie jumped as Jade bellowed, "Kaitlyn, what's that on your phone?"

"Oh nothing." Kaitlyn was obviously hiding something.

Holding out her hand, Jade said, "Let me see."

The girls made a deal after they returned from the PKO that whenever Kaitlyn obsessed over her phone that she would allow her friends to check her messages for accountability.

Biting her tongue to keep from arguing, Kaitlyn said, "It's just the Gram, Girls."

"You're not talking to Batman again, are you?" Rachel asked.

The reference to Noah, her crush from last summer caused Kaitlyn to crinkle her nose. "No, but there is someone."

"Wait, who's this someone? You didn't tell me about no

someone." Hands on hips, Jade wasn't going to let this one go.

"His name is Brad. He works at The Coffee Bar. We met when I was studying for the SAT."

"Wait a minute, isn't that where Jackson Reese works? Whatever happened to him, Rach?" Maddie asked.

Blushing, Rachel mumbled, "I forgot about him."

Putting her hand to her ear, Maddie asked, "What'd you say?"

"I think she said she forgot about him. You're failing the vibe check, Girl." Jade said sarcastically.

"Leave her alone, she's interested in someone else now." Maddie exclaimed. "Oops!" Sending a nonchalant wink toward her friend, she covered her mouth in amusement.

Rachel shot the look of death toward Maddie. "She doesn't know what she's talking about. And Jackson is still around, he just hasn't had much time to talk because he's preparing for boot camp."

"Hold up, Jackson's going into the military?" Jade asked incredulously.

"Yes, they're going to give him a full ride to college, but he's going to boot camp first. He'll start workups this summer. After graduation, he'll go straight into boot camp and then enter college after."

"What about the worship team?"

"He's taking a break for the summer." Rachel said.

Interrogation ready, Jade asked, "You sure do know a lot about Mr. Reese. How do you know so much about him so far away?"

"We talk." Rachel smiled.

"Oooooohhhh, Kaitlyn chimed in. Okay, I'm with Jade, somebody's telling a story. Just two minutes ago you said you forgot about him, but now you're talking. Mm hmm."

"You Ladies have completely missed Maddie's slip of the tongue, so who is Rachel interested in, now?" Emma asked.

Maddie looked at her friend mischievously as she shrugged her shoulders. "Well, his name is Rory. And I wouldn't say Rachel is exactly interested in him, but he is sure interested in her." Maddie winked.

A chorus of oohs filled the air as everyone turned to Rachel.

Aunt Lisa walked up and leaned against the doorframe to the room. She said, "Okay, girls, it's time to get this shindig on. Maddie, there's somebody named Rory askin' for ya."

"Oooooohhhh." All the girls harmonized as they parroted their friend.

Before she knew it, Grammy's backyard was filled with half of Wild Rock. Maddie didn't know half of the people who came to celebrate her, but she was okay with that.

Taking a break from dancing to grab a drink, she noticed Jacob and his friends standing across the yard as they took a break from playing their instruments. Maddie decided to test Rachel's theory about Jacob as she gave him a good long stare. He caught her eyes and before she knew it, Rory and Jared were punching and elbowing Jacob into blushing himself. Maddie shook her head as she looked for her friend in response.

A whisper in her ear caused her to jump, "You owe me a dollar." Rachel laughed.

"You are not right!" Maddie laughed.

"I don't know, the dollar you owe me seems to say that I'm pretty right."

Before they knew it, the boys found their way over to them.

"I see ya don't have a drink, Ms. Monroe. Would ya like a dope?" Rory asked.

"A what?" Rachel looked at Maddie with alarm on her face.

"A dope, ya know, a soda?"

Rachel and Maddie both cracked up laughing as Rory stood with a soda can in his hand.

"Thank you, Rory. I would love a soda." Rachel said.

"My Pap is playin' fer me, so I have a few minutes." Eyes laser-focused on Rachel, Rory asked, "Would ya like to take a spin around the fire?"

Maddie watched her friend squirm a little. "I think that'd be a great idea. Go on Rach. I'll hold your soda."

"No ma'am, it's yer turn ta take a spin." Jacob laid down his banjo and grabbed Maddie's hand. "I've got dibs on a dance with the birthday girl."

Maddie felt alive from her head to her dancing feet. She loved everything about this night and hoped it would never end. As the song died down, a banjo echoed the slow pick of a guitar. Everyone stopped dancing as they watched the two pickers copying one another. Maddie's mouth dropped as she watched her dad play the banjo. Shaken, she was afraid to close her eyes, or else she would miss something. All around her some were clapping as others clasped arms and began to dance in circles.

"That's called The Dueling Banjo," Grammy whispered from behind her granddaughter.

"Since when does Dad play the banjo?" Maddie asked.

"Oh, my boy started playin' as a tike. It's bred in 'im, it is."

Maddie's mom placed her arm through her daughter's. "He's quite good, isn't he?"

"Mom, Dad said he played for you?" Maddie asked, her eyes fixed as the music invited her hands to clap.

Jacque had a faraway look on her face. "Oh yes, we met at a bonfire just like this at UGA. He brought out his banjo and I was smitten."

"But didn't he play football?"

"Yes, your dad has many talents, Maddie."

As they finished, Maddie watched as her dad caught her eye and began playing solo. One of the other guitarists began to sing "The Man Who Loves You the Most" by the Zac Brown Band as her dad played. Maddie knew this song. Memories of her dad picking her up and dancing as this song played in the background filled her with joy. Placing her head on her mom's shoulder, Maddie shed a tear as she enjoyed the moment. This season of life was a beautiful dream that she never wanted to wake from.

"Ya know, memories last a lifetime, Maddie Ruth."

Grammy whispered from behind.

"Yes ma'am."

Before bed, Maddie sat down to write in her journal. She didn't want to forget one single moment of the day. As she wrote about her dad playing the banjo, her eyes filled with tears once more. Her dad was full of surprises. Finishing her entry with a prayer, she knew she had to end this day with gratitude and a prayer of her greatest wish.

> July 16
> Father,
>
> thank you for this day. Thank you for everyone who came to celebrate my birthday. Thank you for my dad. Jesus. Would you do me a favor? Keep my dad safe as he goes back to work tomorrow. I really want to get to know him better. And Lord, please help him find Mike. In Jesus' Name, Amen.

"It's been a long time since we've watched these stars." Jacque said.

Kissing his wife's hand tenderly, David replied, "Yes, it has."

"David . . ."

"Yes, Love?"

"I know you can't tell me about your work, but . . . Is Mike alive?" She asked tentatively.

"Yes, I believe he's alive."

"But is he safe?"

David sat quietly watching the winking stars above them as he pondered the question. "I don't know."

"It's been almost three months, what is taking so long?"

Jacque turned away in frustration.

This was personal. David wanted to share his thoughts with his wife, but he didn't want to place her in danger. "Jacque, I can't give you all of the details, but I want you to know that I'm not going to let anything happen to our son."

"I don't know if I can take any more surprises." Jacque whispered.

Quiet as heavy as the humid night settled around them. David was worried. Lucien Baldur was playing a game with him, and unfortunately, he did not have any backup. Admiral Rick Osborne, David's superior, did not believe David's suspicions of Lucien Baldur and made it clear he was on his own. David was certain a human trafficking ring was only a small part of Lucien's portfolio. But he couldn't get anyone to believe him. David was incensed with the final report from the PKO fiasco: In-state kidnapping: no federal jurisdiction. Everything was pinned on the boy who lured Maddie's friend into a relationship and the other girls were caught in the crossfire. All bad actors were investigated and taken into custody by local officials. Case closed. There was no evidence of human trafficking. David smelled a rat but would need backup to prove the case. David knew that he couldn't be there for his wife and work through this mess at the same time.

"Would you like to stay here with Mom and the kids for the final weeks of the summer? I'm sure she would enjoy the adult company."

Jacque seemed to want to say something, then thought better of it. "Yes, I would like that."

After kissing his family goodbye, David made his way to the car. It was probably best that Jacque decided to stay behind as he had some phone calls to make on the ride back to Atlanta. Closing the car door behind him, David hit the speed dial to Israel.

"David, shalom! I have been awaiting your call, how is your

morning faring?" Mordecai Oronoff greeted.

"It depends on what you have to tell me." David replied expectantly.

"Our friend is on the move."

David shuddered. "He is anything but a friend, Mordy."

"Yes, yes, we must chat soon. When can I expect you?" Something was up for his friend to resort to code words. "Give me an hour and I will call you back."

"Good, that's good. Shalom, shalom." The line went dead.

Navigating through the thick fog as he made his way down the mountain, David sought a secure location to stop. Finding an empty parking lot on the northern side of the Cherokee National Forest, David connected to a secure line and re-dialed his friend.

"Hello David. It is good to hear your voice."

"So, what's up?"

"An operative of the Mossad sent me a garbled message that we have a mole."

David moved his seat back as he nodded to an empty car. "I expected as much."

"You knew? But how?"

"I had an interesting meeting with our friend." Uneasy, David decided to play the game.

"Really? And what did he have to say?"

"Apparently, it's not me he wants, but you."

"Me? What would he want with me?"

"I haven't a clue. He said something about information that would save the world. He wants me to partner with him. And before you say anything, no he is NOT A FRIEND!"

Chuckling at David's scornful tone, Mordecai said, "Come now, he's very rich."

Ignoring his banter, David asked, "What is this intel that he is so interested in?"

"Eh, you tell me. I'm an old, retired boat captain. Unless it has to do with sails and engines, I don't know what he would want with me. Unless . . ."

David watched as a doe with two fawns crossed the parking

lot in front of him. Incredulous at their lack of fear over his presence, David waited for the rest of his friend's statement. "Unless?"

"This is top secret information, David."

"Okay."

"Israel is working on a plan to extend the Iron Dome."

"The Iron Dome? Do you mean, the air defense system that intercepts rockets over Israel? How would he know about the plan? Why would he care?"

"Perhaps he wants to destroy it?"

"But he lives in Israel, doesn't he? Why would he want to destroy his homeland?"

"David, his homeland isn't Israel. As I understand, he is from Armenia."

"Hmm, interesting. Iran is just next door to Armenia. Do you know if his family has ties to Iran? You don't think he is in cahoots with them, do you?" David asked.

Uncertainty was heavy within his friend's inhale. "I don't, but I can find out. David, it would not be good for Israel if this information fell into Iran's hands."

"I understand. So, what should I tell him?"

"When are you meeting him again?" Mordecai asked.

"Monday morning."

"Give me until the weekend and I will forward you intel that you can share."

"It must be good, Mordy. My son's life is at stake."

"You know me, David. I'm the best at dreaming up a tale."

CHAPTER 7

A Persuasive Proposal

The morning sun promised a hot July day as the girls ate breakfast on the back porch. Maddie smiled as she watched her friends reminisce over the events from the night before. "Hang on, what is that?" Maddie asked as Jade shared a blurry pic from her phone.

Kaitlyn cackled as she announced, "Oh yeah, that boy Jared thought he would be funny and took me for a spin."

"Wait, you've got a thing for Jared?" Rachel asked.

"Naw, he's cute, but not my type AT ALL."

"What is your type?" Jade asked as she gave her friend the side eye.

Kaitlyn frowned as she looked off into the distance. "I don't know anymore. I'd like to start by having a guy just return my text messages. Oh, and not kidnap me."

Everyone was silent after Kaitlyn's declaration.

"I thought we weren't talking about it?" Emma asked quietly.

"Hey Maddie, look at what your friend Jacob gave me!" Interrupting the awkward silence, Matthew showed off a bright red pick. "It's a real guitar pick!"

Rachel winked at Maddie as she and the girls oohed and awed over Matthew's new toy.

"What are you going to do with this, little Bro?" Maddie asked.

Matthew beamed in response. "Jacob said he'd show me how to play his banjo."

"I think you'd make a great banjo player, Matthew." Jade tipped his cap forward in encouragement.

"Yeah, that's what Dad said, too! Hey, Mads, did Dad leave this morning?"

Giving her brother a dirty look for daring to use the hated nickname, she replied, "He did."

"Oh man, I wanted to ask him something."

"He said he hoped to be back next week."

"Yay!" Matthew went running back into the house.

"How's your mom and dad doing, Maddie?" Emma asked.

Pushing her plate away, Maddie said, "They're doing okay."

"I saw your mom smile more last night than I've seen in a long time," Rachel said.

"I know, right? I think she's doing a lot better. She's worried though, I can tell."

"About what?" Jade asked as she popped a blueberry in her mouth.

Wanting to stay low-key, Maddie whispered, "I overheard Dad say that he knew Michael's location."

"Wait, really?" Rachel asked.

"Shh, yeah. He didn't give any details though." Gesturing toward her mom and Grammy in the kitchen, Maddie placed her index finger on her lips.

"Is she worried that he's in danger?" Emma whispered.

Shrugging her shoulders, Maddie mumbled, "Yeah."

Placing her hand on her friend's shoulder, Rachel asked, "Hey, what do we do when we're worried?"

"I know. I've been praying a lot lately."

"Well, let's do it right now. Place your hands out."

The next few minutes were spent with Maddie placing her dad and brother in her hands as they prayed for Michael's rescue. She asked God to protect them both as he gave her family peace in the wait. After she said amen, she basked in the sun, feeling as if God was shining over her. She didn't know if that was possible, but she hoped so.

"Better?" Rachel asked when Maddie opened her eyes.

Smiling, she said, "Better, thank you, Rach. You always know exactly what I need."

A haunted look passed over Kaitlyn's face as she watched the exchange. Catching a glance out of the corner of her eye, Maddie wondered what Kaitlyn was thinking.

"Hey, Girl, would you like to talk about the nightmares you're having?" Maddie asked her friend.

Kaitlyn looked away. A tear escaped as she began to shake her head. "Yeah, I think so."

Everyone sat still as Kaitlyn struggled to continue. Emma grabbed a hand as Jade grabbed the other.

"The dream begins with a scream. But I can't see the person who's screaming. It's dark and foggy and I can barely see five feet in front of me. I'm running down row after row of sunflowers, but I can't see anyone or anything. The dream ends with the sunflowers wilting and then I wake up." Rubbing her nose with her arm, Kaitlyn took a deep breath. "Several times, I've woken up screaming. Mom is worried about me, but I tell her I'm fine. I'm always fine. I just want to be fine!"

Everyone sat still for a moment as Kaitlyn composed herself.

"Kate, do you think you're trying to find the person screaming? Is that why you're running?"

Shrugging, she looked at Jade and said, "I guess so. I'm not sure."

"Remember when we were looking for the opening in the fence?" Jade asked.

"Yeah."

"You had a look of terror on your face. I think you would have dug through the brush with your bare hands if I had let you. I had to talk you out of it." Looking intently into her friend's eyes, Jade nodded. "Remember?"

"I just remember being so happy to see Maddie." Kaitlyn grabbed Maddie's hand as she remembered the feeling of relief.

"You were almost giddy, Kate. Like you had come from a party." Maddie added.

"Panic," Rachel said.

"My mom calls it fight or flight," Emma said quietly.

"What's that?" Jade asked.

"It's a survival instinct. When your mind senses danger, your body responds in fight or flight mode. There are others too, freeze, I think. The way she explained it to me is, like, your body protects you from danger by responding in a way that makes you focus on something other than the threat."

"So, in your dream, if you're the one screaming, maybe it's your mind's way of letting go?" Rachel asked.

"I don't know. I just want it to stop!"

Maddie could see her frustration building as she balled up her fists.

"It sounds like you need to let go, Kate," Emma said.

"But how? It won't go away."

"We can pray," Rachel said quietly.

Throwing her a dirty look, Kaitlyn said, "Yeah, no. What has God ever done for me?"

Rachel nodded at her friend's rebuke.

Feeling the need to do something, Maddie jumped up and said, "Hey, I have an idea." Running down the back stairs, she ran to her aunt's house.

"Where's she going?" Jade asked.

Rachel held up her hands. "Don't look at me."

Out of breath, Maddie ran toward the backyard with boxing gloves and a small speed bag.

Laughing, Emma said, "Now, that is genius!"

Kaitlyn looked at her friend with a blank stare. "And what am I going to do with that?" She asked cynically.

"You're going to hit it. Trust me, this bag has been through a lot." Hanging the bag on a hook, Maddie put on the gloves to model how to hit the bag. Giving the gloves to her friend, she said, "Your turn."

Placing the gloves on her hands slowly, Kaitlyn looked at the bag timidly and said, "How do I hit it?"

"First, you get a picture of what you want to hit. Then you swing. Don't worry. You're not going to hurt anything."

"Can the "what" be a who?" Kaitlyn asked.

Maddie looked at Rachel.

"Well, David did hit Goliath," Rachel said.

"Your mission, Kaitlyn Brown, if you choose to accept it, is to hit this bag and allow your pain to release through each punch. Like this." Maddie stood in boxer formation with her eyes firmly fixed on the bag and let out a controlled yet powerful punch.

Mimicking her friend's form, Kaitlyn did the same.

"Well, I guess she just accepted the mission." Jade declared with a laugh.

ATLANTA, GEORGIA

David had twenty minutes to spare as he sat in his car with the engine running. He looked at the envelope sitting on the passenger seat. This wasn't the first time he was involved in collusion, but it was the first time he did so without his superior's knowledge. When he realized that help to find Michael wasn't forthcoming, David took an indefinite leave of absence from the military reserves. He gained administrative approval from Admiral Osborne, who took little issue with the understanding that once Jacque was stable, he would check in.

David's loyalty to his country was of the utmost importance to him, but his family meant more. The contents of this envelope could lead to a dishonorable discharge and possible court martial. These threats were nothing compared to Michael's life, however.

Looking in the rearview mirror, David tightened his tie and grabbed the envelope, remembering the prayer his mom prayed over him before he left Wild Rock,

"Father, give my son yer word. Protect 'em and keep 'em safe in yer hand. In Jesus' Name, Amen."

I'm not sure what good your words will be to me now, God, but if they

rescue Michael, please give them to me. He prayed.

As the elevator door opened, David directed his attention to the desk. "Good morning, Zoe." He had the gift of remembering names and faces. A lucrative talent, this tactic had gained him the trust of many in his career.

"Good morning, David. Mr. Baldur is expecting you."

Leading him into a spacious conference room, Zoe indicated where he was to sit. "May I get you a coffee?"

Placing the envelope on the table, David responded, "No, thank you."

"Very well then, I will let Lucien know you are here." Zoe smiled warmly as she closed the double doors behind her.

David was surprised at the sudden familiarity. He had learned early on that image was key and maintaining the pretense of formality led to respect. In addition to names and faces, David had become very good at discerning body language, and he was curious at this change of tone.

"David, my friend, it is good to see you again." Lucien Baldur walked into the room, commanding authority while offering both hands for a friendly handshake.

David stood as he offered his hand in return. "Mr. Baldur."

"Please, call me Lucien."

Nodding his head, David replied, "Lucien."

"Please have a seat. Would you like a coffee or water?"

"Neither thank you. Zoe was kind enough to ask but I am fine."

David watched as Lucien poured himself a glass of water and sat down. Once again, David was surprised by the youth emanating from his adversary. His body language suggested this was nothing more than a friendly meeting, but David was reminded who he was dealing with as Lucien looked at him with a penetrating gaze.

"So, David. Have you considered my offer?"

"I have, but I have a question."

Lucien looked at David quizzically.

"When we met last, you made mention of a partnership. What did you mean by this?"

"Ahh, did I capture your attention?"

"I would be lying if I said no."

"Good, good. I assume you have heard my speech before the World Trade Organization?"

"I have."

"I do not have to tell you about the humanitarian crisis with food insecurity worldwide. I have a plan to end world hunger and require someone with your, shall I say talents, to help me bring this plan to fruition."

"What does this have to do with Mordecai Oronoff?" David asked.

"Oh yes, our dear friend Mordecai. As I understand, he has information that will help me persuade the great nation of Israel to join in this humanitarian effort. They have been very stubborn to date."

There was that cold David experienced before. *Did Lucien's eyes change color?*

"Persuade? And how exactly do you intend to persuade Israel to do anything?"

Looking at the envelope on the table before David, Lucien asked, "I think I have shared enough information with you, Mr. Bennett. Do you have something for me there?"

David picked up the envelope and held it in his hand. He slowly opened the flap and looked inside. There was a single white piece of paper with a yellow note stuck to the top. Closing the envelope, he answered, "Yes, I do. But first, where is my son?"

"Tsk, tsk, and we were having such a lovely conversation, David. Give me a moment and I will get the coordinates for you directly. I do hope you will have an answer for me when I return."

As Lucien left the room, David tapped the table with the envelope. Mordecai had not briefed him on the information he had given him. David knew it was a long shot, but if anything, he could pretend to be oblivious if Lucien called his bluff. Pulling out the piece of paper, he glanced at the note. *What? What is this?*

> *And Jesus answered and said to him, "It has been stated, 'You shall not put the Lord your God to the test.*
> Luke 4:12

Is this a joke? Beads of sweat dripped down David's face as he re-read the note. The white piece of paper was blank. Quickly pulling the yellow note off and placing it in his pocket, David tapped the table again with the envelope. *How am I going to play this one?* As he watched Lucien walk into the room, he calculated his exit. Apparently, Plan B was going to be necessary. Suddenly, his mother's words popped into his mind, *Father, give my son yer word.* Placing his hand in his pocket, he felt the sticky yellow note and had a crazy notion as he chuckled under his breath.

Sitting in the leather chair at the end of the table, Lucien interlaced his fingers in front of him and said, "Well, David? Do we have a deal?"

Sitting back in his chair with an air of confidence, David responded, "Actually, Mr. Baldur, I will have to decline your offer of partnership but thank you for the vote of confidence. I am certain you will find someone qualified to help you. You are quite persuasive as I understand. Regarding the information from Mordecai Oronoff, I am not personally aware of the information you refer to; however, I did ask Mr. Oronoff to send me a memo with the details, and he was happy to oblige. But first, where is Michael?"

Lucien paused as David engaged him with a cynical gaze. They were at an impasse and Lucien knew it. If he wanted what was in this envelope, he would have to give something in return. Sitting back in his chair, Lucien took a deep breath and said, "You are very persuasive yourself, David. Your son is in California, but that is all the information I have now. I will put my man in touch with you to pick your son up. The envelope?"

David had to work quickly. Sliding the envelope to the other side of the table, David prepared to bolt.

As Lucien pulled the paper out of the envelope, he looked

perplexed as he turned it over. Looking up at David, he said, "There is nothing here."

With as innocent a look as he could muster, he shrugged and said, "As I said, I am not personally aware of said information. I guess he's not working on anything now. Oh, but there is another message I have for you."

Lucien's eyes flashed red as he glared at David, "And what is that?"

Pulling out the note in his pocket, David read, "It has been stated that you shall not put the Lord your God to the test. Thank you, Lucien, it has been a pleasure." David turned and walked toward the elevator. Reaching the first floor, he pulled out his phone and dialed. "Hey, it's me. Nope, it's Plan B. Yes, San Bernardino, California. How soon can you be there? Great, I'll be waiting."

SAN BERNARDINO, CALIFORNIA

Exhausted, Michael didn't think he could keep his eyes open another minute, but he didn't have a choice. From the first moment of his return to PKO-CA, he was under constant watch. His every movement was added to his file. Trust from his CO was usually elusive, but for Michael, it was impossible. When he first joined the PKO, his interview did not go well. He was hung over from a party the night before and determined to leave the state of Georgia after an argument with his dad. The PKO policy was complete inclusion, so anyone who showed the tiniest interest in the program was accepted and indoctrinated. *Oops, did I say that out loud?* He thought to himself as his counterpart looked at him funny. Since he was adamant about leaving Georgia and didn't have a passport, they sent him to California. When he heard the news, Michael was ecstatic! His idea of California was sun, sand, and girls. It was going to be a blast. Unfortunately, time would tell that none of this was to be. *I was so naïve.* Remembering his interview with CO Thomas, he knew he didn't leave a good impression, and the hangover noted in his file certainly didn't help matters. So, the sixteen months of his training had been spent as a lackey, always working in the shadows of someone else's glory and under the constant sight of CO Thomas, who clearly didn't trust Michael Bennett.

"Bagman, you've got fifteen minutes!"

"Yes Sir, I'm almost finished, Sir."

"CO will confirm every piece is still intact."

"He will not be disappointed."

"Good."

After finishing his task for the night, Michael made his way to his bunk. The thought of his pillow was enough motivation to keep moving. As he walked the breezeway to the bunkhouse, he looked up at the stars. Breathing deep the night air, a fleeting thought of home made him feel homesick. Suddenly, everything went dark as a hood was thrown over his head and he was picked up from behind.

CHAPTER 8

The Gift that Keeps on Giving

Walking toward the kitchen, Maddie and Rachel stopped as they heard Grammy's strong sure voice. The door to Jacque's room stood ajar. Grabbing Rachel's hand, Maddie placed her index finger on her mouth in silence.

"Father God, yer el Shaddai, the Almighty One. Lord, we don't know where our David and Michael are, but you do. Lord God, we need yer peace at this moment. Be with my Dorter Jacque here and let her know you've got her son in yer hand. We trust ya, God. In Jesus Name, Amen."

Rachel whispered amen and nodded toward the kitchen to signal their quiet retreat.

Swinging their clasped hands together, they stopped short when they entered the kitchen to see Jade and Emma looking through the sliding glass doors. "What'cha lookin' at?" Maddie asked.

"Shh, look," Emma whispered.

Peering around their friends, Maddie gasped as she saw Kaitlyn destroying the punching bag. The tears that fell down her red face and sweat-soaked shirt revealed the agony she was experiencing.

Maddie stepped forward and grabbed the door handle.

Placing her hand on top of Maddie's, Jade said, "No."

79

"But she's crying." Maddie's eyes darted anxiously toward her friend.

"Let her cry. She needs this. It's been a long time." Jade placed her forehead on the glass.

Four pairs of eyes watched as their friend, exhausted, fell to her knees and began to scream.

"Ok, no more waiting." Maddie opened the door and ran to her friend.

"Who's that screamin'?" Grammy asked as she ran to the back deck with Jacque tagging behind.

"It's okay, Grammy. We're having a moment." Rachel answered.

"Whew, I thought I was gonna have to pull out my baseball bat." Grammy said as she plopped into a chair.

"Rachel?"

"Yeah, Kate?"

"Will you pray over me? I can't do this anymore. I just want these dreams to go away."

Rachel sat down in front of Kaitlyn and grabbed her hands. "Of course, I can, but Kate, praying doesn't always make the bad things go away. We're inviting Jesus in to give us strength and courage to face the bad things."

The tears began to flow again. Suddenly, Rachel and Jade began praying over their friend. They were praying quietly, separate yet together. Emma placed her hand on Kaitlyn's back, and she joined in the prayer. Maddie wasn't quite sure what to do, so she placed her hand on Kaitlyn's knee and began to pray. The words inside of her began to bubble up. One minute, she didn't know what to say; the next moment, the words were coming out like water. She just said what she wanted to tell God on behalf of her friend. Hearing the prayers of her friends and her Grammy from behind gave her confidence.

As she opened her eyes, Maddie watched as Kaitlyn wrapped her arms around Rachel's neck. It was a quiet yet tension-filled moment as their friend released the pent-up emotion she had been carrying. Nobody knew what to say, but knew it was okay to just sit and be quiet. Maddie was learning that it was okay to not always have the words. Sometimes, she just needed to be still.

Kaitlyn pulled back and wiped her face. Grammy, ever prepared, gave her a handful of tissues. Kaitlyn smiled as she said, "Thank you, Grammy."

"A'course, a girl's always gotta be prepared fer a good cry. Them tears are a gift from God, ya know."

"A gift?" Grammy, I don't know about that; they're more like a curse."

"Naw! The Good Book says God keeps bottles of our tears in Heav'n. Ever'time I gotta let 'em out, I see him holding a bottle under my swollen eyes and I know he's with me."

Kaitlyn chuckled, "Yeah, I guess."

Maddie remembered Grammy telling her the same. She had to remember to ask where in the Bible she could find this.

"Grammy, you're pretty old. I bet your bottle is way big." Matthew said as he gestured wide with his arms.

Jade fell out in laughter at Maddie's brother. Maddie shook her head as she let out a little giggle.

Grammy joined in with her own chuckle, "Bottles is more like it, Boy." I 'spect there's a whole room of 'em with Grace Bennett in big red letters."

"Red, why red, Grammy?" Jade asked as she composed herself.

"Why, 'cause the blood 'a Jesus covers me," Grammy said.

Later that night, the girls sat in a circle on the floor of their shared room.

"Do we really have to leave tomorrow?" Emma asked.

"I really think you should stay," Maddie said.

Weaving yarn around her fingers, Rachel replied, "I can't. I have a summer project to finish before school starts. I haven't even started." Giving Maddie a glance she continued, "But, I wouldn't trade a moment. Thank you, Maddie, for inviting us up."

"Grammy sure is amazing," Kaitlyn said. "You're lucky to still have your grandma around."

Maddie smiled as she said, "Yeah, she's pretty great."

"What about the blood that she was talking about, Rach?" Jade asked as she attempted to stick her finger in the loop Rachel was working on.

Swatting her friend's hand, Rachel said, "That was cool, wasn't it? Jesus shed His blood on the Cross so we would be set free from sin."

"But how does it work? I mean, didn't he, like, die over two thousand years ago?" Maddie asked.

"The way my dad explained it to me, it's a spiritual exchange. When we say yes to Jesus and choose to follow him, he covers us with his blood. When he died, our sin was on him, and he exchanged our sin for his blood."

Kaitlyn looked perplexed. "But why blood? I mean, we're not talking about sacrifices like with witches and stuff, are we?"

Rachel laughed. "No. The human sacrifices you see in the movies you like to watch," Rachel winked, "are rituals. The person performing the sacrifice believes they must kill for protection or to get some kind of reward. And the sacrifice is neither perfect nor willing. Jesus was both perfect and willing to sacrifice himself. Where a ritual takes a life, Jesus gave life. And it must be blood because sin entered the body by the fruit eaten by Adam and Eve."

"Was the fruit cursed?" Kaitlyn asked.

"Maddie, open the Bible app and read Genesis three."

Maddie began to read. Once she read verse seven, Rachel said, "Stop. Read that last verse again."

"Then the eyes of both of them were opened, and they realized they were naked . . ."

"Do you see? They ate the fruit and then their eyes were opened."

"So, the fruit was cursed like in Snow White?" Kaitlyn repeated.

"Maddie read earlier that the fruit came from the tree of the knowledge of good and evil. So, let's say you go to a store and see a top that's fire, but you don't have any money. There's a sign at the front of the store that reads: theft will be prosecuted. You know that if you take the top, you'll be breaking the law, but you do it anyway. You then have a choice to make, take the top or leave it alone. God made them aware the tree of good and evil existed and told them not to eat from it. The serpent lied to them and essentially said that God was holding out on them. They disobeyed and then their eyes were open to evil."

"And that's sin?"

"Yes, their sin was falling for the lie and disobeying God."

"So, you're saying that if I steal the top, I've sinned right?"

"Yes."

"But Jesus shed his blood to cover that sin, so I'm good?"

"Well, not exactly."

"Rach, in science, I use a method to test a theory. The test will either pass or fail to prove the theory. So, if you tell me that Jesus shed his blood to cover my sin, then it is either true or it isn't."

"Kate, we all sin. Jesus shed his blood to cover all sin. But the missing variable here is whether you choose him. To be covered by his blood, you are saying, 'I choose you, Jesus' and then he covers you and your sin."

"So, let's say I choose Jesus, and he washes away my sin; what if I decide that I want that top anyway?"

"Jesus forgives all our sins, but we still must turn back to him. Listen, Kate, when you follow Jesus, you don't want to take something that isn't yours, but if you do, he will lead you to make it right and to turn back to him. That's called repentance."

"Okay, go back to that evil thing. I'm confused. Why would God plant an evil tree if he had no evil in him?"

Maddie brightened as she said, "I know this one! Grammy told me she thinks it was there to remind us there was evil. She said that God gave us free will to choose good or evil and the tree was like a red light to remind them of danger."

"Wow, that's a great analogy. I never thought about it like

that." Rachel stopped to rework a loop she had mistakenly reversed.

Agitated, Kaitlyn asked again, "But where did the evil come from?"

"Grammy said an angel named Luc, Luci. What's his name, Rach?" Maddie asked.

"Lucifer. He was the angel that was kicked out of Heaven because he was prideful and wanted to take God's throne."

"Yeah, that one." Maddie agreed.

"So, this Lucifer was prideful and was kicked out of Heaven. Then God created a garden, placed two people in it with a tree, and said, 'Hey, don't touch that tree, or it'll make you evil.' Sounds like a setup to me." Kaitlyn wrinkled her nose in disgust.

"That's not all the story, Kate. God loved his creation. Remember the variable. He didn't create Adam and Eve to follow him blindly. He created them for companionship, and while he wanted them to follow him out of love and obedience; he gave them the free will to choose good or evil. But don't you think he had to warn them of the enemy? Remember when Ms. Sonya told us about the armor of God? She said that our battle isn't against flesh and blood but against the spiritual forces of evil in the Heavenly realms. That's the same thing, right? God was only trying to protect them from what he knew they would face."

Quiet during Kaitlyn and Rachel's exchange, Jade interjected, "Kate, check it out. Why would God set them up if he loved the world so much that he sent his Son to die to make it right? That's what you're talking about, isn't it, Rach? He sacrificed himself to right the wrong in the garden and gave the gift of eternal life in the process." Looking down at the half-finished bookmark in her hand, she said, "I don't know anybody else who'd give their life to love me like that, especially for something I did."

Rachel nudged Jade's foot and said, "Hey, I remember somebody daring to climb a tree to save me when I stupidly got stuck. It seems to me that you've known his love all along."

Sitting with their thoughts, the girls were suddenly mesmerized by the rhythmic motion of Rachel's fingers.

"What are you making, Rach?" Emma asked.

"A bookmark. It's super easy. Do you wanna try?" Giving each of them a handful of string, she proceeded to show them how to form the loops repetitively.

Rachel watched intently as each girl attempted their own loop.

Jade was struggling. Each time she attempted to pull the strings through the loop, she seemed to mess them up. Frustrated, she looked at Rachel who giggled at the knots she had formed.

Emma tore through the loops like they were nobody's business.

Kaitlyn decided the straight loop was too boring and decided on a more extravagant pattern.

Maddie decided she liked the calming repetition as she copied Rachel's hand movements. She had never seen Rachel do this before. "Where did you learn to do this?"

Grammy showed me. When you went to help your Aunt Lisa for the day. She's quite the crocheter.

"Wait, this is crochet? I thought you had to use a hook to crochet."

"I wanted to start small, but I'm sure I'll graduate to a hook soon enough. Check it out, Jade, you're getting it!"

Jade beamed at Rachel's praise.

Maddie noticed a knot in her weave and began to back it out. "Oh, by the way, no big deal, but apparently, I have a date on Saturday."

"Wait, what?" Everyone's hands went limp as they all stared at Maddie.

"I thought we were waiting to date." Kaitlyn peered at her friend with fear in her eyes.

"Well, I don't know if it's really a date. Apparently, there's a group going to Sycamore Lake on Saturday, and Jacob asked me to tag along." Maddie answered.

"Tag along, huh?" Jade asked.

"Is Rory going?" Rachel asked as she concentrated on her bookmark.

Jade, Emma, and Kaitlyn giggled as Maddie smiled at her friend. "I don't know. Why? Would you stay if he was?"

Frowning, Rachel answered, "Hm, I can't."

"I don't know, Rach; it seems to me you're interested in Rory," Emma said.

"Okay, Ladies, focus. Maddie, who is going on Saturday? Kaitlyn asked.

Maddie shrugged her shoulders. "All I know is some people from church."

"Will you find out, please?"

"What's wrong, Kate? Are you worried?"

Looking down at her hands, Kaitlyn said, "I just want you to be safe, okay?"

Maddie placed her hand on her friend's. "I will. Promise."

"Maddie Ruth?"

Maddie looked around to see her Grammy standing in the doorway. "Yes, ma'am?

Grammy held out her phone as she said, "You've got a phone call."

Jade gave her friend a look as she said, "Hm, wonder if it's Jacob?" She whispered.

Laying down her yarn, Maddie stood and took the phone from Grammy, "Hello?"

"Hey, little Sis, what'cha doin'?"

Her eyes widened in astonishment as she yelled, "Michael!"

ATLANTA, GEORGIA

Michael was exhausted. Relieved to see his parent's house, he couldn't believe he was home.

The minute he was picked up at the PKO, he fought with all his might. But the man who held him was not budging. The hood was removed once he was securely thrown into a vehicle.

"Michael Bennett?" The deep voice seemed to boom inside

the cabin of the vehicle.

"Shouldn't you have checked before you placed the hood over my head?"

"David Bennett sent us. You are safe, but there is no time to waste. Put your head down. I expect we are being followed."

Michael followed the man's instructions. Dad sent them! He immediately felt relief to know his dad had something to do with this.

The next seventy-two hours found Michael in and out of sleep. He overheard the driver and passenger talking about losing someone, but he was too tired to worry about it.

Snapping back into the present, Michael watched as his dad walked down the stairs from the house. Opening the door to the SUV, he ran up to his dad who hurled himself at Michael, nearly pushing him over. Michael felt like a little boy again as his dad squeezed him tight.

"Are you okay?" David asked as he released his son.

"Yeah, I'm good, Dad."

"Commander Bennett, Wes Malone. Good to meet you, Sir."

Shaking the extended hand, David replied, "Thank you, Mr. Malone. I am forever in your debt."

"Call me Wes, and no debt owed here. Tom and I go way back. I know all about how you saved his life. It is we who are in your debt."

David snickered, "Does Tom know you're here?"

"Yes sir, but we must get back. Let him know we will debrief him tomorrow."

"Will do. Thank you again, Wes."

As they walked into the house, Michael noticed David looking behind them.

"Is everything okay, Dad?"

David closed the door and said, "Yeah, you can never be too careful. Are you hungry?"

Michael's stomach growled in response. "Starved."

"Make yourself a couple of sandwiches for the road," David said.

"The road? Where are we going?"

"Tennessee."

CHAPTER 9

Who Can we Trust?

Awakened by the slam of the screen door, Maddie grabbed her phone from the bedside table and groaned, "5 am, UGH!" Sitting straight up in her bed, she excitedly whispered, "Dad!" Rachel murmured something unintelligible beside her and rolled over. Not wanting to wake anyone, Maddie slid out of bed quietly and tiptoed into the living room.

Relief filled her whole body as she saw her dad and brother laying bags on the couch. "Dad, Michael!" Maddie ran into her dad's arms as he picked her up and swung her around.

"What are you doing up, Ruthie? You weren't waiting for us, were you?" David asked.

Maddie pulled her hair back into a bun and said, "No, Sir, the door woke me."

"Oops, sorry about that, my fault," Michael said.

Maddie turned around to hug her brother. "It's okay, I forgive you." Emotion overwhelmed her as she realized she never wanted to let her brother go.

"Maddie, um, I think I need to go to the bathroom?" Michael said with an amused look on his face.

A little embarrassed, Maddie mumbled, "I wasn't sure I'd ever see you again."

Tousling her newly formed bun, Michael said, "You didn't think you could get rid of me that fast, did you, Little Sis?"

Watching him walk down the hallway, Maddie giggled. It

89

had been a long time since she had laughed at her brother's wry sense of humor.

"Ruthie, we've had a long night. Why don't you go back to bed, and we'll catch up in a couple of hours?"

"Yes sir." Making her way down the hall, she turned around and said, "Thank you, Daddy."

"I love you, Ruthie, Girl."

Three hours later, Maddie woke the girls and told them the news.

Jade let out a loud breath. "Finally, we can have closure."

Walking into the kitchen, Maddie's heart skipped a beat as she saw Grammy, her dad, mom, and brothers sitting at the table.

"Whooee, I sure am glad we have an extra-long table. We're gonna have a crew to feed this mornin'." Grammy beamed as she began to make breakfast.

"Can we help, Grammy?" Rachel asked.

"Why a'course, Love. Maddie, you work on the biscuits. Jade and Kaitlyn can crack and stir up some eggs. Emma you and I can fry up some bacon.

"What can I do, Grammy?" Matthew stood at attention waiting for his orders.

"Here's a bowl; why don't ya go fetch some blueberries and blackberries from the garden? Don't forget ta clean 'em when ya bring 'em in."

"I'll help you, Son," Jacque said as she followed him out the back door.

"Grammy, I was wondering, is the table in the dining room homemade? It looks like someone carved it." Emma asked.

Smiling from ear to ear, Grammy said, "Yessiree, that'd be my George. Took 'im nigh to six months to build that monstros'ty." Leaning toward Emma as if to tell her a secret, Grammy continued, "If truth be told, I thought he was crazy making somethin' so long, but lookee here, the Lord knew what we needed this mornin' and made sure ma George made it jes' right."

"I remember when Dad made the table. The slab must've weighed a thousand pounds."

"Yup, it took six men to rig 'er up. Oh, I'll never ferget that first Christmas. R'member David when yer dad took us ta the Christmas tree farm? That'd be a'fore Lisa was born, a'course. You were knee high to a grasshopper, but there weren't nothin' that could stop ya from helpin' yer ole' dad. We brung that tree in and made a wreath right thar in the middle of that table. I'll never ferget the way that fur smelled or how the candlelight shone." Grammy's voice softened as she looked off into the distance.

David gave a slight smile as he snickered. "Yeah . . ."

"Grammy, look at what I picked!" Matthew ran in with a bowl of berries and a face that had suspiciously tasted a few.

"Why lookee thar. Ya 'bout ate as many as ya picked, did ya, Boy? Go on, warsh 'em up, now."

As Matthew and Jacque washed the berries, David's phone rang. The girls looked at each other as he decided to take the call outside.

Maddie watched Michael as her dad went outside. A sleepless night had added to the haunted look in his eyes. She shivered as she remembered his demeanor the Christmas before. Did he know what was going to happen?

"I think that biscuit has had enough." Rachel elbowed her friend. "Penny for your thoughts."

Nodding toward her brother, Maddie whispered, "He looks worried."

Rachel glanced at Michael and back at Maddie. Closing her eyes, she whispered a prayer of protection over the two.

As David walked in, he grabbed Jacque's hand and walked her toward the back of the house.

"Okay, now I'm worried," Maddie whispered.

"I'm sure it's fine," Rachel replied.

Grammy peered over their shoulders and said, "What'cha Girls goin' on 'bout? Them biscuits ain't gonna bake themselves."

"We're putting them in now, Grammy," Maddie said.

David and Jacque walked back into the kitchen hand in hand.

Maddie noticed her mom seemed to have the same haunted look as her brother.

"Girls, we have some news. I spoke to your parents and you ladies get to stay on an extra week."

"Wait, what? YAY!!!!" Flour and eggs went everywhere as the girls shared their excitement.

As their excitement died down, Maddie asked, "What happened, Dad? Is everything okay?"

"Everything is fine. We just want to take extra precautions with Michael back in town."

"Why? Is he in danger? Are we in danger?" Maddie began to feel a fire in the pit of her stomach.

"Ruthie, look at me." David placed his hands on his daughter's face and peered into her eyes. "You are safe. We just want to let things die down before we send everyone home. I promise, Ruthie, I will never let anything happen to you or your friends."

Her dad's use of her nickname never failed to calm her. "Pinky promise?" She asked.

David grabbed his daughter's pinky and smiled.

After breakfast, the girls decided to walk through Grammy's Garden. Maddie loved every inch of this garden. Even the dirt.

"Maddie, do you think Grammy would let me plant something here before we leave?" Emma asked.

Maddie was excited at the thought of planting with her friend. "Sure. What are you thinking?"

"I don't know yet, but I'll think of something."

"Hear that?" Rachel asked.

"Hear what?" Jade replied.

"The Cicadas. Listen to them sing." Rachel moved her

hands as if to conduct the symphony of insects.

Maddie placed her hand on a nearby tree and said, "Grammy said they come out of the ground every seventeen years."

"How cool is that? The last time they were here was the year we were born," Jade interjected.

"Grammy said they remind us of Jesus' resurrection and our future resurrection," Maddie added.

"What do you mean, resurrection?" Kaitlyn asked.

"One day, Jesus will return as King and those who followed him in life will dwell with him in eternity," Rachel answered.

Kaitlyn sat on a bench and said, "Rach, I'm having a hard time with all this Jesus stuff. Will you please explain to me plainly from start to finish what you believe?"

Grabbing a stalk of bee balm, Rachel sat in the grass and caressed the soft petals as she said, "Gladly."

Jade sat down next to Kate as Maddie and Emma sat cross-legged on the ground beside Rachel.

Placing her nose in the bloom, Rachel said, "I love this plant. This color is scarlet, right? Doesn't it remind you of what Grammy told us about the blood?"

"My momma uses it for bee stings," Emma said.

"You can make tea out of it, too," Kaitlyn added.

"Have you ever wondered why this plant? I mean why not a daisy or a sunflower even? Why does the bee balm have this color, shape, and function?"

"What does this have to do with Jesus?" Kaitlyn asked.

"In the beginning, God created the Heavens and the earth."

Looking around them, Maddie thought, *isn't it ironic to be talking about a garden as we sit in a garden?*

"Now there's a lot of good stuff that comes after the garden, but I'm going to jump straight to Jesus. The New Testament begins with the birth of a baby born to a virgin." Rachel continued.

Kaitlyn raised her hand. "Okay, stop. How does that even happen?"

"Well, the Bible says that God's Spirit came over Mary,

Jesus' mother, and gave her a baby. This is how Jesus was perfect, with no sin. If Jesus had the blood of his mother, then he would have been exposed to sin." Rachel waited for another question.

"Alright, go on," Kaitlyn said while waving her hand.

"Jesus lived thirty years on earth in obscurity. When he was thirty, he began his ministry, choosing twelve disciples to follow him. In the three years that followed, Jesus fulfilled his purpose just like this flower, teaching many people, performing many miracles, and making many people angry." Rachel grimaced as she pulled a leaf off the plant.

"Why?"

"Because he was upsetting the traditions built by the religious establishment."

Kaitlyn smirked. "Hmm, now that's something I can get behind."

As Rachel talked about the conflict between Jesus and the religious leaders, Maddie grabbed a piece of grass and wrapped it around her finger.

"Jesus came in and flipped everything on its head," Rachel said. "Dad said he wanted the people to know that God was love and justice— not one or the other, but both. After three years, he showed them what he had been teaching, by giving of himself on the cross. Kate, this wasn't an easy death. Jesus died brutally. Dad told me that he suffered in seven ways. Literally every drop of his blood was spilled." The girls watched as Rachel began to pick the flowers off the head, dropping them to the ground.

As everyone sat quietly in their thoughts, a butterfly landed on the remaining flowers. Everyone froze as they watched the butterfly sip its nectar and fly away.

"Whoa, that was cool," Jade said.

Rachel looked surprised as she said, "I don't think that's ever happened to me before."

The other girls nodded in agreement.

"For three days, Jesus stayed in the tomb, but then he rose again and went to Heaven to be cleansed, after which he became our High Priest. Then he returned to earth and hung out with the disciples and his followers until he returned to Heaven."

"What's a high priest?" Jade asked.

"The way my dad explained, it's like an attorney," Rachel said. "Remember when we talked about Jesus exchanging our sin for his blood?"

"Yeah."

"Well, when we say yes and receive this gift of cleansing, he becomes our Savior and Redeemer but also our High Priest."

"So, all a person has to do is follow Jesus?"

"Yes."

"But what if all this is some crazy guy's idea of a bad dream?"

"Kate, Jesus asks us to follow him, to trust him, and to love him. Who do you know is crazy enough to ask such a thing?" Jade asked.

Irritated, Kaitlyn stood up, walking to a nearby bush to pull at the leaves. "What about that guy who started a cult and killed everybody? What about the PKO? Isn't it the same thing?"

Rachel looked at her friend with compassion, "Kate, no, it's not. Those people who died were not given a choice." Placing her hand on her friend's shoulder, she said, "We were not given a choice. Jesus gives us a choice, along with the promise that we can trust him, no matter what."

Grabbing a handful of leaves, Kaitlyn threw them to the ground. "Everyone I've trusted has let me down! How can I trust this guy I've never even seen?"

"Everyone?" Jade asked.

Sighing as she grabbed a bloom off the same bush and lifted it to her nose, Kaitlyn said, "No, not y'all; but you know what I mean." Giving the bloom to Jade, she continued, "We've been through stuff together, but I've never even met this Jesus. I don't understand how I'm supposed to follow him."

Placing the bloom behind her ear, Jade said, "I get it, Girl. This is scary. But Jesus doesn't ask us to do something he wouldn't do himself. That's why he came to earth. I promise you can trust him. But you have to give him a chance."

"I'll think about it, okay?"

Rachel raised an eyebrow as she looked at Kaitlyn's crossed arms.

"I will, truly," Kaitlyn repeated.

Taking a deep breath, Jade decided it was time to change the subject. Flailing her arms out to her sides, she looked around and said, "Okay, okay, time to lighten the mood. Who is going to call out the elephant in the room?"

Everyone turned to look at Jade standing in a commanding pose with her hands on her hips.

"Maddie, your dad said that we get to stay another week. Does that mean we're all invited to your little shindig at the lake?"

Maddie clapped and squealed, "Oh, my goodness, I forgot all about the lake!"

Later that evening, Maddie sat with her Bible and her thoughts. Journaling, she wrote, *God, can I trust you? Kaitlyn is right; so many people have let us down. How can we know that we can trust you?* Looking toward the mountain, a familiar sound surprised her. Walking to the railing, she saw Ms. Carolina Wren singing her familiar song on a nearby feeder. Looking up, Maddie said, "Well, I guess you haven't let me down yet."

Sneaking up behind her friend, Rachel asked, "Who are you talking to?"

"Look." Maddie pointed toward the feeder.

Gasping, Rachel said, "Hey, look, it's Ms. Carolina."

"Guess what just happened?"

Rachel turned to grab some birdseed for the feeder. "What's that?"

"I asked God if I could trust him and then she flew up. What do you think it means?"

Rachel laughed. "I don't know. What do you think it means?"

Sitting on the picnic table, Maddie asked, "Don't you think it's interesting that she shows up when I need God?"

Spreading the seed through the feeder, Rachel said, "You told Ms. Bonnie that every time you see her, you know God is with you. I know that when I need a reminder of God's presence, he places something or someone in my path to encourage me."

"Like what?"

"Like the flower earlier. There's something about flowers that reminds me of the work of his hand. Sonya told me that every flower has its own unique bloom, kind of like a fingerprint."

"Whoa, really?"

Extending her hand, Rachel said, "Yeah, and every time I look into the bloom's center, it's almost as if I'm looking at the heart of the flower in God's hand."

"But how does this remind you of God's presence?"

"If he created this unique flower and provided it with all it needed to grow, then why wouldn't he do it for me, too? Think about it. This flower grew from a seed, a little bitty seed that was planted in the ground. Do you know that seed had to die before it could live? And yet it grew a stalk, sprouted leaves, and produced amazing scarlet flowers that would supply nectar for butterflies and balm for bee stings. Now, apply that to everything you see around you. Yeah, God is here."

"I guess. When we were at the PKO, I saw her every day. I swear she would always lead me to the sunflower garden. Maybe God wants to remind me of moments in the past when he was there for me?" She asked, a little uncertain.

Rachel smiled, "That's a gift, Maddie. But he may not always send a physical sign."

"What do you mean?"

"God isn't a genie in a bottle. He is our Creator, and he's already provided everything we need to know that he is with us." Sitting on the picnic table beside her friend, she asked, "What if, in choosing to trust the Lord, our eyes are opened to see his goodness all around us?"

Suddenly, the back door opened behind them, and their friends surprised them with a monstrous pizza. "Now that's what I call good." Maddie winked at her friend.

"David, who was on the phone?" Jacque grabbed her husband's hand as he led her into their bedroom in the back of the house.

"That was Tom. Someone is watching the house."

Alarm covered Jacque's face as she shook her head. "I'm scared, David," she admitted.

Drawing his wife close, he smelled deeply of her hair. Closing his eyes, he thought to himself, *just one moment, can we have one moment without worry?* "We're safe here, Love. But I'm going to have to close this loose end."

Jacque flinched and pulled away. "Can't you call Rick? Surely, he will believe you now that you have Michael back."

"I'm thinking about it. I need to call Mordy first. I may need some legal backup. Tom graciously supplied a group of Navy Seals he's been coaching to help break Michael free. I'm not sure they would be willing to lay their jobs on the line by sharing what they did for us."

"What about the guys from Baldersville? Wouldn't they be willing to share what's going on?"

David placed a strand of hair behind his wife's ear as he shook his head. "They're undercover, Love. I doubt very seriously they would break their cover, else lose all they've worked for."

"Oh, David, this is all hopeless!"

"Never hopeless. As Momma says, if we have breath, we have hope. We don't have a choice, Jacque; we must believe this is true."

A Servant's Heart

As Maddie and the girls awoke Saturday morning, the house was abuzz with activity. She was thankful to have extra time with her girls but worried about the "extra precautions" her dad mentioned.

While preparing for the big lake day, Maddie realized she was excited and nervous all at the same time. *What if he decides he really doesn't like me?* She wondered. *What if I do something stupid?* Contemplating all the things that could go wrong, Maddie decided to take her thoughts captive and just enjoy the day. Straightening her shirt, she thought, *well, at least Rachel and the girls will be with me.*

"Up or down?" She asked Emma as they peered at their reflections in the mirror.

"Definitely up," Emma answered.

"You Girls 'bout ready?" Grammy asked.

"Yes ma'am, almost." Maddie grimaced as she finished brushing her hair.

"Are you nervous?" Rachel asked as she pulled a tendril from Maddie's bun.

Looking at her friend, Maddie said, "A little. What if he asks me a question, and I don't know what to say?"

"You say I DON'T KNOW," Jade said sarcastically.

"Leave it to Jade to be compassionate." Rachel threw a wadded-up napkin at her friend.

"I'm just sayin'. It's not a big deal, Maddie. Just be yourself."

"And when did you become a dating expert?" Kaitlyn asked.

"Ha! Wouldn't you like to know?"

"I do know, that'd be never!" Kaitlyn laughed.

Parading across the room, Jade said, "You just think you know. I could have a whole other life you don't know about." Gesturing for Kaitlyn to look her in the eyes, she continued, "007 Jade, now that's what I'm talkin' 'bout."

"Yeah, except we're joined at the hip, and you couldn't burp without my knowing about it!"

In response, Jade let out a great big burp for effect.

Maddie shook her head. "Alright, y'all, let's get this date started!"

"Do y'all think it's weird that we're going on Maddie's first date?" Emma asked with a giggle.

Maddie was surprised to see the bus in the church parking lot. Breathing a sigh of relief, excitement began to build as she realized more people were going than she expected.

Aunt Lisa pulled up behind the bus to let the girls out. Catching her eye, Jacob stood on the side of the bus and waved. A smile revealed a dimple on his right cheek, enough to make the butterflies in her stomach go crazy.

Jade grabbed her hand. "You'll be okay, Maddie. Remember, just be yourself." Smiling, she stepped out of the car.

"Hey," Jacob said.

Tucking a curl of hair behind her ear, Maddie mimicked, "Hey."

"Do ya wanna sit with me?"

"Sure," Maddie said as she looked back at her girls.

Kaitlyn blew her a kiss as Jade yelled, "Bye Honey, you look great!"

Maddie giggled as she followed Jacob onto the bus.

Walking toward the back of the bus, Jacob sat down and began chatting immediately. Maddie halfway heard him say something about fishing but was distracted by the boy named Rory staring intently at Rachel.

"Oh yeah, Rory's really into yer friend," Jacob said.

"I see that. Hey, what were you saying about fishing?" Changing the subject, Maddie listened to Jacob describe the big bass he caught the last time he went to Sycamore Lake.

"Are we fishing today?" Maddie asked.

"I brought two fishin' poles. I was hopin' ya'd like ta fish with me."

"Sure, but I've never fished before."

"That's alright, I'll teach ya. It's easy."

I didn't know Kaitlyn could fish! Inspired, Maddie cheered on her friend as Kaitlyn reeled in a little blue catfish.

Deciding it was time to cast her line, Jacob grabbed Maddie's reel and pulled out a container of worms. "Yer turn now, Maddie. Worm?"

Maddie peered into the container and then gave Kaitlyn a side glance.

"It's okay," her friend encouraged.

Maddie was used to seeing one at a time when she gardened with Grammy, but seeing so many in a plastic container was disconcerting. "There are so many of them," she replied.

Picking one out of the plastic container, Jacob looked at the worm as it curled around his finger. "Lookee here, see, they won't hurt ya."

"Are you sure? This doesn't hurt them, does it?"

"Naw, they like being eaten by fish, Maddie," Jade whispered behind her.

"Go away!" Maddie laughed.

"I think you're scared." Jade teased.

"I am not! I can do this." With eyes closed, Maddie placed her fingers in the container and pulled out a worm. She was surprised at how wet they were. The worm apparently did not like being picked up as it suddenly began squirming between her fingers. Surprised by the motion, she let go and watched the worm fall to the ground.

Jacob laughed. "Well, look at that. Ya just saved one from bein' eaten. Alright, let's try 'er agin."

Determined, Maddie picked up another worm and held it in her hand.

"Alright now, yer gonna take the worm and hook it like this," Jacob said, showing off that little dimple again as he demonstrated hooking the worm.

Maddie looked at her worm and said, "Sorry, little guy, there's a fish who needs to eat now." Concentrating, she stuck her tongue out of the corner of her mouth and placed the worm on her hook. "I did it!" She exclaimed.

Jacob smiled as he said, "Shore looks that way. Alright, now ya gotta cast it like this. Ya want yer hook to go way out to the middle of the worter. Then yer gonna reel 'er back in slow like."

Maddie copied Jacob and cast her hook into the middle of the lake just as he showed her.

"Now what?" She asked.

"Now, we wait. When ya feel a tug, start reelin' 'er in. Til then, keep tension on yer line with the tip of yer rod up high. See thar; ya want yer line ta stay real straight."

Anxiety bubbled up as she realized she had no clue what to do next. "Reel her in? What do you mean?"

"Watch. See how I'm spinnin' the reel? If I had a fish on the other end, I'd be spinnin' the reel as I pull the rod back in the opposite direction the fish is swimmin'."

Suddenly, Maddie felt a tug. Spinning quickly, Maddie's heart pounded as she worried over what was on the other end. Spinning, spinning, spinning, an empty hook was all that was left as the hook hit the end of the pole. Maddie groaned.

"It's alright, Maddie. I ain't never known nobody who reeled a fish in the first time," Jared said. "Ya just gotta be patient."

"Yeah, and reel 'er in slowly. Ya want the fish ta get tired." Jacob added.

Adding another worm to her hook, Maddie cast out again, determined this time she would catch a fish. When her hook arose empty again, Maddie watched, disappointed, as Jacob caught a fish and Kaitlyn another.

One more time, she thought to herself. Perhaps fishing just isn't my thing. Suddenly, the rod lurched forward. If Maddie hadn't been holding it tightly, she would've lost it, but Jacob saw the movement and set his rod down quickly so he could help her.

Standing behind her, Jacob guided her hand as she started to spin the reel. "Slow like. R'member, ya wanna pull 'er back the opposite direction she's swimmin'. If she goes left, yer gonna pull back to yer right."

Maddie methodically reeled in the fish by pulling the rod back and turning the crank according to Jacob's instructions. She was afraid her heart would beat out of her chest. After about fifteen minutes when she felt like she couldn't hold on anymore, she began to see the splash of the fish as it flopped on top of the water.

"Yer almost thar, Maddie. Just keep reelin' 'er in slow like. Don't let go 'a the tension."

Pulling the rod back again, Maddie reeled in the biggest fish she had ever seen.

Jacob grabbed the line as she said, "Whooee doggee, look at that smallmouth bass. I'll bet she's a good foot and a half!"

Ms. Bonnie and her husband, Mr. Bruce, came over to help.

Relieved, Maddie let Jacob take over.

"We gotta take the fish off the hook now, Maddie. Do ya think ya can?"

Looking at the fish flopping in Jacob's hands, Maddie asked, "How do I do it?"

Jacob opened the fish's mouth as Mr. Bruce held the body. Taking a pair of plyers from Jacob's hand, Maddie clipped the line and pulled the hook out of the mouth.

Mr. Bruce held up the fish and asked, "Do ya wanna take a

picture?"

Worried, Maddie asked, "What happens to the fish?"

"As much as I'd love to take this beauty home, today we're catchin' and releasin'. So, she'll live to swim another day."

Excited, Maddie said, "Yes, can we get a picture?"

Mr. Bruce handed her the fish and showed her how to hold it from the bottom. The fish fought for a moment but then seemed to know that Maddie wouldn't hurt her as she held her firmly.

Standing beside Jacob, Maddie smiled as Ms. Bonnie took a picture of them both. Then, they threw the fish back into the lake.

Maddie watched the fish swim away. She couldn't believe she'd caught a fish!

As the sun set over the lake, Bonnie and Bruce had the students help put dinner together. They had rented a home for the day that had a huge upper deck and a grill. As Bruce grilled burgers and hot dogs, a group of students gathered firewood for a bonfire.

"Beautiful sunset," Amy Jayne said as she helped Maddie and Rachel set the table. "Have ya ever seen all that color over water?"

"We went to the ocean on July fourth, and it was just like this," Maddie closed her eyes in remembrance of the night.

"I ain't never been ta no ocean. What's it like?" Amy asked.

"Oh, the water goes on forever!" Rachel exclaimed. "And the sand is soft and rocky all at the same time."

"And the waves are bigger than these," Maddie added as she gestured toward the lake.

"Oh yeah, the waves are much bigger," Rachel agreed.

"It sounds like a dream." Amy Jayne said.

"Hm, yeah. Hey Amy, how are you doing? When we saw you at church, you seemed a little down. Is everything okay?" Rachel was never one to forget when somebody needed help.

"It's nothin'. Just a little home trouble."

"Would you like to talk about it?" Rachel asked.

"Naw, there ain't nothin' gonna change, so thar's no point in mullin' it over."

I wonder if I should tell Amy Jayne about Mom, Maddie wondered. She could just hear her Grammy respond in her thoughts, *All part a yer story, Maddie Ruth. Don't ferget yer story is God's glory.*

"Amy, you know my mom tried to commit suicide?"

Curious eyes looked up at Maddie as Amy Jayne stopped in her tracks.

"Anyway, Rachel helped me realize that I couldn't change what my mom did, but I could allow God to help me process my feelings about it."

"What'd you do?" Amy asked.

Looking at Rachel, Maddie placed her hands before her and said, "I put my mom and my feelings in my hand and laid it all at the Cross, and then I prayed for God to help me."

Amy set the silverware down and asked nervously, "Did he?"

Maddie looked up as she thought about the last year and all she'd been through. "Yes, a whole lot."

Rachel smiled at her friend.

"I don't know what you're going through Amy Jayne, but I believe God wants to help you too," Maddie urged.

"Hm, maybe."

After placing the last plate on the table, Maddie touched Amy's shoulder as she said, "If you want, we can pray later."

Amy Jayne nodded and turned toward the kitchen.

"Bonfire pit is ready, Mr. Bruce," Jacob called out as he, Rory, and Jared walked up the stairs.

The conversation around the big picnic table was lively. Mr. Bruce had quite a sense of humor, and the boys loved him.

"He reminds me of Dad," Rachel said as she watched him joke around with the boys.

"Do you miss your dad?" Maddie asked.

"Yeah, I do. Do you think we'll get to go home next week?"

"I don't know. Guess we need to ask my dad tomorrow."

Ms. Bonnie called out from the kitchen, "You'ns throw away yer plates and meet us down at the fire pit."

As Maddie was cleaning up, Jacob whispered in her ear, "I'll save ya a seat," as he walked past her and down the stairs.

"So, what do you think of Jacob?" Rachel asked.

Maddie blushed and shrugged her shoulders, "I don't know. He's nice. He taught me how to fish."

"Rory, too," Rachel said. "I sat and talked with him while y'all were fishing."

"Wait, really? What's he like?"

"Very serious. Have you noticed that he doesn't smile much? He's nothing like Jackson . . ." Rachel trailed off.

"Yeah, maybe he's had a hard life."

"I guess."

"Hey, the last one to the fire pit has to make S'mores." Jade laughed as she ran down the stairs.

"Now, how is that even fair?" Kaitlyn asked.

"And when has Jade ever played fair?" Emma laughed as she raced around the girls to keep from being last.

The chair next to Jacob was empty. As he pointed to it, Maddie felt butterflies in her stomach again. Why do I get so nervous around him? Determined not to let her nerves get the best of her, she followed his lead.

"Did'ya have fun today?" He asked shyly.

"I did. Thank you for teaching me how to fish."

"I still cain't believe ya caught the biggest fish 'a the day. Some kinda luck ya got. My Pap's gonna be so jealous."

Laughing, Maddie said, "She was pretty big."

"Perty big, she was the biggest fish ya ever did catch!"

Giving him the side eye, she said, "The only fish."

"Details, details. It was a good catch, Maddie."

With a smirk, Kaitlyn gave Maddie a S'more as Jared followed behind.

"Awe, look at little Jared helpin' Kaitlyn." Jacob laughed as Jared gave him a S'more.

Standing tall, Jared said, "Well, at least I'm helpin'."

"Alright Boys. Thank you, Kaitlyn, and Jared, for serving your friends so well," Mr. Bruce said. "Jacob, would you like to share about yer trip to Kentucky?"

Maddie looked at Jacob. *Did they go on their mission trip already?*

"It was a great trip. We helped repair a roof and served in a soup kitchen."

Ms. Bonnie leaned forward to roast a marshmallow. "And where did ya see the Lord move?"

"I got to talk to a homeless man," Rory answered. "He asked me to pray over him."

"What was that like?" Ms. Bonnie asked.

"I was skeered at first, but it wasn't so bad. Ya shoulda' heard his story." Glancing Rachel's way, he looked sad.

"Do y'all go to Kentucky every year?" Rachel asked.

As he cut up a stick to give to Amy Jayne, Mr. Bruce answered, "Yes, ma'am. The Lord called us ta Picker's Hill 'bout ten years ago. Ever' year, we take a group ta serve."

"What do y'all do there?" Kaitlyn asked.

"We rebuilt a porch last year," Jacob answered.

"Hey, r'member when we had to clean ole' Mr. Johnson's cistern?" Jared asked.

Jacob pinched his nose as he said, "Pewee, that thing smelled ta high Heaven!"

"What's a cistern?" Maddie asked Jacob.

"It's like a well, but it collects rainwater."

"Do you drink from it?"

"Not this one. Mr. Johnson used it to water his field. But ya can buy 'em."

"Doesn't Mr. Johnson have a drinkin' water cistern delivered?" Jacob asked.

"I'd say that's 'bout right," Mr. Bruce said.

"Wait, so they don't have water from the city?" Kaitlyn asked.

Ms. Bonnie stuck another marshmallow in the fire as she said, "They live in the mountains, Kaitlyn. Thar ain't no pipes goin' up the mountain. So, they rely on the springs and the rainwater for their water supply. The town that provides their water collects it from the local spring, treats and then delivers it to the local communities."

Fully engaged in the conversation, Kaitlyn placed her chin on her hands and said, "That's cool. So, they're living off the grid? What about electricity?"

"Nope, daylight, fireplaces, candles, and bonfires give 'em all the light they need."

"Wait, so they don't have pipes. What about plumbing?" Jade asked.

Chuckling, Ms. Bonnie said, "No indoor plumbing."

Aghast, Jade asked, "Well, what do they do with the, um, ya know."

Cackling, Jared asked, "The poop?"

"They use outhouses."

"Outhouses? I thought those were used in the old days!"

"Well, they still use 'em in Picker's Hill."

With a serious look, Kaitlyn asked, "Ya know, I've always wondered. What do they do when, ya know, the hole fills up?"

"They dig a new hole and move the outhouse."

Ms. Bonnie decided it was time to change the subject. "Rory saw God move when he prayed with a homeless man. Anybody else?"

Staring at the fire, Jared quietly said, "Thar was this little girl we gave a bowl 'a rice and beans. You'd a thought we'd given her a Christmas ham; she was so happy."

"They don't eat three meals a day like we do, but they consider themselves blessed to have one meal from the soup kitch'n."

Maddie noticed Rachel listening intently to the conversation. "Jade, weren't you talking about food lines in New York?"

"Yeah, Momma said she's starting to see them in Atlanta, too."

"What did y'all do to help, Ms. Bonnie? Who provided the food?" Rachel asked.

"The local farmers give to the soup kitch'n who use the food to make one meal a day for those who have nothin' ta eat.

We came in ta help where we could. It was the hands and feet a Jesus that served these people."

"Wow, that's exactly what Jesus told us to do," Rachel wiped away a tear from her eye.

"Yes ma'am, that's a servant's heart."

As the embers died off, Ms. Bonnie asked the boys to carry the remaining wood under the back deck and the girls to carry the dishes to the kitchen. After everything was put away, the girls walked to the railing.

Looking at the moonlight shining on the gentle waves of the lake below, Maddie realized she was sad they had to leave.

"Boy, I could live here forever," Jade said as she leaned over the railing.

"Yeah, me too," Kaitlyn said.

"Hey Maddie, that was really cool what Jacob, and his friends did in Kentucky."

"Wasn't it?" I didn't know they already went; I was hoping I could go too," Maddie said, disappointed.

"I don't know if I could live without indoor plumbing," Kaitlyn whispered.

"Girl, we gotta talk about your priorities!" Jade laughed.

"I'm just sayin', I wouldn't know what to do."

"You'd bring a roll of toilet paper to an outhouse and close the door," Jade said very matter of fact.

"I thought it was cool how they served as the hands and feet of Jesus," Emma said softly.

"Right? That's what I'm talking about," Rachel exclaimed. "Think about what Jesus did while he was on earth. He called us to do the same. I only wish I knew where we could go."

"Well, my mom found a shelter in Atlanta that she's been working with. Maybe we could serve with her."

Maddie could see Rachel's wheels turning as she thought about serving.

"Could we do something like that?" Emma asked quietly.

Rachel's eyes widened as she nodded her head and smiled. "Yeah, I think so. Jade, can you ask her?"

With a salute, Jade said, "Yes, General."

CHAPTER 11

A Counterfeit Plan

The unknown tune Maddie was humming was a sweet surprise. *What is this song?* She wondered. Trying to remember, she grabbed her brush and thought maybe Emma would know. Suddenly realizing she was alone, she hurried to catch up with her friends.

The knots in her hair proved to be as stubborn as her conflicted thoughts. As she fought her hair, she reminisced over her conversation with Jacob the night before. He made it very clear that not only did he like her, but he also wanted a relationship. Smiling, she remembered how he held her hand. Working out the last knot, she looked in the mirror and asked the reflection, "Do I really want to be in a relationship with him?"

After the quarrel over her hair ended, she set out on a quest to find her missing friends. Walking into the kitchen, she was surprised to find them quietly concentrating on the back porch.

"Why, good mornin' to ya, Maddie Ruth. How'd ya sleep?"

Peering out of the back window, Maddie turned and answered, "Good. What are they doing?"

Grammy shrugged her shoulders and turned back to the stove. "Ya got me. They all tiptoed down the hallway at the crack 'a dawn sayin' they had some 'portant work to be done."

"Probably homework. I'm not ready for all that," Maddie said as she peered over her gram's shoulder. "What'cha

110

making? Can I help?"

"Ya can always help, my Girl. Grab a spoon. Yer brother's over thar makin' toast."

"Cinnamon toast, Maddie!"

Wiggling her eyebrows at her granddaughter, Grammy said, "More 'n like cinnamon on Matthew toast."

Matthew beamed as he popped a finger full of cinnamon sugar in his mouth.

"Grammy, I've been meaning to ask. How do you put up with all these people for so long? Me, Matthew, my friends, Mom, Dad, and now Michael." Maddie couldn't believe her eyes as she counted, "Nine people! How do you do it?"

Chuckling, Grammy said, "The Good Book says to always show hospitality fer ya never know when yer entertainin' angels." Turning to look at Maddie, she said, "So I'm always ready fer whatever the Lord brings."

Excited, Matthew jumped to the floor and began looking around the chairs. "Angels! Can I see them?"

"Boy, ya better not get any sugar on them chairs." Grammy held her spoon teasingly.

"Mmmm, something smells good in here, Momma." David grabbed Matthew as he attempted to look under the island.

"Well, good mornin' to ya, David, my Boy. How'd ya sleep?"

"Pretty good, but Momma, can we please talk about getting a longer bed?"

Popping a grape in his mouth, Michael agreed, "I wasn't going to say anything, but since you mentioned it. . ."

"Michael Ryder Bennett, you come give yer Grammy some sugar. Yer lookin' better and better ever' day!"

Kissing Grammy on the cheek, Michael investigated the pot she was stirring and asked, "What is that?"

"That'd be a mess 'a oatmeal, stick ta yer bones oatmeal, in fact."

"Hmm, looks like a whole bunch of mush to me," Michael said as he stuck his finger in the pot and took a bite.

"Boy, don't make me use this." Holding the wooden spoon,

she threatened, "Ya ain't too old for a whoopin'. My David grew up on this oatmeal, and he grew up 'jes fine. Apparently so well that he cain't sleep on the bed I gave 'im."

"She's not wrong," David said with a laugh.

Calling the girls in, Maddie and her family sat around the table. As Grammy said grace, Maddie thanked God for placing everyone she loved around the table once again.

Barely taking a breath after everyone said amen, Michael asked, "Dad, when are we going to talk about the PKO?"

Kaitlyn's face lost all color as each girl looked at one another.

"Not now, Michael."

"Okay, but Dad we can't wait much longer. It's only a matter of time."

"After Church. We'll talk then."

As the girls walked into Ms. Bonnie's Sunday school room, Amy Jayne awaited them.

"Hey, Maddie, Rachel."

"Hi, Amy Jayne!"

With her voice lowered to a whisper, Amy asked, "Hey Maddie, I was wondering, um, if you'd pray fer me like you said yesterday?"

Maddie looked at Rachel who smiled at her friend. "Of course. Do you mind if my friends pray with us?"

Shrugging her shoulder, she said, "I guess. They don't know me from Tom's housecat anyway."

Pulling together a circle of chairs, Maddie looked at Amy who was wringing her hands anxiously. "Rachel, would you like to pray?"

Winking at her friend, Rachel answered, "You've got this, Girl."

Maddie was nervous yet excited. She had never had anyone ask her to pray for them before. What should I say, God?

A quiet voice inside her head answered,

"Ask her what she needs."

Taking a deep breath to calm her nerves, Maddie asked, "Amy, what do you need us to pray for?"

Amy looked around and answered quietly, "My dad's missin'."

Alarmed, Maddie inched to the edge of her seat and intently looked at Amy. "What do you mean, missing?"

"Awe, he's probably just layin' off drunk somewheres," Amy said as she looked at the floor, "but I'm worried 'bout 'im. He's all me and my brother's got. If people find out he's gone agin, we're off ta the home."

"The home?"

"TCH. It's a home for children. We've been thar before. It's nice and all, but I don't want ta lose my brother. I cain't lose 'im!" Tears fell silently on Amy Jayne's pale white cheeks.

"Amy, can we go look for your dad?" Emma asked.

"Naw, I don't want nobody ta know. Can we jes' pray?"

"Okay, let's pray." Taking a cue from Rachel, Maddie asked, "If God were sitting here now, what would you ask him?"

Biting her lip, she looked up and thought for a moment, then whispered emphatically, "I'd ask him ta fetch my dad home and take that blasted bottle out a his hand!"

Maddie sat a moment, collecting her thoughts. As everyone closed their eyes, she bowed her head and looked at Rachel who opened one eye and nodded in assurance.

> *"God, thank you for Amy Jayne. She needs you, God. Her daddy needs you."*

As Maddie prayed, she thought of her own dad and how scared she was when she didn't know where he was, or if he would ever come back. This seemed to give her confidence.

> *"Just as you brought my daddy home, God, will you bring Amy's home too? And Lord, please heal him. We ask that you help him turn away from alcohol forever and to know*

how much you love him. In Jesus' Name, Amen."

After everyone said amen in agreement, Maddie worried if she did it right. Glancing at Rachel, she breathed a sigh of relief as she winked at her.

"Okay, Girls, let's get started. Looks like y'all already have a good circle goin'." Ms. Bonnie said from behind. "Come on in, Esther, we're talkin' 'bout the least of these today."

On the ride home, Maddie found herself deep in thought about Amy Jayne and the message Ms. Bonnie taught. Looking at Rachel, she could see her friend grappling with similar thoughts.

Before Jade told them about the soup lines in New York, Maddie never considered that there were people who didn't have food to eat. Feeling guilty, she realized she took a lot for granted.

"Rach?"

"Yeah?"

"Is it bad that we always have food to eat?"

Rachel looked at her curiously. "No. Why do you ask?"

Staring out the car window, Maddie answered, "Well, it just doesn't seem fair that other people don't."

"It's not fair," Jade interjected emphatically.

From the front seat, Grammy turned around and peered at her granddaughter. "What'cha goin' round 'bout, Girl?"

"Grammy, were you poor growing up?"

"Here we go," David commented, looking in the rear-view mirror.

"Poor, no ma'am, we were rich in love. That's all ya need."

"But like, you know. Did y'all ever go without eating?"

"Shore nough. Ya worked ta eat. When I was a tot, I'd work with my momma in the garden from early in the mornin' til the sun'd go down. We grew up hard."

"But was there ever a time you didn't have food?"

"Hmm, I r'member when I was 'bout ten or 'leven. 'Bout little Matthew's age, I guess. We'd been plantin' fer weeks and one afternoon when we were settin' up a row fer plantin', the sky turned all sinister, like. You'da thought Satan 'imself were flyin' in. My Pappy called us in and set us all in the storm cellar. I was skeered as anythin'. But my Pappy, he said, 'The Good Lord is here. Nothin' to be 'fraid of, Gracey.' Suddenly, the boards above our heads started rattlin' somethin' fierce. I thought fer sure they'd come flyin' off, but then it stopped."

"Was it a tornado?" Kaitlyn asked.

"Yes, ma'am. It was the worst I've ever seen. When we stepped out, everythin' was gone. Everythin' we'd worked fer was gone. But worse than that thirty people lost their lives that day."

You could hear a pin drop; it was so quiet.

"What did you do?" Emma asked.

"What do ya mean what'd we do? We did what the Good Lord tole us. We pulled together and helped each other. That year, we raised more barns'n I can ever r'member. My Pappy had to go and work in the coal mines to get us some money; then he'd bring food home, and we'd have a hootenanny with the whole town! But we'd go days waitin'."

"Who's Andy?" Matthew asked seriously.

Grammy chuckled, "Why, Boy, that'd be a party with lots a music and dancin'. We'd raise a barn and throw a hootenanny better 'n the last one."

"Sounds like my kind of fun," Jade snickered.

"Them were good ole days. When ever'one comes together to help one another, ya got God's love in the center. Thar ain't nothin' better than that."

"Grammy, what do you do today if somebody needs a helping hand?" Rachel asked.

"Why, we do the same thang we always done. We give 'em a hand. What's all this 'bout bein' poor anyway?"

"Ms. Bonnie taught us about the least of these in Sunday school today. I guess I feel a little guilty that we aren't poor."

"Now ya look at me, Maddie Ruth. Thar been people goin'

without since the garden. The first thang ya gotta know's God is our Provider. His word says he'll provide fer all our needs accordin' to the riches of his glory in Christ Jesus. Thar ain't nothin' promised on this earth 'cept that, and thar ain't no time in my life when he didn't fulfill that promise. Second, God tole us ta work, so we work. God provides but he calls us to partner with 'im. We have a choice, we give up an die, or we can get up an go. Lastly, when God gives ya plenty, then ya give from yer plenty. Servin' the least 'a these is one way the good Lord provides.

After a moment of reflection, Grammy continued, "Ya know what we did in those days, we didn't know when we'd eat again?"

Bending forward to place her chin on the back of her Grammy's seat, Maddie asked, "What's that?"

"We praised the Lord, Maddie Ruth. A heart full a gratitude cain't be anxious or worried 'bout the future. It was gratitude my Pappy and Mammy poured into me no matter if we had a little or a lot. Never ferget that, Love. Gratitude'll help ya in the hard times and it'll serve ya in the good. It's all part a God's perfect plan."

Anxious to hear the promised conversation between her dad and brother, Maddie decided to stick close by.

"Girls, why don't y'all help me fetch some 'maters for supper?" Grammy asked as she grabbed her basket.

"Do we have to? I was hoping to talk to Dad."

"Girl, I don't think thar be anythin' ya need to be hearin' from those two."

"It's okay, Mom. It's about time we bring this thing to an end. Kaitlyn, Jade, are you ladies okay with this?" David looked intently at Maddie's friends. She was thankful that he thought of their feelings.

"I think I'll go punch a bag," Kaitlyn answered leaving the glass door ajar after stepping on the back deck.

"Where do you want to start?" Michael asked.

Setting her basket down, Grammy sat down and said, "The beginnin' is usually the best place to start. Don't'cha think?"

"Senior year, a group of men had a booth on Career Day." Glancing at his dad, he continued, "Dad, you know that I didn't want to go to college, and there was no way I was going to follow in your footsteps. Anyway, the guys and I started talking to these men, and they said everything we wanted to hear. They said the government was jacked up and they knew how to fix it. They talked about a new life where we could change the world. It was everything I was hoping for, Dad." Michael frowned as he looked down at his hands.

Maddie could see the sadness on his face.

"Go on," David said.

"Our first couple of visits were a dream. We met up with a group of guys who were top notch. They were the main character, Dad. They had all their … stuff together."

Maddie couldn't help but giggle at her brother's almost slip of the tongue. Grammy would've had his head.

"When they gave me a cell phone, I began to feel like I was part of the team. It was when I was invited on a mission that I was hooked. They paid me two hundred dollars for four hours of work."

"I'm not sure I want to know, but what was the job?"

Michael's fingers twitched with nervous energy. It was obvious to Maddie that he did not want to answer the question.

"Do you remember hearing about the expansion at the Port of Brunswick?"

"Vaguely."

"The PKO imported cars from their plant in the Philippines. The Case Officer for Baldersville worked a deal with the GPA to allow their employees to "inspect" incoming shipments before the customs examination. I was on a team that performed the inspection."

"And what did you find?"

"Every car on the ship was filled with ghost guns."

Maddie breathed in sharply at the thought of her brother

handling guns, even as she heard David's monotone voice's dry, dulcet tones. While the revelation shocked her, her dad was completely calm.

"I assume you were responsible for unloading these guns?"

"Yes, sir. Every month, a new shipment. It was an easy transition into becoming Bagman."

"Tell me about that. Did you deliver guns?"

"Not always, but when we did, we would take them to California which was the hub for firearms."

"Hub? What do you mean?"

"Baldersville and San Bernardino are two of twelve compounds in the United States. San Bernardino handled firearms and Baldersville handled farmed goods. That's just in the states. There are compounds in every major country within the WTO."

"Wait, what?"

"Yeah, I don't know all of them, but I know the US is largely responsible for distributing food and firearms. Another Bagman told me that Asia is responsible for bioweapons. The Middle East trains and sends out mercenaries. Europe handles communications. Africa handles mineral resources and South America is responsible for drugs.

"Then there are the people." Michael looked at the girls.

It was time for a break. "Girls, why don't you help Grammy."

"No, Dad, we need to hear this, too." Maddie wasn't sure where the courage came from, but she knew she needed to hear the whole story.

"You can't shield us from it, Mr. Bennett. We've seen a lot." Jade added.

Taking a deep breath, David looked at Michael. "What about the people?"

"Every compound has a human trafficking branch. Babysitters trained to brainwash people brought into the compound."

"What kind of people are we talking about?"

"Mostly the unwanted. The homeless, foster children,

runaways, nonconformists, teens, and young adults from broken homes. Many people like me who wanted a chance at a better world. Even veterans who were rejected by society were welcomed into the PKO. Every person worked while having their physical needs met."

Maddie noticed Kaitlyn standing in the doorway. She was white as a sheet but listening intently.

"Hey Kate, are you okay?" Rachel asked.

"Yeah, I'm fine."

Michael looked at Maddie and asked, "Does Dad know how y'all were taken?"

"It was me," Kaitlyn answered quietly.

Worry plastered on Jade's face as she said, "It's okay Kate, you don't have to say anything."

"No, I want to."

"It's okay, Girl. Yer in a safe place," Grammy assured her.

"I was coming off the Noah rejection. You know, Batman?" She said half-jokingly. "After Maddie's encounter at the mall, I started researching "Birdwatcher" online and found this account with a bajillion followers. That's when I started talking to Todd."

Jade and Rachel both grabbed a hand to encourage their friend.

"He was so nice, and I was so stupid."

"Not stupid. You didn't know!" Jade exclaimed.

"No, I was stupid. I should've listened to you and Sonya when you warned me about him. He kept pressuring me to meet up. I should've known something was up because he always wanted to meet privately. He said it would be romantic if we could be alone together." Kaitlyn shook her head in disgust.

"Is that how you ended up at the Boba Tea Shop?" David asked.

"Yes, sir. He wanted to meet me in a more private place, but I truly thought I would be safe there. I never thought about the parking lot behind the building." Kaitlyn began to sob.

Jade laid her head on her friend's shoulder as Rachel

squeezed her hand. Maddie and Emma drew close to their friend as Kaitlyn released the pent-up emotion she had held for so long.

The room was heavy with the pain of four girls who shared in the trauma of that night. Grammy's kitchen clock struck an hour in time that served to turn the page for each one as they allowed the tears to flow.

After a few moments, David asked. "Kaitlyn, do you remember the account name where you met Todd?"

"It was PkNO and something after, but it's been deactivated. I looked."

"Are you sure it wasn't just relabeled?"

"I searched every which way and could not find it. But I guess it could have been."

"Dad, can I ask a question?"

"Of course, Ruthie."

"Were we trafficked?"

David inhaled sharply. To hear his daughter say the words brought a wave of guilt he hoped to never experience. "Yes, Ruthie, you were."

"What is the difference between kidnapping and trafficking?" Rachel asked.

"Well, human trafficking can include kidnapping as it did for the three of you. But often, it is instigated using manipulation or tricking, as Kaitlyn experienced. Then the victim is forced into some type of labor. Michael, is this how fosters and runaways are brought into the compounds?"

"Mostly, yes. But Dad, I don't have proof of this, but there was talk that the local governments were making deals with the PKO to clean up the streets."

With her hands on her hips, Grammy exclaimed, "Wait a doggone minute. Do ya mean ta tell me the city was sellin' the homeless?" Grammy's lips tightened as she grunted in anger.

"Yes ma'am, and children caught up in the foster system. If they couldn't find a family, the PKO would take them. They sold the idea to the government by telling them they would teach them a vocation and help them find jobs in the real world. But the only jobs they found were those working directly for the PKO.”

“I’ve got to say, this is a well-planned and lucrative organization,” David said.

“Well-planned, my patudie!” Grammy exclaimed. “More ‘n like a counterfeit plan. This is EVIL straight from the pit a Hell!”

“Whatever it is, I need you Girls to listen to me. You can’t share this with anyone, okay? Jacque and I will talk to your parents. We want you girls to heal. In fact, I think it would be a good idea if the five of you went to see Dr. Coleman when you get home.” Looking at his wife, he said, “We’ll pay for it. Dr. Coleman is a good man, and he’ll help each of you work through your trauma.”

Kaitlyn raised her hand. “Mr. Bennett, thank you for the offer, but I’m good.”

“Are you sure, Kaitlyn?”

“Yeah.”

“Well, the offer stands if you change your mind.”

CHAPTER 12

A Shaking is Coming

Sunday afternoon, the weather reflected everyone's mood. Maddie and her friends didn't seem to have much to say after Michael's heavy conversation with Dad, so they sat quietly on the front porch as a storm rolled in. She loved the sound of raindrops hitting the metal roof. Peace in the storm, Grammy called them.

"I was excited to go home last week, now not so much." Lightning flashed across the sky as Rachel expressed her disappointment.

Maddie nodded as she rocked, "I know. I wish we could all stay. But at least we get to go together."

"I can't believe school starts next week." Emma groaned as a boom sounded in the distance.

"Yeah, it seems to cut more into summer every year. What's up with that?" Jade asked.

"Well, let's not get torn up about it. Let's talk about the soup kitchen. Jade, have you talked to your mom?" Rachel said.

Maddie was thankful for the change in subject.

"Yeah, she's talking to a non-profit she works with. They're going to schedule a Saturday for us to serve."

Rachel's melancholy expression turned to joy. "Yes! Thank you for that. Where do you think it will be?"

"I'm sure somewhere downtown where she works."

"Wait, downtown? Are you sure it's safe?" Kaitlyn asked.

"As safe as sitting under this metal roof," Jade answered.

Suddenly aware of the lightning coming closer, Emma asked, "Wait, is it not safe to sit under a metal roof?"

Kaitlyn narrowed her eyes at Jade as she said, "It's fine, Girls. A metal roof is safer than shingles because it's non-combustible. A metal roof can't ignite because it's made of steel. But seriously Jade, will we be okay in downtown Atlanta?"

"We'll be fine. They do this all the time, so I'm sure there will be security," Jade answered confidently.

"Just in case, I'll ask my dad to join us." Rachel looked at Maddie and asked, "Can you ask your dad to come?"

Maddie shrugged. "To be honest, I don't know where he'll be. But I can ask."

Later in the day, after the girls were out of earshot, David gave his son a glass of tea as he asked, "Michael, I need you to be straight with me. What is the PKO using ghost guns for?"

"As far as I know, the Birdwatchers and B&Bs are using them for demo missions."

"What's a B&B?" David asked.

"Bang and Burn. They're the guys going into cities to riot and demo. Typically, on the tail end of a peaceful protest which they use as cover."

David was disappointed that his team's intel didn't share this data with him. "You call them demo missions. Why?" David asked.

"The plan is to demolish grids of infrastructure in an attempt to sabotage local government and force dependence on the PKO."

David nodded. "Let me guess. Someone comes behind them to shake hands and kiss babies while making deals in back rooms."

"Something like that. I've only participated in one operation. It was a small town in California. It was weird, Dad, almost as if the mayor was happy to have us there. Even after our B&B Team burned down their shopping center."

"Terror cells using mob tactics. This is totalitarianism at its finest." David said. "The MO is to instill fear, then take control. Cults like this will sever authority—parental and governmental. Then they will substitute their own authority over those they've terrorized.

"So, who's in charge?" David knew the answer to his question, but he wanted to see how his son would answer.

"The Case Officer. He's responsible for all the teams coming in and leaving the compound."

"But who oversees him? To have twelve compounds in the states and more spread out worldwide, somebody must control the whole operation."

Focusing on the empty space between them, Michael was quiet. "Honestly, Dad, I'm not sure. There was this one time when a group of VIPs visited San Bernardino, but I never could get close enough to find out who they were. And nobody was willing to talk."

Peering intently at his son, David knew he was telling the truth. It was for the best. Michael didn't need to know who was behind the operation. As it was, David was going to have to pull some strings to keep him out of harm's way. "Tell me Son, how do you know so much about the PKO? As I understand, the Bagman is nothing more than a logistical runner."

"Everyone who enters the PKO is put through a series of tests. Since I had graduated, I entered a boot camp. One of the tests was an introduction to small-scale missions. I guess it was to see what I was good at. Anyway, as I understand, my response determined the role I was placed in. As you said, a Bagman is considered logistics, but there's a hierarchy. I began as a runner, but gradually would have worked my way up the food chain to missions with more responsibility. My goal was to negotiate the big deals." Feeling ashamed, Michael turned away from his dad for a moment and then turned back with a pained look on his face, "Dad, I really thought this was my chance to make a difference in the world, ya know? A Bagman knows everybody. They had the best opportunity to really inspire change because they had their hands in every mission."

As Michael placed his head in his hands, David looked at his son with compassion. For the first time ever, he saw his son as a man. It took courage to tell this story, knowing it could come back to haunt him. Placing his hand on his son's shoulder, David said, "I believe you, Son. You know, I haven't even taken a moment to ask, but how are you holding up?"

Michael grabbed his glass and took a sip. "Relieved, but if I'm honest, I can't shake that this isn't over."

"I know the feeling, but I've got a plan and a few cards up my sleeve."

Looking at his dad expectantly, Michael said, "I was hoping you'd say that."

Dinner was a somber affair, with Grammy and Matthew making much of the small talk. Maddie was grateful to Grammy for trying to raise everyone's spirits.

"Grammy, can I ask a question?" Matthew asked.

"You shore can, My Boy."

"When we were at Uncle Tom's today, I overheard him talking to a man who wasn't very nice. The man was asking him things about Wild Rock. Uncle Tom told him he couldn't have his town. What did he mean by that?"

Grammy looked at David who was ready to answer. Placing her hand on her son's, she said, "Well Matthew, there are some bad people out thar who want to come into our lil' town and tell us how to run it. Uncle Tom is protective over us here."

Maddie and Rachel exchanged glances with Jade, Emma, and Kaitlyn. Maddie began to feel a familiar burning in her stomach.

"Are they the bad people that took Maddie?" Matthew asked.

Dad squeezed his fist as Maddie's mom turned away.

Anger swept over Grammy's features for a split second, but

then a look of compassion took over as she grabbed her grandson's hand and squeezed. "Okay Family, it's time we let the elephant out."

"Elephant, where's the elephant? Is he with the angels?" Matthew asked innocently.

The girls giggled as Matthew looked under the table.

Ignoring his question, Grammy looked around with a fierce glint in her eye. "This family has been through it in the last year, and pardon my sayin' so, but we're all actin' like we're skeered. Now," raising her hand when she saw David attempt to interject, "I know it ain't been easy fer none of ya, me included. Everythin's gone all catawampus on us. But we're Bennetts, by golly, and Bennett means blessed, not fearful. I watched ma family torn in two when the enemy tried to take us out, but I ain't ne'er gonna do that again! I declare that fear has no place here! Are ya with me? Now, we're facin' a shakin', but ya gotta know on whose foundation you stand!"

She lifted her Bible and said, "This tells us who we are! It tells us that thar ain't nothin' promised in this life. It tells us we'll face trials, but more 'n that, it tells us Whose we are! And we are the Lord's. From the first moment he formed ya, he knew this day would come. Nothin' surprises the Lord our God. And his book gives us promises to stand on. Never doubt it! Our God is with us, fer us, and he sees us. He is our Strength and Shield, which means he is our Protector, and we need to start actin' like it!"

"Grammy, what do you mean that we're facing a shaking?" Maddie asked.

Nodding at David, she said, "Go on, Son, tell 'em. Ain't nothin' to be skeered of here. The truth is the truth."

"Your Grammy is right. We don't have anything to be afraid of. Our family has gone through a lot, and we've come through it stronger every time."

"That's right." Grammy nodded.

"Girls, you experienced a lot at the PKO, and for whatever reason, you were protected from an experience that could have been much worse."

"That'd be the Lord, David, that'd be the Lord." Nodding, she motioned for him to continue.

"The people who run the PKO are not good people. They have purchased property all over the world and are staging terror attacks in major cities to take over local governments."

Maddie and her friends mirrored expressions of shock.

"The riots you have seen on television have been staged by this organization. They come behind a peaceful protest and stage attacks that damage local businesses. Their sabotage is designed to stir up fear and anger so they can take over control."

Maddie and Rachel looked at one another as they remembered the protest at the military base they visited.

"Why aren't they in jail?" Jade asked.

"Good question. The crimes they commit are treated as small, in the name of whatever is being protested at the time. Local governments see the PeaceKeepers as petty criminals looking for their day in the sun, not as terrorists threatening a global takeover."

Angry, Jade exclaimed, "How can they not? It's happening everywhere! Mom told me about an attack near Kansas City just a couple of weeks ago."

"Uh, Dad, Rachel, and I saw a bunch of people carrying signs that said NO ORDER, NO PEACE when we went to the lighthouse. Are they the same people?"

"I would say so, Maddie. The FBI is looking into the PeaceKeepers, but unfortunately, they haven't recognized their connection to the PKO yet."

Kaitlyn was visibly shaken as she heard this news.

"Is this what you worked on when you left last year?" Maddie asked.

"Yes, Ruthie, there was a threat to our country that was said to have originated through this organization; however, since there wasn't a crime committed, there have yet to be any arrests."

Jade's eyes filled with tears. "Don't they know what happened to us? How can they not see that they're related? Did our testimony account for nothing?"

Kaitlyn grabbed the hand of her friend.

"Jade, your testimony was right on. And because of your courage, four people have been imprisoned for a long time."

"I don't get it. If the PKO and the PeaceKeepers are all the same organization, why doesn't the FBI get the guy at the top?"

"That's a very good question, Rachel. One I have asked myself. Unfortunately, there isn't anything to tie the two together, yet."

"I 'spect yer gonna tie up that little loose end?" Grammy asked.

David chuckled, "I'm trying Momma. The admiral hasn't been too happy to see me lately."

"Why?" Kaitlyn asked.

"Well, I disobeyed a direct order, and took matters into my own hands."

"And rescued five people!" Jacque cried out. "If it weren't for you, we wouldn't be sitting here with our son and daughter now!"

"Well, they don't know about Michael yet. I expect that revelation will bring its own consequences."

"Again, I don't understand why you would suffer a consequence for saving your own children. After everything you've done for this country. . ." A sob broke from Jacque's throat as her voice trailed off.

"Love, I know this is confusing, but it's the way of things. As a Commander, I am obligated, by oath, to follow orders I willfully disobeyed. But I would do it all over again because my family is my priority." David looked at all three of his children with a steely-eyed gaze. He was serious.

"Dad, are you going to go to jail?" Maddie didn't want to consider this possibility but felt she had to ask.

"There will be an inquiry, but with the Warriors of the Way and Tom's help, I should be fine. I spoke to Jack's attorney, who doesn't think they have any recourse considering the circumstances. I will probably face demotion if not a forced discharge."

"But what did you do wrong? I don't understand it!" Jacque cried.

Drawing his wife close, he said softly, "I disobeyed orders, and I broke into private property."

"And got shot fer it," Grammy said.

"Is my dad in trouble, too?" Rachel asked.

"No, Rachel. The local law enforcement let us off because we were there to rescue you and exposed a human trafficking scheme in the process. They were grateful. It is the Navy that isn't too happy with me. There are ways to go about what we did. I took matters into my own hands. There is a consequence for that."

"Alright, now that we've beat that dead horse, let's talk about what's really goin' on. Now Jacque, I know ya don't wanna hear 'bout this, but thar thangs happenin' right in front of our eyes that we cain't ignore."

"What do you mean? What's happening?" Jade asked.

"The Good Book tells us we're gonna go through tribulation, but John encourages the church to patiently endure seven times. We cain't be skeered! Jesus has overcome, so we'll overcome, which calls fer trust. Them's our marchin' orders."

"What is tribulation?" Maddie asked.

"Great trouble or sufferin'. We all been goin' through it, hadn't we? What you girls went through was tribulation. The riots in the streets and the civil unrest all point to somethin' bigger'n us. We know that the whole world'll go through it when a man'll rise who'll pretend he's the savior of the world. He'll establish a world order that promises the counterfeit peace we discussed, and then tell the world to bow down to 'im. Then, we all decide who we're gonna worship."

"Is that man here?"

Grammy looked at David who looked away.

"Is that man here, Dad?"

Ignoring his daughter's question, he turned to his mom and said, "I love you, Mom. I really do, but I just don't know if I believe like you do."

Grammy placed her hand on her son's and said, "It's okay,

Son. I got enough faith fer the both of us. But yer gonna reckon with the Lord one way or 'nother. Seek 'em, ask 'em to reveal 'imself. But don't ignore him. Judgment's comin'. Those who don't know the Lord will know the real sufferin'. What the antichrist is gonna do is nothin' compared to bein' judged by an almighty God."

"We don't even know if this tribulation is here. We've faced terror before, Mom. That doesn't mean we're in the middle of tribulation."

Grammy looked at her son with compassion as she said, "I know, I know, and yer right. It's the mercy a God that we're all sittin' here today. What I know ta be true, is the Lord is patient, fer he wants no one to perish. And sometimes, he lets us go through tribulation to get our 'ttention. It may not be the great tribulation, but the signs are tellin', and I hear 'im sayin' that it's mighty time we start listenin', don't ya think?"

Maddie had a hundred questions as the girls prepared for bed. She didn't know where to start. "Hey Rach, what do you know about the tribulation that Grammy was talking about?"

Applying lotion to her hands, Rachel offered some to Maddie as she said, "Honestly, not much. It's not exactly my favorite subject to study."

"Do you think that Sonya would know about it?" Maddie insisted.

"Why don't we read about it so we can come up with some questions?" Jade asked.

"Oh hey, how about your dad, Rach?" Maddie asked excitedly. "Didn't your dad tell you we could be in the last days?"

Yawning, Emma burrowed under her covers as she asked, "I'm with Jade. How about we read it and come up with a list of questions?"

"Okay but be prepared. It's a hard read. About as hard as Moby Dick." Rachel winked at Maddie as she mimicked

Emma's yawn.

Monday morning arose bright and oppressively hot. A cotton shirt and shorts were the fit of the day as Maddie and her friends faced the mugginess left behind by the storm.

Sitting with their Bibles and journals, the girls decided to read the scripture aloud—well, most of them anyway. Kaitlyn protested but argued that since they were twisting her arm to read on her summer vacation, she would make it into a science project. Before they started, however, Rachel encouraged them to read a summary on tribulation from Got Questions, a website that answers questions people have about the Bible.

After Rachel read the summary, Kaitlyn said, "Oh look, now we don't have to read the Bible."

"Don't be snarky, Kate. We said we would do this, so let's do it."

Rachel reached out to Sonya, who told them to break it down into seven sections, which was perfect since they would be together for the next seven days before school started back. Today, they began with chapters one through three. After each girl read her section, she passed it off to the next one. Emma was voted scribe.

Surprisingly, Kaitlyn was the first to have a question. "Is John writing to the churches of his day or churches in the future?"

Rachel couldn't answer the question.

Jade said the letters must have been written to the churches of John's day since it specifically says, "gave him to show his servants what must soon take place."

But Maddie disagreed because Jesus told John to write about what is now and what will happen later. "Why would Jesus limit this revelation only to the seven churches of his day?" She pointed out.

"Do you notice that each church has a strength and a weakness?" Rachel asked.

"Yeah, what if each church represents a type of person?" Emma said.

"Well, all I know is I want to be like Philadelphia, so I don't have to go through the hour of trial!" Jade said with a dramatic sigh of relief.

"Which do you think is the most like the people of our day?" Rachel asked.

"Definitely, Laodicea," Maddie replied sadly. "Lukewarm, wealthy, blind, I wish everyone could see what's happening around us. We're so concerned with having the latest fit or the newest phone while our cities are burning down, and people are going hungry."

"Yeah," Rachel said, "but look, he gives us hope in chapter three when he says he stands at the door and knocks. If anyone hears his voice and opens the door, he will come in and eat with that person. So, it's not all lost. We just need to pray that people will open their eyes and the door of their hearts to him."

That afternoon, they studied Revelation four through seven. Rachel was in awe of God's throne room. "Can you imagine, we will stand before him one day!" She exclaimed.

"But who is this Lion of the tribe of Judah? Who is the Lamb?" Kaitlyn asked.

Rachel smiled as she answered, "Jesus is the Lion and the Lamb."

"That makes absolutely no sense. How can he be both?" Kaitlyn asked.

"That would be a question, 'How is Jesus both the Lion and the Lamb?'"

"Got it," Emma replied as she wrote down the question.

As they read through the seals, each girl felt profound grief over what was revealed—conquest, killing, scales, and earthquakes. "I'm sorry, but this is just too much," Kaitlyn pointed out. "This makes it sound like God is some cosmic King ready to destroy what he created."

"Kate, is there a question in there? I told you this would be hard. You said you would make it into a science project. Just pretend you're in school." Rachel said.

"Who are the 144,000?" Jade asked.

"Well, considering they come from Jewish tribes, I would say they are Jews," Rachel answered.

"So, they will be protected through this seal an angel places on their forehead?" Emma asked.

"Yup, looks like it."

Watching Rachel, Maddie realized her friend had the patience of a saint as she fielded everyone's questions.

After writing down the 144,000 Jews, Emma asked, "And these in the white robes? Who are they?"

"In verse fourteen, it says they are the ones who came out of the great tribulation."

"Wait, did they die?" Maddie asked as she closed her Bible. "I'm done. I don't think I can read anymore."

"Hey, what did your Grammy say?" Rachel looked intently into Maddie's eyes. "It's time to stop being afraid, right?"

Maddie gave her friend the look as she re-opened her Bible.

Scrolling through her phone, Kaitlyn called out, "Hey, y'all, I looked up the question about Jesus being the Lion and the Lamb, and here's what Wikipedia says, "In Christianity, according to a sermon by Augustine, the Lion stands for Christ resurrected, the Lamb for Christ's sacrifice." Okay, but you guys realize this is a paradox, right? In nature, a lion is a hunter while a lamb is gentle and meek." Looking at Rachel directly, Kaitlyn added, "You can't be both."

"You sure are spending a lot of time on something you don't believe in," Jade asked sarcastically as she picked up her books to walk to their room.

Kaitlyn stuck her tongue out as she threw a wadded-up paper from her journal at her friend.

CHAPTER 13

The Challenge of Revelation

Over the next four days, the girls read through all twenty-two chapters of Revelation.

"Yes, I am coming soon. Amen. Come, Lord Jesus. The grace of the Lord Jesus be with God's people. Amen," Maddie read as she closed her Bible.

"Hang on, Jesus is coming back?" Jade asked.

Rachel looked ready to jump out of her chair. "Yep! Isn't it awesome?"

"Well, my head hurts," Kaitlyn said as she shook her head. "I can't believe we read that whole book. I have more questions now than I did before! Why didn't we just stick to Got Questions?"

"Do you want to upload the questions and see how it answers?"

"Naw, I think we should talk to Sonya," Jade said.

"How about we ask Grammy, too?" Rachel asked.

"What y'all wanna ask yer ole Grammy?" Grammy asked as she joined them on the back deck.

Maddie was excited to see her walk out at just the right time. "Grammy, we've been reading Revelation this week."

"I was wonderin' what y'all were chewin' on. And whatcha think?"

"I think I have a headache," Kaitlyn said.

Grammy chuckled, "That's about right. I had ta read it

134

several times 'afore it clicked."

Kaitlyn held her head in a vice. "Whoa, I don't know if I could do that."

"We have a couple of questions. . ." Emma looked up shyly as she turned the page of her notebook.

"Well, I cain't promise to have all the answers, but maybe I can help with a few. Shoot."

"Were the letters to the churches written just to those in John's time or future churches?" Emma asked.

Grammy smiled, "Revelation is a book where Jesus revealed a prophetic message to the Church, which is fer all time. But diff'rent people read it diff'rently, so while I'll answer as best I can, I ain't Jesus. Let's be clear on that."

"So, the letters are for all time? What do the names mean? Like Philadelphia?"

"Well, Philadelphia was a real church in John's time."

Irritated, Kaitlyn asked again, "I'm confused, was the letter to the local church or all churches?"

"Let me ask ya a question, did ya ever read The Lion, the Witch, and the Wardrobe?"

"I love The Chronicles of Narnia!" Rachel exclaimed.

"Well, I'll bet ya didna' know that C.S. Lewis wrote the first book fer his goddaughter?"

"No way, really?" Rachel asked.

"That's right, and now thar are seven books enjoyed by people fer all time. How do ya reckon that happened?"

"I guess because it had a message others needed to hear?" Rachel asked.

"That's right. Them letters have a message all need to hear a'fore they reach fulfillment. Tell me, what did ya read that spoke just ta you?"

"When Jesus wrote to Philadelphia, he said, 'Hold on to what you have, so that no one will take your crown.' What did he mean by that?" Jade asked.

"Well, Revelation's filled with word pictures." Grammy placed an invisible crown on her head, saying, "The crown was a picture reflectin' our reward a vict'ry. Through Christ, we have faith, hope, and love, right? So, if ya hold on ta Christ, operatin' through the faith, hope, and love he gives ya, nobody can take yer vict'ry, nobody can take yer crown. Now, to answer yer question, Kaitlyn, I believe Jesus wrote these letters to the local churches listed at the top a each letter, but I also believe he intended 'em fer all believers. If ya think 'bout it, the whole Bible is a letter to the Church, even though many of the books were written to the Jews."

"Just like The Lion, the Witch, and the Wardrobe."

Grammy nodded. "Does that answer yer question?"

"Yeah, I think so," Kaitlyn answered. "Can I ask another question?"

"You betcha!"

"Who are the Jews, and how are they different from the Church?"

"That's a mighty good question, Girl! The Jews were God's chosen people. In the Old Testament, he made a cov'nant with a man named Abraham ta raise a fam'ly that'd usher in the Savior of the world, his Son Jesus. After Jesus went back ta Heaven, some believed in him while others didna. Those who believed in him became the Church. That'd be a big "C" 'cause it represents the bride a Christ."

"So are the Jews still God's chosen people?"

"Yes, ma'am, they are, and those who aren't Jewish are also chosen since they're grafted into God's fam'ly."

"Grafted in? What does that mean?"

Grammy pulled a stick out of her apron. "See this here, branch? This came from the rootstock of an apple tree last summer. I been hibernatin' it in the icebox." Pulling her gardening gloves on, she grabbed a knife and a roll of black tape from the gardening box on the bench behind them. She then made a long straight cut in the wood.

"Now walk on over here with me." Grammy walked off the back deck toward the garden. The girls followed her.

"This, Dearies, is an apple tree. We're gonna cut what looks like a tongue right'chere." Demonstrating the cut, Grammy placed the loose branch inside. "This branch here'll fit just like a glove. See? That's called a tongue and groove. Now, we're gonna wrap it with tape. I'll take the tape off in the fall, and we'll have a grafted branch."

"So, a grafted branch is cut in to become one with the tree?" Rachel asked.

"You got it, Girl! God wanted a big fam'ly. So, he started with himself, added the twelve tribes of Israel who'd be the Jews if ya didna know, and then he grafted in the gentiles, that'd be you and me and anyone who ain't Jewish."

Maddie began to empathize with Kaitlyn. This was a lot of information.

Walking back to the house, Grammy asked, "Alrighty, what's next?"

Everyone settled back around the table. Kaitlyn sat forward in her chair and said, "So, there are seven seals. Is Jesus the one who breaks the seals?"

"Yes, ma'am, he shore is."

"Why? The seals have destruction and suffering. If God is love, why is he pouring out suffering on the world he created?"

The joy-filled lines on Grammy's face suddenly reflected a haunted sadness. "God is a lovin' God, but he's also just. And the truth is, Ms. Kaitlyn, that justice is the other side a love. Tell me, what do you think justice is?"

Picking up her phone to search online, Kaitlyn spoke as she typed, "What is justice. . . This says that justice is just behavior or treatment."

"Okay. And who gets to decide what behavior is good or bad?" Grammy asked.

"A judge?"

"Whooee, doggie, give her a cookie! Now, what does this judge use to determine what's fair?"

"I know, I know! The law," Emma said.

"Okay, so yer standin' in a court a law fer somethin' ya did. The judge compares yer actions to what the law says, and he says, she is guilty! What happens next?"

Kaitlyn let out a loud sigh. "I know the answer to this. I ran a stop sign, and my mom made me go to court. I got a ticket."

"And ya had ta pay fer it, didna' ya?"

"Yes, ma'am."

"Alrighty now, the Bible says we've all sinned an fallen short a God's glory. As sinners, we'll stand 'afore God ta speak to the sins we've committed, right?"

"But didn't God send Jesus?" Jade asked.

"Yes! He did! And our Jesus stands as Defense Attorney when we choose to foller him. But if we don't, then we stand alone, right?"

"Yeah."

"Jesus took God's judgment meant fer us on himself at the Cross. Justice and love poured out for all who call on the name a Jesus. That is our vict'ry ma young friend. If God doesna' declare justice over sin and evil, then love has no power. The seals in this book pour out God's judgment over evil, and since Jesus took God's judgment on the Cross, he's the only one who can pour out the judgments. But unfortunately, those who don't choose him will stand in judgment on their own power 'cause they rejected his."

With a pained look, Kaitlyn asked, "If judgment was poured out on Jesus at the Cross, why does it need to be poured out on the earth?"

Placing her hand on Kaitlyn's, Grammy asked, "What is it yer 'fraid of Kaitlyn?"

Closing her eyes, she began to rock. "When we were at the PKO, Todd said something to me I'll never forget. . ."

The sound of the creaking chair filled the quiet room as she continued to rock. "He said that nobody on the campus mattered. He said that we were all replaceable. If one was lost, they'd find another who worked just like them." The grief that held Kaitlyn captive for so long once again poured out of her like a flood. "We were nothing to them!"

The emotion was too much to hide. The room was heavy, and it was clear to Maddie that each of them had to find release.

As their tears began to subside, Grammy opened her Bible and began to read.

> *Fer God so loved the world that he gave his one and only Son, that whosoever believes in him shall not perish but have eternal life. Fer God did not send his Son into the world to condemn the world, but to save the world through him.*

After pausing for a moment, she continued, "When ma David decided ta go in the Navy, I didna' know how I could stand another season a worry. Eight years I struggled with ma George bein' gone. I r'member cryin' out, 'Not again God, WHY?!?' It was in that thar season the Good Lord showed me he would ne'er leave nor forsake me. I could trust 'em with my son. Girls, sufferin' is real, and it's this ver' reason Jesus came. He suffered to save. Now, r'member that crown Jesus tole' us 'bout? He said ta hold on ta what ya have. Well, when ya hold on ta Christ, ya endure the sufferin' with him by yer side. His plan from the beginnin' was ta deal with the brokenness of the evil in this world. But look at what this verse says, 'God did not send his Son into the world to condemn the world, but to SAVE the world through him.' Now, does anyone r'member what he said in the last chapters a Revelation?"

"Oh, I know! He said he's coming again, and we will dwell with him forever!" Emma answered.

"That's right. Jesus gave us vict'ry by takin' our judgment on the cross, but ONLY when he defeats evil on the earth will our vict'ry be complete. Ya understand?"

Rachel's eyes were laser-focused on Grammy as she said, "So, it's like a two-part process. Jesus took our judgment personally on the Cross and then he'll pour judgment on everything else when the seals are poured out?"

"Yes ma'am, that's right. After Jesus returns, sin and evil won't have dominion over this earth nomore. There'll only be one more time the enemy can strike."

"Wait, when is that?" Kaitlyn asked.

"Jesus returns, and a great war takes place, right? That'd be Armageddon. The beast and the false prophet are captured and thrown into the lake of fire. The Bible goes on ta say that an angel comes down from Heaven, he seizes that ole' no count bugger Satan who is the dragon, the serpent, or the devil, whatever ya wanna call 'im; and he bounds him fer a thousand years. At the end a that thousand years, he'll be set free and allowed to deceive once again and gather those who choose to foller 'em into battle, but only fer a short time. As I read it, this is a second battle at Gog and Magog. The Good Book says that Satan and his minions march across the earth and surround the camp a God's people, but fire'll come down from Heaven and devour 'em, and Satan and his followers'll be thrown into the lake of fire ferever. Then comes the White Throne judgment."

"That was another question I had, Grammy. Revelation twenty verse twelve says, 'The dead were judged according to what they had done as recorded in the books.' What are the books? I see the Book of Life mentioned, but I don't see any other books?"

"I cain't rightly say what they're called. What I do know is the Book a Life will have the names of all who said yes to Jesus and follered 'em. Now, I heard Pastor say once there's somethin' called a Bema Seat where Jesus'll reveal what we did after we said yes to him. I think it was Paul who said, 'He'll bring to light what is hidden. And at that time, each'll receive their praise from God.' Now, I 'spect that's what these books are. R'member those crowns we're talkin' 'bout? On earth, the crown is vict'ry in Christ, but in Heaven, we'll receive real crowns that speak to what we did fer him. And we'll give 'em back to him."

"I was reading about the crowns online," Rachel added. "There's an imperishable crown, the crown of rejoicing, the crown of righteousness, the crown of glory, and the crown of life. So will we all get every crown?"

"You Girls are just full a questions, ain't ya?" Grammy sighed. "I ain't no scholar, Ladies, but I know my God is good, and he'll assign our reward as he sees fit. Not shore I can answer this one, 'cept to say go see what God says about it." Picking up her Bible, she said, "This book here is full a ever' answer you'll ever need. So, ask 'em, and see what he says.

Alrighty, now, I think that's enough. Let's get dinner on the table so y'all can pack."

"Ohh." Kaitlyn groaned. "Do we have to leave?"

Standing, Grammy touched Kaitlyn's shoulder and said, "Ya know, yer welcome back anytime."

"Thank you, Grammy."

Later that night, Maddie and Rachel decided to skip the game the other girls were playing to gaze at the stars.

Maddie, tracing an imaginary line from the North Star to the Big Dipper, said, "We go home tomorrow."

"I know," Rachel said.

Wanting to see how her friend felt, Maddie asked, "Are you sad?"

Copying Maddie's movements, Rachel blurted out, "Hey, look, a shooting star. Do you ever wonder why we place more importance on the stars that move than those that stay in place? God used the North Star to lead the wise men to Jesus, but the North Star never moved; it only shined brightly."

Maddie shrugged her shoulders. "I never thought about it."

Rolling to her side, Rachel placed her head in her hand. "Yes, I'm a little sad. This summer has been great. Thank you, BFF."

Leaning back on her elbows, Maddie said, "You're welcome. I love it here. Sometimes, I wish I could stay forever."

"Yeah, me too."

"Hey, Rach?"

"Yeah?"

"I'm really worried about Kaitlyn. She's struggling, isn't she?"

"Yeah, she is."

Sitting up and placing her arms around her knees, Maddie squeezed tight and said, "This last year has been the hardest of my life, but you guys made it easier to get through. Honestly,

Rach, I can't remember the last time I had a panic attack. I want Kaitlyn to find peace, too."

Rachel breathed in deeply and sighed. "Yeah, me too. Why don't you tell her?"

"Tell her what?"

Sitting up, Rachel said, "Tell her what Jesus did for you."

After crossing her legs, Maddie looked down as she began to braid her hair. "Oh, I don't know if she wants to hear it."

"Hey, remember that verse we read that said they overcame him by the blood of the Lamb and the word of their testimony?"

"Yeah."

Placing her hand on her friend's shoulder, Rachel said, "Dad told me once that we can never persuade a person to follow Jesus by our words, but that we can lead them to him by shining his light and sharing our testimony."

"What is my testimony?"

"A testimony is our story, how we met Jesus and how he changed our life."

"But she already knows," Maddie said.

"She knows her perspective of your life, not yours. There is power in allowing yourself to be vulnerable and share and show the hard stuff."

"Oh, I don't know if I can do that."

Rachel looked at her and said, "Maddie, do you think Jesus was vulnerable when he laid down his life?"

"Yeah, but that's different."

"How? He left Heaven and came to Earth as a baby. He grew up with all the hard things in life that we face. Then he walked to a cross to suffer and die as people rejected him— sounds vulnerable to me."

Maddie didn't like the direction of this conversation. The thought of being vulnerable brought back old feelings. Destroying the braid she had worked so hard to create, she nervously began again, saying, "But he's God. He knew what he was doing."

Rachel laughed, "And you think that makes it easier? He

shed blood in the garden as he considered his next." Pointing toward her friend, she continued, "And he did that, Maddie, thinking about you, me, Jade, Emma, and Kaitlyn. Think about it. If Jesus could be vulnerable, then so can we."

"Yeah, I guess you're right."

"Hey, I was just thinking. Maybe that's why the North Star was so bright. It gave the wise men confidence in their journey while revealing the One who would give them confidence. Let Jesus be that for you, Maddie. Remember how you said that Ms. Lorna taught you to focus on the One who would heal you from anxiety? Let him give you confidence to share your story as he reveals his light through you."

"David Bennett, here."

"David, my good friend, shalom! How are you?"

"I am well, thank you, Mordy. I wanted to thank you for all your help. We were able to secure the package efficiently."

"That's excellent news! Oh, there goes my connection. Can you return the call?"

Mordecai Oronoff was always to the point, but his brevity clearly showed something was up. Walking to the back room, David closed the door and opened his laptop to secure a line. "Mordy?"

"Hello, David. Thank you for calling me back. I don't have long and have essential information to share with you."

"How can I help?" David asked.

"My house is being watched. Do you remember the man who chased us from the bar on Hillel Street last year?"

"As I recall, he had an interesting tattoo."

"Yes, I saw him talking to Ambassador Cohen last week."

"Well, that is an interesting development. Did you hear what was said?"

"No, I was leaving with a cohort and happened upon them in the corridor."

"Do you think he is the one watching your house?"

"He and another, yes. I saw a nondescript black car across the street with two men just yesterday. I sent my wife and children to be with her Ima."

David took a deep breath. "Tom informed me that my house is also being watched. Jacque and I decided a well-earned vacation was needed."

"That sounds splendid. I think we should do the same. It's about time to take the boat for a jaunt."

"Mordy, you don't think Ambassador Cohen is involved with Lucien Baldur, do you?"

"He is the one who revealed the case to you, is he not?"

"Yes, he was."

"Well, that's the challenge of revelation, isn't it? That which is revealed was first concealed, and only when you find that which is concealed, the truth is revealed."

David chuckled, "That sounds like something my mom would say."

"It is Biblical. For there is nothing hidden that will not be disclosed, and nothing concealed that will not be brought to light. I expect something Adonai is revealing to us, but we will have to find that which is concealed first."

"Speaking of revelation, Lucien Baldur was not too pleased with my response to his proposal."

Mordecai laughed as he asked, "He did not take it well when you declined his offer?"

Remembering Lucien's quick change in countenance, David said, "Let's just say his eyes breathed fire."

"And here I thought you were the persuasive one."

David snorted. "Do you think he will find another way to get the information he wants?"

Clearing his throat, Mordecai said, "Back to your earlier question, if he is working with Ambassador Cohen, it's possible he already has."

"Ambassador Cohen has sworn an oath to protect and defend the United States Constitution. If he is in cahoots with Lucien Baldur and is sharing Israeli secrets, then he is in blatant violation of this oath. I would need proof of this allegation."

"Yes, and so the reason for my call."

"How would you like me to proceed?" David asked.

"Hm, it's about time my family and I take that long-awaited vacation. Perhaps you could contact Ambassador Cohen in my absence to see if additional communiques have been received?"

"I'm on it. But do you think the Ambassador would speak to me?"

"You are the most persuasive man I have ever met, David Bennett. I have complete confidence in you.

CHAPTER 14

Schoolhouse Rock

Maddie and her friends climbed into the SUV for the long ride home to Atlanta.

The initial quiet that filled the cabin revealed the effects of the long Appalachian goodbye. Everyone who is anyone knows that saying "bye" just isn't enough for those who call Appalachia home. Grammy didn't know how to just wave and send off; no, she had to give rib-crushing hugs. Nothing would be left behind, of course. And Max wouldn't be forgotten either as he made sure all her friends hugged him properly. Maddie couldn't help but smile as she remembered Grammy's final goodbye to Kaitlyn when she ran up for one last hug, "Bye, Grammy, thank you so much for letting us stay here! I hope we can come back soon."

Cupping Kaitlyn's face in her hands, Grammy replied, "Good Lord willin' and the creek don't rise, and ya will. You'ns know y'all are welcome 'ere anytime."

Interrupted from the memory, she listened as her brother broke the silence with conversations of bows, arrows, and boomerangs. He was becoming quite the archer.

While Matthew kept everyone occupied, Maddie wrote in her journal. It had been a minute since she had written her thoughts and processed them with God. She was surprised over how much she missed it. When she told Rachel that everything changed after following Jesus, she was serious. *It's as if you know my every thought*. She wrote. There seemed to be a release when she talked to God. When she wrote down and prayed over her anxious thoughts, the worry disappeared. She just wished she could remember to do it every time.

Maddie did still struggle with anxiety, but thankfully, the panic attacks had subsided. She just continued to do the things she had learned. She would breathe, then pray. Afterward, she would call out what she could see, hear, touch, smell, and taste. Then if she was in a place to do so, she would journal what she was thinking and experiencing. Mr. C told her this was very helpful to him when they were processing.

In their last video call, Mr. C asked her to read through her journal and find common themes in her thoughts and feelings. After her rescue from the PKO, they worked a lot on facing fear. If she were honest, she still struggled with fear a little. *Why can't it just go away?* She thought. Grammy told her she ruminated too much on things. When she looked up the meaning of ruminate, she had to admit Grammy was a little right, as always. She did have a habit of thinking about the same thing again and again.

"Hey Rach, what was it that Sonya told us to do with our thoughts at Woodlands?"

Rachel looked up from the picture Matthew was drawing. "Take them captive," she said.

"Oh yeah, thanks."

Writing the words: *"take my thoughts captive"* in her journal, Maddie drew a picture of the thoughts she would typically have and wrote in words she remembered Rachel saying about them.

"What'cha doin Maddie?" Kaitlyn asked.

"Journaling. I've been slacking lately."

Pointing to her book, Kaitlyn asked, "What does that say?"

"'I don't think I can do it' and right here it says, 'God will help me.'"

"What can't you do?"

"I've just been thinking about the thoughts I have when I struggle with anxiety. Mr. C wants me to write them down and write the truth beside them." Maddie drew a flower in the corner of the page.

"You're taking them captive," Rachel said.

"I guess. I just wish I could do it better when they pop into my mind."

"Are you feeling better Maddie?" Kaitlyn asked.

Nodding, Maddie answered, "Yes, a lot better."

"This happens to me a lot." Kaitlyn pointed toward the circles representing Maddie's frantic thoughts.

"What do you mean?"

"I'm having a hard time concentrating on one thing. I feel all scattered."

"I get that. Is there anything that helps you not feel so scattered?"

"Well, being at Grammy's really helped. I didn't always have a signal, so I couldn't check my phone all the time."

Maddie laughed, "Yeah, me too. We could hold each other accountable to stay off our phones if you want."

"That'd be cool. But you know we'd have to be on our phones to hold each other accountable."

Maddie didn't think about that. "Well, let's just take a picture of our screen time before bed."

"So, what's your screen time at now?"

Maddie opened her phone to settings to check. "One and a half hours. Wow, I didn't realize I had already used it that much on the car ride. How about yours?"

"Two hours. What should our goal be?"

"I would say two hours a day. What do you think, Rach?"

"What did you average before going to Grammy's?"

Changing the date to the end of May, Maddie said, "Ouch, seven hours, and nine minutes. What am I doing for that long?"

Kaitlyn laughed, "Check mine, ten hours, and twenty-five minutes. That's crazy. No wonder my thoughts are so scattered! Alright, so two hours a day?"

Kaitlyn fist-bumped her friend. "Two hours a day." But what will I do for the other twenty-two hours of the day?"

"Sleep, I hope," Jade interjected.

Closing her journal, Maddie leaned forward and placed her chin on Kaitlyn's chair. "Kate?"

"Yeah?"

"How are you doing?"

Kaitlyn shrugged her shoulders. "It's hit or miss. Hey, but that punching bag really helped. Your Aunt Lisa was so nice to let me have it."

Maddie smiled. "Can I ask you a question?"

"Sure."

Nervous, Maddie hesitated momentarily before asking, "Do you remember when you were on the back deck punching the bag?"

"Yeah."

"What did you see when you hit the bag?"

Kaitlyn shrugged. "Honestly, I don't remember."

"Are you still having nightmares?"

"Yes, not as often though. Why?" Kaitlyn asked, looking at her friend.

Maddie sat quietly, thinking what to say next. "Do you remember when Rachel said that when we pray, we invite Jesus to give us strength and courage to face bad things? I wanted to tell you that he's done that for me. He's helping me to let go of things I'm afraid of."

"So, you're not afraid anymore?"

"Oh, I'm still afraid, but before, when I was afraid, I didn't know where to go. Like, I was in a dark hole and couldn't get out. But now, I know where to go." Maddie shrugged. "I guess that's what's different."

"But what does he do for you? Rachel said he doesn't take away the bad stuff, so how can he really help?"

"Just like she said, he gives me strength and courage. I don't know. . . Hey, remember when we ziplined at Woodlands? Right before I jumped off the platform, I remember feeling so anxious. But something happened before I jumped."

Curious, Kaitlyn turned toward Maddie and asked, "What happened?"

"First, I realized how high up I was, but then I realized I had a guide who knew his stuff. He showed me all the pieces of the gear and what they did. That gave me the confidence I needed to jump. When I pray, I feel the same thing. Like, I'm talking to somebody who knows me and knows what I'm going through. But he knows what I need to get through it."

"That's wisdom," Rachel said.

Crossing her arms, Kaitlyn looked at Maddie and said, "Thanks, Girl. I appreciate you, really, I do. And I believe that you believe this, but God hasn't done anything for me except allow me to be in a broken home with a mom who's too busy for me. When Grammy confirmed that Jesus pours out suffering and judgment, I felt it all the way to my bones. How can I expect Jesus to save me after hearing that?"

The car got quiet at that moment. Maddie had no idea what to say. She knew he helped her, but how could she help her friend see that he wanted to help her, too?

Tell her I love her.

Maddie shook her head. Is that you, God?

Tell her that I love her. Tell her I see her. She needs to know that I am with her.

Nervously, Maddie placed her hand on her friend's arm as she said, "Kate, God loves you. He sees, and he loves you. I don't fully get the suffering part, but Grammy said that he'll make everything right. I believe he'll do that for you, too."

Kaitlyn sat quiet and stiff with her arms folded before her.

A little embarrassed and worried she didn't handle things right, Maddie sat back in her chair. She realized her friend probably felt trapped. She didn't want her to feel that way.

"And we love you, Kate," Rachel said. Winking at Maddie in reassurance, she said, "What I think Maddie wants you to know is he's here to help you when you're ready. It's okay if you're not. We love you just as you are; and are here for you, too."

Kaitlyn's countenance softened as she uncrossed her arms. "Can we change the subject?"

Quiet through the exchange, Jade piped up and said, "Hey, I know, let's play Name that Tune!" Jade began humming a tune.

"Don't Stop Believing!" Emma said.

Before long everyone was laughing and crying when Matthew broke into song with them. Kaitlyn looked at Maddie and smiled. Everything would be alright.

The first day of school was a blur. Maddie was excited to be entering her sophomore year with her friends.

After the chaos of the previous semester, the school administration decided to let Maddie and her friends pass; however, they all had to take a retention test to confirm they were ready for the new school year. Thankfully, they all passed. *School is totally gonna rock this year!* She thought.

Maddie was most excited to go back to church. Rachel invited her to come to Sunday church in addition to Wednesday. Before Summer, she and Sonya met for a short time to talk about the Bible and stuff. She was hoping she would be willing to meet up again. She had so many questions.

Walking into her first-period class, she felt self-conscious. While the news stories stopped months ago, there were still those who had questions about their experience at the PKO. She couldn't help but feel as if everyone was talking about her when she walked into a room.

Suddenly, as she took her seat, she heard, "Hi Maddie!" Turning around, Maddie saw Ashley Gordon, the girl who had bullied her in middle school.

"Hi, Ashley," she said.

"How was your summer?" Ashley asked.

"It was good. I hung out at my Grammy's."

Leaning over the desk to whisper to Maddie, Ashley asked,

"That's cool. Is she in Marietta?"

"No, she lives in Tennessee. How was your summer?"

"I went on a mission trip with the church. It was so awesome!"

Softening when she saw the sincere look on her face, Maddie asked, "Really? Where did y'all go?"

"Guatemala. We served in a medical mission. It was so fun." Ashley held up her phone to show a picture of the medical mission team.

"That sounds really cool."

Lowering her whisper even further, Ashley asked, "Hey, how is your mom doing?"

Maddie smiled and looked back at her classmate again. "She's better. Thank you for asking."

As the bell sounded, Ashley passed a note. Reading the number and smiley face on the page, Maddie felt at ease. Perhaps not everyone was talking about her.

As the weeks passed, Maddie settled into a normal rhythm. Believe it or not, she and her mom were getting along. Maddie followed Mr. C's recommendation to spend an hour a week with her talking over the things they were each struggling with. Before the suicide attempt, her mom was annoying, but she was strong. The past year proved that even her mom struggled with overwhelming feelings. And so, they chose to process their feelings together. Maddie still didn't like her mom telling her how to dress and wear her hair, but she was learning how to stand up for what she wanted, respectfully, of course.

Dad was wrapped up with work, but at least he came home every night. Maddie could tell something was bothering him, but he kept it to himself. After the revelation at Grammy's house, she wondered if he was worried about being arrested.

Michael decided to stay at Grammy's to help her with a project. Maddie was happy that he decided to stay in Tennessee. One thing she knew was that Grammy would keep him busy, and perhaps he could heal, too.

Matthew jumped right into the new school year. Maddie couldn't help but laugh as their mom sternly told him he could not take his new boomerang to school. "But all my friends want to see it!" He cried out. Mom did not think middle school was ready for boomerang Matt.

In September, Maddie received her first letter from Jacob. Due to their long distance, they decided to just be friends, but they agreed to stay in touch through letter writing. Opening the letter, she read of his school antics. He wrote how he, Jared, and Rory were leavin' their mark on high school. Those were his words. Oh, and how Rory was pining for Rachel.

She was a little jealous that her friend had two guys liking her. Rory was so intense in the looks he cast Rachel's way over summer, and now Jackson Reese was at her door the moment she came home, well, soon after anyway. They had gone out on several dates since. Rachel was keeping Jackson at arm's length, but he was insistent.

As they got older, Maddie half expected Rachel to move on since she was a year ahead, but she never did. She had a few friends who were her age, but she chose to hang out with Maddie and the girls most often. When she asked her about it, Rachel would say, "Y'all are my tribe!" *I wonder if things will change now that two boys like her.* She pondered. Suddenly, the ring of the doorbell pulled her out of her musings. Setting her letter and journal down, Maddie opened the door.

"Surprise!"

Rachel and Jade came rushing in as she closed the door. "I don't know, Jade; we should stick to the plan."

"Come on Rach, this is the Kingdom, right? Let's serve the people of Atlanta well!"

"Hang on, what are we talking about?" Maddie asked.

"There's this parade in Atlanta on the day we serve at the soup kitchen. I think it would be great to participate in both. What do you think, Maddie?"

"What's the parade about?"

"It's a walk to bring awareness to homelessness in Atlanta.

There will be a speaker at the end who will commemorate the day with a candle lighting for every homeless person in Atlanta."

Looking at Rachel, Maddie said, "That doesn't sound so bad, does it?"

Rachel said, "But, we have already committed to serving the homeless. That's what we're called to do. I'm not saying that marching is a bad thing; I just want to stay focused on what we've already committed to and what Jesus called us to do."

Shrugging, Maddie looked at Jade.

"So, what do you think, Maddie?" Jade persisted.

"I think Rachel is right. We've already committed to serving, so we should serve."

"Hey, Maddie, can you come help me in the kitchen?" Maddie's mom peered into the living room. "Oh, hi Girls, when did you get here?"

"Hi, Mrs. Bennett!"

Jade continued to insist they could do both as they walked into the kitchen.

Spread out over every counter was a plethora of cheeses, meats, olives, and fruit. Maddie had never seen so much cheese in one place. "What'cha doin', Mom?" She asked.

"I'm making a charcuterie board for the party your dad's company is holding."

"Wow, that's a lot of cheese. How many kinds are there?" Jade asked.

"Well, we've got brie, gouda, cheddar, monchego, and goat cheese. And here we have salami, prosciutto, coppa, soppressata, saucisson sec, and bresaola. Would you girls like to help?"

"Sure."

After they washed their hands, Jacque put them to work cutting up cheese and meat for the display. She had drawn out a plan and meticulously put each group in their perfectly set place on the board.

"Mom, you really like doing this stuff, don't you?" Maddie asked.

"I do. I've been talking to your dad about going back to work. I think it's time."

"What would you do, Mrs. Bennett?" Rachel asked.

"Well, my degree is in Interior Design. I'd like to do that, but I really think I would enjoy party planning. There are so many facets to creating a beautiful space for an event."

"Sounds awesome, Mrs. B!" Jade exclaimed.

"I realized I've been spending too much time sitting around worrying about everyone else. It's time I take care of myself," Jacque said

Giving her mom a side hug, Maddie laid her head on her shoulder as she said, "Nothing would make me happier."

After they finished, the girls went back into the living room. Jade couldn't help but bring up the subject of the parade once more. Holding both hands as if holding scales, she asked, "Okay, Girls, soup kitchen and parade, or soup kitchen?"

"How about we serve at the soup kitchen, and then we walk the next parade? I'm sure they'll do it again," Maddie said.

Jade hesitated for a moment, then thought better than to argue. "Okay, it's a plan."

ATLANTA, GEORGIA

"Answer," David said to the ringing phone while driving home. "David Bennett here."

"Hi, David, it's Tom."

"Hi, Tom."

"Are you ready for the hearing?" Tom asked.

"As ready as I'll ever be. Will you be able to attend?"

"Yes, I'll be there. Have you spoken to Pastor Joe?"

David turned into the neighborhood and answered, "I have, Joe has offered to be there. I am eternally grateful to you, Tom. You have been a good friend through all of this."

"Of course, but you did save my life. I am forever indebted to you."

"Well. . ."

"David, there is something we need to discuss."

The tension in Tom's voice was unmistakable. "What's that?"

"The girls have decided to serve at a homeless shelter in Atlanta. Jade's mom set it up. Dave, I'm not sure I like it."

"I haven't heard anything about this. When is it scheduled?"

"A week from Saturday," Tom said.

"Hm, let me talk to Maddie, and I'll get back to you."

"David, I think we should be there."

"Why? Is there a problem?" David didn't like where this was going.

"Yes, there is a *peaceful* protest planned for the same day."

CHAPTER 15

The Making of a Disciple

After talking to her fam, Maddie texted Sonya with a question that led to Sonya inviting her to coffee on Saturday. It had been months since they had met, and Maddie realized she had so much to share with her mentor.

She had no idea what a mentor was until Sonya asked if she would like to be mentored. Realizing she was surrounded by mentors, she was grateful to have people she could turn to with her questions.

After coming home from Grammy's, Maddie began having dreams. She had never been much of a dreamer, but lately, they were coming frequently. As she dreamed, she had a sense that there was something she needed to do, but she couldn't make sense of the dreams. She thought she would start with that.

Saturday morning came quickly. The familiar song of Ms. Carolina Wren outside her window reminded her that she had important business to attend to. Throwing on a white tee and a pair of jeans, she grabbed her journal and ran downstairs. "Hey, Mom, I'm ready. Can you take me to The Coffee Bar?"

"Give me ten minutes, Maddie."

Maddie sat on the kitchen stool as she watched her mom put together a fruit concoction. "What are you making?"

Jacque smiled. "It's a fruit flower. Do you like it?"

"I love it! Is that a strawberry?" Maddie went to touch the luscious chocolate-covered fruit.

157

Jacque smacked her hand lightly. "Don't you dare! That's for a client."

"You have a client? That's so cool! Who is it?"

"It's a woman I met at your dad's party. She's holding a small gathering and wants a sample of what I can do. So, here we go. Do you think she'll like it?"

"I think she'll love it, Mom! I am so proud of you."

Jacque beamed at her daughter's praise. "Yeah, I'm proud of myself, too. Let me wrap this up, and I'll be ready to go."

Mom was quiet as they drove to The Coffee Bar, so Maddie took the opportunity to read the questions she had for Sonya in her journal. She didn't want to forget anything.

"Hi, Sonya!"

"Maddie, it's so good to see you! I'm so glad we could meet today."

"Me too."

"I've missed our coffee dates," Sonya said. "What would you like?"

Realizing she forgot to ask her mom for money, Maddie said, "Oh, I'll just take a glass of water."

"Oh, Girl, it's on me. Now, what would you like?"

Looking at the sign, she was giddy as she whispered, "Iced Mocha. Can I have whipped cream?"

"Make that a large, iced mocha with whipped cream. And add a couple of chocolate shavings on the top." Sonya winked at Maddie.

Walking over to their table, Maddie sat down and waited for Sonya to bring their drinks.

"So, how was your summer?" Sonya asked as she set the biggest mocha in front of Maddie.

"It was awesome! We spent the summer at Grammy's. Rachel and my friends practically stayed the whole summer with me."

"I wondered where everybody went. What did y'all do?" Sonya took a sip of her iced coffee.

"Oh, we went to the ocean and saw fireworks, we had a pick'n' grin'n, and we went fishing. . ."

"What exactly is a pick and grin?"

Maddie laughed when she realized Sonya's confusion wasn't much different from hers when Grammy introduced her to the idea. "Essentially, it's a bonfire with music and lots of dancing."

"Oh, now that sounds like fun!"

"It's a blast!" Maddie said.

"I've never seen fireworks over the ocean. What was that like?"

"Crazy! The ocean seemed to go on forever and here are these lights out in the middle of nowhere."

"And fishing, huh? Did you catch anything?" Sonya asked.

"I did! I caught a smallmouth bass. Jacob said it was a good foot and a half!" Maddie pulled up her phone to show the picture.

In awe, Sonya said, "No way! You reeled in an eighteen-inch fish? How did you do it?"

"It was hard, but I had help."

Sonya chuckled, "I would've needed help too."

"What did you do this summer?" Maddie asked.

"Well, my kids had a lot of activities. So, next to working, I was playing chauffeur. We went on vacation, too. We took the kids to the lake. They got to go jet skiing and play with their cousins for a week."

"That sounds like fun." Maddie wondered what it would be like to have so many kids around.

Opening her Bible, Sonya said, "So, Maddie, I wanted to start with the question in your text, and then let's chat about the semester. Does that work?"

"Yes, ma'am!"

"The question in your text was, 'Have I seen the Lord move.' That's a whole question right there, and my answer is absolutely. In fact, you're proof."

"Me?"

"Of course, you! Look at how far you've come since you met Jesus."

Once upon a time, Maddie would have been afraid to talk about dreams and fishing, but Sonya was right; she had come a long way. Nodding, she said, "Yeah, I've learned a lot, I guess."

Sitting back in her chair, Sonya tilted her head and smiled as she said, "I must admit, I am curious about the reason for your question."

Maddie paused for a moment, looking at a tree outside the window. "The day we went on our fishing trip, we hung out with some people who talked about watching God move, and I just, well, like, I wondered what that looks like?"

Sonya placed her arms on the table and looked directly at Maddie. The serious expression on her face gave Maddie chills. "Do you remember the painting you told me about?"

Playing with the napkin on the table, she said, "The one with the girl holding up her hands?"

Nodding, Sonya answered, "That's the one! Would you say that girl was expectant?"

Uncertain where her mentor was going, Maddie asked, "Do you mean, like, she expected something to happen?"

"Exactly."

Maddie remembered the peace the girl seemed to have. "She had a lot of peace on her face."

Sonya leaned forward and asked, "Do you know where that peace comes from?"

"God?"

Opening her journal, Sonya turned to a blank page and began to draw. "Yes, but specifically, how does God give us his peace?"

The rough drawing of the girl looking up captivated Maddie's attention as she said, "Through prayer, I guess."

"Yes, that is true. But not just in prayer. His spirit gives us peace whenever we ask, but his peace falls as we surrender to him. We surrender to him because we know he is faithful. We know he is faithful because he has moved before and are expectant that he will move again. It's a matter of trust, right?"

Maddie looked up with a questioning expression. "But how do we know when he moves?"

Sonya smiled at her refreshing curiosity as she said, "We watch, we listen, we surrender. Be still and know that he is God."

Maddie about jumped out of her seat as Sonya recited the verse she learned from Ms. Bonnie. "I know that verse!" She exclaimed as she opened her Bible and read from Psalm 46:10 and then proceeded to tell her mentor about the awe and wonder she and Rachel experienced at the beach.

"Look at you! See you've already seen God move. That, my friend, was a move of his Spirit."

Sonya laughed as she watched her take in what she learned. "So, Maddie, what would you like to do this semester?" Sonya asked.

Reeling over the revelation that God could have given Sonya such an important word, Maddie wondered if this would be a good time to bring up her dreams. "Well, I have a lot of questions."

"Really now? Do tell."

"Do you know anything about dreams?" Maddie asked.

"Do you mean to ask if I'm a dream interpreter? No, I'm not, but I've had quite a few dreams myself, and I believe God talks to us in our dreams through symbols."

"How do you find out what the symbols mean?" Maddie asked.

"Well, I pray, then I look in the Bible to see if I can find the symbols. Do you mind if I ask what the dreams are about?"

"They're different except for one thing. Almost every dream had a crown in it. But different crowns, mostly made up of sunflowers."

"That sounds interesting. In your dreams, are you or is someone else doing something with these crowns?" Sonya asked as she took another sip of her drink.

"That's the thing, neither. They're on things, or they're growing from the ground. It's like, I'm supposed to pick or find them, but I can't."

"Hmm, that's very interesting. So, what does God say about it?"

"What do you mean?" Maddie asked curiously.

"Have you asked him what the dreams mean?"

"Yeah, but I haven't heard anything. Rachel researched five crowns that believers will receive in Heaven. I was wondering if my dreams are related?"

"Well, let's see what God says about it."

Opening their Bibles, Sonya asked Maddie to read First Corinthians 9:24-25.

Maddie was confused as she read that everyone who competes will get a crown that will not last, but we do it to get one that will last forever. "Wait, what? What does that even mean?"

"Hang on a moment." Sonya left the table and walked up to the hostess. She ordered an iced mocha with a glass of ice water. Coming back to the table, she sat down and set them side by side.

"What do you see?" She asked Maddie.

"I see they left off the chocolate shavings," Maddie crinkled her nose in jest.

"Oh, I forgot to ask," Sonya laughed. "These glasses both have something in them." Pointing at the mocha, Sonya said, "This one has a yummy drink that if I were to drink every day, would send me into a diabetic coma and would eventually kill me. This one, however, has life-giving water that will nourish me and sustain me for my whole life. Both drinks impact my eternity based on how they affect my body. Do you agree?"

Shrugging, Maddie said, "Sure."

"This is a visible representation of what we just read. You can determine to live for this life," she said as she pointed to the mocha, "with all its pleasures, or you can determine to live for eternity and discipline yourself accordingly."

"Oh, I see."

"Now, the five crowns Rachel researched are crowns we will receive in Heaven. Do you remember what they were?"

"Maddie pulled up the notes on her phone and read: imperishable crown, crown of rejoicing, righteousness, glory, and the crown of life."

"Alright, so these crowns are all rewards for what we did in this life. So, if you discipline yourself to drink water and eat healthy, you will hopefully lead a healthy life that allows you to participate in activities that have eternal reward, such as chasing after four rugrats over summer vacation."

Maddie laughed at the thought.

"That's a physical analogy; now let's look at this spiritually. If you are chasing after worldly things, then you'll only receive a worldly reward, like this ten-thousand-calorie drink here. But, if you chase after eternal things, you will receive the Heavenly rewards you just read about."

"Do you think that is what my dreams have been about?"

"I don't know. That's something you must ask the Lord. But, if they were, what do you think God might be telling you?"

"Well, since I can't pick the crowns, maybe I'm chasing the wrong things?"

"Wow, that's wisdom. Jesus said to ask, seek, and knock. I think this is a great opportunity to do just that."

The next two hours were spent by the two women talking about calling and discipleship. Maddie was so grateful to her mentor for spending time with her. She had so many questions, and while Sonya couldn't answer all of them, she always pointed her to places where she could find the answers.

"Okay, Maddie, I see your mom waiting outside. I have a challenge for you. I want you to read Proverbs 18:10. And bonus points if you memorize it. I think it'll help as you ponder this prophecy. Are you up to the challenge?"

"Yes, ma'am."

"Awesome, I'll see you Wednesday."

Walking to the car, Maddie opened the door as her mom started the engine and asked, "How was your meeting?"

Unable to contain her excitement, Maddie said, "It was awesome, Mom! Sonya is mentoring me."

Jacque frowned as she asked, "What do you mean by mentor?"

Sensing her mom's disapproval, she softened her tone as she said, "She wants to read the Bible with me. Thank you for letting me go, Mom. Sonya is nice. She lets me ask a hundred questions."

"Does she answer all of them?"

Maddie thought for a moment. "Not all, but most."

"Well, be careful, Sweetie. There are a lot of crazies out there who would love to mentor you right into a cult."

"She's not like that, Mom. You should meet her. She's a nurse with four kids. She asks me questions and teaches me to read. She reminds me of Grammy." Giggling, she added, "Without the accent, of course."

Jacque let out a quiet grunt.

Picking up her phone, Maddie sought to distract herself from the uncomfortable quiet.

"Your dad wants to talk to you tonight." Turning to look at her daughter with an arched brow, Jacque asked, "He said something about a homeless shelter?"

Placing her phone back down, Maddie answered nervously, "Oh yeah, I almost forgot! Jade and her mom are taking us to serve at a soup kitchen next Saturday."

"When were you going to ask us?" Her mom's tone was filled with disappointment.

With an anxious dart of the eye toward her mom, Maddie said, "I completely forgot, with school starting and all. But Jade's mom knows all about it. I can call Jade and ask if her mom can video chat with us tonight?"

"That's fine. We just do not appreciate finding out from one of your friend's parents."

The angry glare bore a hole through Maddie's seat. "I'm sorry, Mom," she said sadly.

"It's okay, but I will expect your homework to be finished."

"Yes ma'am."

Later that afternoon, in Maddie's quiet time, she asked the Lord again to show her what the crowns meant. She really felt like there was something she was supposed to do, and it was making her anxious. Unfortunately, she wasn't hearing God very clearly on the matter. *Where is Carolina Wren?* She wondered.

"God, am I focusing on the wrong things?" Remembering Sonya's analogy of the water and the mocha, Maddie wondered what she could be focusing on that was wrong.

Suddenly, Rachel's words popped into her head, "God isn't a genie in a bottle. He is our Creator, and he's already provided everything we need to know that he is with us."

"God, is it wrong to look for signs?" She asked.

The deafening quiet was just too much. Lying down her journal and Bible, she threw on her tennis shoes and decided to go for a run.

At the bottom of the stairs, she looked left and then right, trying to decide which way to go. She felt strongly about turning right, so right she turned. Passing house after house, she admired the orange, red, and yellow hues that brightly colored the landscape. The day was overcast, but the air was clear and clean. Breathing deeply as she turned at a stop sign, she noticed Charlie's Tree standing proudly at the end of the road. As Maddie ran toward the beloved tree, she remembered when Rachel got stuck on a limb, and Jade saved her. Maddie smiled as she remembered Jade's courage. She didn't even think twice about it; she knew exactly what to do.

Maddie was grateful for her two courageous friends, Jade and Rachel. They were never afraid to boldly go forward. If she were honest, she wished she were more like them.

Standing in front of the beloved tree, Maddie looked up. The trunk was solid, and the limbs were strong. Perhaps she needed to do a little climbing herself.

Grabbing the bottom limb, she pulled herself up and sat on the horizontal branch. The solid feel of the wood beneath her swayed slightly but felt strong enough to hold her. After a moment, she began to swing her legs back and forth. *Oh, to be a child again.* She pondered. Once upon a time, she didn't have a care in the world. Anxious thoughts were never a thing because she knew she was safe.

"Wait! Is that it, God?" She asked into thin air.

That's what Rachel was trying to say: "What if, in choosing to trust the Lord, our eyes are opened to see his goodness all around us?"

"You're already here, God. I'm waiting for a sign from you to know that I can trust you when you're already here!"

Maddie jumped down from the limb onto the soft, manicured island below. Getting on her knees, she grabbed a handful of dirt and mulch and rolled it around in her hand. *God has made everything around me, so if I can trust him to hold me in the things that I can see, then perhaps I can trust him in the things that I can't see.*

"Trust, is that it, God?"

Looking up from her kneeling position, she watched as an opening formed in the clouds, and bright sunbeams shone through. *That's it.* Smiling as she realized God had moved once again, she jumped up and took off at full speed toward the house.

"Admiral Osborne, thank you for returning my call."

"David, it's good to see you."

Peering through the video within the secure uplink, David said, "I was hoping to speak with you privately before the hearing. Do you have some time on your calendar next week?"

"I have an hour on Monday. Robin has decided we need a long-awaited vacation. So, we're taking the twins and the new baby to New Hampshire."

"That sounds good. What time?"

"How does nine a.m. sound?"

"Thank you. That will work."

C HAPTER 16

Preparing for Battle

Tension filled the dining room as the rivalry of family game night ensued. The game was "Sushi Go!" and Dad was winning.

"That's not fair!" Maddie yelled as her dad laid down the nigiri she passed to him. She realized she had a wasabi card which would have tripled her points had she kept it.

"You snooze, you lose," He laughingly replied.

At the end of the round, her mom added up all the points, and her dad won again. "Ugh," Maddie groaned as she whispered to her brother. "We need a strategy to beat Dad!"

"Matthew, can you please go into the living room? We have something to discuss with Maddie."

"Do I have to?" Matthew whined as he re-ordered the cards.

"Go on, we'll join you in a moment. We can watch that new movie you were telling us about."

"Yay!" Matthew ran into the living room to leave Maddie behind with the parents.

Maddie was worried. She forgot to ask about going to the soup kitchen with the girls. She hoped her dad didn't say no. She really wanted to go.

"Maddie, Rachel's dad told me you and the girls plan to go to a homeless shelter in Atlanta next Saturday?"

Wringing her hands under the table, Maddie said, "Yes, Sir.

167

Jade's mom found a place where we can serve. She works with the people there through the hospital and said it's safe and everything."

"I trust Alisha's instincts, but that's not the issue. I just wish you would have asked us about it before assuming you could go."

"Yes, Sir, I'm sorry. I completely forgot what with school starting and all."

"Maddie, you are growing up. Your Mom and I realize that keeping you from experiencing life is unhealthy for you. However, you must learn to be discerning and watchful. Check a place out before you go, even if someone tells you it's safe."

Tugging on her bottom lip, Maddie argued, "But it's Ms. Alisha. She wouldn't allow us to go somewhere unsafe after all we went through."

"That's not always true, Maddie. What is safe for Alisha may not be safe for you. We live in a violent and distracted world. You and your friends are lucky to be sitting in your homes today. Many don't come out of situations like you found yourselves."

Maddie looked down at her shaking hands. She never considered those who were never rescued.

Placing his hand across the table, David said, "Ruthie, look at me."

Maddie looked into her dad's serious eyes. The clench of his jaw was unmistakable. *I hope he isn't mad at me.* She worried.

Releasing the tension he was holding, David said, "When I realized you were missing, I felt helpless for the first time in my life. I knew how to rescue and protect others, but I never thought I would have to do so for my own family. I had time to think about the things I never taught you. It's time that changed. Tom and I have decided to show you and the girls some techniques we have learned over the years for protection. Now, I'm not saying anything bad will happen to you, but we want you to be prepared in case you are ever threatened. I won't always be around to protect you."

A year ago, Maddie's response to this would have been to

argue out of fear. But today, she realized this was necessary. "Okay."

"There is something else. A protest is scheduled in Atlanta for that Saturday. Tom and I have decided to escort you girls and stand guard. We don't expect anything to happen, but we want to be around just in case. Now Maddie, the first thing to do in any situation is to be aware. Situational awareness begins with being aware of your surroundings. Everywhere you go, pay attention to where you are and who is around you. Don't let this strike fear in you. Just use your senses to pay attention to what is happening around you. Okay?"

The ghost of a smile rose on Maddie's face as she murmured, "Okay."

On Sunday, Maddie's friends came over to her house. Maddie's and Rachel's dad invited a woman who was an expert in Korean martial arts.

"Girls, this is Laura. She owns a martial arts facility in Atlanta."

The girls were excited, Kaitlyn especially. Giving her phone to Jade, she pretended to box as Jade snapped photos.

In the girl's distraction, Laura stepped in, grabbed the phone, and grabbed Jade in a flash.

"Lesson one: no phones. Let's talk about situational awareness. This," Laura held up the phone, "is your own worst enemy. While you are snapping selfies and scrolling through your feed, an attacker could be watching and possibly tracking you."

Gasps filled the room.

"Your phone can be a tracker if you don't set it properly. So, the first lesson is to be aware."

Maddie remembered her dad's warning about being aware of her surroundings.

"What if my mom needs to talk to me?" Jade asked.

"If you're walking alone and your phone rings, find a public place to answer it discreetly. You don't have to be loud and obnoxious. Just answer it, have your conversation quickly and quietly, and then hang up. This isn't the time to have a long-drawn-out conversation. You must be street-smart. Awareness can prevent anything from escalating. And these," Laura pulled an earbud out of Kaitlyn's ear, "are a disconnecting danger. If you can't hear what's happening around you, you'll set yourself up for disaster."

Embarrassed, Kaitlyn took the earbud and placed it with its twin in her pocket.

"Lesson two: look around and be aware of your surroundings. Especially if you're walking alone." Laura walked in front of the girls and looked long and close into their eyes. "Steer clear of dark alleys and places where you can be cornered. You want to stay in well-lit public areas. Pay attention to landmarks and places where others are congregating. If you see anything dangerous occurring, walk away and call 911."

Concentrating on the teacher, Maddie wondered what she would consider dangerous.

"Lesson three: when walking in unknown places, walk with friends. Your security matters. If you do find yourself alone, call someone to pick you up.

"Lesson four: body language can make or break a potential attacker." Laura stood tall with her shoulders back. "When you're walking, walk with purpose. Have your shoulders, back, and head up, and always make eye contact. You don't have to mean-mug them, but confidently show that you see them."

Jade giggled, "Mean mug," she mocked under her breath.

"Do you think this is funny, Jade? Because I promise you, an attacker will not stop for your amusement."

"No ma'am!" Jade answered loudly.

"Lesson five: if you think you're being followed, don't go home, or turn away from crowds. Instead, walk into a store or coffee shop and ask for help."

Stopping in front of Emma, Laura said, "Lesson six: if someone tells you to come with them or threatens you in any way, use a very loud and assertive tone and tell them to back off. A potential attacker expects fear and submission, using a harsh tone will throw them off. Let me hear you say stop, Emma."

Emma answered in her soft demeanor, "Stop."

"Not loud enough. I want you to pretend you are yelling at someone across the parking lot."

"STOP!" Emma yelled.

"That's what I'm talking about." Laura was pleased with Emma's yell.

"Now, final lesson seven: if someone actually tries to grab you," Laura grabbed Jade again, "Bend both of your legs and drop down. And don't be afraid to use these." Laura balled her hands into fists to the giggles of all five girls. "Now, Jade, grab me."

Jade grabbed Laura from behind. Jade was a good six feet tall to Laura's five-five. But Laura dropped down, playfully punched Jade in the belly, and escaped her grasp.

"I know the movies show the tough guys laying the attacker out, but I want you ladies to concentrate on getting out of there. If you must hit, aim for just below the eyes, nose, throat, or groin, but only to deter the attacker long enough to get away and get help. The key is establishing as much distance as possible between you and the attacker.

"Remember, Ladies, your dads won't always be there to help you. So, it's up to you to learn to defend yourself."

Over the next two hours, Laura, David, and Tom worked with the girls on situational awareness and self-defense moves. The girls learned how to protect themselves by using their car keys, knees, the heel of their palms, and elbows.

By the time the lesson ended, the girls were really into it and asked if they could do it again. After saying their goodbyes and thanking Laura, the girls left the adults to their conversations and headed outside.

"That went well," Tom said.

Frowning, David rubbed his jaw as he said, "Let's just hope it stuck."

"Do you think we should send the girls to Laura's dojo?"

"Not a bad idea," David answered.

"That was so cool!" Maddie declared as they walked toward the park in the back of the neighborhood.

"I thought Laura was going to take you out, Jade," Kaitlyn said while punching the air.

"The look on your face when she took your phone! Priceless!" Jade laughed.

"Girls, you know this is serious, right?" Rachel asked.

"I'm not sure if I can hit anyone," Emma said quietly.

"Yeah, me neither," Maddie agreed.

"Rach, did Jesus ever fight anyone?"

"Physically? Not that I know of. But he did drive out the moneychangers and overturn their tables in the temple."

"Why?" Kaitlyn asked.

"They were buying and selling with pagan money in God's holy place."

"I would've liked to have seen that!" Jade said.

"My dad told me that the moneychangers worked where the Gentiles were allowed to worship. Can you imagine how sad that made Jesus to see people blocked from being able to worship?"

"Would Jesus be okay with self-defense? Grammy said that God teaches us to turn the other cheek."

"Let's look it up," Rachel said as she grabbed a swing on the playground. "Here, it says that turning the other cheek has to do with personal offense, which may lead to retaliation. That is what is wrong. It also says that the Bible doesn't forbid self-defense; believers can defend themselves and their families, but we need to rely on God's wisdom to know when to do so."

"Where does it say we can defend ourselves and our families?" Maddie asked.

Rachel looked at a scripture found on the page she had read from. "Here, look at Nehemiah 4:13-14. Nehemiah tells the people to stand knowing that God is great but be ready to fight for your family if needed."

Performing a search for defending your family, Maddie said, "Look at this one in Psalm 27, 'When evildoers assail me, though an army encamp against me, my heart shall not fear; though war rise against me, yet I will be confident. For he will hide me in his shelter in the day of trouble.' So does that mean that God will hide and protect us?"

"Yes, but isn't our protection sometimes in the wisdom he gives us?" Emma asked. "Read what David says in Psalm 144, 'Blessed be the Lord, my rock, who trains my hands for war, and my fingers for battle.' So, God will prepare us for those moments, right?"

Each girl had their phone out, searching for scriptures about self-defense.

"Can I ask a question?" Kaitlyn asked. "You guys talk about how you trust your Jesus. Wouldn't you trust him to help you in the moment? Isn't that the point of your faith?"

Rachel smiled at Kaitlyn. "Kate's right. God will prepare us for any circumstance, but it is up to us to ask Jesus to help us in the moment. I thought you didn't believe in Jesus?"

Kate shrugged one shoulder. "Just asking for a friend," she said.

"Hey, by the way, what was that Laura said about your phone being tracked?"

"After our rescue, Mom taught me to turn location services off on my phone," Jade said. "You can turn it back on if you need it for maps. Then set all the apps to never use location services, except for, like, maps. And only when you're using it. Mom said our photos have a location stamped on them if we don't turn it off."

"Whoa, are you serious?" Kaitlyn asked as she checked her boxing photo. "You're right. It shows the map of your house, Maddie. That's crazy! Turn this puppy OFF!" She said as she disabled Location Services.

"Does Find My app work with location services off?" Looking at her settings, she said, "Yes, it looks like it does. I have to check who has permission," Rachel said.

"Also, check Google Maps," Maddie added.

"Should we set each other up to share?" Emma asked.

"I wouldn't. Just add your parents," Jade said. "You never know who might get their hands on your phone."

"Good thought," Rachel said.

"Are we being paranoid?" Kaitlyn asked.

Swinging her legs from the retaining wall, Maddie said, "I don't think so. What if God is giving us wisdom to prepare us for battle, just like he did David?"

Maddie looked up with a secret smile, wondering if God was moving once again.

"Hey, Girls, can we pray?" Rachel asked.

Circling up, Rachel led each of them into a prayer for protection and wisdom.

David awoke with a grimace on Monday morning. He was not looking forward to his conversation with Rick, but he wanted to know where he stood.

Boarding the elevator to the office of Jack's attorney, David looked over his notes. He was thankful for his father-in-law's connections. The calling of a nine a.m. meeting on a Monday morning was no different than asking someone to have coffee for the powerful Jack Ruby.

Walking into the foyer of the law firm, David introduced himself to the receptionist and sat down. At the attorney's request, he was fifteen minutes early so they could debrief before the call.

"Come in, David," the attorney called. Where Jack was tall, ruddy, and boisterous, his long-time friend, Curtis, was short and quiet but sharp as a tack. He wore a tailored dress shirt with suspenders and dress slacks. The suit coat and round glasses matched his square jaw and pronounced features. It was obvious that nothing could stump Curtis Stiles. Adjusting his glasses, Curtis shook David's hand and offered him a seat.

"Good morning, Curtis. Thank you for making time for me this morning."

"You are welcome. Anything for Jack's son-in-law. Did he tell you I beat him by four solid points in golf on Saturday?"

David laughed, "No, he did not."

Jack was a man to be reckoned with, and on Saturdays, everyone who was anyone knew that if you wanted to soften the man up, it would be on the golf course.

"Well, let's get to it then." Pulling out a file folder, Curtis read through a document and looked at David. "The video chat with the Admiral will be secure, correct?"

"Yes, I have the machine here."

"Good, that's good. Can we record the meeting?"

"We can. I just need to advise the Admiral that we are doing so."

"That's acceptable. Remember, David, you are not being tried here. You are under investigation, which is standard protocol."

"Is there anything I need to say or not say?"

"Just the facts."

"I can do that."

As the secure uplink rang, David flicked at a piece of fluff on his pants. He wasn't nervous, but it was strange being on this side of the desk.

"Admiral Osborne, here. David, good morning."

"Good morning, Admiral Osborne. This is my attorney, Curtis Stiles."

"Good morning, Mr. Stiles. I am glad you have joined us."

"Admiral, will it be permissible to record this meeting?"

"I see no issue with that. Please provide a copy of the recording to me afterward."

"That is no problem."

David started the recording and motioned to Curtis.

"Admiral, thank you once again for meeting with us. My client and I are here to go over a few questions we have regarding the inquiry."

"Go on," Rick responded.

"Where are we on the investigation?" Curtis asked.

"An email was sent to PERS for a Show Cause determination. Commander Bennett was flagged for no service. A recommendation was made to detach your client for cause after which he received a notification of such determination pending a board of inquiry."

"Considering my client's station, do we know who will be on the board?" Curtis asked.

"I understand that a closed-door senate judiciary hearing is set for October third."

David looked at the attorney with surprise. "On what basis is a congressional hearing required?" He asked.

"A particular senator is interested in your case and has asked to serve on the board. Since the three board members must consist of senior officers, the request was granted."

"Who is the senator?" David asked.

"I am not at liberty to say," Admiral Osborne responded.

"Rick..."

Curtis lifted his hand to silence David.

"If that will be all Gentlemen? I have a plane to catch," Admiral Osborne stated.

"Yes, Admiral, thank you for your time," David said as the uplink ended.

"Do you have the recommendation letter that was sent to you?"

"Yes, I have it here." David pulled the letter out and gave it to Curtis.

Curtis read over the letter and looked at David. "So, the options you are being given are to resign or retire with an unfavorable characterization of service. You also have the option to contest. What are you thinking?"

"My gut tells me to challenge, but honestly, resignation seems rather enticing. After all the years I have given the Navy, this is a slap in the face."

"Remember, this is not a court-martial; this is only an administrative hearing with relaxed rules of evidence. We can bring our own witnesses. I cannot tell you what to do, but if it were me, I would contest the determination."

"The charge was a dereliction of duty under article 92. Listed here is 'Failure to obey a lawful order.'"

"What order did you disobey?"

"When I advised Admiral Osborne of the properties obtained by BALDR Industries, he shut me down and told me to allow the police to do their job."

"Did he order this?"

"Well, any instruction is considered an order from the Admiral of the United States Navy. But he also told me that if any credible evidence was found that she was being held against her will, he would send in the cavalry, his words."

"So, did you give him evidence once it was found?"

"Honestly, when he shut me down, I assumed he didn't believe me. So, I took matters into my own hands."

"Well, we don't want to say that in a hearing," Curtis said. "Was there any information shared about these locations that should have resulted in an investigation?"

"Yes, I sent the list of locations to the Admiral through a secure connection."

"Did the Admiral respond to you?"

"He did not. In fact, I didn't hear a thing until he told me the case was closed once the PeaceKeepers were rounded up."

"Is it possible that he used your correspondence to find the PeaceKeepers?"

"It's possible, but I have no proof."

"Well, if you choose to contest, we can use the defense that the Navy had knowledge of your daughter's captivity and did nothing to stop it."

"I don't know. It's a long shot. I have no proof."

"Well, leave that to me. We have a lot to do before October third, Mr. Bennett. I suggest you prepare for battle."

CHAPTER 17

A Season of Suddenlies

A flurry of nerves and excitement catapulted Maddie out of bed early Saturday morning. She had never served before and was curious what it would be like. Listening to Jacob talk about his experiences encouraged Maddie to pursue her own.

Jade told the girls that they needed to wear jeans and a sweatshirt. Oh, and they had to wear their hair up. The shelter had a full commercial kitchen, so they would be expected to wear hairnets and smocks for health and safety.

A light knock on the door surprised Maddie as she arranged her hair in a bun. "Come in," she said.

"Are you ready, Ruthie?"

"Yes, Sir, almost."

Grabbing her phone, she turned off her bedroom light and met her dad in the hallway.

"What are you feeling about today?" Dad asked.

"I'm so excited!" She said, "But I have no idea what it'll be like."

Maddie noticed her dad seemed a bit off. *Should I be worried?* She wondered.

Popping his head out of his bedroom door, Matthew asked, "Hey, Maddie, can I go with you today?"

Dad interjected, "No, Sport, I need you to care for your mom today."

Yawning, he replied, "Oh, okay."

"When do you think you'll be home?" Mom asked as they walked into the living room.

"Alisha said they'll finish around two-ish, so we should be home between three or four, depending on traffic." David walked up to Jacque and kissed her forehead. "How do you feel about going out to eat tonight?"

Jacque's eyes sparkled as she gazed into his eyes and nodded in agreement.

Giving his wife a proper kiss, to Maddie's chagrin, he smiled and turned toward the door. "Okay, Ruthie, let's go."

Running down the front stairs, Maddie jumped into the front passenger seat. Since they had the SUV, Dad was the designated driver for the day.

After picking up her friends and Tom, Rachel's dad, they ventured onto the expressway. The ride to Atlanta was a relatively smooth one. It was early Saturday morning, and everyone was still snug in their beds as they ventured into the big city. Maddie laid her head back on the seat and watched the overhead lights that pierced the early morning quiet. Living in such a big city, she was fascinated by the early morning stillness of a city that was typically hustle and bustle.

As they drove up to the facility, Maddie was surprised by the security guard who checked them in. She wouldn't have expected a soup kitchen to have security. The guard waved them through after checking her dad's ID.

"See Dad, I told you it's gonna be good," Rachel said.

The nondescript building looked like any other warehouse. There weren't many windows, but the windows that were present had pretty decorations with children's handprints in a multitude of colors.

"Oh, how cute is that?" Emma asked as she looked at all the names.

"Hey, wait up!" Jade ran up the stairs to meet them with Alisha not far behind.

"Look at you! I love your hair. Going for a Princess Leia look?" Kaitlyn asked.

"Oh shush, I'm a trendsetter. You just watch; everybody

will be wearing their hair like this."

Kaitlyn laughed ironically, "Yeah, we'll see about that."

"Hi, Alisha, is this your crew?"

"Hi Bob, yes, meet my team." Alisha introduced them to Bob, The Refuge's Saturday team lead.

Motioning for them to follow, he said, "Come on in. We'll get right to it; our residents will be up around seven am."

"I thought this was a homeless shelter," Jade whispered to her mom.

"It is. The Refuge houses women and children who do not have a home. They give them temporary housing, three healthy meals a day and the chance for training and work opportunities. It's a spectacular program that serves the City of Atlanta."

Bob showed the girls around the kitchen and put them on serving duty. Each girl received a hairnet and a pair of gloves. The metal lids to the deep pans were hot to the touch. As they lifted them, Maddie caught a whiff of the piping hot feast of eggs, sausage, and grits. Her stomach reminded her that she hadn't eaten breakfast.

Rachel threw her a glance that suggested she, too, was hungry.

"Girls, meet our chefs, Bill, and Toby. They've been at it since five am."

Maddie gave a shy wave as Jade and Rachel engaged in conversation with them, asking where they lived and how often they served.

The first group of people to come up were older women. Bob showed Maddie how to pick up a tray and dip a spoonful of eggs into the primary slot. She would hand the tray to Rachel, who would add the grits, and Jade would follow up with the sausage. Kaitlyn and Emma would offer milk and orange juice in square paper cartons.

As she worked, Maddie caught the glance of a woman with kind eyes. The lines on her face suggested she had seen a lot in her life, but her genuine smile set Maddie's nervousness at ease.

"Thank ya, kindly," she said.

Maddie smiled as she heard a voice very similar to her Grammy's.

Throughout the morning, the girls served a diverse group of people of varied ages. Emma loved getting on the kids' level and asking their names.

The last person walked through the line around nine am. Maddie stood up and stretched. She was starving.

"Here you go, Maddie." Toby gave her a tray.

"Oh no, I can eat later."

"No, you ladies eat. Get what you want and go hang out with the residents in the dining area. You've earned it."

"But what do we say?" Jade asked.

"Just be yourself," Toby said. "Many of them have girls your age. They'll enjoy talking to you."

Walking into the dining area, five pairs of eyes looked over the tables. Jade recognized her mom in the back of the room and ventured in her direction with Kaitlyn and Emma in tow. Maddie noticed the woman who smiled at her in the line and went to talk to her. Rachel joined her.

"Can we sit here?" Maddie asked.

"Why a'course. What's yer name?" The woman asked.

"I'm Maddie, and this is Rachel," Maddie said. "What's yours?"

"My name is Hazel. Are y'all from 'round here?"

Grabbing her napkin, Maddie said, "Yes ma'am, we live in Marietta. Where are you from?"

"Born and raised in Kentucky, but I'm makin' ma rounds in Atlanta."

"What brought you to Atlanta?" Rachel asked.

"My daughter, but she ain't 'round no more."

"What happened to her?" Maddie asked.

Rachel elbowed her and gave her a look.

"It's okay. She came down with cancer. I came down ta help, but the good Lord decided he needed 'er more." Hazel looked sadly at the remaining piece of sausage on her plate.

"My Grammy lives in Tennessee," Maddie said. "You sound like her."

Hazel looked at Maddie and smiled. "Whereabouts?"

"She lives on Wild Rock Mountain."

"Oh, I know Wild Rock. Got me an ole schoolmate thar named Clyde who ended up in them parts."

"I know Mr. Clyde," Maddie remembered him as the burly man who argued with Pastor Ron in the kitchen last summer.

Hazel chuckled. "Oh, that man had a sharp mouth on 'im. I reckon he still does?"

Maddie giggled as she nodded.

"So, what brings you ladies' round here this mornin'?" Hazel asked.

Rachel leaned forward excitedly and said, "We wanted to serve. Jade's mom," she pointed to the table where their friends sat, "connected us, and here we are."

Hazel squinted her eyes, "Whatcha thinkin' ta gain by servin' 'round here?"

"We just follow Jesus, Ma'am," Rachel answered quietly.

Hazel's warm brown eyes rested on them with a smile. "You keep servin' others and you'll be servin' him. And it'll be costly, mind ya, but he'll be with ya ever' step of the way. That'd be a word fer ya."

Rachel and Maddie looked at one another in shock. She had no idea that was exactly the message that led them to decide to serve.

"Well, Girls, I gotta run. There's a bus with my name on it. Mr. Bob over thar, he's a good man. He got me a job at the hospital gift shop. I catch the bus ever' mornin' and work the afternoon shift. I'm a hopin' to have my own place here soon."

"It was nice to meet you, Hazel," Maddie said as she stood up. "Can I get your tray?"

Standing, Hazel grabbed her cane, "No, ma'am, we all serve ourselves here. Can't give up, ya know? God gave us two hands and two feet to keep goin' fer as long as we have breath. Thank ya kindly, though."

Maddie and Rachel watched as Hazel hobbled to the garbage can to empty her tray and put it away. As she slowly approached the front door, she stopped by the table where

Jade, Kaitlyn, and Emma sat. After chatting briefly, she waved bye and left the building.

"Wow, she was so nice!" Maddie said.

"Yeah, she was. Isn't this so cool?" Rachel asked. "Everybody here has a story."

"It's weird, though," Maddie said. "I feel like she served me more than I served her."

Rachel looked at her with a grin, "That's Jesus."

The rest of the day went by quickly. The girls helped the remaining residents sweep and clean up. Then they suited up to serve lunch. After they finished, they hung out with some of the kids. Emma quietly braided the girl's hair while Jade and Kaitlyn played basketball with the boys. Rachel and Maddie split up and talked to some of the younger women.

Maddie found everyone to be quite reserved. It wasn't much different from High School in that everyone kept to themselves unless they knew someone. It was hard at first getting them to talk, but she followed Rachel's lead and began by asking their name and where they were from. She decided to keep the conversation light unless they had something to share. Maddie found the women talked more when they had children she could connect with.

Two o'clock came much too soon. Maddie was sad that it was already over. Putting the broom away, she joined the group.

"Well, you girls did a great job today. Tell me, who did you meet?" Bob asked.

Each girl spent a couple of minutes sharing the names of those they met.

Bob shared how Jesus taught us his model of love was to "be with." "Every person is made in the image of God," he said, "Imago Dei. They are all worthy of love and respect. We treat each one as the image bearer they are."

"Image bearer?" Kaitlyn asked.

Pulling a coin out of his pocket, Bob said, "This quarter here bears the image of George Washington. When I look at it, I remember how he served our country well and set us on the path to freedom. You, my friend, are an Image bearer of Almighty God. This means that when I look at you, I see the imprint of the One who created you with purpose. No matter where you are in life or what challenges you may face, you will always have the love of your Creator. It is my honor and duty to pour out that same love that God poured into me."

"That's really awesome, Bob."

"Hey, would you like to tour of the facility?"

"Thank you, Bob, that is kind of you, but we need to get back," David interjected.

"Next time. You girls are welcome anytime. Just let Alisha know to give me a call."

"Thank you, Bob!" Each girl placed their smocks on the kitchen wall and walked toward the exit.

David drove out of the parking lot, waving to the security guard as he passed by. Turning toward the capitol, he concentrated on the road as the girls chatted in the back. Stopping at a traffic light, Tom grabbed his attention and nodded to the right. David saw a group of people coming their way. This must be the peaceful protest Tom warned him about.

David decided to wait and allow them to pass. "Everyone buckled up?" David asked as he made sure the doors were locked.

"Yep!" The girls called out in unison.

David looked in the rearview mirror to memorize where everyone was sitting. Tom in the front, Maddie and Rachel in the center, Jade, Kaitlyn, and Emma in the back. He had a bad feeling about this but couldn't place his finger on what was bothering him.

When the march began to pass, the girls all leaned forward to watch. Colorful signs with the messages such as: "Food not Fines," "Homeless doesn't mean Worthless," "The end is near," and "We are all Homeless" were lifted as people raised their voices to anyone who would listen. Traffic began to back up as people stood to watch.

"I wish we were out there," Jade said.

"Girls, this is not the time," David replied.

"Mr. Bennett, how will anything change if we stay silent?" Jade asked.

"There are ways to speak your voice without walking down a dangerous street surrounded by strangers," David said.

Jade was visibly irritated. "But a march gets the attention of those who can do something about it."

"We can all do something about it, Jade. What you girls did today was a perfect example of what we all should be doing," Tom said.

Jade crossed her arms and sat back in a huff.

Maddie could tell she was frustrated. "Maybe we could start an online petition?" She asked quietly.

"Yeah, I guess," Jade said as she looked out the window.

"Hey, what's that?" Rachel asked. "Maddie, isn't that one of the signs we saw in Virginia Beach?"

The colorful signs began to change to black-and-white signs that said NO ORDER, NO PEACE. The people carrying them did not have the same countenance as the ones excited to share their message. These men were angry and were yelling, just like the people in Virginia.

"I don't like this," Emma said.

"It's okay, Girls. Just stay where you are. The doors are locked. We'll be fine."

Suddenly, the men carrying the signs started running. There were so many; it looked like a sea of men running down the road in front and beside them. Maddie's heart was beating so fast. Looking at her dad, she thought, At least Dad is here.

A murmur became a cadence beside her as Rachel began to pray. "Father, protect us, Father, please hold us in Your Hand." Rachel prayed this over and over as the SUV was surrounded by the angry crowd.

"Girls, I need you to put your heads down. Do not move. No matter what you see, do you hear me?"

Everyone placed their heads down. Maddie saw her dad

slowly grab something out of the glove box. Her heart began to beat even harder as she realized he had a weapon of some kind.

When the SUV began to rock, Kaitlyn began to scream. David shushed her and told her to stay down. Maddie saw him hold up a gun so the people that surrounded the vehicle would back off. This seemed to only stir up the mob even worse. As the rocking continued, Rachel's prayer became louder. Jade, Maddie, and Emma joined her.

Suddenly, Maddie heard a crash as someone broke the back window.

"You stay here, Tom." David climbed over the center console and went to the back of the truck.

Before they knew it, Kaitlyn was grabbed from behind and dragged out of the truck.

"NOOOOO!" Maddie heard herself scream as she watched her dad jump through the back tailgate and begin running.

"Stay down!" Tom yelled at the girls.

And just like that, as if a wind blew them away, the mob was gone.

"Where is she?" Jade yelled.

Tom placed his finger on his lips as he looked around the truck.

Emma began crying as she looked in the empty seat to her left. Jade pulled her friend close and wept with her. Rachel continued to pray. Maddie didn't know what else to do but pray. A shiver went down her spine as she experienced a feeling of déjà vu. A feeling of dread she hoped never to experience again swarmed her like a ton of bricks, but she joined Rachel in begging God to bring their friend back.

Suddenly a surge of relief filled Maddie when she saw her dad running to the truck with Kaitlyn in his arms. "Call 911!" He cried out. "Call 911!"

"Stay in the car!" Tom said. He exited the vehicle and dialed 911. Maddie's dad laid Kaitlyn on the ground and tore a piece of his shirt.

It was then she noticed the red stain on Kaitlyn's white

sweatshirt. It was getting larger as she watched. "Oh no! Rachel, look!" Maddie cried out.

Rachel paused from her prayer and looked at her friend.

As David put pressure on her abdomen, the blood seemed to come out of nowhere, covering her, his hands, and his shirt. Nobody could believe what they were seeing.

"Move, I'm going to help," Jade said.

"NO! Dad said to stay put!" Rachel said.

"She NEEDS US!" Jade yelled.

"Listen!" Emma said.

Sirens, far off in the distance, came ever closer. Rachel grabbed Maddie's hand as the ambulance drove up beside the truck. The girls watched as the first responders took over from David, and as swiftly as they came, they were gone—with Kaitlyn.

Wishing they could hear the conversations outside of the SUV, the girls peered through the side window.

"Hey, look, where did all the people go?" Emma asked.

Maddie looked around. Where there was a sea of people before, they seemed to have all gone. *Yeah, where did everybody go?* Maddie wondered.

Popping his head in the driver's side door, David said, "Girls, Tom is going to escort you with these officers to the hospital. I will join you soon," He kissed Maddie on the forehead.

Opening the door of the patrol car for Maddie and Rachel, Tom encouraged, "It'll be okay, Girls, I'm right behind you with Jade and Emma." Closing the door, he walked to the car behind them, and the officer started the engine.

The quiet in the car was unnerving. Maddie didn't know what to say. Just a few hours ago, Kaitlyn played basketball with a couple of kids. Now. . .

Everyone piled out of the cars once they reached Atlanta Memorial. Running into the ER, Tom found the nearest nurse to tell them who they were. Kaitlyn's mom, who was not far behind them, ran in crying, "Where's my baby?!?"

Uncertain what to do as they watched the adults discuss

Kaitlyn's condition, the girls crowded close together, holding hands. Maddie was shaking. Rachel was praying, and Emma and Jade held the group together tightly.

Maddie didn't want to close her eyes. Afraid to let go for even a moment, she looked on hoping to catch a glimpse of her friend's status. She wasn't the best lip-reader, but she asked God to help her just this once. "It will help me know how to pray." She pleaded quietly.

Her heart dropped when she saw the ER doctor look to the floor. *Oh God, please no*, she thought as she watched Kaitlyn's mom suddenly yell NO!!!! and fall into a heap on the floor.

CHAPTER 18

Winter's Affliction

"Can you describe the perpetrator?" Officer Burns asked David after the girls left.

"White male, dark hair, all black clothing. He was wearing a mask, so I couldn't see his face," David repeated.

Looking at David, the officer asked, "Did he have any markings that you remember?"

"Not that I remember, no. Very little skin was uncovered. The mob he was with carried signs that read NO ORDER, NO PEACE. I believe this group is a faction of the PeaceKeepers."

Stunned, Officer Burns peered at David with wide eyes. "What do you know about the PeaceKeepers?" He asked.

David didn't want to show his federal ID since he was under investigation. "Do you remember the four girls kidnapped and held against their will in Baldersville last spring?"

"I recall hearing something about it." Suddenly the officer was very interested in what David had to say.

"The four girls your officers took to the hospital were the same. One of them is my daughter. It was a PeaceKeeper who kidnapped them."

After vigorously writing a note on his pad, Officer Burns asked, "Tell me again how the girl was shot?"

"I told you. Somebody broke out the back window. I heard the crash and climbed over the seats, and she was gone. I exited

189

through the tailgate and ran down the street. When I turned the corner, I saw the man in the mask arguing with another man. I came up from behind them and knocked the other man out, grabbing Kaitlyn. I then swept the man's feet out from under him, and his gun went off. I ran as fast as possible to my truck and asked Tom to call 911."

"And you didn't know the perpetrator even though you believed him to be a PeaceKeeper?"

Frustrated, David answered, "For the third time, no, I did not."

Hesitating, Officer Burns stroked his jaw looking warily at his witness. After a few moments, he said, "I'm having a hard time understanding why this PeaceKeeper busted out your back window. Did you threaten him in any way?"

"No, I did not. When the mob of PeaceKeepers started rocking the SUV, I showed my firearm so they would know I was armed, but the man who grabbed Kaitlyn was not visible at that time."

"How many people made up this mob?" Officer Burns asked.

"I would say seventy-five to a hundred?"

Curious, the officer looked around and asked, "Where did they all go?"

David could feel his blood pressure rising as they spoke. "They scattered after Kaitlyn was taken. I followed them to an empty parking lot."

"And you did not recognize any of them?"

"No, I did not."

"What makes you think these men were PeaceKeepers?" The officer asked.

"It was the signs. The message was the same as the message they spouted when they held my kid hostage."

"Okay, Mr. Bennett, that will be all for now. We will need your firearm for ballistics testing." David pulled his gun from the back of his pants and handed it to the officer. "Thank you for your time. We have more witnesses to interview, and we will get back to you. If you are needed for additional questioning, do not leave town."

After verifying the safety lock was in place, the officer secured the gun in a baggie and said, "Right now, it's a crime scene. We will tow the vehicle in for evidence and call you when it is ready for pick up."

"Thank you. Can I get a ride to the hospital?"

"Sure, give me ten minutes, and I can take you."

Pulling his cell phone out of his pocket, David called Jacque to tell her what had happened. After hanging up, he closed his eyes. He knew going to Atlanta was a bad idea. *Why didn't I listen to my gut?* He ruminated.

"Mr. Bennett, I'm ready." Officer Burns said.

ATLANTA MEMORIAL HOSPITAL

Crossing her arms across her chest, Maddie closed her eyes as the moment's shock began to wear off.

"But we prayed!" She heard Rachel cry out to her dad before running down the hall.

Shaking the heaviness, Maddie chased her friend into the courtyard where she watched her fall to her knees. Approaching from behind, she knelt beside her friend and gently touched on her back. Maddie could feel the violent sobs that racked through Rachel's body.

Unintelligible whispers ascended into a crescendo of desperate prayer. "No! God! No! You can't have her! She didn't say yes to Jesus yet!"

Sharing her friend's desperation, Maddie prayed, "God, please, please help us." She had never seen her friend like this. Rachel was the strong one. Sitting quietly by her friend, she remembered Bob's words about being with. Suddenly, a familiar melody bubbled up from her belly.

> *God, you are faithful.*
> *My source of strength.*
> *Father, I thank you,*

For giving me peace.

A continuous chorus flowed from Maddie. She had no words, but perhaps she didn't need any. Perhaps the song of her heart was enough.

Rachel looked up, her sobs subsiding. Her flushed face gave away her anger. "I'm not sure I'm very good company right now," Rachel said as she looked at her hands.

"It's okay, we can just sit here," Maddie said. "Or if you want, we can pray?"

Shaking her head, Rachel said, "I'm all prayed out. God's not listening." With a blank stare, Rachel focused on the sculpted bush before them.

A bolt of fear stabbed Maddie in her stomach. *What should I say, God?*

I am in this.

Rubbing her sweaty hands on her jeans, Maddie said, "God is in this, Rachel."

An invisible wall separated them as disbelief settled on her friend's face. "I don't see him," Rachel said cynically.

Maddie turned as she heard the automatic door behind them. "Hey, I'm going to go talk to Emma and Jade. Will you be okay?"

Rachel nodded.

Crossing her arms tightly around her middle, Emma asked, "How's she doing?"

"Not good," Maddie replied, staring off into the courtyard. Looking back at her friends, she asked, "Any news?"

Emma hesitated, "She's in a coma. They aren't sure that she'll make it through the night."

Not willing to give up, Maddie asked, "So, there's hope, right?"

"We don't know."

"Well, then, we need to keep praying, right?" Grabbing her friend's hands they walked over to Rachel.

"Hey, Rach," Maddie said, "I know this is hard, but let's pray right now, okay?"

Rachel took the offered hand and stood. The four bowed their heads and lifted a tear-filled plea to Heaven. "Thanks," Rachel said after they finished. "Can y'all give me some privacy? I think I need some time alone."

"Sure, come on girls," Jade said. Lifting her friend's chin, she said, "We love you, Girl."

Rachel attempted a half-hearted smile and turned away.

Maddie followed Emma and Jade into the ER where Kaitlyn's mom was talking to her dad. Relief flooded her as she saw Sonya stand up and walk toward them.

Maddie ran into her mentor's arms who hugged her tight. Tears she had been holding onto poured out of her.

"Rachel's angry," she whispered to Sonya.

Sighing, Sonya said, "I would be angry, too."

Maddie looked at Sonya with a look of worry. "She's angry at God," she replied in anguish.

Sonya placed her arm around Maddie's shoulders. "You know God's got big shoulders, don't you?" She asked.

Looking at Sonya, she nodded.

"He can handle our anger. But we must surrender it to him."

Looking at her feet, Maddie said, "I'm not sure she will."

Sonya squeezed her shoulders and said, "Give her time. She's in shock. She's been carrying a heavy load for a long time. But God's bigger. Give her to him."

Maddie watched her dad walk toward them.

Bending down, David looked his daughter in the eye and said, "Ruthie."

An attempt at a smile fell just short of her eyes as she looked at her dad.

"Kaitlyn's alive, but she's in a coma."

"Will she be okay?"

"We don't know; she's lost a lot of blood."

Cocking her head to the left, Maddie asked, "What happened, Dad?"

Standing up, David answered, "We'll talk about it later. I need to finish up with the officer over there. Your mom is on the way. Sonya, is she okay with you?"

"Of course," Sonya said.

Maddie closed her eyes and placed her head on Sonya's shoulder.

"Maddie," Sonya said.

Groggy, she opened her eyes. Looking at her watch she realized an hour had passed.

"Maddie," Sonya repeated.

Looking up, she noticed the woman they had met earlier at The Refuge.

"Ms. Hazel?" She asked.

"Well, hi thar. I didna expect ta be seein' ya here. I understand thar's been a bit of a commotion."

"I'll be back in a bit. Do you need anything?" Sonya asked.

"No ma'am, I'm good," She responded.

Hazel took Sonya's seat and sat in silence. Placing her chin on the head of her cane, she sighed. "Do not be 'fraid, little one. God's in this."

Surprised to hear her repeat the words she just heard in her thoughts; Maddie looked down as she remembered Sonya's words about God moving. "How do you know?" She asked.

"I got ma ways. R'member what I tole ya this mornin'?"

Maddie looked at her as she tried to remember. "You said to keep serving others, and we'll serve him." Pausing, she added, "That it would be costly, but he would be with us every step of the way."

Looking at her proudly she said, "Look at you! That's a mighty fine mem'ry ya got thar."

Blushing, Maddie looked down at the floor.

"When my daughter came down sick. We brought her here. Six months later, the good Lord decided ta bring her home. I'd sit in that courtyard over 'thar and watch as the butterflies would flit all 'round. I even had one land on me! I knew the good Lord was thar, encouragin' me. I didna' know how I'd ever live without ma girl, but the Lord had a plan. Maddie, he's always got a plan, and he's always with ya and yer friend."

Maddie looked sadly at Hazel, "I don't think she knew Jesus."

"Do ya really think that's gonna stop the Almighty? I've lived a long time, I've seen many thangs, and the one thang I know fer certain, is ta never put limitations 'round ma God. The Bible says that nothin' is impossible fer God. And if Jesus could save the thief on the cross the ver' day of his death, then I 'spect he could do the same fer anyone else. So, what do we do when we want our loved one to know Jesus?"

"We pray?"

"Yes ma'am. Let's do it now."

After talking to Maddie, David walked over to Officer Burns who had just interviewed Tom.

"Sad about the girl," Officer Burns said.

"Yes, Sir, it is. Have you had any luck catching the perpetrator?"

"Actually, we do have someone in custody. We will need you to ID the person. Can you come to the station tomorrow?"

David sighed as he realized another Monday morning would be spent away from work. I hope management will understand. "Yes, I will be there," David said.

"David!" Jacque walked in with a panicked look on her face. Olivia, Tom's wife, followed close behind her.

Grabbing her in a big hug, David held her close and whispered, "We're all alive."

Jacque pulled away and asked, "Alive?"

"Kaitlyn is in a coma," David said. "We have a long night ahead of us."

"Oh David, not again." Jacque wept into her husband's shoulder.

"Mom!" Maddie ran up when she saw her mom. David pulled them both close A nagging guilt tore at David as he remembered the promise he had made to his daughter to keep her and her friends safe. Shaking the thought, he was thankful to have his daughter safe in his arms.

"Where is Matthew?" Maddie asked.

"He's with Caleb. They're giving Thor a bath."

The image of two eleven-year-olds bathing a Great Dane caused Maddie to laugh sadly, "That ought to be interesting."

Tucking a tuft of hair behind his wife's ear, David said, "They're towing the truck for evidence. Jade and Emma's parents are coming, and we'll need to ride home with you."

Nervous over her appearance, Jacque pulled her hair back and over her shoulder as she said, "That's fine. Olivia told me there's a big group coming from the church to pray."

"Oh, hey, Mom, Sonya is here. Do you want to meet her?" Maddie interrupted.

"Sure, in a minute, Maddie. Let me talk to Dad and we'll be right over."

"Okay." Maddie walked over to the chairs where Sonya sat with Jade and Emma and sat beside them. "Mom said a group from the church is coming to pray."

Sonya smiled. "Yes, you girls have quite the contenders standing in the gap for you."

Suddenly, a group of about ten students walked into the ER waiting room. Maddie was grateful to see Jackson Reese heading up the charge.

Over the next twenty-four hours, Maddie and her friends sat in the waiting room. The doctor said these were the most critical hours. They spent their time praying, listening to worship music, and talking. Maddie watched Rachel soften as her church family surrounded her in prayer. She realized that this was the first time she saw the church in action, and it was nice.

She asked her mom to bring her a change of clothes, her Bible, and journal. This was as good a time as any to write down her feelings, and she knew Mr. C would want to read them.

> *September 23*
> *Father,*
> *To be honest, I am not sure what to write. Sonya told me to write my thoughts, so here you go. I don't understand why this happened to us. I believe in you, and I have faith, but how could you let this happen? I'm not angry like Rachel is, but I am confused. I know you love us, but I just don't get how a loving God could allow these bad people to hurt us. Will you help me understand? Sonya said we're going through a winter season, and in the winter season, we are to dig deeper.*

Maddie drew a tree with roots in the shape of a face. The sketch echoed her feelings as perfectly drawn teardrops fell to the ground.

> *Sonya told us the story of a tree that lost all its bark in the wintertime. To the eye the tree looks afflicted, dead even, but underneath was where all the magic happened as the roots dug deep into the earth to find food. She said that after the winter season passed, the tree would be ready for its spring reveal, but until then, it had to trust it would receive all it needed from its creator. She said that in our winter seasons, we are to trust you to provide all we need, and that spring was right around the corner. Is this true, God? In Jesus' Name, Amen.*

After drawing question marks around her prayer to serve as a frame, Maddie closed her journal and fell to her knees. "Coffee?"

Maddie looked up to see Ashley Gordon holding a cup of coffee for her. After getting back in the chair, she took the cup. "Thanks," she said.

"Don't mention it. Have you heard anything about Kaitlyn?"

Stirring some cream and sugar into the black coffee, Maddie said, "Not yet."

Ashley sat quietly for a few moments. "How are you holding up?"

"I'm tired."

"Hey, I know this is a weird time to say this, but I wanted to apologize for being so mean to you in Middle School."

Maddie looked up in surprise. "It's okay," she said.

"No, it's not okay. I was a jerk." Ashley said, looking down in shame.

Remembering Grammy's encouragement to pray for her, she said, "I accept your apology. I forgave you a while ago."

Ashley blinked, "Wait, really?"

"Yeah, you were nice to me when my mom, you know. Afterward, I prayed to forgive you."

"I'm so glad, thank you." With a shaky smile, Ashley asked, "Can we start over?"

Maddie said, "Of course. Hi, I'm Maddie."

"I'm Ashley, nice to meet you, Maddie."

Emma and Rachel walked over as they shook hands. "It's nice to see you two talking," Emma said as she sat beside Maddie.

"Yeah, we're all good," Maddie smiled.

"You know, if it weren't for you, Ashley, Maddie, and I may not have met," Emma said as she elbowed her friend.

"That's right!" Maddie exclaimed. "You were quite the rescuer. Thanks, Friend," she said as she laid her head on Emma's shoulder.

Ashley blushed in embarrassment.

"Hey, God works all things to the good, right Rach?" Emma asked.

"Yeah," Rachel said quietly, agreement not quite reaching her eyes.

Maddie looked at her friend and whispered, "Are you okay?"

Rachel nodded her head. "Hey, Jackson is going to start a prayer vigil, he brought his guitar. Do y'all want to come over?"

"Sure, do you want to come, Ashley?" Maddie asked.

"You betcha!"

Overnight, the students took turns leading worship. When they weren't leading, they were sleeping. Maddie was surprised the hospital allowed them to take so much of the waiting room, but there weren't many waiting to be seen. Taking her turn to rest, she curled up in a ball within her sleeping bag and closed her eyes. As she slept, a vivid dream would begin.

> *Maddie was in a garden. She knew this garden as one she had dreamed about before. There were rings of sunflowers that looked like crowns planted in opposing rows. Admiring the sunflowers, she saw one that caught her eye. Bending down, she felt underneath the ring to find the root. To her surprise, she could pull the crown out with ease. Looking at the gift in her hand, she lifted the crown and saw a huge tower before her. Kaitlyn stood in the window with someone standing next to her. She had the most peaceful look on her face as she lifted her hand to wave at Maddie. Looking at the crown in her hand, she immediately began to run toward the tower calling her friend's name.*

"Maddie, wake up." Someone was shaking her.

"Kaitlyn," she mumbled.

The shaking became more pronounced. "Maddie, wake up."

Still half asleep, she recognized Sonya and said happily, "Sonya, I picked the crown. And I saw Kaitlyn. I think she's going to be okay!"

Sonya paused and placed her hand on her shoulder. Maddie, Kaitlyn's gone."

Confused, Maddie was suddenly wide awake, rubbing the sleep from her eyes. "Wait, she's gone?"

Maddie looked across the room at Rachel who was fighting

tears. She immediately jumped up and ran to her friend.

"I'm so sorry, I tried," Rachel cried.

"What do you mean?"

"I prayed, but it just wasn't enough."

Maddie didn't know what to say. Remembering Hazel's words, she said, "Hey, remember the woman we met at The Refuge? I saw her yesterday."

"You did?"

"Yeah, she said that nothing is impossible for God. Hey, maybe he saved her before she. . ."

Letting go of her friend's hands, Rachel turned away. "Please don't."

"She'll be okay." Sonya placed her arm around Maddie's shoulders. "Just give her some time."

CHAPTER 19

Mercy Revealed

October 3
US Capitol
Washington DC

Stepping out of the taxi, David, Tom, and Curtis Stiles lifted umbrellas to protect themselves from the torrent of rain. After going through security, they worked their way to the Senate Floor. The men walked quietly as they made their way to a specific room designated for closed-door hearings.

It had been a rough week. After the grievous weekend, David had to ID the man who shot Kaitlyn. When he looked into the dead eyes of the suspect holding a four, he knew right away they had the right man.

After the shooting, David and his family were at the hospital all night long. He wished the outcome had been different. He didn't pretend to believe that he could shield his family from death, but he had hoped that he could protect them from the atrocities of it.

They missed the fireworks that followed when the same men who brashly walked in front of his truck torched several blocks in town. It seemed as if half of Atlanta was burning down to hear the officer tell it, and these guys acted as if they wanted to get caught. "Easiest arrest I've made in a year!" Officer Burns boasted. But David couldn't think about that right now.

David found it ironic that the building where he was confirmed as Commander twelve years prior could be the same to change his career forever.

As they were ushered to a seat outside the hearing room, Mordecai Oronoff walked up to join them.

"David, good to see you, my Friend," Mordecai said as he shook his hand.

"Thank you for coming," David replied as they took their seats. "I am grateful to you, Mordy."

Pulling out his notes, David reviewed the order of events from May fifth in preparation for the hearing. He had never been present in a hearing but had briefed himself on the protocols.

"Commander Bennett, they are ready for you now."

As they walked into the hearing room, David noticed four tables pulled together into the shape of an O. At the far end of the room sat three senators from New York, California, and Georgia, each with a brown placard that displayed their names. At the table closest to the door were four chairs for David, his counsel, and witnesses. Senate reporters were stationed behind their representatives to record the hearing events.

David was in full uniform, including three stripes and multiple service metals that spoke to his honored service. Sitting in his seat, he laid his paperwork before him.

"Good morning, Admiral."

David stood and saluted the senior officer.

"You may stand down, Commander," Admiral Rick Osborne, Director of the NSA, said as he smiled at his protégé.

David was surprised to see Daniel Reese, the Deputy Director of Communications at the US Embassy in Israel, standing behind the admiral. *What testimony can he possibly give to the events that happened in Baldersville?* David wondered.

"You may all be seated," the representative from New York began as he read from a script. "We are here today to hear testimony regarding the Show Cause Determination of dereliction of duty under article 92 for Commander David

Bennett.

"This is a hearing only. This committee will determine if Commander Bennett violated a direct order on May 5th. If found guilty, this committee will decide whether Commander Bennett's separation from the US Naval Reserves is warranted. We will now receive remarks from the representative of Georgia."

"Commander Bennett, thank you for your time and cooperation during this hearing. We understand you are a highly decorated US Naval Commander and are grateful for your service to our nation. I concur with the representative of New York that this is a hearing only and will be utilized to obtain testimony on your behalf. Once we have heard the testimony, a decision will be made whether you will be released from your obligations to the US Navy. Do you understand?"

"Yes, I understand," David replied.

Over the next two days, David felt like a frog in a slow-cooker. The evidence against him was great, and to hear Deputy Daniel Reese tell it, David was a cowboy in the Old West as he led the investigation against the PeaceKeepers. The information he and his team provided to the FBI that resulted in thwarting a global coup did not appear to have any weight on David's actions.

On the third day, Tom and Mordecai laid out their part in the investigation while speaking to his integrity, excellent moral aptitude, and service. The questions asked of them were brief and did not seem, to David anyway, to have any impact, good or bad, on the hearing itself. Unfortunately, Joe with Warriors of the Way could not attend. While this disappointed David, he understood the extenuating circumstances of the current case Joe and his team were working on. However, he felt they would have had intel into the inner workings of the PKO that could have been helpful to his case.

After their testimony was complete, the representative from New York said, "Commander Bennett, we would now like to hear your testimony as to the events of May fifth in Baldersville, Georgia."

David laid out the events preceding Friday, May fifth. He led up to the night and confirmed the girl's location and rescue. He advised of the information shared with Admiral Osborne regarding the PeaceKeeper locations and their connection to the PKO.

"Senators, my team did an extraordinary job of thwarting a coup of global proportions. But it is my belief this was only a smokescreen. I believe the PKO is a training ground for the ongoing riots and attacks to our food supply."

"Commander Bennett," the representative from New York interrupted, "what does any of this have to do with your disobeying a direct order?"

"Nothing, Sir, except that my participation in this investigation allowed me to find my daughter, but only by accident. And when my ask for help was denied, I did what any of you would have done for your own daughter. I went in. I'm not excusing the misconduct, Sir. I am only explaining it."

The Representative from Georgia peered intently at David as he asked, "Commander Bennett, you mention accidentally finding your daughter. Did it not occur to you that this may not have been an accident?"

The room went quiet as David sat in shock. "Sir?"

"Pardon me for interjecting here, but I find it interesting that the daughter of the Commander investigating members of an organization planning a global coup comes up missing and then is found to be held by the same members of said organization." Looking at his cohorts, the Senator continued, "Does anyone else on this board think this is worth further investigation?"

"Gabe, I do not think one thing has anything to do with the other. This hearing is to determine whether Commander Bennett is fit for future service. This PKO has nothing to do with this hearing."

"I understand, Senator, and I think the extenuating circumstances require further investigation. Especially with the information Commander Bennett is submitting regarding the PKO." Looking at David, the representative from Georgia asked, "Do you have proof of the PKO being a training ground for the riots and attacks on our food supply?"

The only proof David currently had was his son, and he did not want to involve his children in this fiasco. "No, Sir, unfortunately, I do not. This is only a hunch based on what I have physically seen and investigated."

With his nose contemptuously pointed upward, the representative from New York asked, "Well, we cannot accept testimony based on a hunch, can we?" Looking directly at David, he asked, "Commander Bennett, is there anything further that you or your witnesses would like to add?"

Clenching his jaw in frustration, David returned the representative's gaze as he said, "No, Sir, that will be all."

"Then we shall reconvene tomorrow morning with our decision. Thank you to everyone for your time." As he squared up the papers in front of him with a loud tap, the representative from New York nodded as if to announce that the hearing was over for the day.

Thursday night, Mordecai, Tom, and David met for dinner. Debriefing the details of the hearing, Mordy asked his intentions.

The dark circles under David's eyes displayed his regret, "What would you do?"

"David, I would not have done anything different. Five people are alive today because of the heroic efforts of you and your team."

"Would you resign or contest?" David asked.

After a sip of ice water, Mordecai said, "You have performed your duty to the United States of America; your duty now is to your family, David. Perhaps God's mercy in saving your family reveals God's plan for you. I cannot tell you what to do, but perhaps it is time to ask the Lord what his priority is for you next."

Later that night, David called Jacque to let her know his decision. He was grateful to hear her agreement, considering the impact it would have on their family.

The final call of the night was to his mom. His heart was

heavy, and he needed spiritual encouragement to reassure him that he was doing the right thing.

"Hey, Mom."

"David! It is so good to hear yer voice. But it's kinda late, ain't it?"

"Sorry, Momma, but I needed to run something by you."

"A'course, a'course, what is it ma boy?" Grammy asked.

After telling his mom about the events of the last three days, he asked, "What do you think, Mom?"

Grammy let out a loud sigh on the other end of the line.

"Oh Son, I am so sorry. I shore did love that Kaitlyn; she was a sweet girl, full a questions. How's Maddie Ruth holdin' up?"

"Better than I would have thought, but she is struggling."

"They've all been through a lot this past year."

"Yeah." David hesitated before adding, "Hey Mom, there's something else." Explaining the events of the hearing, he added, "What do you think?"

"I was readin' in Luke 13 jes' this mornin'." Grammy said. "Ain't it interestin' how God works a word in jes' when ya need it? Anyhow, Jesus is grievin' the rejection of his people while the Pharisees are tauntin' him. Now David, ma Boy, I want'cha ta read them red letters a Jesus. The same One that Isaiah proclaimed would set the captives free said that he wouldna give up even though his people rejected 'im! This was Jesus! And he didna let anythin' get in the way a his goal. Not them Pharisees or that nasty little bugger Satan. Yer work in these last twenty-seven years was important, but it's only part a the story. The goal God has fer ya, it ain't done yet Son, and neither are you. Now, I cain't tell ya what to do or not to do, but I can say the Lord has a plan fer you. My advice is ta seek him."

After walking into the hearing room on Friday morning, David sat down with Curtis to his right.

The representative from New York opened the proceedings by reading the determination. "Do you, Commander Bennett, wish to contest this determination?"

David stood with his counsel, "No Sir, I do not wish to

contest."

"Then we will hold the determination of separation to a vote. Each senator will vote yay or nay for separation."

"Will the representative from Colorado share his vote?"

"I vote yay for separation."

"Will the representative from Georgia share his vote?"

Looking intently at David, he said, "I vote nay for separation."

"Commander Bennett, as a commissioned officer in the United States Navy, you have sworn to support and defend the constitution of the United States against all enemies, foreign or domestic. As an officer, you have the duty to obey all orders as directed by your superior officer and as you have freely admitted, you have failed to do so. I, the representative of New York, also vote yay for separation and declare the yays at two and the nays at one. Commander Bennett, it is the decision of this committee that you must separate from the United States Navy. You have the option to either resign with an honorable discharge or to retire with an unfavorable characterization of service. A resignation does not allow for retirement pay or benefits, and you will become a civilian, whereas retirement will allow for lifetime retirement pay and benefits along with the option of the US Navy to call you back in an emergency. What say you?"

"I will resign, Senator."

"Very well. As of today, October third, we accept your resignation, Commander Bennett. Our administrator here has a copy of the formal request to NAVPERSCOM for you to sign."

It was done. David exhaled slowly as he pondered, *twenty-seven years erased just like that.*

As Curtis filled his briefcase and stood to leave, David looked at the vacant chairs behind the formal brown placards. The names of men he would probably never see again were engraved in each one—men who declared a decision that wiped out his whole Naval career.

When David told Jacque of his decision the night before,

she asked why he chose resignation. His answer seemed clear in his mind at the time. To contest would be to lie and say he obeyed a direct order from the Admiral. He couldn't do that. Integrity was woven into every cell of his body. To accept retirement, while it would provide for them financially, would be to accept the unfavorable characterization that came with it. He would spend the rest of his life explaining his misconduct so he could fight for benefits. No, resignation seemed to be the only way. He could cut clean from the Navy and prioritize his family while placing more energy into Magnum Lock Security. His management team would appreciate that. And who knows, perhaps he could even start his own security company. The way the world was going, it seemed a clear option.

As David's career flashed before his eyes, his friend Tom touched his shoulder. "It's not over, Dave."

David shook his head, "Yeah."

The next few days passed by in a blur. Once again, the girls were thrown into a media craze that stirred up a great deal of attention at school. The parents agreed the girls needed to stay home, so they decided to study together during the day at Rachel's house under her dad's supervision. Since the girls had no desire to be alone and did not want to be surrounded by strangers, this seemed to be the perfect arrangement.

Jade was trying to keep everyone's spirits up. The room would be completely quiet when suddenly a disturbing sound coming from Jade's direction would leave everyone in stitches. Then, out of the blue, she would tell a joke that would cause each of them to question her sanity.

Immersed in her writing, Emma was quiet most of the time.

Maddie was walking on eggshells around Rachel. She wanted so badly to be able to talk to her about Kaitlyn, but her friend would have none of it. She couldn't stop thinking about the dream she had in the hospital. She could still see Kaitlyn waving in her mind's eye. It was as if she wanted her to know that she was okay. *Maybe she is with Jesus,* she thought. *But God, how can I share this with Rachel?*

Just wait, my child. She needs time.

Maddie was growing accustomed to the still, small voice. It sounded like her own but wasn't. It was comforting, at times convicting, but always encouraging. She found her child-like faith growing in this winter season. She never realized how much she relied on Rachel's faith until she stood alone. Sonya told her there would be seasons for which she would need to borrow another's faith, but since faith is the assurance of things hoped for, it was time for her to decide for herself who she would trust.

Trust. She would never forget Grammy's visual of sitting in the chair. If she could hope the chair would hold her, sitting in the chair would reflect the trust she had to move forward; trust is an action, a verb. Drawing a chair in her journal, she wrote the word TRUST around it.

"What's that?" Jade asked.

"Hm?"

"What's the chair about?"

Glancing at Rachel uncertainly, she looked at Jade and answered, "Grammy showed us the difference between faith and trust. She used a chair to show how she could have faith that the chair would hold her, but trusting would involve physically sitting in the chair. I was just thinking about what I was trusting God for."

"And what are you trusting him for?" Jade asked curiously.

Looking at Rachel again, she had a jolt of courage as she answered, "I trust him to get us through the next week and the next. And somehow, I believe something good will come from all of this."

Rachel got up and turned toward the kitchen.

"Rachel, please don't leave." Maddie pleaded.

Pacing the floor angrily, she retorted, "I'm sorry, but I just can't. Do you understand? Nothing is impossible for God, right? If that's true, why didn't he save Kaitlyn?"

"How do we know he didn't?" Emma asked quietly.

Rachel turned around and plopped in a chair, defeated. "When my momma almost died giving birth to Hannah, I prayed for God to heal her, and he did. I don't understand why he didn't hear our prayer for Kaitlyn," she cried.

"Do you remember what you told Kaitlyn when she was angry over the dreams she was having?" Jade asked.

Rachel looked at her friend blankly.

"You told her that praying doesn't always make the bad things go away, but that we're inviting Jesus in to give us strength and courage to face the bad things." Jade grabbed the hands of her friend and asked, "Have you invited him into this situation?"

The room was so quiet you could hear a pin drop. Suddenly, Rachel put her face in her hands and began sobbing.

One by one, each girl encircled her and began to pray. Maddie only knew to pray for peace, and it was peace she asked for. As the sobs lessened, Jade knelt before Rachel and encouraged her to look her in the eye.

"I've been studying a word Grammy said in Wild Rock when she talked about tribulation. She said it was the mercy of God that we were all sitting there. I looked up the word and learned that while God could punish us, it's in his love and mercy that he chooses to save. Now, I'm not educated like you, but I've got enough faith in me to believe that God had enough mercy to save Kaitlyn. Emma's right: maybe he saved her, but not in the way we would've wanted."

"Mercy, huh?" Rachel laid her head back against the chair and closed her eyes. "But what if he didn't? How do we know?" She pleaded.

As Maddie looked at the expressions of grief, hurt, and anger on the faces of her friends, she knew it was time to share the dream she had been keeping a secret. She moved closer, "Hey guys, there's something I want to tell you." Maddie said. "Do you remember the dreams I've been having about the crowns? The day Kaitlyn died, I dreamed of her. I went to pick a sunflower crown and I could pick it from the root. Afterward, I saw a huge tower before me, and Kaitlyn was standing in a window with someone next to her."

Rachel's eyes widened in astonishment as she asked, "Wait what? You had a dream about Kaitlyn?"

"Yeah, she waved at me and everything."

"Have you dreamed of her since?"

"No, but I felt like she was telling me that she was okay. I know, it sounds weird," Maddie looked away nervously.

A myriad of facial expressions revealed the apparent battle Rachel was fighting in her mind. Closing her eyes, she took a deep breath and let it out slowly. Suddenly, a weary smile peaked through her grief-stricken eyes as she bent down and said, "No, not weird at all."

CHAPTER 20

Giving the First

As she stared at her reflection in the mirror, the bright pink top over black pants clearly showed that she had never been to a funeral. Her mom was stunned that she was not going in all black, but she and her friends decided this was a moment to reflect Kaitlyn's spirit. She could almost feel Kaitlyn smiling down at the bright pink flower she used to clip her hair into a bun. She was ready.

Grabbing her journal, she walked downstairs and stopped on the landing. As she gazed into the living room, she reminisced the days when she and her friends laughed in this very room. *How will I survive this?* She wondered. It was then that she heard the comforting voice.

I am with you.

Lost in the moment, she was surprised when a hand slipped into hers. Looking down into her brother's curious eyes, she couldn't help but smile.

"Are you okay, Sis?" Matthew asked.

She nodded, "I will be."

Suddenly enfolded in the biggest little brother hug ever, she knew everything would be okay.

"Are you ready?" Her dad asked, his eyes not quite making hers.

"Yes, Sir." Dressed in a black suit with a navy-blue tie, her dad looked handsome yet distant. He had flown in early that morning. Maddie didn't know the results of his Navy hearing but had overheard her mom talking to him the night before, and it didn't sound good. "Hey, Dad, thanks for being here," she said.

A sigh escaped him as he put his arms around his daughter, placing his chin on her head. "Of course, Ruthie. I'm so sorry I haven't been around to help you this week. There's been a lot going on."

The familiar scent of his cologne reminded her of innocent days, simpler times. Breathing deeply, she decided she could wait to ask how the hearing went. "It's okay." She spoke. "You're here now."

As they walked into the Church, Pastor Derrik and Sonya pulled the girls aside and prayed with them. Ever prepared, Emma gave each of them a pack of tissues with a reminder of Grammy's words that God held a bottle of their tears. The memory of Kaitlyn's fallout with the boxing bag was almost enough to send them into sobs, but they pulled themselves together to walk into the sanctuary.

Maddie wasn't surprised to see so many people in attendance. Kaitlyn was an introvert, but her vigorous intellect and unique perspective on life drew others to her. Today was no exception as so many people spent their Saturday paying tribute to their beautiful friend.

Kaitlyn's mom sat in the front row, surrounded by her family. When the girls sat in the row behind her, she grabbed Jade's hand and whispered, "Thank you." Squeezing Momma Brown's hand, Jade nodded, her smile not quite reaching her eyes. Jade and Kaitlyn had a special friendship that only they understood. Where Kaitlyn was introverted, Jade was extroverted. Where Kaitlyn was nerdy, Jade was a jock. Where Kaitlyn was analytical, Jade was bold and quick-thinking. Jade sat in the chair, looking a little lost. They were all dealing with grief in their way, but with Jade, it was almost as if a piece of her was missing.

The following two hours were sweet yet sad. A video including Kaitlyn's best pictures played as the worship team played songs that encouraged hope and peace. Pastor Derrik gave the eulogy, after which Maddie and Rachel both spoke.

When Sonya asked if Maddie wanted to speak, she didn't think she could. But the more she thought about it, she realized this would be a good time to share some of the things God had placed on her heart.

> *"I thought I would be down there with all of you, looking up here as Kaitlyn gave the valedictorian speech for graduation. When Sonya asked me to speak, I didn't know how I could ever live up to her wittiness, but Kaitlyn would never have let me get away with that. She was one of the smartest people I knew but would never keep it to herself. You see, she wanted everyone to love learning as much as she did and gave of herself first, to make that happen. Kaitlyn refused to leave anyone behind. That's who she was. She read more books and asked more questions than anyone, and I believe this curiosity led her to God."*

Looking at Rachel, she smiled and said,

> *"I expect he's answering many of her questions, even now. I know many of us are sad for her, but she wouldn't want us to stay there. She would tell us to find a soft patch of grass and watch the moon come up. She would encourage us to check out every constellation and to seek every shooting star. She would tell us to get up, figure out what we can learn from this life, and keep living. That's who Kate was and what she would have done. Thank you."*

As she walked off the stage, the confidence that had driven her just moments ago suddenly vanished. Rachel squeezed her shaking hand as she sat down. Returning the favor, she added an encouraging nod as Rachel walked up to share.

It's funny what people choose to remember about a person. Maddie remembered her friend's nerdy attributes, whereas Rachel remembered her courage. As Rachel spoke, memories of when Kaitlyn refused to let her quit flooded her. Maddie wasn't a quitter by nature, but there were too many times when fear made it easy to walk away from something. Rachel reminded her how Kaitlyn would never let them do that. *I will miss you, Kate.* She looked toward the ceiling and blew a kiss.

"That was a beautiful testimony, ma Girl," Grammy said as they entered the house.

"Thank you, Grammy. I'm just sad I had to give it. Thank you for coming. Kaitlyn loved you so much." Maddie said as she gave her a big side hug.

"Why a'course! I wouldna have it any other way."

As Grammy walked into the kitchen, Maddie sat on the couch. Surprise distracted her from a wave of grief as a soft throw pillow hit her on the side of the head.

Mike stood there cautiously, silent. His narrowed eyes looked warily at his sister. Maddie could tell that he didn't know what to say. Thankful for the interruption of her sad thoughts, she decided to play along. "Mike!" she yelled, throwing the pillow at his head.

As Maddie, Michael, and not to be left out, Matthew made a mess of the living room; Dad commanded, "Hey Guys, keep it down!"

Plopping back down on the couch, she focused on the television as her dad turned up the volume.

"Once again, Bob, Lucien Baldur has shown outstanding prowess for solving real-world problems.

When he enacted a treaty with the nations to declare an end to world hunger, many doubted, but today he has put his money where his mouth is."

"Susan, what do we know about the PeaceKeepers Organization? Do we have any information about these facilities?"

"I'm glad you asked, Bob. Our team had an opportunity to tour one of the facilities in San Bernardino, and we were impressed with how down-to-earth everyone was. The facilities are clean, the farm grounds are immaculate, and everyone works well together. You might even call them—extended family."

Maddie couldn't believe her eyes. She was looking at a well-manicured complex that looked too much like the PKO. The way they were describing the farm made her stomach churn. If the look on Michael's face was any indication, he felt the same.

"Susan, tell us more about this Kindness Tax. What changes can we expect from the TKT?"

"Well, that's the most interesting part of this plan, Bob. Every American can participate in this amazing plan by giving the first ten percent of every dollar they spend for food. When you buy groceries, you will automatically give ten percent to the PeaceKeepers Organization. For every dollar you spend, you will help an orphan find a family or a food-insecure family a meal. Every ten percent you give will provide a homeless person with a roof over their head. And the most exciting thing to me, Bob, is the unemployed, who will receive real-world training so they can enter the workforce. This is a win-win for the American people! Just think about the money the US Government will save by dismantling programs that are no longer needed because of the generosity and management of Lucien Baldur. And since he is combining the programs that he manages in the US with those in other countries under the WTO, this will allow for a diverse community of workers who are all trained with the best of the best."

Maddie watched as her dad turned the television off and sat on the couch. Everyone was speechless. She didn't understand what the reporter said, but it didn't sound good.

"It appears the American people will be paying a new sales tax," he said.

"Ten percent is a lot of money," Grammy said. "Where do they think people are gonna get it from?"

"This is a farce!" Michael exclaimed. "Dad, you know they're selling a load of c…"

"Watch your language, Son."

"I can't believe they walked through the PKO and thought the people were, what did she say, down to earth? Who are they fooling?" Michael's face was flushed as he paced back and forth.

"Michael, sit down, please. Let's take a deep breath and think about what we just saw."

Maddie watched as Michael sat down, but he made it very clear it was under protest.

"Dad, was that place like the PKO where we were taken?"

With hooded eyes, David nodded, "Yes, Maddie."

Suddenly, what the reporter was saying dawned on Maddie, an agony arose in her throat as she remembered the "orphans" the reporter spoke about. "Dad, will this sales tax be used to fund this place?"

Rubbing his forehead with his hand, David closed his eyes as he thought for a moment, then said, "Yes, Maddie. This Kindness tax is slated to pay for the PKO."

Suddenly, everything was falling into place. The words of the Georgia Senator rang in David's mind, *"Did it not occur to you that this may not have been an accident at all?"* David went to his office. He needed some time to think. He was not one to place much stock in coincidences, but it seemed like one big coincidence that his daughter ended up in the PKO, the same organization his son worked for. And now he was being "invited" into this very organization? Who was Lucien Baldur truly after, anyway? Reviewing the pad that held a synopsis of each conversation he had regarding the PKO, his phone rang.

"Mr. Bennett, please hold for Mr. Baldur."

Coincidence, huh? He thought.

"Mr. Bennett, it is good to talk with you again. I am so glad you have your son back safe and sound. I do trust he is well?"

"Let's not play games, Mr. Baldur. What is it that you want?"

"I expect you have heard the news?" Lucien asked slyly.

"I have."

"This is a good time to discuss a potential job opportunity, David. As I understand, you have time on your hands now."

David could not believe he was having this conversation. *Was this man insane?* "And how would you know that?" David asked.

"Oh, word gets around, David. When you know as many people as I do, you make it your business to stay informed about what's happening. I do hope your loss wasn't too great."

Not wanting to give this man even an inch, David asked, "You mentioned a potential job opportunity?"

"Yes. When we spoke last, I requested assistance procuring a sensitive package from Israel. I understand that you perhaps had a conflict of interest since you worked with the Ambassador. Now that you are no longer working with the US Navy, I should think that your allegiance has changed. I would like to offer you a substantial employment package in exchange for your help to obtain what I need."

"For a man as connected as you, I don't understand why

you need a man like me."

"You flatter me, David, but to be clear, you have an investigative skill that I need. I always say a good businessman surrounds himself with even better people. That is the secret to his success. I invite the best of the best into my circle, Mr. Bennett. And you are the best."

David was incensed. If he was right, this man lured his son into employment and drug abuse. He kidnapped his daughter and her friends. He dangled his son like a carrot for David to help him. He was potentially the one responsible for the death of Maddie's friend and now dared to invite him to work in his organization.

I would be insane to say yes. David mused. But he had to tread lightly. One thing his training had taught him was to wait to show his cards.

"What skills do you need exactly?" David asked.

He almost heard Lucien rub his hands together in glee over the phone.

"Well, I understand that you and Mordecai Oronoff are close friends. I expect I insulted you by asking you to obtain his information, so I will not ask again. But there are ways that you can obtain the information I need without involving your friend, no?"

"Exactly what are you asking of me, Mr. Baldur?"

"David, I need a right-hand man who has exceptional skills for obtaining information that I do not have. You, my friend, have such skills. I am asking you to consider a partnership, a marriage of sorts. If you provide me with information, I'll provide for you and your family for the rest of your lives.

"How about this, David? Take the night to think about it. Talk to your wife and I will call you in the morning."

David sat back in his chair with his eyes closed. Several times in his career, he had to use espionage to gain intelligence on a case. Just thinking about it made his skin crawl. He never did anything to risk his marriage, but several times, he risked his moral integrity. This was one of the reasons that resigning from the Navy was attractive to him. No longer would he have to place himself in positions where he had to make a decision that could harm his integrity or his family.

Submitting to Lucien Baldur would change all that. David wondered if Lucien knew that he was on to him. *Doubtful.* He thought.

Picking up the phone again, David called his friend Mordecai. If he was back in Israel, it would be early morning there, but he had to take the chance.

"David, my friend." His greeting was interrupted by a long yawn. "Is everything okay?"

Perhaps this isn't the best time to do this, David thought. "Mordy, I apologize for calling so early, but there is something very important I need to discuss with you. Can you call me when you have had your coffee?"

The laughter on the other end of the line caught David off guard. "And what is the indication that I haven't?"

"Well, the yawn, for one."

"It's the boat life, my friend. The waves have a way of lulling you to sleep. So, how can I help you?"

He must be on a cruise, David thought. "Do you recall when the representative from Georgia asked if the kidnapping was not an accident?"

"I do."

"We had another incident here a couple of weeks ago. One of Maddie's friends was taken and shot."

Mordecai gasped. "I am so sorry, David. Is everyone okay?"

"No. The girl died from her wounds. And strangely enough, I had an interesting phone call this evening."

"Let me guess, Lucien Baldur."

"Yes, how did you know?"

"Well, since he has released to the news his plan for the Kindness Tax, I expected he would come back around to calling you."

"How will this impact Israel?" David asked.

"Since Israel signed the treaty enacted by Mr. Baldur and the WTO, pressure has mounted for Israel to provide national secrets to their food production. International relations have been strained to say the least. The Prime Minister is incensed about this tax. My guess is Baldur will be desperate for them to agree, or he may lose his influence with other nations."

"So, you don't think this is about The Iron Dome?" David asked.

"Honestly, I'm not certain of anything anymore. But I find it mighty curious that Baldur is so intent on getting to you, considering you have worked so closely with me and my country in the past."

"About that," David began, "I know this sounds crazy. I'm starting to wonder if I'm going a little crazy, but I'm starting to wonder. . ."

"If he's been after you all along?"

"You think so too?"

"There's no such thing as coincidences, David."

"My thoughts exactly."

"This Kindness Tax is only the beginning. What I know about Lucien Baldur and his business dealings is that he will dangle a carrot in front of his potential business partner. He will provide a service that looks shiny and clean on the outside while engaging in back-door transactions. Once he is in, he will work his way into every nation, every company, and every home until he has you. David, he doesn't just want the first; he wants it all."

Chapter 21

Not on My Watch

Maddie was angry. She could not believe what she had just heard. Running upstairs, she slammed the door and plopped on her bed. Picking up her phone, she began to type.

> Maddie: "Hey."
>
> Rachel: "Hey, you."
>
> Jade: "Hola."
>
> Emma: "zzzzzzzzzz."
>
> Maddie: "Are y'all watching the news?"
>
> Jade: "No, why?"

Searching for the local news channel online, Maddie found the article representing the story she watched and texted it to her friends.

> Jade: "What is this?"
>
> Maddie: "Exactly what it says. We just watched it on the news."

Rachel: "Let's chat tomorrow. Meet by the gym at 3:30. I'll ask Mom to take us home."

Maddie: "Okay, but I'm lowkey salty right now."

Rachel: "I know. This is too much to process tonight. Saying a prayer."

Irritated that she couldn't talk about this news immediately, Maddie went over what she heard as she paced her bedroom floor. I can't believe some guy wants to hand taxpayer money over to the PKO. Who made that decision? Weeks of wondering why so many bad things were happening around her took their toll as she collapsed into the middle of her bed, exhausted. "God, where are you?" She cried. "You KNOW these people are evil! Why would we ever want to give money to them?"

Maddie, do you trust me?

Surprised at the miraculous calming of her heart, she asked the same question of herself while realizing how much she yearned for the soft and comforting voice that spoke from deep within. *Do I?* She wondered guiltily. When listening to or for God, Sonya told her to listen for the voice that was convicting, not condemning, and always lined up with scripture. She knew that it said God was with her somewhere in the Bible. *Grammy and Rachel tell me that all the time*, she thought. *And there was a scripture somewhere that said something about trusting in the Lord, right?* Lying back on her pillow, Maddie pulled up the Bible app on her phone and searched for trust in the Lord. Scrolling down, she found what she sought in Proverbs 3:5: "Trust in the Lord with all your heart and lean not on your own understanding."

"God, I'm so sorry, but I need your help with this trust stuff," Maddie said as she drifted off to sleep.

The rings of sunflowers were dying. She had to do something! Bending down, she felt for the root of one of the rings. Remembering how she had successfully picked one before, Maddie pulled the crown out of the ground and watched it wither in her hand. Running to the next one, she attempted to pull it out of the ground and watched it wither again. Over and over, she tried, but nothing she did would change the outcome. Looking up, she saw the familiar tower where she felt such joy before. The need to present a sunflower crown was strong, but they were all dying. She felt helpless.

Shaking her head from right to left, Maddie was in and out of consciousness. "God, no!" She cried, waking herself up. Getting on her knees, she wondered, *what was that?* After what she saw the night before, she didn't know what else to do. "God," she whispered, "I need help learning to trust you. Please, show me what to do."

The following Monday, the girls returned to school. Harboring so many feelings over losing Kaitlyn and now this PKO thing, Maddie didn't want to talk to anyone, so she decided not to make eye contact as she navigated her classes.

At the end of the school day, she had to work to stay awake as she waited for the minute hand to reach the six. She could hear the second hand as it ticked by interminably slow, tick-tock, tick-tock. Yawning, she wondered when the magic bell ending the last period would set her free until she heard RRRINNNGGG. *Finally!* Maddie thought as she grabbed her bookbag and ran out of the room.

"No running, Ms. Bennett."

"Sorry, Ms. Truett." Maddie changed her pace to a fast

walk.

As she reached the courtyard for the gym, she looked around for her friends. Not seeing anyone, she found the closest bench and decided to work on math homework as she waited.

"Hey Girl," Emma called out from behind her.

"Hey." Distracted, she went back to the word problem in front of her.

"Maddie, are you okay?" Emma asked.

Sighing, Maddie closed her math book and looked at her friend. "No, I'm not. When is this thing ever going to end?" She asked as Rachel and Jade walked up.

"Did you watch the newscast?" She asked Rachel.

Pulling her books tight to her chest, Rachel said, "Yes, I did."

"What do you think?" Maddie asked anxiously.

Sighing, Rachel looked into the distance and answered, "I think there isn't much we can do about it."

"What! We can go tell them what's really going on down there!"

"And do you think they would believe us?" Rachel asked. "What proof would you be prepared to give?"

"Well, we could tell them how everyone looks like zombies," Jade interjected.

Shaking her head in exasperation, Rachel asked, "Since when is that a crime?"

"What about the ghost guns that Michael talked about?" Maddie asked.

"Again, how would you prove it, Maddie?"

Maddie huffed as she crossed her arms. "All I know is I don't want us ever returning to the PKO. And if I have anything to do with it, it won't happen, not on my watch!"

Placing her hand on her friend's shoulder, Rachel said, "Look, I know this is a lot. I've been so angry at God over Kaitlyn's death that I walked away for a minute. But I realized something. I thought I had a responsibility to bring Kaitlyn to Jesus, and when she died, I felt guilty, like I had failed. But

Maddie, I couldn't save her, spiritually or physically. I had to lay that down. We have no control over anything but ourselves. We can learn all things, such as self-defense or self-awareness, but at the end of the day, we must trust that all of this is in God's hands. We do what we can and let him do the rest."

Exasperated, Maddie yelled, "How do we know he is doing anything?! Look at what's happened to us in the last year. Look at what happened to Kaitlyn!"

"Maddie, look at us. We are right here despite everything that's happened," Emma said softly.

Sighing, Maddie looked at her hands and said, "So, are we just supposed to sit and wait? How do we know when to trust God and when to do something ourselves?"

"Well, what can you do right now?" Jade asked.

Maddie thought for a moment, "Pray?"

Nodding, Rachel agreed, "Yeah. Dad told me once that God will place in your hands everything you need to do the job. Until then, you do what he told you to do last, trust him, and pray. I've had to do that. I spent time repenting this weekend for allowing hopelessness to set in. I get to choose. We all get to choose if we are going to trust him."

"Trust." Maddie sighed. "I'm just so angry because all this bad stuff keeps happening. First, my mom, the PKO, and now Kaitlyn. I don't understand why God allowed these bad things to happen. I keep going back to the seals that we read about in Revelation. UGH! Are we being punished?" Looking off into the distance, she blinked to clear the tears she was fighting.

Jade moved to the ground so she could look up at her friend. "Girl, I've spent a lifetime wondering if I was being punished for my dad's death. When my auntie told me, she swore me to secrecy. When I met God, I could finally talk about it."

Looking up at her friend with a sad smile, Maddie asked, "And what did you hear?"

Jade snickered as she cocked her head upward, "That God had him." Blinking quickly to clear her moist eyes, she smiled.

Closing her eyes as she breathed deeply, Maddie asked, "But

why us? Do you guys ever wonder, why us?"

"Why not us?" Rachel asked. "Maddie, we live in a bubble. There are people across the world who have it much worse than we do. Seriously, search for 'The Persecuted Church.' Think about the woman we met at The Refuge, the people in Kentucky. We've been through some hard stuff, but they've had it much worse."

"You're right," Maddie said. "I guess I'm just struggling with fear again."

Rachel pulled out her phone and said, "Let's read Psalm twenty-seven."

Looking around, Maddie whispered, "But we're at school."

"So? God's here, why can't we read his word? Come on, let's do it together."

The girls each read several verses, Maddie being the last to read. "Wait for the Lord; be strong and take heart and wait for the Lord. . ."

"Do you remember the song Ms. Lorna wrote? She wrote that God was her Deliverer. She used a verse from Psalm 144 that says that he is her stronghold and Deliverer."

"What's a stronghold?" Maddie asked.

"I've got it," Emma said as she looked it up on her phone. "The dictionary says a stronghold is a place fortified to protect it against attack."

"Like a tower?" Maddie asked.

"Yeah, I guess."

Remembering the sunflower crowns in her dream, she said, "Hey, remember the dreams I told you guys about? In the dream I would pick the crown and present it to a tower."

"NO WAY!" Three voices yelled.

"And there's something else." Maddie searched her phone for a text Sonya had sent her. Finding the text, she looked up at her friends in awe. "What is it?" Emma asked.

Maddie showed the text to her friends.

Sonya: Maddie, before we meet next, read, and memorize Proverbs 18:10: The name of the Lord is a strong tower; the righteous run to it and are safe.

"Have you memorized the verse Sonya sent you?"

Maddie laughed, "That would be a big fat no."

"Well, there you go. It sounds like you've got some homework to do."

Later that night, Maddie decided to video chat with Sonya and run by her what she and her friends had talked about.

While waiting for Sonya to pick up, she made notes to share with her mentor.

"Hey Girl, what's up?"

"Hey, Sonya, sorry to call you after dinner, but I need to run something by you."

"No worries, the kids are with their dad doing homework. Let me go into another room."

Maddie watched as Sonya closed the door behind her. "Do you remember when I told you about the dreams I'm having?"

"About the crowns? Yes, I vaguely remember."

Maddie described what the girls had come up with when they dissected the dream.

"Okay, so in your dream, you're picking crowns to present them to the tower. If the tower is God, do you feel you must present something to him?" Sonya asked.

Thinking back to what she was doing in the dream, she said, "I guess."

"Tell me what you feel when you try to pick a crown and it dies."

"Sad."

"How did you feel when you presented a crown that didn't die?"

"Happy."

"If I had to guess, you're happy when you can give something to God that is beautiful and intact. But whenever you prepare to give him something that dies, you're sad. Do I have it right?"

"Yes, ma'am."

"Okay, as a reminder, I'm not a dream interpreter, so I want you to take everything I tell you to God in prayer. My guess is that the crown is a symbol of works. When you do something good, you're happy, so you present it to the Lord as a good work. But when you try to pick a crown that won't come up, perhaps that is not your calling. And the crowns that wilt, perhaps those are the things that won't last. Do you remember when we talked about the fruits of the Spirit?"

"Yes."

"Anything you do for God will produce one of these fruits, but the fruit comes from him first. For example, the fruit of love—God pours his love into you, and then you pour his love into another person by doing something for that person. That is a fruit that will last. But if you do something for someone out of desperation or people-pleasing, then there is no love, and that person's response is all the reward you will receive."

"So, what do you think God is telling me?"

"Before I answer that, have you memorized Proverbs 18:10?"

Maddie groaned, "I haven't yet."

"That's okay, but let's start there. I feel God is going to reveal much to you through his word."

After hanging up the phone with Mordecai, David's mom walked into his office. "Son, it's time we talk."

"Now is not the best time, Mom."

"Well, I don't know when there'll be a better time, do you?"

David opened his mouth to share a million reasons why he thought there was a better time, but instead, he thought better of it, stood up, and walked over to sit next to his mom on the loveseat.

"Now, I know ya been under a lot of stress lately. And Son, yer ole' mom is worried that yer tryin' ta carry the weight a the world on yer shoulders. You realize this whole thing is much bigger 'n you, don'tcha?"

"What I know is that my family is in danger. Four young girls have been unfairly caught in the middle. One girl has lost her life. I've lost twenty-seven years of security, and now a man I barely know is subtly threatening extortion."

Grace placed her hand on her son's. "David, this has nothin' to do with ya. Yer only a pawn in a much bigger story."

"Wow, thanks for giving it to me straight, Mom."

Chuckling at her son's sarcasm, Grace said, "I shore do miss yer Pa. Do ya 'member what he always tole ya?"

"Do it afraid."

"That's right. Do ya know where he got that from?"

"The Navy."

"Yep. Yer Pa went into the Navy in 1971. His first deployment was the USS Gideon, a guided missile frigate. In 1972, the Gideon was off the coast of North Vietnam. Now, yer Pa said they were protectin' planes from attack. One night, the sky was pitch black. The clouds so thick that ya couldna see the moon ta throw a lasso 'round it. Now, his Cap'n had a hankerin' that an attack was comin', and he asked fer air patrol but was dee-nied. Late that night, when yer Pa was on watch, two enemy planes were comin' at 'em fast. They fired at one of 'em and took 'em out, while the other one turned 'round. A few minutes later, two more planes came at 'em, and do ya know they must've had angels protectin' 'em cause one crashed and the other couldna even drop a bomb on 'em. That moment marked yer Pa. He could ne'er ferget how calm the Cap'n was or how brave the men he served alongside were. From that moment on, he faced everythin' with courage and grit knowin' he couldna control nothin' but his own response."

"I remember Dad talking about that Captain, Joseph E. Lain, correct? He became Rear Admiral and served as the Naval Inspector General. He was a good man."

"Yes, he was, so was yer Pa, and so are you, David Bennett. Now you get ta decide how ta face yer enemy. You can get chewed up an' spit out or you can say 'Not on my watch.'"

"But isn't that taking control?"

"Only of yerself. Everythin' else yer puttin' in the hands a the only One who's sovereign."

"Mom, I cannot give up protecting my family."

"Oh, my country alive, who tole ya ta do that? I ain't suggestin' that at'all! I'm sayin' lay all that stress down, Son, and let yer Creator give ya wisdom on what ta do next." She whispered, "It's what he's good at."

The following day, David busied himself with research on a new case he was working with Magnum Lock Security. Engrossed in the details of his latest client's facility, he was disgruntled as the sudden vibration of his phone interrupted his research.

"David Bennett."

"Good morning, Mr. Bennett; please hold for Mr. Baldur."

He knew the call was forthcoming but wished the man would choose better timing.

"David, my Man, how are you this fine morning?"

This man is insane! He thought to himself. Deciding to play his game of familiarity for now, David replied, "I am well, and yourself, Mr. Baldur."

"Well, it is a beautiful morning if I do say so. Have you decided to accept my gracious proposal?"

Gracious, huh? David grunted softly. "While I am honored by your request, Mr. Baldur, I must graciously decline. My wife and I have decided that it is time to prioritize our family."

The silence on the line was deafening. David had experience saying no and found that an enemy's response could range from acceptance to downright violence. He had no idea how Lucien Baldur would respond.

"Well, Mr. Bennett, I must say, I am surprised. But you are all alike. I find it distasteful that you people think you can have your way, but that's how you've been trained, isn't it, free will and all." The sinister laugh haunted the airwaves between them. "What a joke. You silly little people who believe they can run from order. You people want peace, but peace hinges on bowing to order. And the world will bow, David Bennett, make no mistake. Now, I have been more than patient with you, but my patience runs thin. Cherish your priorities for now. Good day."

David sat back in his chair, phone in hand, as the line went dead. *What did he mean by the world will bow?* Writing down Lucien's words, he sat back in his chair and thought, *not on my watch.*

The Strong Tower

Life was crazy as Maddie and her fam studied for the PSAT. She wasn't the best test taker. If she were honest, she was a little worried, despite Rachel assuring her it wasn't a big deal.

As she pondered an algebra problem, memories of Kaitlyn flooded her thoughts. Kaitlyn was the queen of all facts and never failed to help her friends when they struggled to learn them. Oh, how she missed her friend. *Would this grief ever end?*

On the morning of the test, Sonya sent a group text to the girls. The prayer she sent reminded Maddie of the scripture she gave her to memorize. *After the test,* she thought, *I'll have time to focus and hopefully memorize this verse for Sonya.*

She couldn't believe it, but she breezed through the hundred and thirty-nine questions and left the test room feeling pretty good.

"How'd you do?" Jade asked as she surprised her from behind.

"I think I did okay," Maddie said. "You?"

Jade shrugged, "Eh. I don't know if I'm going to college anyway."

"Yeah, I'm not sure if I want to either, but my mom, well, you know," Maddie said.

"I know, mine too. Dr. Alisha Jackson would be shocked if her daughter decided not to go to Georgetown."

Maddie laughed as Jade dramatized her mom's reaction. "Why Georgetown?"

"That's where she went to school. Can you believe she's already started emailing professors about me?"

Shaking her head, Maddie laughed. "My parents would want me to go to UGA, considering they both went there."

"Oh, the horror!" Jade said as she fell against the locker next to Maddie's.

"Come on, it wouldn't be that bad to be a Georgia Bulldog." Maddie laughed.

Jade gagged. "The only dog for me is Smokey. I love that little coonhound! Yep, if I go anywhere for football, it would be Tennessee."

"So, if we go to college, it'll be for the football team?" Maddie asked.

"Why else would you go? Well, gotta run; my ride is waiting!"

As Maddie waited for her mom, she pulled her phone out and read Proverbs 18:10, "The name of the Lord is a strong tower; the righteous run to it and are safe." Writing SOAP in her journal, Maddie worked through the Bible-reading method Sonya taught her.

Writing an "S" for Scripture, Maddie read the scripture several times and then wrote it down. Writing it down helped her to memorize. Then she added the "O" for Observation. What did she observe in the text? Reading through a fourth time, Maddie wrote down, "The Name of the Lord (Jesus) is a strong tower." Looking up the word tower, she read: a building or structure higher than its surroundings stands apart, one that provides support or protection. *God, is your name a strong tower, or are you the strong tower?* She wondered.

Drawing a tower, she colored in a moat and added other buildings, trees, and stuff in the distance. The first thing she observed was that the tower was tall and served as protection. It would be hard to attack this tower. Writing her thoughts down, she wrote the second half of the verse, "The righteous run to it and are safe." A bridge took form above the moat, drawing people safely into the tower.

Whoa. Wait a second. When Ms. Lorna prayed over her, she

remembered her ending the prayer weirdly, "In the strong Name of Jesus Christ." At the time, Maddie wondered why she prayed like that but didn't question it. Realizing there was something to it, she added a big S to the right as she thought, *I need to ask Sonya.* When she saw her mom drive up, she quickly closed her books and waited by the curb. "Hi, Mom," Maddie said as she entered the car.

Jacque looked at her daughter expectantly. "How was the test?" She asked.

"Better than I thought, but I'm glad it's over."

"Do you think you did well?"

Maddie realized they weren't going anywhere until she answered her mom's hundred questions. "Yeah, I think so."

"College 101 classes are in a couple of weeks. Are you signed up?"

Mom's gaze was penetrating as she waited for an answer. "Not yet."

"Maddie, you don't want to wait until the last minute. Getting into a good school gets harder the longer you wait."

Rolling her eyes, Maddie said, "I know, Mom. I'll sign up. I promise."

Her mom placed the car in gear which meant the Q&A was over. Maddie breathed a sigh of relief.

Opening her journal, Maddie wrote a big "A" as she thought about how to apply the scripture. Looking at the people who ran into the tower, she wondered, *is that me, God? Should I run into you? What does that even look like?* Writing that in her journal, she placed an S next to it so she could ask Sonya. Next to a big "P," Maddie wrote a simple prayer asking God for help.

October 25
Father,

I am struggling. I have these dreams and know I'm supposed to trust you, but I don't know how. Please help me to memorize this verse that Sonya gave me and show me how you want me to apply it. How do I run to you when

I can't even see you? I want to trust you, God. I really do. In Jesus' Name, Amen.

On Saturday, Maddie and Sonya met for coffee. She was so excited to finally have an opportunity to share the things she was struggling with and hopefully get answers. Sitting at the table with her mentor, she opened her journal to her list of questions and waited for Sonya to start.

"A lot has happened since we met last. How are you doing?" Sonya asked.

Shifting in her seat, she looked down as she answered, "Not sure. If I'm honest, I've been pretty angry."

"That's real, tell me about it."

The tiny flame of doubt Maddie had been harboring became a forest fire as she blurted out, "I just don't understand why God is allowing all these bad things to happen to us. He's a God of love, right? If he loves us, won't he keep us safe?"

"You know, there was somebody in the Bible who asked that very same question. His name was Elijah. Have you ever heard of him?" Sonya asked.

Maddie shook her head no.

Sonya proceeded to share the story of Elijah in First Kings eighteen and nineteen: "The takeaway," she said, "is to know that bad things will happen, but God is above our circumstances, so we can take our focus off the bad thing and place it on Jesus. This is where our peace and safety come from."

"Oh, the scripture you gave me says, 'The name of the Lord is a strong tower; the righteous run to it and are safe.' What does that mean exactly?"

"Just what it says. The name of Jesus is strong, victorious, protective, and when we run to him, we will find safety."

"When Ms. Lorna prayed for me, she prayed in the strong and mighty name of Jesus Christ. Is that the same thing?"

"Yes, ma'am. Every time we pray in Jesus' name, we believe

he will move on our behalf. Jesus said, 'Whatever you ask in my name, I will do it so that the Father may be glorified in the Son.' So, in this prayer, we find protection, peace, and safety, just as you drew in your tower there." Sonya pointed to the drawing in Maddie's journal.

"But it's not like real protection? Like the police?"

"Let me ask you a question. When Kaitlyn was shot, where were you?" Sonya asked.

"I was in my dad's truck."

"Safe?" Sonya asked.

Maddie shifted again in her seat, remembering the day she wanted to forget. "Yes."

"And what were you doing?"

"We were praying."

"That's right, and were you saved?"

"Yes, but Kaitlyn wasn't."

"How do you know?"

Puzzled, Maddie looked at her mentor, wondering how to answer her question.

"Maddie, the Word says that God's thoughts are not our thoughts, and God's ways are not our ways. We may not understand the why, but we can trust the Who. For all we know, this may have been God's way of saving Kaitlyn, and in so doing, he saved the rest of you by keeping you safe in the truck."

"But she died, so how was she saved?"

Sonya paused to take a drink before answering. "Do you remember when Jesus died on the cross?"

Maddie nodded.

"There were two other people who died that day. They were thieves sentenced to death for their crimes. One thief mocked Jesus, yelling at him to save himself and them if he was truly the Christ. The other asked Jesus to remember him when he came into his kingdom. Do you know Jesus' response?"

"No, ma'am."

"He told the thief who believed in him that 'today he would be with him in paradise.' I can't pretend to know the thoughts of God except to know that he is a merciful God who sent his Son to die so I could live. He is patiently waiting because he doesn't want anyone to perish. And just as he did for Elijah, I believe he rescues those in their darkest hour who genuinely want to know him deep in their hearts."

Looking at the watery mess of her drink, Maddie frowned. "But Kaitlyn didn't believe like the thief, and we prayed for her to believe and be saved."

"Maddie, look at me." Pointing to her journal, Sonya asked, "May I?"

"Sure," Maddie said.

Picking up the pen, Sonya wrote the word HOPE above the tower Maddie drew. "You can ALWAYS ask. You can ALWAYS seek, and you can ALWAYS knock. He has you and your circumstance in his hand, even if he doesn't answer your prayer as you hoped."

Focusing on the word HOPE, Maddie asked, "Sonya, was there ever a time when God didn't answer your prayer the way you wanted?"

"Actually, yes. I lost my first baby."

Shocked, she asked, "What happened?"

"Well, when I was eight months pregnant, I went into labor. We went to the hospital, and I could see on the doctor's face that the baby wasn't doing well. After a complicated delivery, baby Malachi went home to be with Jesus. We begged God to save him, but we realized that if he had answered our prayer exactly as we asked, Malachi would have suffered greatly. I will always cherish the eight months I carried my boy." Smiling, Sonya added, "If truth be told, God saved me through that sweet little babe as he taught me to trust in him."

"I'm so sorry, Sonya."

"It's okay, Girl. The good Lord has blessed me with four hooligans for which I am grateful daily. And we know we will see Malachi in Heaven. Do you want to know what running to my strong Tower looked like?"

"What?"

Sonya drew a rough sketch of a woman kneeling on the

ground, "It looked like getting on my knees and saying, 'God, I trust you, whether you choose to heal Malachi on earth or in Heaven, I trust you.' The righteous surrender to the Lord when they call on the name of Jesus, and they find comfort and safety in his arms, knowing that as a strong Tower, he is their refuge, their fortress, and their God in whom they trust."

Later that night, Maddie sat with her notes and her Bible. Looking at the sketched drawings, she was moved by the woman on her knees. *What was it like to lose a baby so close to term?* She wondered. Closing her eyes, Maddie pondered the question Sonya left her with: *"Where is God?"*

Rachel said that God is all around us. Grammy said that God is everywhere. Maddie knew that God was with her when she visited Grammy and Ms. Carolina Wren visited her. But did she truly believe he was with her always? Highlighting the outline of the tower, she thought, *Can I trust that my Strong Tower will be with me no matter what I face?* And with that, she drifted off to sleep.

> *Walking through the familiar garden, Maddie looked all around. In addition to the rings of sunflowers that grew all around her, she could see bright pink flowers that reminded her of Kaitlin's hair. Luscious blades of green grass reminded her of the feel of the football field after a fresh cut. She took off her shoes and wiggled her toes in the soft grass, feeling the cool, gentle earth beneath her bare feet. Maddie playfully skipped through the garden and was surprised to see Ms. Carolina Wren flitting around her. "Where have you been?" She asked as the bird seemed to play hide and seek. Following the bird through the garden, Maddie was suddenly so happy to see*

the tower in the distance. She longed to go in the tower and raced Ms. Carolina Wren to the moat's edge.

The bird suddenly stopped and perched carefully on the edge of a bridge. Cocking her head, she began to sing. Maddie knew that tune! Singing Peace, the lyric that she and Emma had written, the bird seemed pleased that she had chosen her song to use for the melody.

Joy filled Maddie in that moment. When the bird stopped her song, she stopped as well. Ms. Carolina Wren seemed to be waiting for Maddie to do something. It was a quandary, but she just didn't know what to do next. Seemingly tired of waiting, the bird flew away and left her staring at the top of the tower. The only thing separating her from the curious tower she had dreamed of so often was the brown drawbridge in front of her. What to do? She thought. Realizing it was time to do something, she attempted to take a step but suddenly realized she couldn't move.

The day after the unsettling call with Lucien Baldur, David was called into the office of Jim Scott, CEO of Magnum Lock Security.

"David, how are you doing?" Jim asked.

"Pretty good. I think I'm getting my land legs back."

"I'm glad to hear that. What do you think about the case I gave you?"

"It's very complicated, but I don't think it will be too difficult."

"How long do you think it will take?"

"About a week?"

"Good, that's what I like to hear. David, you are a stellar

hacker, and we are so grateful for all you have done for Magnum Lock."

David did not like where this was going, "But. . ."

"Well, I didn't want to tell you like this, but we have to let you go." Raising his hand, Jim rushed to continue, "Before you say anything, this is not about you. The board has decided that we will have to close our doors."

"Why?"

"It's complicated, David, but this Kindness Tax has everyone in a panic. We've had ten clients cancel their contracts just this week."

David couldn't believe his ears. When he decided to resign from the Navy, he never imagined that he wouldn't have a position at Magnum Lock. "When does this take effect?"

"We have a month of contracted work on your books. If you can give us thirty days, that would be great After thirty days, you'll receive a year's severance package and a letter of recommendation. It's the least we can do after your impeccable service. And David, you are the best of the best. The board and I are beyond upset that we must do this, but I have no doubt you will land on your feet."

CHAPTER 23

Shedding the Grave Clothes

Where is God? Sonya's question haunted Maddie over the weeks leading into Thanksgiving. She could see God in nature but struggled to see him in her pain.

After Kaitlyn's death, Maddie's parents scheduled an appointment for all the girls to meet with her counselor, Mr. C. It was an opportunity for them to speak about their shared trauma and hopefully move past their pain. Listening to each of them share reminded her that she wasn't alone in this whole mess.

Asked if she wanted to share what they had been working on in their sessions, Maddie decided to share about radical acceptance. Sonya's story about Elijah helped her see that God wasn't inside the storm, but as the One who controlled the storm, he would also comfort her in her pain. In radical acceptance, Mr. C was teaching her that she was stuck to her pain like glue and couldn't see outside of it to find her healing. Once she stepped out of it, she could acknowledge the trauma that happened to her, including the fear, the worry, and the pain, accept them as they were, and place them in God's hands. "It's weird, but I keep coming back to this place of giving it all to God." Looking at Rachel, she added, "I guess that's where he is."

As the girls left the session, they climbed into Rachel's van. "Mr. C's awesome. Thank you, Maddie," Jade said.

"Yeah, he's helped me a lot."

242

"When he gave us permission to feel, wow, just wow!" Jade said as she placed her hands above her head, signifying that Mr. C blew her mind.

"Did you really have to respond to Mr. C with "that cooks?" Maddie shook her head at the memory.

Emma laughed, saying, "I wish Kaitlyn were here with us."

Rachel leaned on the back of her friend's seat. "Me too. Hey, Emma, what's one memory you have of Kaitlyn?"

"Hm. The sleepover where Kaitlyn made a fort out of blankets and pillows."

"That was so fun! I will never forget the white lights that she hung inside. They reminded me of Christmas morning. Do you remember? I will never forget her stories of the stars," Maddie said.

"Oh, how about the time that she challenged us with starting every sentence with the next letter of the alphabet?" Jade asked.

Crossing her arms, Emma cringed as she said, "That was the worst! I seemed always to get stuck with the X. How do you start a sentence with X, anyway?"

"Xylophonists just wanna have fun!" Jade belted out.

Maddie bust out laughing. "Now, that is something Kate would say."

Suddenly, the van got quiet. After a few moments, Rachel's mom said, "I am thankful you guys have one another. And remember, you'll always have Kate right here." Patting her chest, she smiled into the rearview mirror.

"Yeah, thanks, Mom," Rachel said.

Later that night, Maddie sat alone with her journal. Finding God in her pain was a game changer. Mr. C affirmed their pain was real, but they didn't have to be controlled by it or the emotion it triggered. Writing this down, she followed his lead, recorded a moment when she felt pain, and then wrote down where God was in it. As she drew in the corners of the page, the picture of the tower in her dreams popped into her mind. Opening her Bible to Proverbs 18:10, she read, "The name of the Lord is a strong tower, the righteous run to it and are safe." Yes! Remembering the moment at Charlie's Tree when she realized she could trust God, she felt like God was teaching her about himself one thing at a time. Writing the things she had learned in her journal, she began:

> *God is all around me.*
> *See my trauma, my fear, and my pain in my hand and lay it on the Cross.*
> *I don't have to be afraid.*
> *Faith is not a feeling but a choice.*
> *God walks with me when I walk in faith.*
> *God's got me.*
> *Be still and know that he is God.*
> *I can trust God.*
> *God isn't my pain; he is with me in my pain.*
> *God is my strong tower.*

After the last line, she added a heart at the end. She then began to thank God for all the things she had learned. As she did, she felt like God was sitting right beside her. Looking up, she asked, "Is this the awe and wonder Ms. Bonnie told us about? Grammy was right; a heart full of gratitude can't worry about the future." *Something to add to my list,* she thought as she wrote the word GRATITUDE in all caps.

The following Saturday, Maddie shared her revelation with Sonya. She was thankful for her mentor's willingness to meet and listen to her strange thoughts. While she was close to her dad, she didn't think he would understand any of this.

As they chatted, Sonya asked her what she thought about baptism. It had been over a year since she had said yes to Jesus, and Sonya wondered if she would like to take this next step toward Jesus.

She had seen others baptized but didn't know if she would be asked to do this or if she could do it on her own. "I think so," she said.

"Awesome! I wanted to surprise you, but I'll go ahead and tell you. Jade has decided to get baptized as well. So, you guys get to share in your baptism day."

"No way!" Now, Maddie couldn't wait.

Jade and Maddie sat down with Pastor Derrik separately to discuss baptism. When Maddie sat with him, he asked her to share her testimony. Maddie shared how Jesus helped her through a hard year. She told him about Grammy, Ms. Carolina Wren, and her amazing friends who walked with her. She told him that even when they were at the PKO, she knew Jesus was with her.

When the subject of her friend group came up, Derrik noticed something was off. "Maddie, you didn't say anything about Kaitlyn. How are things?"

Suddenly filled with dread, Maddie had hoped he wouldn't think to ask. Old, familiar feelings churned within her stomach as she hesitated. Looking down at her hands, she focused on her PKO scars. *Am I okay?* She wondered.

Pastor Derrik sat patiently as she processed her feelings. After a few moments, he broke the awkward silence, saying, "It's okay if you don't want to talk about it. But if you do, I'm here."

"No, it's okay. Honestly, I don't know. Just the other day, I thought I had a breakthrough when Ms. Sonya asked where God was when it happened. I was feeling better. But now, I just wish she was here. I wish she could see all this." Looking out the door's window toward the sanctuary, she sighed.

Pastor Derrik paused and asked, "Tell me what you're feeling."

"Sad, angry. . ." Taking a deep breath, she wanted to run out of the room; but she knew this was something she needed to work through. *God, please take away these anxious thoughts,* she prayed silently.

"Those are real and valid feelings, Maddie. Anything else?" He asked.

She shook her head no.

Cocking his head to the right, he looked up and said, "Hm, I think I would feel those things; I would probably also feel confused and maybe a little helpless?"

She looked up at him again as he put words to her confusing thoughts.

"Yeah." she agreed.

"You girls suffered a trauma, Maddie. I can't imagine what that experience must've felt like for you. And the feelings you're having are completely normal. What you're feeling is grief. For every trauma, there is a loss that must be grieved. It's okay to feel sadness and anger."

Maddie looked up nervously, "What if I'm mad at God?"

Derrik chuckled, "He can handle it, just don't hold it in."

The diagonal pattern on the arm of the couch gave her an excellent excuse to keep from looking up. "I'm just ready for it all to be over," Maddie admitted.

"I get it; grief is exhausting, isn't it?" He asked.

She nodded in agreement.

"The truth is, Maddie, that grief is work, and you will feel tired both emotionally and physically. And that is okay. Remember, grief is God's way of relieving the pressure."

Maddie held out her hands and said, "Rachel taught me to put my pain in my hand and lay it at the cross."

Nodding, he said, "That is very wise. Would you like to do that right now?"

"Yes, Sir." Closing their eyes, he led Maddie in a prayer of surrender where she laid down her sadness and her anger. He then prayed peace and healing over her.

After praying, he smiled at her and asked, "You're sixteen, right?"

"Yep."

"Well, you've experienced a lot at your age. I'm impressed with how far you've come." He paused for a moment and then asked, "Do you understand what baptism is?"

"Washing everything bad away?" She asked.

"Well, kinda, but not like a bath. It's so much more. When we say yes to Jesus, we choose to follow him. When Jesus started his ministry, he was baptized by John. He was saying, 'I'm all in to follow God.' For us, baptism is a public declaration of faith that we have placed our lives in the hands of Jesus. The physical action of being dunked under water signifies laying down your old life. We'll call it a shedding of the grave clothes. As you are raised out of the water, you are raised with him into a new life. This is what we call the resurrection. Do you have any questions?" He asked.

"What do you mean by shedding the grave clothes?" Maddie asked.

"That's a good question. Romans 3:23 says, for all have sinned and fall short of the glory of God. When we say yes to Jesus, he forgives us of our sins and imparts his Spirit to transform us into his likeness. Every transformation is like a shedding of the grave clothes—death to sin. Our baptism is a symbol of that shedding. I can take a bath but then need to take another. But, when I was baptized, I was raised to new life. Does that answer your question?"

A new life, she liked the sound of that. "Yes, sir," she answered.

Pastor Derrik smiled and asked, "Good, now, who would you like to baptize you?"

"I get to choose?"

"Absolutely, the great commission calls all believers to baptize."

"Can I ask Sonya?"

"Sure. I did want to mention that Rachel is going to baptize Jade."

Maddie's eyes widened in astonishment. "Wait, students can do it?"

"Sure, why not?"

"Then, I would like to ask Sonya and Rachel if that's okay."

"Great! So, when they baptize you, we'll have one of them read your testimony, and the other will physically dunk you. Talk to Sonya and Rachel, send a copy of your testimony to Sonya and me, and we'll get you signed up for our next baptism."

"Yay! Thank you, Pastor Derrik."

Excited yet nervous, she walked away, wondering what she would write. Rachel shared her testimony of how she met Jesus, how he changed her life, and how she didn't feel hopeless when bad things happened. She had someone to go to when it felt like the world was falling apart. Now, it was time for Maddie to write her own. Confident she had a plan; she added a reminder to her phone and walked toward the lobby to find her friends.

Maddie was so happy to come home to see Grammy and Michael the following Wednesday. They had come into town just so they could join the rest of her family and watch her get baptized.

Just that morning, Maddie prayed, "God, will you draw my parents to you? I want them to know Jesus, too." She didn't hear God say anything, but it felt good to know that perhaps tonight would bring a breakthrough for her whole family.

Wednesday night was a blast. Maddie and her friends worshiped as her family stood beside Rachel's and Jade's parents. Grammy and Matthew clapped their hands while Maddie's parents stood perfectly still. She wondered if she should have said something about the music, but at least they seemed to enjoy some of it.

Jade was baptized first. As Rachel read her testimony, she shared the life of a young woman who had overcome adversity.

Jade's mom wept as Rachel read how much her daughter wanted to know her dad but was blessed with a mom who served as both mom and dad.

When Rachel got to the part of the shooting and the loss of Kaitlyn, she almost broke. Maddie could tell that her friend didn't expect to have to read this part, but Sonya's encouraging hand helped Rachel to go on.

As Jade rose out of the water, Maddie had to smile. She could see joy in the smile that extended from ear to ear. Her friend was a new person, just like Derrik said. She whispered a prayer of Thanksgiving and blessing over her friend as everyone clapped for her.

Maddie was up next, and boy, was she nervous; watching a baptism and participating in one were two different things. As she entered the warm water, Sonya, and Rachel, both gave her a smile of encouragement. *What am I thinking? I'm getting baptized!* she thought.

As Rachel read her testimony, her melodious voice highlighted everything Maddie struggled to write. The enthusiasm she brought to her friend finding faith in the face of fear brought Maddie back to that place of joy when she realized fear no longer had a hold on her.

"Maddie, I have two questions for you," Sonya asked. Have you placed your faith in Jesus Christ as your Lord and Savior?"

Maddie looked at her mentor and smiled, "Yes."

"Do you promise to trust and obey Jesus and follow him all the days of your life?" Sonya asked.

"Yes, I will."

"Then it is my honor, my sister, to baptize you in the name of the Father, Son, and Holy Spirit."

As Maddie went under the water, time seemed to stand still. The water felt like a grave, just as the pastor said. Opening her eyes, she could see above the water, the freedom just on the other side. Colorful lights danced in rainbow colors as she rose. Remembering Pastor Derrik's words about being raised with Christ, Maddie felt one with Jesus for the first time. She no longer had to be everything for everyone; he was with her! Exhilaration filled her as everyone clapped around her.

Stepping out of the tub, Rachel gave her a towel. Suddenly, she and Jade had a mob of girls hugging them. It felt good to be loved, and Maddie couldn't remember the last time they laughed and cried like this.

"That was pretty awesome ma Girl!" Grammy said as they walked into the house.

"Wasn't it? I am so happy you were able to be here, Grammy!" Maddie said as she gave her a big hug.

"Well, all I have to say is the Gaggle is real," Michael teased his sister.

Punching him in the arm, she yelled, "Whatever!" as he ran up the stairs.

"You've come a long way, Maddie Ruth," Grammy said.

"Yes, ma'am."

"Do ya recollect what I tole ya last year 'bout yer name?"

She had forgotten all about the prophecy that surrounded her name. "What was it?" She asked, barely remembering.

Grammy grabbed her arms and looked into her eyes, "You, ma Granddaughter are the little blessed one who'll be a companion ta many. Now, yer first name means high tower, but yer not the high tower, do ya hear?"

Maddie couldn't believe her ears. "What did you say, Grammy?"

"Yer not the high tower, it's almighty God who is yer Tower, but he's gonna use you to draw others ta him."

A wave of relief flooded over her. "Grammy, I love you so much!" Hugging her beloved gram, she kissed her on the cheek and ran upstairs.

Grabbing her journal, she plopped onto her bed and read her dream entries regarding the crowns and the tower. She had an epiphany as she realized the dream and the prophecy were related. She had to walk into the tower! The Tower was God, and she had to run to him. Like Sonya said, 'the righteous run into it and are safe.' Of course! Excitedly writing everything from the night in her book, she drew the tower again and said, "I trust you, God." And with this, she went to sleep.

The garden was especially beautiful. Bright pink flowers cut a path alongside sunflowers shaped like crowns. Walking in the grass, she could feel the soft earth beneath her toes. As she turned a corner, Ms. Carolina Wren flew up beside her, landing on her shoulder. Together, they sang the song the bird had inspired so long ago.

"You knew, didn't you, Ms. Carolina Wren?" She asked after they finished their song. The bird cocked its head curiously and looked at her. As the bird turned its gaze back toward the path, Maddie's gaze followed. There it stood. The Strong Tower she had dreamed about, The One where the righteous run to it and are safe. "This is it, isn't it, Ms. Carolina Wren? I am to meet the Lord here and trust in him?"

As they reached the moat, the bird flew away while singing her song. "You led me here, didn't you?" Stepping onto the drawbridge, she looked around and noticed the people behind her. Looking up, she knew what she had to do. The water underneath was rough and treacherous. Somehow, she knew that she shouldn't look down but up. Suddenly, the bridge began to move. She grabbed the railing and looked up, and the water suddenly became still.

CHAPTER 24

Hope for a Prosperous Future

The last day of school before Christmas was always the best. Tests were over, the break was here, and the promise of a Peppermint latte gave Maddie much to be thankful for. After school, Mom dropped her off at The Coffee Bar to wait for Rachel.

As Maddie looked around the shop, Jackson called hello to her from behind the counter. Happy to see a familiar face, she went over to catch up. Rachel and Jackson had been seeing one another off and on over the last several months, which gave Maddie and her friends a chance to get to know him. She could see what Rachel saw in him: He was kind, loved music, and was a hard worker. These were qualities that Maddie knew her friend appreciated.

"Hi Jackson, what'cha making?"

"I'm trying my hand at a Caramel Macchiato; would you like one?"

"Sure."

Maddie sat at the bar and watched as Jackson carefully poured the espresso to make the mark on top of the foam and then drizzled caramel in the form of a grate on top. One thing she could say about Jackson was that he was intentional and creative.

"Here ya go. Let me know what you think." Jackson pushed the drink over to Maddie and walked back to the sink.

"Hey you." A familiar chin leaned over Maddie's shoulder

252

as she took her first sip. "Whoa, what is that?" Rachel asked.

"A Caramel macchiato, here try it, it's amazing!"

"How long did it take you to draw the top?" Rachel asked as she smiled at Jackson with a perfectly manicured milkstache.

Jackson leaned over the counter and said, "At least ten minutes; you know me. Do you want one?"

"Sure, but let's make it five, okay? Wouldn't want you to be accused of slacking on the job."

Jackson grabbed his heart, "Me? Never!" He shouted with gusto. Maddie and Rachel grabbed a table as Jackson spent the next ten, no five minutes working on Rachel's drink.

Laughing at her friend's gaze, Maddie asked, "When are you going to make it official?"

"What?"

"Your relationship with Jackson."

Staring at the pattern on the table, Rachel replied, "We're just talking."

Maddie laughed; Rachel never could hide her signature blush. "Yeah, ricgggght."

"So, what are your plans for the holidays?" Her friend asked, changing the subject.

"Oh, I see, we're going to play that game, are we? Did I not tell you? We're going to Tennessee. Dad finished his last project and said we're going this weekend."

"That's awesome!" Excited for her friend, Rachel's smile soon turned to a frown of disappointment, "Wait, so, you won't be home for Christmas?"

"Probably not. Dad said we weren't on a schedule, so we could stay as long as we liked. Can you believe it, Rach? I can't remember Dad ever saying that! Even when we went on vacation, he was working."

Jackson placed a perfectly formed drink in front of her and said, "One Caramel Macchiato."

"This is really good," Rachel said as she looked up in awe."

Maddie giggled when the look lasted just a second too long. "Friends," she said under her breath.

After Jackson walked away, Rachel turned back to her like

nothing had happened. "Hey, so did you hear? There was another riot the other day."

Not wanting to talk about it, Maddie murmured, "Mm, hmm," to her drink.

"You know we can't ignore this, right?"

"How about selective memory?" Maddie asked.

"Don't play therapist with me. I overheard Dad telling my mom that nothing will be left of Atlanta if this keeps up. It seems the rioters are trying to burn the city down."

"They're going to jail, though, right?"

"Yeah, but then more come right after them. Hey Maddie, can you keep a secret?"

"Sure."

"Since we lost Kate, I've been overwhelmed by thoughts that something bad might happen."

"Like, what?"

"I don't know but look around us. Dad says we might be in the end times; and I'm beginning to wonder if he's right. I just wish Jesus would come back already."

Maddie didn't know what to say. She had never heard her friend talk like that before, but she wanted to help her in any way she could, so she reached out her hand and said, "Hey, Rach, I love you."

Looking off into the distance, Rachel smiled weakly and said, "I know. Hey, can we talk about something else? I'm sorry, I don't mean to be such a Debbie Downer. Tell me what's going on with you?"

"Well, I keep having these crown dreams. It's almost like God is talking to me through them."

"What do you mean?"

Maddie laid out the sequence of dreams to her friend. "At first, I thought it was all about the crowns, but now I think he is leading me into the tower, but it isn't just me. The last couple of dreams have included other people. You and the girls were in one of them."

"So, everyone is following you?"

So far, just me. But I feel like the Tower is God, and I'm

moving toward him."

"That's cool. What about the other people?"

"It's weird, Rach, but I could swear they were waiting on me."

"That is strange. What do you think is keeping you from crossing?"

"I don't know, but can we pray about it? I need to figure this out."

"Sure, you go ahead, and I'll follow."

After they prayed and finished their drinks, the girls walked around the shop admiring the Christmas décor.

Suddenly, something caught Maddie's eye as she was looking at the jewelry. A small pewter keychain held the words from Matthew 17:20 in a circle: "Faith of a mustard seed." In the middle of the keychain was a little seed. Glancing over at her friend, who looked deep in thought, Maddie grabbed the keychain and quickly took it to Jackson to ring it up. *This is the perfect gift for Rach,* she thought happily.

Walking back to her friend, Maddie asked, "What'd you find?"

With wide eyes, Rachel stood staring intently at a plaque before her.

"Is something wrong?" Maddie asked as she wondered at the inscription of Jeremiah 29:11.

Her gaze stuck, Rachel said, "No, I'm just wondering about our future." With a pained look, she asked, "What good can come in the next year with all the bad things happening around us?"

Maddie didn't know what to do with this discouraged Rachel. Her friend was always encouraging others, but now she seemed to be the one who needed encouragement. "I don't know, Rach, but don't you always tell me to lay it down? Maybe we need to do that and ask God to help us trust him for our future." Placing the gift that she purchased deep in her pocket; she held out her hands.

Rachel hesitated as she looked at her friend.

Did I say the right thing? Maddie wondered. A boldness came over her in that moment as she remembered how the rhythm had helped her. "It's okay, Rach. We can do it together."

David's plans were going awry. He had hoped to persuade Admiral Osborne to begin an investigation into the PKO, but after the hearing, David's former mentor would not give him the time of day.

After Mordecai saw Ambassador Cohen speaking to their impromptu follower from Hillel Street, David attempted to contact the Ambassador, but was unsuccessful. Now, he was unemployed and looking for work. Everything felt like it was falling apart.

As Christmas drew near, he realized he would have to make some hard decisions for his family. Thankfully, Magnum Lock Security provided a hefty severance package to get them through the next year, but David needed to decide his next move. He knew too much about the PKO and could not let this information lie. Desperate times called for desperate measures, so he decided it was time to place a call to an unexpected ally.

After David's hearing, the Senator of Georgia clapped him on the back and told him to give him a ring if he needed anything. Figuring this was a good time to make that call, David picked up the phone.

"Senator Hawke's Office." The young man on the other end of the line couldn't be older than Michael.

"Good afternoon, this is David Bennett. I would like to leave a message for Senator Hawke to return my call," David said.

"Mr. Bennett, Senator Hawke has been waiting for your call. Hold, please."

"Gabe Hawke here."

"Good afternoon, Senator; this is David Bennett."

"Hello David, I was hoping you would call. How are you doing?"

"I'm well, thank you. I was wondering if we could meet?"

"Of course, let me check my calendar. Are you available on Friday? I can meet at The Lunch Spot at eleven."

"Yes, I can be there. Thank you for your time."

David spent two days wondering why the Senator of Georgia would be waiting for his call. Whatever the reason, David was thankful for the Senator's quick response, and eager for their meeting.

Turning into an older shopping center, he looked for a restaurant called The Lunch Spot. He could see it on his GPS but was having trouble locating it. Driving around to the west side of the center, he finally saw a little stand-alone hole-in-the-wall building tucked neatly into the back corner. *Interesting place for a Senator to eat,* he thought.

David was surprised as he walked into the little sandwich shop. It reminded him of a diner from the 1950's, complete with a soda fountain behind the bar. The painted applique on the back concrete wall stopped him in his tracks, "For I know the plans I have for you, declares the Lord, plans to prosper you and not to harm you, plans to give you hope and a future – Jeremiah 29:11." David knew that quote, he read it every time he walked into his mom's kitchen. *Interesting to find it here.* He thought.

"Mr. Bennett, it's good to see you again." Senator Gabriel Hawke interrupted his gaze to shake his hand. The firm handshake matched the intent gaze he threw to David after looking around him to say, "Thank you, Mom."

David was surprised yet again as he noticed a petite older woman locking the door. Raising an eyebrow, he turned to look at the Senator.

"Safest place I know. Mom, meet David Bennett, a hero to our country in every sense of the word. David, meet my mom."

"Pleased to meet you Mrs. Hawke."

"The pleasure is mine. Let me know what y'all want, Gabe.

I'll be in the back."

Sitting at the Senator's booth, David said, "I never would have known this place existed had you not invited me."

"We like to keep a low profile here. My parents have owned this diner for fifty years, and their clientele know them well. They don't advertise, every customer they have is by word of mouth."

"Wow, how do you maintain a low profile in Atlanta?"

The Senator laughed, "We manage."

"I am curious, you mentioned hoping I would call. Why?" David asked curiously.

"I am very interested in what you have to say about the PKO. I've heard much about a certain compound in Baldersville, and I would like your take on it."

"What have you heard?"

"Oh, you know a little here, a little there." Gabe looked David up and down as if to size him up. "Do you know of a group called The Way?"

David laughed as he nodded, "Do you mean Joe and his mighty men?"

"That would be them. Joe's an old friend of the family."

"Really now, do tell."

"I served with him in Vietnam."

David paused, remembering that Joe met his dad shortly after being released from the Navy. "You wouldn't happen to have met George Bennett, would you?"

"Not only did I meet him, but I know him well. Your dad was quite the man. Joe introduced him to me shortly before I ran for my first term as councilman."

"So that would make you…"

Chuckling, Gabe asked, "Are you trying to figure my age?"

"I was more interested in your mom's age."

The burst of laughter nearly shook the place. "Hey, Mom, David wants to know how old you are!"

"Now, Gabe, we proper women don't speak of such things," Mrs. Hawke replied with a twinkle in her eye. "But for you, Mr. Bennett, I'll be eighty-six next week."

"Wow, eighty-six years old? You don't look a day over sixty."

The boisterous hoot from the "proper lady" standing in the kitchen doorway with an apron and a hairnet nearly knocked David out of his seat.

After ordering two sandwich plates, David and Gabe spent the next hour sharing what they knew about the PKO. David went on to share the information he had received from Michael, with the understanding that it was all conjecture. He had no physical proof of any of it.

"This is all very interesting, David. Thank you for taking the time to share it with me. So, what are your next steps?" Gabe asked.

"Well, I was released from my job a month ago, so I am officially unemployed."

"Oh, I am sorry. Do you have any prospects? I can investigate some opportunities for you."

"Thank you for the offer, but I have some ideas. First, I must figure out the safest place for my family."

"I understand. Do you plan to leave Atlanta?"

"Yes, I just need to find a way to keep Maddie's friends and families safe in the process. A colleague of mine and I are working on it."

"That sounds like a good plan. David, you mentioned concern about the PKO at your hearing. One of the main reasons I wanted to meet was the testimony of the Deputy Director. He really played you off to be a cowboy in the wild west, but based on my investigation of your service history, that is furthest from the truth. Did he lie?"

Sitting back in the booth, David considered his next response. A man of integrity, David was unafraid to speak the truth, but he was curious about the intent behind the question and the knowledge of the man behind it. "Before I answer your question, I have one of my own, if you don't mind. At the hearing, you asked if it occurred to me that finding my daughter may not have been an accident at all. Do you recall this statement?"

The Senator leaned forward, looked David straight in the eye, and said, "Yes, I remember."

"Do you have intel that would lead me to believe that none of this was an accident?"

"Just a hunch, honestly. Experience tells me there are no coincidences, yet your story places you and your family in the wrong place at the wrong time much too often. Whenever I listen to the testimony, I look for the common denominator, and David, you are it. It seems to me that you've been lured into a spider's web for some reason. So, my question is, are you the cowboy the Deputy Director made you out to be?"

"Every decision I have ever made has been with the knowledge that my family and my country's freedom hung in the balance. You said it yourself I was a highly decorated Naval Commander; a man doesn't get to that level impulsively."

"Yes, I agree, and what should have been said in that room was that your impeccable service record speaks for itself. So, I ask again, why would the Deputy Director say otherwise? Was there conflict during the investigation?"

"No, Sir. I've known Dan for a long time. We've worked together on several cases. He is the one who called me in for the job and briefed me on the facts of the case. He told me a foreign terrorist organization was suspected, and he even referred to the Nazi party."

"Well, that's strange."

"I was certain that a ruse was at hand. Whomever was guilty of sending the communications was covering for something else, I just couldn't put my finger on it."

"Well, your team did an excellent job of uncovering a potential global coup. The United States of America is forever in your debt."

"I must wonder, Senator, what if this was all a ruse? "What if someone deliberately provoked an international incident so they could be the ones to resolve it?"

"And in comes Lucien Baldur promising the world a prosperous future as he rides in on a white horse."

"Exactly."

"If that was the case, is it possible that Daniel Reese is in on it?"

"Are we on the record?"

"No."

"Then I would say that yes, it is possible. Now that I look back on it, Daniel mentioned that tension in Israel was rising and that he had to send his wife home. I should also mention that Mordecai Oronoff saw Ambassador Cohen speaking to a man who was seen chasing us through town last year. I thought it weird at the time, but now, I wonder."

"Well, it's time we open an inquiry into Deputy Reese and Ambassador Cohen. I am also interested in the PKO; however, with the fiasco of this Kindness Contribution, Washington has become a disordered mess, so I'll have to work covertly."

"Let me know if you need help," David said.

Gabe chuckled, "Be careful what you offer."

"Speaking of this new tax, how exactly is this supposed to work?"

"The PKO becomes an instrumentality of the federal government—an independent, non-governmental agency, but the government backs its actions because it provides a public service. Like Fannie Mae or the American Red Cross. In the case of the PKO, retailers will add a ten percent surcharge to every dollar of food sold; the money will be collected federally and then dispensed to the local PKO organization."

"And Congress agreed to this?"

"Yes, in fact, congress passed this bill with bipartisan approval. I have never seen a bill pass this smoothly."

"Perhaps there needs to be an inquiry of Lucien Baldur."

"I've tried, but nobody wants to go there."

"Why?"

"I couldn't tell you even if I knew. But he has developed a following unlike anything I've seen. And he has the world wrapped around his finger."

CHAPTER 25

Worth Fighting For

As she sat on her bed packing, a question asked a year ago as part of a school project weighed heavily on Maddie's heart. *What are you willing to fight for?*

Folding the last shirt into her suitcase, Maddie glimpsed the keychain she had purchased for Rachel. Holding it in her hand, she focused on the words, "Faith of a mustard seed." The actual mustard seed in the middle was so cool. She had no idea they even existed, but when researching them, she learned that the tiny seed grew to be a large leafy tree.

A year ago, her Grammy told her, "Ya only need faith as big as a mustard seed." She called this a promise that such a little faith could grow into a beautiful tree within the garden of our hearts. "A garden," she said, "has ta be tilled, planted, watered, weeded, and harvested. And let me tell ya, the Gardener ain't lackin' fer work in this here heart. But ya know what. Somethin' amazin' happens when my faith is feelin' a might puny. He plants another right'chere and says, Gracie, if ya need a little faith, borra some a' theirs. In the gardenin' world, that's called companion plantin', but in faith, that's called standin' in the gap. And that faith, my Girl, well, that's worth fightin' fer."

Smiling at the memory, she knew Grammy would tell her to share her faith with her friend. So, with the keychain in hand, Maddie ran downstairs to the kitchen. "Hey, Mom, do you have a gift box?"

"In the back closet," Jacque said as she returned to her project.

After grabbing the box, Maddie sat at the kitchen island to write a card and wrap the little gift. Chewing on the edge of her pen as she thought of what to write, she noticed her mom putting together a Christmas wreath. "Who's that for, Mom?"

"I have a client who hired me to make a wreath for them; isn't it beautiful?"

"It is. Mom, you're so creative."

"I know, and it's so much fun! I've wondered if I need to concentrate on one thing, but I love it all. Bringing a client's dream to life is very rewarding."

"So, are you going to start your own company?" Maddie asked.

Jacque looked up and smiled, "I'm thinking about it."

"What would you call it?" Maddie asked.

"Hmm, that's a good question. I'll have to think about it." Turning to wrap a piece of holly through the wreath, she asked, "What are you doing?"

"I'm running to Rachel's for a couple of hours. I want to give her the Christmas gift I bought for her before we leave for Tennessee," Maddie replied.

"That's a good idea. Dinner is at 6:30, be home before then."

"Yes, ma'am."

After she finished writing her note, Maddie left for Rachel's. She was so grateful to live close to her best friend. Walking down the street, she noticed several houses going up for sale. That's strange. There seemed to be a lot of people moving lately. As she wondered what it would be like to have neighbors she didn't know, Maddie walked up her friend's driveway and made her way up the stairs.

Opening the door, Rachel greeted her friend with a big smile. "Hey, BFF! I saw you coming up the way. I thought you were getting ready for your trip?"

"I wanted to see you before I left." Maddie followed her friend into a beautiful Christmas mess.

"You're just in time; we're wrapping gifts," Rachel said.

"Maddie!" A flurry of blonde curls and child-like energy ran into the living room.

Maddie twirled her around as her friend's sister jumped in her arms. "Hannah! Wow, you've grown!"

"Look!" Sticking her tongue through her two missing front teeth, Hannah smiled from ear to ear.

"Well, I'm impressed. Did you pull them out all by yourself?"

"Nope, Daddy did! And I didn't cry once."

Maddie bopped Hannah's nose, "I am very proud of you." Setting her down, she sat on the floor next to her friend.

Rachel gave Maddie a rectangular box as her mom walked into the room.

"Hi Maddie. Would you like something to drink?"

"Thank you, Ms. Olivia, I'm good."

"We've got hot chocolate," she pressed.

"With marthmallows!" Hannah lisped from the kitchen.

"Okay, I'll take one hot chocolate with a marthmallow," Maddie said loudly so little Hannah could hear.

Rachel giggled at the exchange and then pointed to the present.

The wrapping was exquisite, with a unique red bow on top. Rachel didn't believe in buying pre-made bows, she loved giving gifts so much that he had to manually tie the bow herself.

"It's so pretty, I'm not sure I want to open it," Maddie said.

"It's fine, I'll make a hundred just like it. Open it!" Rachel said as she clapped her hands.

Tearing the paper gently, Maddie opened the box to find a beautiful burgundy leather Bible.

"Rachel!" She exclaimed.

"I love my study Bible and wanted you to have one too. There are a lot of good notes at the bottom, along with scriptures you can use for study. It really helps me to go deeper."

Opening the front cover, she read the dedication inside.

"To Maddie, Psalm 144:1-2. Father, please train my sister for her calling."

Navigating to the middle of the book to find the referenced scripture, she read the verses, "Praise be to the Lord my Rock, who trains my hands for war, my fingers for battle." Maddie ran her finger across the highlighted words Ms. Lorna shared with them over the Summer. Holding the Bible to her chest, she looked at her friend and exclaimed, "I love it!"

Remembering the gift she had brought, she picked up the little box she had neatly wrapped and handed it to her friend. She hoped she would like it.

Rachel opened the card first. "I know how much you love words, so I'm going to read this first, okay?"

Blushing, Maddie said, "Yes, of course."

As she read the card, Rachel's countenance fell. The note included Maddie's thankfulness for her friend and all she had taught her. She wrote a prayer to God thanking him for delivering her from fear and using her friend to show her the way. A tear settled on Rachel's cheek as she opened the little gift box. Pulling out the keychain, she read the verse. "Whoa, is this real?" she asked.

"Yes! Did you know that little seed grows to be a big tree?"

Rachel chuckled, "Yeah, my dad told me that once."

"Rach, you taught me that God was faithful. You told me that he would never let me down. Do you remember?"

Looking down at the pewter keychain, Rachel nodded.

"You were the one who told me that I had to give all my anger over my mom to him. That has helped me so much." Pulling a rock out of her pocket, she extended both hands before her. "Do you remember the rocks?"

"I remember Jackson giving us a whole vase full of them."

Maddie laughed at the memory. "Well, now it's your turn. Can you name the rocks you're holding onto?"

Taking a deep breath, Rachel held out her hands and closed her eyes. Maddie joined her by closing her eyes while waiting for her friend to take the next step.

Suddenly, Rachel spoke softly, "Anger, fear, worry, doubt."

Her voice broke with the last word.

Maddie opened her eyes to see her friend quietly crying. She wasn't sure what to do except to let her friend know she wasn't alone.

"I have never doubted God, ever. Even when Hannah almost died, I knew God would be faithful. But when we lost Kaitlyn. . . You have no idea how often I prayed for Kaitlyn to find Jesus."

"But Rach, what if God did save her?"

With a half-hearted smile, Rachel nodded. "I lied to you, Maddie."

"What do you mean?"

"I don't know if I can say that God will never disappoint you. I mean, look at what happened to Hazel, your mom, us, Kaitlyn," Rachel trailed off as she played with a piece of ribbon.

"You didn't lie to me, Rachel. If I'm learning one thing about this faith, it's that we trust God to be with us when things happen, right? Hey, do you know that verse Sonya had me memorize? She told me something that didn't make sense at first, but I think I'm starting to understand what it means."

Rachel looked at her friend curiously.

"The verse says, 'The name of the Lord is a strong tower; the righteous run to it and are safe.' I couldn't understand how God's name was a tower, but I think it means that when we call on his name, we are safe because he is our protection."

"I know all of this, but we weren't protected."

"But we were! I know it sounds weird; Sonya had to tell me this too. But every moment God was with us, right? While we prayed, as the paramedics worked on Kaitlyn, even when we found out she was dead, God was with us."

Holding the keychain in her hand, Rachel squeezed tightly. "Thank you."

Maddie smiled. She loved her best friend so much and wanted her to find the peace she had helped her find. "When Grammy told me about the mustard seed, she said we could borrow faith from each other. Did you know that?"

Looking up, Rachel shook her head.

"She said that sometimes God plants us next to each other to hold us up." Playing with the bow on her gift box, Maddie added, "Well, I guess that's what you've done for me anyway, and I'd like to do that for you."

"I always knew you'd be an intercessor," Rachel said candidly.

Tilting her head quizzically, Maddie asked, "What's an intercessor?"

"It's a prayer warrior. Someone who intervenes for somebody else. Go read the story of Moses, Aaron, and Hur, you'll see what I mean."

Shrugging, Maddie answered, "I don't know about all that, but I think I can finally answer what's worth fighting for, Rach. It's faith and friendship. When I was struggling, you helped me find faith; now I can help you."

WILD ROCK, TENNESSEE

David was glad to be home as he inhaled deeply of the cold Tennessee air. He wasn't too keen for his mom to know, but for David, Wild Rock was home. And he felt like he could breathe for the first time in a long while.

The year had been a whirlwind. It was time to relax and enjoy his family for a moment.

When Jacque insisted on the trip, David wasn't sure. There seemed to be so many unknowns about their future, but she was adamant that the Bennett's needed a break.

As he pondered the drama they had left behind, David recalled the conversation he had with the Senator of Georgia. Finally, someone was taking an interest in their case and for that, David was grateful.

Looking up at the star-filled sky, he realized he was beginning to lose faith in the country he loved dearly. It seemed everywhere he turned, evil was winning. To hear his mom and Mordecai tell it, there was some cosmic spiritual battle around them, but David only saw greed and complacency, not to mention unsettling precursors to war.

While The Kindness Tax may have received bi-partisan approval in congress, it divided the country into factions.

There were establishments that wanted no part of the distribution. Small mom-and-pop grocery stores just couldn't afford the up-front expense required due to all the paperwork and government intrusion.

Low-income workers, already struggling from crushing inflation, were protesting the extra ten percent they were expected to give.

Then, there was the other side of the coin. Greed was fickle and ugly, and those in her clutches were coming out of the woodwork. As news of the tax spread, people looking for a handout were on the doorstep of every PKO establishment. The media had a field day with everyone they were "helping." It made David sick to his stomach.

A group of Pastors called this an apocalyptic tax; they called it the beginning of the end.

Then, there were the law-abiding citizens who felt like the PKO was serving the community. If they only knew, he thought.

David thought it interesting that the US wasn't alone in this divide. Nations all over the world were realizing the cracks in their systems as this forced taxation took effect.

How did we get here? He wondered. *Senator Hawke felt Lucien Baldur had the world wrapped around his finger, but how?* It was David's experience that things like this didn't just happen, yet this did. An old quote by Robert Greene nagged at him, *"Hasty climbers have sudden falls."* With the haste in which the world was moving at Lucien Baldur's beck and call, David could see a nasty fall coming. *Hmm, it's not too much different from the fall of Rome.* He contemplated.

Surprised by the vibration in his pocket, David pulled out his phone and said, "Hello?"

"David, shalom, my Friend!"

"Hello, Mordy. It's been a long time since we talked. How

is the Mediterranean?" Mordecai was on an extended holiday, as he called it.

"Bluer than the bluest sapphire. Truly, David, you and your family must join us on a cruise."

"Jacque would love that," David replied.

"Then it's settled! We will plan a date."

"Whoa, wait a minute now. Jacque would love it, but we have quite a lot happening here. I would need to figure some things out first."

"Speaking of figuring things out. I understand you have some friends in high places," Mordecai said.

"What do you mean?" David asked.

"Have you not heard? Ambassador Cohen and Deputy Director Daniel Reese have been relieved from duty at the US Embassy in Israel."

David couldn't believe he didn't know this; he was losing his touch. "When did this happen?" he asked.

"Just yesterday, my friend. A certain representative of Georgia, Gabriel Hawke, headed up a US task force that worked with the Israeli government and found evidence of espionage. They have both been detained pending an investigation."

Stunned, David asked, "I don't understand; what did they steal?"

"You will never guess," Mordy teased. "Do you remember Lucien Baldur's ask of you?"

David didn't like where this was going. "Yes, but he never actually asked me for anything."

"Our Israeli Technology Team has been working on a highly sensitive project. I was under specific orders not to divulge the name, but I can share it now that this news has leaked. David, I believe he planned to get you to steal secret intel for Project Manna."

"What is that?"

"Project Manna is a digitized financial system that Israel is building to eliminate credit cards and ease the flow of electronic transactions."

"How were the Ambassador and Deputy Director exposed?"

Mordecai chucked, "It's quite ironic, really. This Senator Hawke called in looking for information on you. A request was made for all emails within a certain timeframe. Through an internal review, emails were found that leaked the trade secret. The Senator sent in a task force to investigate every email the two had sent over the last two years. That is when the coup was discovered."

"Was there any evidence of Lucien Baldur's involvement?" David asked.

"Not that I have heard, no. And neither the Ambassador nor the Deputy Director are willing to give up their accomplice."

"Then why do you think he was involved?"

"Who else could it be? Just think about it, my Friend. Israel is the only country in the WTO that refuses to have anything to do with this tax. It only seems logical that to involve them, he would hold their technology ransom while dangling it for global use to the highest bidder. Now, if you planned to hold the world by their purse strings, what would you use to control them?"

"So why would he want me? Why wouldn't he have used the Ambassador and deputy director from the beginning?"

"Your reputation precedes you, my Friend. He knows that you will stop at nothing to solve a problem. I expect he knew your hacking skills were worth fighting for."

CHAPTER 26

Hunting for Treasure

Joy filled Maddie and her brother as they enjoyed the colorful lights adorning Main Street. Holding the door to the café open for Matthew and Grammy, she gazed in awe at the decorations adorning the window. She couldn't believe she was in Wild Rock for Christmas!

The ambiance immediately reminded her of The Coffee Bar. *Are all coffee shops the same?* She wondered as the robust aroma of coffee beans danced around her. Maddie watched as Grammy engaged with the barista over her festive smock. Smiling over her Gram's attention to detail, she walked around, looking at the handwritten notes on the wall. *This is different,* she thought. Her love for words drew her to each message of hope and encouragement. One such message stopped her as she leaned in to read it.

> *"I was so lost, and then I met Jesus. He set me free from fear, anxiety, depression, and suicidal thoughts. I hope that you, too, will find your hope in him. Call on him today; he is waiting."*

"Hey Grammy, look at this," Maddie called out. After placing their order, Grammy walked over and read the note. Smiling, she gave her granddaughter a hug. "God is good, ain't he?"

"Yes, ma'am. Grammy, can we pray for this person?"

"Why a'course! Matthew, come 'ere Boy." Matthew walked over, and the three held hands as they interceded for the person in the letter.

Sitting down to their coffee and hot chocolate, Grammy asked, "Maddie Ruth, how'r ya doin' with yer readin'?"

"Good. Sonya has me reading a Psalm and a Proverb a day."

"That's a good combination. What'cha ya learnin'?"

"David prayed A LOT."

"Yes, ma'am, he did. I like ta think he showed us how ta do it."

"When Rachel was here, Ms. Lorna told us about David being a man after God's heart. Do you remember that?"

"I shore do."

"I've been studying what it means to be a woman after God's heart."

"And what'd ya learn?"

"It's all about trust, right?"

"Oh, and David gave God his all!" Matthew interjected.

"That's right, Boy, good job! But I'd say yer only tellin' part a the story. R'member, David was a lil' shepherd boy left by 'imself to hunt while his brothers went off ta war. The Lord was his ev'rthin'. I 'spect faith and trust were built in those lonely moments with the Lord."

"Sonya said that David showed us what it was like to be with God."

"He shore did. The Psalms is full a David's musin's. I like ta think ole David shows us what it's like to seek the good Lord's presence in love and worship. He teaches me a thang or two."

Pausing to collect her thoughts, Maddie said, "Grammy, I feel God with me when I worship and when I see Ms. Carolina Wren. I feel like he sends her to me when I need him. But I don't know how to seek his presence."

"Well, Girl, that's somethin' ya can start today. Thar's a scripture in Psalm 46:10 that tells us ta be still and know that he is God. It starts right thar."

Maddie remembered that verse from Ms. Bonnie's class.

"What does it mean to be still? Is that looking at nature?"

"God created nature, so that's part of it, but Maddie, ya walk with God all day ever' day, bein' still is knowin' it."

"Wait, so God is with me at school?" Matthew asked.

"Yes sirree, he shore is."

"Whoa. I guess I better finish my homework." Matthew mumbled to himself.

"Maddie Ruth, I've got a challenge fer ya. I want'cha ta take that fancy phone a yers and search fer the words seek the Lord. Write down what ya find, and let's talk 'bout it."

The more she read the Bible, Maddie felt as if she was on a hunt for hidden treasure. There was SO MUCH to learn! She wished she had verses memorized like Grammy and Sonya did. Scripture just seemed to roll off their tongues.

Wearing her warmest PJs, Maddie walked on the back deck with a blanket, a cup of coffee, her Bible, and her journal. Pulling out her phone, she opened the Bible app and searched, 'Seek the Lord.' Intentionally gazing at Grammy's backyard, she prayed, "God, where are you?"

Being very still, Maddie watched as her breath formed ice crystals before her. Even though it was cold outside, birds sang their song as they flew from tree to tree. Dad said the air was so thick that it might snow. *How cool would it be if it snowed on Christmas?* She wondered.

As she focused back on the scriptures she found, the first thing she noticed was how many verses there were! *I don't know if I can write down all of these!* She thought to herself. Sticking to those relevant to being still, she first focused on First Chronicles 16:10, *"Glory in his holy name; let the hearts of those who seek the Lord rejoice."* Drilling into the chapter in Chronicles, she read how David called the people to praise the Lord, proclaim his name, sing to him, tell of all he had done, and always seek his face.

After reading ten verses, Maddie wondered if God wanted

to be found. The last verse stuck out to her. Below the verse, she drew a heart and wrote, "God, what does it look like to seek you with all my heart?"

"Why good mornin' to ya, Maddie Ruth."

"Good morning, Grammy."

"It's a bit chilly out here, ain't it? Are ya warm enough?"

Pulling her blanket out, Maddie answered, "Yes, ma'am. I brought a blanket."

"Alrighty then, well enjoy yer study. Don't stay out here too much longer, else you'll get frostbit."

After Grammy returned to the house, Maddie picked up her cup and looked at the landscape. Suddenly, a gentle breeze caused the trees before her to sway. The motion was mesmerizing. There was something about the wind that seemed to speak to her. Inhaling the cold mountain air, Maddie asked, "Is that you, God?" The wind seemed to blow much more, and then it stopped just like that. Her fingers began feeling numb, but this didn't stop her as she searched for wind in her Bible app. Coming across a verse in John 3:8, she read, "The wind blows wherever it pleases. You hear its sound, but you cannot tell where it comes from or where it is going. So, it is with everyone born of the Spirit." Clicking the bubble to read the note below, she read, "The Greek for Spirit is the same as that for wind." *Whoa!* She exclaimed.

"Hey Grammy!" She called out as she ran into the kitchen. Feeling the warmth from the oven, Maddie walked over to warm her cold hands.

"What'cha goin' on 'bout?" Grammy asked as she walked in from the living room.

"I just noticed the wind blowing the trees outside. I looked up the word wind in the Bible app and found a verse that says that the Greek for Spirit is the same as wind. Was that God in the trees?"

Grammy smiled as she asked, "What'cha thinkin'?"

"Well, if God is everywhere, maybe it was him?"

"Ta be clear, God is not the wind; he made and controls the wind. But his Spirit is like the wind. Often, his Spirit moves, and what we think is the wind is truly him."

"How do you know the difference?"

Grammy chuckled, "Oh, Girl, you'll knowed. God's Spirit changes ever'thin'. The whole atmosphere is filled with his glory."

"His Spirit is in me, right?"

"Yes, ma'am."

"When reading the verses about seeking God, I read a lot that said to seek him with all my heart. What does that look like?"

"Well, what did the wind look like?"

Confused, Maddie hesitated. Then she said, "It was moving the trees."

"What did it touch?"

"Everything, I guess."

"When ya seek the Lord with all yer heart, yer lettin' his Spirit get in there and touch ever'thin. Jes' like nothin' can hide from the wind; nothin' can hide from his Spirit. But ya gotta give it all to 'im first. Love the Lord with ALL yer heart, soul, mind and strength, Jesus said."

"But what about my family? If I love God with all my heart, how can I love them?"

Grammy chuckled. "I love you, Maddie Ruth, do ya know that?"

Maddie nodded.

"How do ya think I can do that?" Grammy asked.

Uncertain, she asked, "God?"

"You betcha." She placed her hands in front of her granddaughter and said, "If I place my whole heart in my hands and give it ta the Lord, he gives it back ta me filled with all I need ta love you and ever'body else he gives me. But if I try ta add a whole bunch of stuff in thar thinkin' I can love ya better than he can, then thar ain't much room left fer him to work. R'member, love is a fruit a his Spirit; it's unconditional, and the only love that lasts."

◆ ◆ ◆

That afternoon, Grammy took her granddaughter out for what she called a Dog Day. Walking the long trail, Maddie was winded as they walked and talked, while Grammy, with her walking stick, treated it like a jaunt in the park.

"Grammy, where are we going?" Maddie asked. "I don't remember walking back here before."

"'Tis a special place. One I've been a might selfish with if I'm honest. The Lord showed me this little treasure not long after George and I moved here, and I just haven't wanted ta share it with anyone but him."

Excited to see this special place, Maddie worked to keep up with her Grammy. *Where does she get all this energy,* she wondered?

At the end of the trail, Grammy stopped.

Maddie's breath left her lungs as soon as she breathed it in. The scene before her was like a perfectly painted postcard. What looked to be a large boulder led out to the edge of a cliff overlooking a beautiful valley covered with low-hanging clouds. Snow-capped mountains in the distance whispered a promise of Christmas snow that Maddie could only wish for. "Whoa." Maddie didn't know what else to say.

"Ain't it beautiful?"

"It's amazing! I can't believe we've never come here."

Grammy laughed. "Yep, hidden treasure I only wanted ta share with Jesus."

"How often do you come here?"

"At least once a week in the wintertime, but I try ta come ever' day when blackberry winter sets in. Ya should see it in the springtime, Maddie Ruth. The flo'ers pop out like fireflies in the most beautiful arrangement Father God could bring. I'll never ferget the first time Grandpa George brought me out here. He said, 'Gracey, this here is God's country. His glory is all 'round us.'"

"So, is this where you come to be still?"

"It's one of them places, yes, but r'member Love, God is ever'where. To be still is to know. But in this place, ya'd be a plumb fool not to know it. So, when I need a reminder, I come here—hence ma Dog Day."

"Why do you call it a dog day?" Maddie asked.

"Ya know how Max likes ta sit at ma feet? Well, this is me sittin' at the feet a the Father. It's a day I get right with the Lord. I come and sit in his presence, and I jes' listen. I open his word, and I listen. After a time, I'll talk to 'im. But first, I wanna hear his voice."

"Wait, so you come out here every day just to hear his voice?"

"It's in the quiet; I hear it most. Maddie Ruth, if ya wanna hear the voice of the Lord, ya gotta let go of them distractions. That's what God tole' ole Elijah on Mount Horeb. He wasn't in the storm, the fire, or the earthquake. He was the gentle whisper that came after. Do ya know what that means?"

"What?"

"Ya gotta listen if ya wanna hear the whisper a God. Take yer eyes off all the thangs goin' on in yer world and put 'em on Jesus. Now, let's set fer a moment." Grammy walked Maddie over to a bench just off the boulder's side. Pulling a Bible out of her deep pocket, she opened to a page that was crinkled and well-read. Illegible scribble took up the margin of most of the page, while highlights drew the eye to what appeared to be most important to its owner. Closing her eyes, she moved her lips while taking a deep breath in and out. Opening her eyes, she gave the Bible to Maddie and said, "Read this here."

Maddie read aloud from Psalm 23—A Psalm of David. Her imagination provided a vision of green pastures, quiet waters, and well-manicured paths as she read. The valley before her promised a place where she was safe with the One who comforted her, and she could almost see a table prepared before her. "I will dwell in the house of the Lord forever." After reading the last of the passage, she copied her Gram and breathed in the cool air.

After a few moments, she looked at Grammy and asked, "What just happened?"

Wiping a tear from her eye, Grammy said, "You just heard from the Lord, my Love."

"It was like I was there."

"When ya draw near to the Lord, yer spirit man knows yer in his presence."

"Grammy?"

Grabbing Maddie's hand, she said, "Yes."

"When I pray, I feel like I'm always asking for stuff. But when David prays, it's like he's talking to God. I mean, I talk to God, but it's like their best friends."

Chuckling, Grammy said, "Yep."

"Is that what prayer is?"

Grammy opened her hands wide as she looked up at the sky. "Prayer is sittin' in the presence of El Shaddai, Almighty God, acknowledgin' who he is and who ya are in him. It's surrender, dependence, and trust. Prayer is a relationship. It's takin' yer friends and family ta the Cross, knowin' that Jesus has the answer ta all their woes." Taking a deep breath, she lowered her hands and looked at Maddie, "Now, the love I have fer you, Maddie Ruth, is nothin' compared ta his great love, and when ya seek 'im, you'll find that love, but more. David sought after God's heart, 'cause he knew God was in control and he was faithful."

"When I was reading about David seeking God, I noticed he told the people to do it in different ways. Are there multiple ways to pray?"

"Yes, ma'am. But Jesus did show us how ta pray in the Lord's prayer. Open the Good Book ta Matthew chapter six."

Maddie navigated to the chapter and read verses nine through thirteen. "Do you pray this every day?" She asked.

"Maddie Ruth, the Word a God is alive and active. When ya speak it, ya give it life from yer mouth. Now, I love to pray the scriptures back to God, and I foller Jesus' lead. I want ta pray like ma Rabbi."

Confused, Maddie asked, "Rabbi?"

"Yer bumfuzzled now, ain't ya?" Grammy asked with a twinkle in her eye. He's ma Teacher, Jesus. He's the One who taught us ta pray, ain't he? So, I pray like him. Maddie Ruth, sometimes I jes' wanna praise 'im. Then thar's deep feelin' prayers like the one he prayed in the garden; those are called travailin' prayers, mind ya, cause yer birthin' somethin' like a baby. Other times, I'm thankin' him for all my blessin's. Then thar's the time I ask him to move, to do what only he can do, declarin' the word as I go. Never ferget; what's impossible with man is possible with God. But" with her finger pointed up, she looked into her granddaughter's eyes seriously and said, "I'm always givin' him the honor he's due."

"Grammy, when Mike was missing, I heard you praying for him and my dad." Suddenly embarrassed, she blushed and said, "Sorry about that."

Stunned, Grammy asked, "What'cha sorry fer? I ain't hidin' nothin'."

"Well, you were on your knees, crying." Maddie shrugged as she looked at the ground, "I guess I thought it was private, and I shouldn't have seen it."

Laying her hand on her granddaughter's knee, Grammy said, "Girl, the Lord calls us to pray in the inner room, but that don't mean nobody can hear our prayer. I 'spect he wanted you thar. What'd ya see?"

"You were on your face crying. I was worried you were afraid, but then I heard you speaking promises. I've never heard anyone pray like that. And then Michael came home." Looking at her Gram quizzically, she asked, "It's like God answered your prayer, but Grammy, how did you know what to pray for?"

Taking the Bible from her granddaughter, Grammy held it up and said, "Them promises are in this book, Maddie Ruth. I jes' said 'em back to the One who spoke 'em in the first place."

"You and Sonya know so many verses. It took me a month to memorize one. How do you do it?" Maddie asked.

"It starts by openin' the book and readin'." Placing her hand on her heart, Grammy said, "The Lord says he'll write his word on yer heart. He also says ta ask, and you shall receive. So, if ya wanna learn his promises, ask 'im. Then open his book to hear his voice and speak the promises out loud."

"How do we know which promises we can ask for?"

"That's a mighty good question, Girl. When ya read a promise, ya read the scripture 'round it. You'll see if God is speakin' to a specific person or if he's speakin' to ever'one. But even if he's speakin' to someone specific, we can take comfort from knowin' he's faithful. Ya know the scripture I have in ma kitchen 'bout the plans God has ta give hope an a future?"

Maddie nodded.

"He gave that promise in Jeremiah ta Israel, but I can find peace in it too, even if I cain't claim it specifically."

"So, what is a promise we can claim?" Maddie asked.

"Well, do ya know the scripture that promises his peace?"

Remembering Sonya sharing something like that when she told her about Ms. Lorna's painting, she asked, "Something about lifting my requests?"

"Yes, ma'am. Take a gander at Philippians. Four, I think it is."

Maddie opened Grammy's Bible to Philippians four and looked until she found verses six and seven. After reading, she asked, "So, we can claim this promise?"

"Ya shore can. Let's do it now." Finding a patch of grass, she leaned on her walking stick and slowly bent to her knees. She then closed her eyes and spread her hands out wide.

Maddie knelt and did the same. Following her lead, she praised God for his holiness and his goodness. They both lifted the requests deep in their heart and asked for forgiveness and help to forgive. Grammy asked for protection around her family and then finished by surrendering it all to the Lord. She grabbed her granddaughter's hand and asked for God's peace to surround them in Jesus' Name.

As they opened their eyes, the clouds had cleared like a curtain, revealing a bright blue sky above them. The winter sun shone brightly over the snow-covered mountain, showering the valley with light. As they were praying, Maddie noticed a warmth spread from her belly to the top of her head. Turning to her gram, she said, "That was…" She couldn't communicate what she was feeling.

Grammy looked at her granddaughter and smiled, "Nothin'

like sittin' with the Lord, Maddie Ruth. Now, help me up and give me ma walkin' stick. We gotta git a'fore the sun goes down."

After speaking to Mordecai Oronoff, David spent Sunday morning researching the investigation into Ambassador Cohen and Deputy Director Daniel Reese. The charges of espionage were severe, carrying a maximum prison sentence of ten years. They were also charged with the scheme to conceal, which carried another five.

Shaking his head, David couldn't imagine what Dan's wife Cindy and their children were going through. Dan told him they were considering returning to the States, so hopefully, they were spared the drama of his arrest, but he worried for them, nonetheless.

David and Dan went way back to the academy. When David began working as a cryptologist, Dan went the way of communications. Their paths seemed to cross every two years or so when a data breach was suspected.

Thinking back to his hearing, he still could not believe Dan's testimony. If anyone should know the high degree of integrity that David practiced in his work, it would be him, but he played it off as if David was somehow impulsive and even worse, untrustworthy.

As he recalled, the Ambassador was relieved with the intel provided. *"Israel is grateful for your thorough investigation,"* he said. Yet, David was forced to resign, and the Ambassador was arrested. *None of this makes any sense,* he thought. Unless Mordecai was somehow correct, and Lucien Baldur wanted him. But why? Hackers were a dime a dozen nowadays, but clearly, there was something about David that Lucien felt he needed.

CHAPTER 27

The Theory of Conspiracy

The white tower Maddie had seen in her dreams stood before her in the distance. A strong desire to see inside this time motivated her through a mire of mud and brush. While she felt tired, she knew deep down that what was inside that tower was worth every step, but she couldn't give up. A strong yellow light penetrated the dense fog that settled all around her. The light served as a beacon that penetrated the atmosphere around her and the spirit within her. As she trudged through, an encouraging voice rose from her belly, through her throat, and out of her mouth, "Look to the Lord and his strength; seek his face always."

"Seek his face always." Maddie awoke repeating the very thing she dreamed. Her rapid heartbeat signaled a physical response, almost like she was there. *That's weird.* She thought.

A quiet knock on the door interrupted her thoughts. "Maddie, we're leaving for church in an hour."

"Thanks, Mom." Getting out of bed, Maddie grabbed her brush as she mulled over the dream.

After breakfast, the family jumped in the SUV and went to church. Opening her Bible, Maddie reread Philippians 4:6-7.

How can I seek God's face in this scripture? She wondered as she looked out of the window. *"In every situation, by prayer and petition, with thanksgiving, present your requests to God, And the peace of God, which transcends all understanding, will guard your hearts and your minds in Christ Jesus."*

Walking into Ms. Bonnie's room, Maddie was happy to see Amy Jayne sitting in the circle. Thankfully, she was early and had time to talk with her friend.

Motioning for her to come over, Amy Jayne asked, "Maddie, when'd ya get here?"

"We drove up Friday."

"Are ya here fer Christmas?"

Maddie couldn't hold back her excitement. "Yep, a whole two weeks." She exclaimed.

"I'm happy fer ya," Amy Jayne nodded, a slight smile not quite making it to her eyes.

"Hey, are you okay? Did y'all find your daddy?"

The worried look on her friend's face said it all. "We did. Thank ya fer prayin'. God answered."

Afraid to ask, Maddie took a deep breath and then went for it, "Is he, I mean, your dad, is he okay?"

Amy Jayne shrugged her shoulders and said, "Yeah, he will be. He's in rehab, jes' down the street."

"Did you and your brother have to go into foster care?"

"Nah, Ms. Bonnie took us in."

Maddie looked at Ms. Bonnie, who was standing across the room writing on the whiteboard. "That was nice of her."

"Yeah, I'm grateful. Brother's safe, and hopefully, daddy's dryin' out. I'm jes' sad he won't be home fer Christmas."

Sad for her friend, she looked down at her feet, wondering what to say. "Hey, would you and your brother like to come to Grammy's sometime this week? I'm sure Matthew would love to meet your brother.

Amy Jayne's face lit up at the idea. "Shore! Let me ask Ms. Bonnie."

Both girls were excited when Ms. Bonnie said yes. Plans for a visit on Thursday gave Maddie something to look forward to before Christmas.

After service, everyone went into the fellowship hall for lunch. Still harboring confusion over her dream, Maddie wanted to talk with someone about it and knew just the person who might be able to give her insight.

"Ms. Lorna?"

When she heard her name, Ms. Lorna turned and gave her a big smile. Her cheerful countenance was contagious. "Hey, Girl, good to see ya!"

Her familiar, reassuring smile gave Maddie the confidence she needed as she asked, "Do you have a minute? I was wondering if I could talk to you about something."

"A'course! Let me tell your Grammy, and we'll grab the table on the other side."

As Maddie waited for Ms. Lorna to return, Rory and Jared walked over to talk to her.

"Maddie!"

"Hey y'all, where's Jacob?"

"He's visitin' his grandparents fer the weekend," Rory said. "How long are ya here fer?"

"My family and I are here for two weeks for Christmas and New Year's."

"Great! See ya!"

Maddie shook her head as the boys walked away. "Boys!" She muttered under her breath.

"What's that?" Ms. Lorna asked as she sat beside her.

"Ms. Lorna, why are boys so weird?"

Chuckling, she answered, "Boy troubles, huh?"

"Naw, I just don't understand why they can't finish a conversation. It's like, they walk over, ask a question, and then walk away."

"They're still learnin'. Give 'em time and a lot a grace. I

promise ya, they'll grow up. Now, what would ya like ta talk about?"

Maddie proceeded to share her dreams with Ms. Lorna. "I think the Tower is God?" She hesitated, looking for confirmation. When none seemed forthcoming, she added, "This morning, I woke up saying 'seek his face always.' Why would I have to tell myself to do something I already do?"

"Hm, if the Tower is God, as you say, then perhaps it's Holy Spirit instructin' ya."

Maddie was quiet for a moment. "He lives inside me, right?"

"That's right. David told us he leads us beside quiet waters and guides us along the right path. It's his Spirit doing the guidin'."

"Wait, I read that yesterday." Opening her Bible to Psalm twenty-three, Maddie read the passage Ms. Lorna referenced. "He guides me along the right paths for his name's sake. So, the Holy Spirit can talk to me through my dreams?"

"Why a'course! Think about it: you're quiet and not distracted by the world. Some of my best songs have come in the wee hours of the morning as the Lord wakes me from a dream."

"Could these dreams be from him?" Maddie asked.

Shrugging, Ms. Lorna responded, "Perhaps. Did ya ask him?"

"Not really." Maddie paused as she pulled together her next question. "Didn't you tell us that about David? That he had to remind himself of who God was while giving God his worship? Was that Holy Spirit encouraging him?"

Placing her hand on Maddie's shoulder, Ms. Lorna said, "That's right as rain. You kids never cease to surprise me. Kudos to you for rememberin'."

"Okay, so God might be telling me something, but what?" Confused, Maddie looked at Ms. Lorna, hoping for an answer.

"I don't know, but I know the One who does. Get quiet and ask him to show you. Did ya have anythin' else for me?

"No, ma'am, thank you, though."

"Well, a plate of Ms. Nelly's potato salad is calling my name, but if you ever need ta' chat, I'm here."

With that, she gave Maddie a warm smile and a wink and left her with her thoughts.

While everyone was happily eating their lunch, Maddie was restless after her convo with Ms. Lorna and so she went outside. The sun was shining, and the air wasn't too cold, so it seemed a perfect time to soak up some Vitamin D. Sitting on the grass just outside the fellowship hall, Maddie pulled out her journal and began writing. She thought she had figured out the meaning of her dreams, but they continued to unravel. Frustrated, she wrote as much in her journal.

Distracted from her writing by a colorful pair of birds that flew by her, she set her book down to watch them. Being still was a challenge, but she was enjoying the little blessings found in the discipline. Leaning back on her hands, she focused on the bright yellow and orange mohawk one of the birds sported as she watched them flit through the conifer tree not far from where she sat. Suddenly, she watched in horror as the other flew into a window opposite the tree.

"No!" Jumping up, she ran over to where the bird lay. Kneeling, she wondered what she should do.

"That's a Golden-crowned Kinglet," Rory said from behind her.

Oh!" Maddie wondered how long he had been standing there. "He hit the window and fell. What should we do?"

"Beg'n yer pardon, but that's a she. The male's crown is orange and yellow, the female's yellow."

Should I have known that? She thought, embarrassed. "So, what should we do?"

"Jes' give 'er a minute. She's prob'ly jes' stunned. We don't wanna touch 'er 'less we have ta."

"Oh, okay. How long should we wait?"

"About five or six minutes, and we should know. Here, let's set a spell. Try not ta stare at her," he said as he pointed toward a bench on the side of the building.

"What happens if we stare at her?"

"She's been hurt. Birds can die from the stress. So, ya don't wanna hold it or stare at it and stress it out more." Nodding toward the bird, he whispered, "Look, see thar, she's breathin'."

Maddie knew what it was like to be stressed under a microscope. Saying a prayer under her breath, she stared at the bush across the way, hoping the bird would be okay.

"If she don't get up, we'll get her a box and take 'er ta see Doc Copeland. He's a vet'rinarian."

She nodded in agreement.

After a few moments of awkward silence, Rory said, "Ya know, they eat three times their body weight in insects."

Surprised, she looked at him and said, "No way! How much do they weigh?"

Pulling out some change from his pocket, he said, "Not much more'n these two pennies."

Hearing a bird call out, seet-seet-seet, Maddie said, "Hey, look, there's the other one. He must be the male." As quickly as Maddie saw the bird, he flew away.

Looking down his nose at her, Rory scolded, "They don't like ta be perused. Did ya see that thar mohawk? When they raise their feathers like that, thar tellin' ya ta back off."

Maddie giggled, "Well, I guess I've been told."

Suddenly, the bird on the ground stood up. "Hey, look!" Maddie exclaimed.

"Shh, give 'er a minute."

The bird stood there for a minute, shook her feathers, looked up, and flew away.

"And jes' like that, the bird lives another day." Rory stood up. "Well, Ms. Bennett, I'll be seein' ya later."

Alarmed that he would leave the bird, Maddie asked, "Hey, wait a second. Will she be okay?"

"Prob'ly. Time'll tell. She's gotta lot of eatin' ta do, and so do I." Saluting Maddie, Rory walked back toward the fellowship hall.

Looking up into the tree, she saw the two birds happily flying through the tree. Pulling out her journal, she wrote down what she witnessed. Looking at the words written on the page, she suddenly had a revelation. The bird was encouraged by the other to get up. She was practically dead, but when she heard the call of her friend, she looked up, shook it off and then flew away.

"Are you encouraging me to do the same, God?" She asked as she watched them play. Thinking over the last year, she had been begging God to make everything as it was before things broke apart. She rarely stopped to look up and thank God for helping them through the chaos. Praying with Grammy and watching the bird fly away made her realize that God was with her even as she sought his face. She wrote the words "Seek your face" in her journal and heard Sonya's voice: where is God? Maddie wrote,

> *You were here all the time, watching over me. Thank you, God.*

Jumping up, Maddie smiled as she walked toward the fellowship hall.

Sitting in church with his mom brought many unpleasant memories. David couldn't get past all the conspiracy theories thrown about from the Bible. He respected his mother's belief but wasn't into believing himself. He had seen too much, he expected.

David wasn't sure when he parted with religion. Perhaps he never really believed. He participated in all the events at church before graduating high school, but it didn't seem necessary once he went to college. Jacque didn't mind; she had a love-hate relationship with religion. So, their mutual decision to only visit on special occasions seemed to work for them.

There was one thing that David couldn't shake: his mom's peace. She was solid as a rock through his dad's passing and everything that happened in the last year. Watching her navigate the challenges they faced, he realized how often he appreciated her faith, and she never took the credit; that was God's alone, to hear her tell it. David could admit to feeling a little jealous of her consistent strength.

After the message was over, Pastor Ron came over to talk to the family. He was nice enough and seemed genuine, with a firm handshake. He seemed to love his mom greatly, and the feeling was mutual. If there was one thing David did appreciate about the church, it was their genuine care for their members.

"David, you, and your family are welcome to stay for the town hall meetin'. We'll be serving dinner. Thar's a spread only the people a Wild Rock could drum up."

David's mom didn't seem too keen on the idea. "Oh, I don't know if David would wanna stay, Pastor Ron. But it's mighty nice a ya to offer."

Surprised, David looked at his mom and asked, "Why wouldn't I want to stay?"

"Oh, ya know, they'll be talkin' 'bout Wild Rock stuff. This and that, nothin' you'd be interested in."

If David didn't know any better, he'd think his mom was trying to get rid of him. "That's okay, Mom. We can stay for dinner."

After everyone ate, they pulled the chairs together into several straight lines. Sitting down, they waited for their town hall to come to order.

Working for the military, David had taken part in many such meetings and was curious about the topic. *Perhaps they needed to choose a new color for the flags on Main Street,* he pondered as they waited.

Pastor Ron stood up before the congregation, "Okay, y'all, it's time ta start."

"What'cha holdin' us fer Pastor? There's 'portant business goin' on in ma livin' room," a man said from the front.

Everyone laughed as they nodded in agreement.

"I shoulda been nappin' an hour ago," someone said from

behind.

Holding his hands up, Pastor Ron quieted the room. "Thank y'all fer makin' time ta be here. I know Clyde, I wanna be watchin' the Titans jes' like you. But we got somethin' critical that needs chewin' on."

David was surprised to watch the room get quiet so quickly. Sitting with his arms crossed, he waited with others for the Pastor to share his important business.

"Y'all heard 'bout this Kindness Contribution? Well, it's come 'ere ta Wild Rock. A man threatened Ms. Nelly by tellin' her he'd shut down her store if she didn't participate."

A female voice called out from behind David, "Play nicely is what they said, Pastor. Tell it straight."

Alarmed, Jacque looked at David as an angry murmur rolled through the room.

"So, what do we do, Pastor?"

"Well, the consensus among pastors 'round the country is that this contribution is nothin' more than a counterfeit tithe— the conspiracy of our generation. And it's my understandin' that this contribution is payin' fer smugglers and sex traffickers. You mark my words; this Jasper sellin' this bill o' goods soon'll be standin' in front of the whole world sayin' he's the savior we've been waitin' fer. Pure evil, he is."

"But what should we do?"

"We don't pay 'em," Pastor Ron declared.

"They'll shut us down, Pastor!"

"Then let 'em! This is our town, we've got each other," Grammy said.

Surprised, David looked at his mom.

Grammy gave her son "the look" and continued, "Clyde, we've been through much worse. B'sides, we take care a our own. Ain't nobody gonna come in and tell us how ta live."

"Mom, perhaps we should lay low," David said under his breath.

"Tom, what did that gentleman tell you over the summer?" Pastor Ron asked.

"He said that if we didn't play nice, he would shut our cute little town down."

"Play nice with what?" The man named Benjamin asked.

Clyde wasn't to be left out as he asked, "What do you mean, shut our town down?"

The angry murmurs were slowly becoming a dull roar.

Exasperated, Pastor Ron raised his hands to signal quiet, saying, "Tom, come share with the town what the man asked fer."

The man named Tom walked to the front of the room and said, "An outlander," looking at David, he clarified, "Ya know, a stranger, all dignified like, came ta ma shop askin' a heap o' questions 'bout Wild Rock and the stores on the square. He said somethin' 'bout thar bein' a discrepancy over the number accordin' ta the state records. He wanted to know who the mayor was so he could set the record straight."

"Did ya not tell 'em that yer the mayor?"

Tom looked down his nose at the question. "Some things are better left unsaid, Benjamin."

"Pastor, you always teach us ta give ta Caesar's what is Caesar's and give ta God what is God's. Aren't we breakin' God's law if we don't pay the contribution?"

"That's a mighty good question, Ms. Nelly, and one I've been strugglin' with myself. Personally, I think we should close our businesses 'afore we pay the contribution."

"Close! I gotta feed ma family!"

"How do ya suggest we do that, Pastor?"

"That's the dumbest thang I ever' heard!"

Worried that a riot might break out, David moved to stand. His mother's hand on his leg stopped him.

She shook her head as she motioned for him not to say anything.

The room grew quiet. Suddenly, the back door opened, and Maddie walked in.

As he waved her over, Maddie came to sit down with her family. "Maddie, why don't you go and play with the kids? I think they're on the playground."

"Do I have to? I wanted to tell Ms. Lorna something."

Maddie asked.

David implored his daughter, "We'll be just a little longer. Go check on your brother for me."

In a huff, Maddie turned around and walked out of the room.

"Can I make a suggestion?" Grammy asked as she watched her granddaughter leave. Turning to look at Michael, who had been mysteriously quiet this whole time, she continued. "Several of us have been 'round the world a couple of times. R'member when we re-built yer barn, Clyde? Ever'body thought the world's end was nigh but look at what Almighty God brought us through. Shoot, my Pappy lived through the depression and two world wars." She pointed her finger at Benjamin and said, "You know 'bout it. Yer Pappy practically saved the whole town after the coal mine shut down. Do ya r'member them stories they tole?"

"I recollect he was mad as a mule chewin' bumblebees," Benjamin replied.

"Memaw used to tell stories a how they built a garden bigger than the whole town square. Ever'body took part in growin' a plot chock full a vegetables that fed the whole town." A young man said from the front.

"Yes, Sirree, and I had ta work it!" Grammy said. "And so did you, Clyde. And you, Benjamin. It ain't beyond us ta do it again."

"Now, calm down Grace, I see yer fit ta be tied here, but we need clear heads. So, give it to us straight." Tom asked.

"I'm sayin' if we gotta close the shops that we plant the garden. We all have one, so let's find a plot to share and work together. We'll barter goods instead a usin' money."

"What about everythin' else?"

"Why, I could stockpile salt and sugar," Nelly said. "Paul, you've got pigs; we could buy some more and get ta breedin' 'em."

"We could go on some huntin' sprees and take on some deer fer jerky," Clyde added.

David had enough. Standing, he said, "This is lunacy. Why

don't you just make the contribution?"

"Ya know what yer sayin', don't ya boy? Think 'bout yer girl and where she's been. That'll be somebody else's daughter if we don't take a stand," Grammy said quietly.

"David, this is bigger than just a contribution. Don't ya see it?" Pastor Ron looked directly at Michael. "Ya should know better than all of us what's going down. Jes' look at the chaos all 'round us. The darkness has a hold on this world, and I'm sorry to say that it intends to take us all down with it. So, we gotta choice, ta stand accordin' ta the word a God or ta get sucked into the enemy's plan. We're commanded ta stand and endure. We cain't give in, else we'll be one a them, condemned ta ruination."

Michael stood and looked at his dad. "Pastor Ron is right, Dad. We must stand. They won't stop taking our money. They want control. You know it's true."

David grabbed his forehead to soothe the throbbing in his temple and took a deep breath. *All these people are crazy conspiracy hunters,* he thought. Embarrassed when everyone turned to look at him, he realized his last thought left his lips.

Benjamin stood, his face as red as his sweatshirt. "Boy, I'll show ya a conspiracy hunter!"

"Benjamin, set down ya ole' galoot. He don't know our ways." Turning to her son, Grammy said, "David, what do ya call it when the whole world done jumped on a bandwagon ta force their people into takin' part in somethin' that's evil?" Grammy asked.

Sighing, David sat back down and said, "Okay, so let's say you all go on some bartering system for food. What will the people with restaurants and food stores do for money? They have utilities and mortgages to pay, right?"

"I been thinkin' 'bout that," a man said from behind. "The contribution is fer food, right? They ain't said nothin' 'bout the goods needed ta grow a garden. Wild Rock General Store could sell gardenin' tools and survival supplies. Nelly, you could change yer name to Nelly's Home Store. Ya could sell all them fancy candles ya like ta make."

"I can sell my quilts," a lady beside David added.

Before you knew it, everyone in the room had something to contribute.

Putting up his hands, David realized he couldn't argue with them. This was their town. Looking at his mom, he said, "I just don't want anything to happen to you, Momma."

With compassion in her eyes, Grace placed her hand on her son's cheek and said, "Boy, I'm in the hands a the Lord. Thar ain't no conspiracy on this earth that'll take me out of his hand."

CHAPTER 28

The Heart of Redemption

Something remarkable happened on Thursday morning: Maddie was up early! She was not an early riser, but she was so excited for her friend to come over that she couldn't stay asleep another moment.

Elbow deep in biscuit dough, she and Matthew chatted about the day while Grammy made a heap of eggs, grits, and bacon.

"Boy, yer lettin' that dough whup you," Grammy said as she looked at the mess he was making.

"I'm just not feelin' it, Grammy," Matthew said with a sigh.

"What'cha mean?" She asked.

"I'm stove up," Matthew said as he contorted his face in exaggerated pain.

Shaking her head, Grammy tried not to laugh. "Since when do ya have arthritis, Boy?"

"Uncle Tom said when you have trouble getting going in the morning, you're stove up."

"Did he now? Well, what cain't be cured must be endured." Grammy said with her hands on her hips. Waving her hands toward the dough, she said, "So, quit piddlin' around and get ta work. Stoved-up joints have a mind to heat up when ya work 'em."

Michael laughed at the scene before him as he walked into the kitchen.

Turning to her other grandson, Grammy said, "Boy, yer grinning like a possum eatin' a sweet tater. What's got ya so happy?"

"Good morning, Grammy." Michael said as he kissed her forehead. "Actually, I have a date today."

"Ya don't say!" Grammy exclaimed. "And who might the lucky girl be?"

"Actually, one of Aunt Lisa's friends. Her name is Melissa."

"Might that be Melissa Tate? I r'member her when she was jes' a tot. Are ya sweet on her?"

Maddie turned to see the blush on her brother's face. It seemed Grammy knew something the rest of the world didn't.

"Well now, I think yer datin' her would be mighty nice. She's as pretty as a peach! Ya know she favors her momma." Pointing her wooden spoon at him, she said, "You better treat her right, ya hear?"

Michael chuckled as he turned to walk out the back door. "Yes ma'am. Wouldn't want to face the wrath of Grammy and her spoon!"

"Grammy, what does it mean to be sweet on somebody?" Matthew asked.

"Well, my Grandson, that means that ya like 'em."

"Does Michael want to marry her?" He asked innocently.

Stunned, Grammy stopped in her tracks and looked at Matthew, "Boy, ya don't marry til ya court. Ya don't court til ya go steady. And ya don't go steady til yer sweet on someone. So, yer brother's still got a ways ta go." Turning her spoon in Matthew's direction, she added, "Don't ya be speedin' things up fer 'em, ya hear?"

"Yes ma'am!" He said with a flour-covered salute.

Around lunchtime, Amy Jayne arrived with her brother James. After a timid knock, the two were surprised when Max came up from behind to greet them. When they bent down to pet him, he immediately laid on his back for a proper belly rub.

Opening the door for her friend, Maddie giggled, "I see you've met Max."

"Bye y'all! Thank ya Maddie fer invitin' 'em! I'll be back after supper," Ms. Bonnie said as she drove away.

Waving at Ms. Bonnie, the three went back to properly greeting Max. Deciding he had more important business, Max jumped up and ran down the stairs to chase after a squirrel.

"Come in," Maddie said. "Matthew, they're here!"

Matthew came sliding into the living room, his white socks making quick work of the shiny wooden floor. "Hi!"

James gave a reserved wave as his sister pushed him toward Matthew.

"Hey James, do you want to come to my room? I built a really cool fort!"

James looked back at his sister as he followed Matthew toward the back of the house.

"Would you like some hot chocolate?" Maddie asked Amy Jayne.

"Shore."

Making two cups of hot chocolate, Maddie added the necessary whipped cream and set one in front of Amy Jayne as she cradled the other. "How are you doing?" She asked.

"Hm, okay." Amy Jayne shrugged.

"How is it staying with Ms. Bonnie?"

"Oh, she's cool. She's got a dog, too. Her name's Maggie. I never had a dog a'fore."

"Does Maggie like to play?"

"She catches a ball. Man is she fast! Ms. Bonnie, she's got a flat yard, so we throw the ball way over yonder, and Maggie, she jes' runs and catches that ball in mid-air. It's amazin'! Never seen anythin' like it."

"If we were to throw a ball to Max, he'd probably go off and bury it," Maddie laughed.

"Why hello, Amy Jayne," Grammy said as she and Momma came in from the backyard. Taking off her heavy coat, Grammy said, "I think we might jes' see a skift a snow this Christmas."

"Wait, really?" Maddie and Amy Jayne looked at each other in surprise. Jumping off the stool, they went to the glass door to look up at the dark sky.

"How can you tell?" Maddie asked.

"Well, the air gets really cold like, but wet, ya know. The clouds get all gray, low in the sky, lookin' like rain clouds. See?" Grammy asked as she pointed toward the sky. "Add that ta freezin' temps and ya got yerself a chance fer snow."

Giddy over the idea, Maddie sighed. "Do you like snow?" She asked Amy Jayne.

Shrugging, her friend answered, "I dunno. It's a lotta work."

"Oh, but there's so much to do! Build a snowman, make a snow angel, and then there's sitting in front of the fireplace watching it fall."

"Yeah, then thar's shovelin' it and hopin' yer dad doesn't get into an accident comin' home."

Maddie didn't know what to say. She never thought about the hardships of snow.

"I'm sorry. Too much in ma thoughts, I guess. So, what's yer favorite part 'bout snow?" Amy Jayne asked.

Maddie thought a moment. It had been a long time since she had seen snow. Atlanta didn't see as much as Wild Rock. "Honestly, I think I love the first fall. When everything is quiet, you can see the snowflakes fall in your hand. Did you know that every flake is unique? It's amazing that God can create something so small yet unique."

"Yeah, I guess."

"Hey, do you want to play a game?"

Amy Jayne picked the game of Clue, and off they went. After an hour, Maddie was surprised at her detective skills. Out of four rounds, her friend won three of them.

"Wow, you're really good at this," Maddie said.

"I love researchin'," she said. "I guess it's somethin' I've had to be good at, takin' care a James and all."

She and Kaitlyn would have gotten along great. Maddie thought sadly. Setting up for another game, Maddie asked, "Do you mind if I ask what happened to your mom?"

A far-away look came over her face as she sat real still.

"It's okay if you don't want to say." She shook her head and added, "It's none of my business, really."

"Naw, it's okay. It's not a secret; cain't keep no secrets in Wild Rock, noway. Momma left when I was seven and James was two."

"I'm so sorry," Maddie said as she sat in the moment's sadness.

Amy Jayne snapped out of it and said, "It's okay. It was a long time ago." Drawing the corners of her mouth into a pronounced frown, she looked away and wiped away a tear.

Maddie gave her friend a tissue and waited for her to continue.

"I miss her," Pausing, Amy Jayne offered a cynical smile as she nodded at Maddie. "Ever'body said we coulda been twins. She had bright red hair, too. Daddy said she had a temper that matched that hair. I don't recollect none a that; I jes' r'member how she loved ta dance. Oh, them were the days. Daddy worked as a fireman, and momma worked at the church. He didna drink back then. He went ta church and ever'thin. Momma wouldna have it any other way."

"You said she loved to dance. Do you remember when you invited me to dance around the campfire at the pick'n 'n grin'n last year? Did you get it from her?"

A haunted look overtook Amy Jayne's pale features as she sat quietly in her thoughts.

The desire to ask for details and make everything okay for her friend was strong, but Maddie knew from experience that she couldn't do anything but sit with, encourage, and pray for her.

"Hey, Maddie?"

"Yeah?"

"What happened to yer mom? Did ya tell me once that she tried to commit su'cide?"

"Yes, she overdosed on alcohol."

Amy Jayne nodded, "Then ya know."

"Yeah. But Amy Jayne," leaning forward on her arms,

Maddie looked her closely in the eye, "I found hope. I realized I couldn't fix my mom, but I could help her by giving her to God, the One who could heal her."

"And did he? Heal her, I mean?"

"For the most part. I still see a haunted look in her eyes occasionally, but I haven't seen her pick up a bottle in a long time. Of course, it helps that my dad isn't always gone."

Opening her hands before her, she said, "I've been puttin' ma dad in ma hands and layin' him at the cross, jes' like ya tole me."

Maddie smiled, "Does it help?"

"Yeah. It keeps me from gettin' riled up."

"Me too."

"I gotta believe that ma daddy will dry up, ya know? James don't need ta see his daddy gommin' up his life. He needs a man ta teach him ta be a man and I cain't do that."

"Would you like to pray for him?" Maddie asked.

"Can we?"

Maddie nodded as she grabbed the hands of her friend and prayed. It was a simple prayer she felt deep in her heart. Remembering the words from Philippians, she claimed the promise Grammy said she could claim, that the peace that transcended all understanding would cover Amy Jayne and James in Christ Jesus.

The rest of the day was spent playing games and walking in Grammy's garden. Amy Jayne loved the straight rows that were prepped for the coming spring. She even asked Grammy if she could come back in the spring and help. That request was received with great joy, of course.

After Matthew and James grew tired of playing in their make-shift fort, they joined in the game play, pulling out the bright yellow bag of Bananagrams. Maddie was impressed with Amy Jayne's way of putting words together. Her competitive nature reminded her of her mom. It was to Matthew's great chagrin that Amy Jayne yelled Bananas when he was down to his last letter.

Later that night, Maddie journaled as she reminisced over

an eventful day. Thankful for this new friendship, she felt exceptionally burdened for her friend's dad.

> *December 21*
> *Thank you, Father, for today. I pray for Amy Jayne, and James that they will see a Christmas miracle in the healing of their dad. God, Grammy says that nothing is impossible for you. We believe you can heal Mr. Wright. In Jesus' Name, we pray, Amen.*

Christmas Eve Service at Grammy's church was different from her own. She was accustomed to a service at night, whereas Grammy's was held during the day.

As she and her family walked into the sanctuary, Grammy walked proudly ahead, nodding at people she knew as they fussed over "little" David's return to Wild Rock. Maddie and Matthew couldn't help but giggle at their reference to her dad as little.

As she stepped into an empty pew, she saw Amy Jayne sitting with Ms. Bonnie, Mr. Bruce, and James on the other side. The enthusiastic wave of her hand reminded Maddie of their visit on Thursday; she returned the wave, hoping they could catch up after service.

In the Christmas Eve sermon, Pastor Ron shared the story of the lost son. She had never heard the story, but memories of freedom in her own relit the candle of her redemption as she listened. While they didn't have physical candles to remind them of Jesus' birth, The flame in her heart seemed to serve the same purpose.

Toward the end of the service, Pastor Ron had a special guest to invite. As the man walked up to the podium, Maddie caught a glimpse of Amy Jayne's excitement from the corner of her eye. Curious about who this person could be, she leaned forward.

The man was clean-shaven with wavy auburn hair. He

introduced himself as Patrick—an alcoholic. Looking around her, it seemed everyone knew him as little whispers floated around the room. Amy Jayne and James were smiling with their eyes fixed firmly on the man. Suddenly, Maddie knew who he was! Patrick is Amy Jayne's dad! Suddenly, she had a vested interest in what he had to say.

As she listened to Patrick, tears welled up in her eyes. He told a story of childhood rebellion and redemption when he met the love of his life. He shared how his heart was broken when Amy Jayne's mom left them suddenly. He didn't know how he could live without her, so he buried himself in a bottle. It wasn't long before the addiction took over, as it created a vicious cycle of shame, depression, and guilt that took away everything he loved, including his children.

Suddenly distracted by a vibration on their pew, Maddie looked down and noticed the nervous movement of Michael's leg. A solitary tear fell on his cheek which he violently wiped away. Not wanting to embarrass her brother, she turned her focus back to the front.

As she listened, she noticed Patrick's countenance transformed instantly when he shared how he found Jesus, or better yet, how Jesus found him. The haunted look of sadness was exchanged for pure joy. Maddie remembered that feeling, like nothing in the world could take away the gift God had given. He said he looked straight into the heart of redemption and realized there was no way he could ever go back. Then, looking at his children, he said he found hope and a plan for their family. With the opportunity of a new job, he was grateful for the love and grace given to him and hoped to help others find the grace that he, too, had found.

There was not a dry eye in the place, including every one of Maddie's family members. After Patrick finished, Pastor Ron shared in Jesus' birth. He read from John 3:16 and asked if anyone would like to join Patrick in declaring their belief in Christ. The quiet in the room was deafening. One person, then two, approached the altar. Everyone bowed their heads for this reverent moment, but the swish of clothing could be heard as people walked forward. Suddenly, Maddie felt her pew move. Glancing up, she watched her brother get up and walk to the front. Several men, including Patrick, were at the front praying over those who stepped forward, and Michael went straight for Patrick.

Bowing her head again, Maddie left one eye open and watched her brother as sobs racked his body and he fell to his knees. Patrick and Pastor Ron knelt beside Michael and prayed over him.

Struggling with conflicting emotions, she was grateful to see her brother praying, but wondered why he was crying so violently. Grammy must've have thought similarly as she grabbed her granddaughter's hand and squeezed tightly.

After service, she made a beeline for her friend.

"Can ya believe it?" Amy Jayne asked. "We get to see him on Christmas, Maddie! Yer prayer was answered!" Releasing her dad's hand, Amy Jayne hugged her friend. "Thank ya!" She exclaimed.

"Who's yer friend, AJ?" Amy Jayne's dad asked.

"This is the girl I tole ya 'bout, Daddy. Her name's Maddie. Maddie, this is ma Daddy." Amy Jayne beamed as she looked up at her dad.

Patrick shook Maddie's hand and said, "I understand ya prayed fer me. Thank ya. I'm grateful." Maddie blushed as she was lost for words. Grammy's voice pulled her out of her perplexed silence.

"Go 'head tell 'im that God is good. He's the miracle worker," she encouraged.

Maddie nodded, "Yes, Sir, God is good. I'm glad you're okay, Sir."

Sitting on the front porch with a blanket wrapped around her legs, Maddie rocked slowly as she stared into the darkness. The simple light above her was just enough to allow for the writing of the events of the day in her journal. Flipping through the pages, she realized the book was almost full. Sonya told her that the end of the year was a good time to praise God for all he had done. This would be a good time to read through all he had brought her through.

Feeling the indention of the words on the page, she realized every memory left an indention on her heart. Some were scars, while others were permanent marks of transformation that Grammy said nobody could take away from her. After drawing a heart around her entry for the day, she laid her head back on the rocking chair and closed her eyes.

Jarred by the opening of the screen door, she opened her eyes and smiled when her brother came to sit next to her.

"Hey, Sis."

"Michael! How's Melissa?"

"She's good. Sorry, we didn't stay after service. She wanted me to meet her family."

"Really now? Are things getting serious?"

Michael shrugged. "I don't know, maybe," he smiled as he looked down.

"Hey, I have something for you." With a mischievous look, he gave her a small box.

"What's this?" She asked.

"A little somethin' somethin'. It's not much. I've been saving every penny I've made working for Uncle Tom."

"It's okay. I didn't get you anything this year. I kinda figured . . ." She trailed off.

"I've got your present from last year. So, I thought we could open them together."

"Oh, Michael, really? You never opened it?"

"I was too angry. I'm sorry, Maddie, I was a jerk. But I'm ready to make it up to you and be the brother you deserve. Thank you for never giving up on me," he said, sheepishly looking out into the darkness.

"I could never!" She exclaimed, as she leaned over to hug him over the arm of the chair.

"Okay, okay, don't make a fuss. Open your gift," he said.

She'd have thought he was blushing if she didn't know

better. Excited, she tore the paper off the unevenly wrapped gift. Opening the box, she saw the gold cross lying on white tissue paper. Lifting the cross out of the box, she held the delicate necklace and stared in awe. "Michael, this is too much."

Picking the necklace out of her hand, he said, "No, it's just right." Unclasping the necklace, he offered to put it around her neck.

Lifting her hair out of the way, she allowed him to put it on her and clasp it in the back. She couldn't help but weep as she placed her fingers on the pendant and thought. *My very own cross!*

She glanced at the box on her brother's lap and wondered about the fray around the corners. She couldn't believe he hadn't opened it yet but was grateful that she would get to see him open it.

"Soooo, open it!" She said impatiently after he laid his head against his chair and closed his eyes.

"What, you want me to open this?" He teased as he picked up the box and shook it. "I wonder what's in it?"

"Maybe you should guess," she replied.

"Hmm, a lump of coal?"

Her signature eye roll accompanied a shake of her head.

Looking at his fingernails, he said, "You know, I need a new pair of fingernail clippers."

"Nope," she said.

Shaking it again, he gasped, "Is it a million bucks?"

Punching him lightly on the arm, she said, "Open it already!"

Maddie thought she would lose her mind as he slowly unwrapped the gift. This was her brother; he loved to tease her, and she knew it. By the time the box was uncovered, she was bopping up and down, excited to see his expression when he finally opened the box.

A black leather cord encircled a simple silver and black shield medallion with a sword in the middle. Pulling the medallion out, Michael turned it over and read the inscription, *"Take up the shield of faith, with which you can extinguish all the flaming arrows of the evil one. Take the helmet of salvation and the sword of the spirit, which is the word of God.*"

"What does it mean?" Michael asked as he fingered the sword on the top.

"When I bought it, I thought the sword was cool, but Sonya taught me about the armor of God that we can pray on as protection. This signifies the sword of the Spirit."

"Maddie, I don't need a necklace for protection, you know that, right?"

"Yeah, but it's a nice reminder that God is always with you, right? Isn't that why you bought the cross for me?"

"Hm," Michael sat back in the chair and rocked.

"Hey, Michael?"

His eyes closed, he answered, "Yeah?"

"What happened today?" Maddie asked curiously.

Opening one eye, he said, "You know I can't tell you what goes on between a guy and his girl."

Giggling, she said, "Your girl, huh? So, it's official?"

"We've already settled this, MAY-BE."

Throwing a wad of tissue paper at his head, she said, "That's not fair, Michael Ryder Bennett! But that's not what I was talking about." Suddenly feeling uncertain about asking her question, she sat back and mumbled, "I mean, what happened today at Church?"

"Oh, do you mean when I prayed with Patrick?"

"Yeah."

Rocking back and forth, Michael took a deep breath and stared into the night. "Maddie, I'm not a good guy."

"What do you mean?"

"I mean, I've done a lot of bad things." Hesitating, he turned his head to confirm the front door was closed then looked at his sister. "Do you remember when I told you that people are suspect?"

"I remember."

"Well, I'm one of those people."

"No Michael, you're free from all of that."

"For now."

"So, did you pray today? Did you say yes to Jesus?"

Michael was quiet for a moment as he continued to rock. "I did." Looking back toward the front yard, he added, "It felt good."

Maddie smiled as she pulled out her journal. She drew a picture of her brother's medallion with her cross beside it. After a few moments, she said, "Michael, you know that when you said yes to him, he forgave all of your sins."

"I hope so, Maddie; I hope so."

"What are you afraid of?" She asked.

"Afraid? I'm not afraid," he countered. "Well, maybe a little." Looking down at his little sister, he remembered the moment that he realized she was at the PKO. He never wanted to have to face a moment like that again. "I don't want to go back to the PKO, ever."

"Then don't," she said.

"Little Sis, it's not that simple. At any time, they could find out where I am and come and get me."

"Then we need to pray that won't happen," Maddie said with confidence.

The slam of the front door surprised them as Matthew, followed closely by Max, ran down the stairs yelling, "It's snowing, it's snowing!"

Looking up from her book, her heart leaped as a series of white flurries danced in the night air. A light dusting soon turned into a heavy fall that quickly covered the front yard in a blanket of white. Maddie followed her brothers and stood still. Awe and wonder arose within her as the snow fell to the ground. "Be still and know that you are God," she said as she looked up and felt the flurries of powder caress her cheeks.

Later than night, she sat quiet and listened as soft flurries reverberated the stillness. Where raindrops showered peace, snow blanketed the earth with a promise of hope. Opening her journal, she wrote:

December 24
Father,

Thank you for teaching me to seek you and find you. Thank you for your hope. Thank you for Christmas and the gift of redemption you gave us in Jesus. Thank you for saving me, my brother, and my friends. And thank you for drawing Amy Jayne's dad to you. I pray that like my mom he will be healed. And Father, please encourage my brother that all his sins are forgiven, and he is washed clean. Protect him Lord so that he never has to go back to the PKO. Nothing is impossible for you, God. In Jesus' name, Amen.

She never wanted to forget this Christmas, so she drew a picture of three happy siblings and a floppy-eared dog playing in the snow. In big block letters, she wrote Merry Christmas and drifted off to sleep.

CHAPTER 29

This is War

Maddie had another dream early Christmas morning, but this one was different.

> *She was on a big ship, like a cruise ship. She didn't know where the boat was going but knew it was taking her to safety. While everyone was looking over the railing, she had her eyes on the man at the helm. Drawn to him, she walked up behind him and just watched. He was looking over the bow expectantly. Maddie wanted to ask what he was looking at but decided to watch with him instead. Perhaps there was something they would see together. Suddenly, from behind, people began to jump overboard. The chaos behind her was overwhelming, yet the man beside her kept looking forward expectantly.*

She awoke in a cold sweat. "What do I do with that, God?" She asked after she wrote down her dream in her journal. Conflicted, she laid back down, wondering if she was supposed to help the people behind her or keep looking forward.

After drifting back to sleep, she was abruptly awakened by the insistent bouncing of her little brother. "Maddie, Maddie, wake up! It's Christmas!" He exclaimed.

"Five more minutes. . ." Maddie mumbled as she rolled

309

over.

"But Maddie, there's a whole bunch of snow! Come look!" Matthew ran over to the window and opened the blinds.

Rubbing the sleep out of her eyes, she was wide awake as she sat up, the shimmer of white glowing through the window. "No way!" She exclaimed, jumping up to look outside.

They grabbed their coats and tennis shoes and ran past the Christmas tree onto the back porch. As they prepared to run out into the snow, their mom walked through the back door and asked, "And where do you two think you are going?"

Pointing to the snow, Matthew said, "Um, we're gonna go check out the snow?"

"There will be plenty of time for that; let's get something warm into you two first." Walking back into the house, Jacque waited for them to join her.

"Ugh. . ." Dragging their feet, they reluctantly followed her into the kitchen.

"Well, look at all these presents! I can't believe you guys were more interested in the snow," Dad laughed.

"Whoa. Where did these come from?" Matthew asked.

They couldn't believe their eyes! The living room had been transformed into a Christmas paradise. The Christmas tree they had spent so much time decorating had a selection of neatly wrapped gifts underneath.

Maddie was in awe. When her dad told them he had lost his job, she concluded that presents wouldn't be a thing this year. She didn't mind. To her, the greatest gift was being with her family. But she would be lying if she didn't admit to being a little happy about seeing the gifts under the tree. "But how?" She asked as she opened the first gift her dad handed her.

"We had a little saved up," Dad said. "Don't expect a lot, Ruthie, but there are a few special things under the tree." David smiled at Jacque, who grabbed his hand.

As she gazed at her parents, she couldn't help but wonder about this new normal. They seemed to be in a bubble in Wild Rock that she didn't want to leave.

After lifting the top to the gold box, she ran her fingers on the soft white cotton. Excited to know what was inside, she lifted the corner and was stunned as she saw a simple silver bracelet with the word faith engraved on the front.

"Like I said, it's not a lot, but we've watched you grow in your faith this year. And your mom and I," he turned to look at his wife who nodded, "are very proud of you and how far you've come."

"It's perfect, Dad, Mom, thank you!" Maddie ran to them both and hugged them tight. This was the first time they affirmed her belief in God, and she saw it as hope that perhaps they would come to believe in him, too.

After they opened presents and ate breakfast, everyone layered up in coats, hats, thick socks, and boots and went outside. The snow was blindingly bright as it reflected the sun's rays, but Maddie didn't care. Aunt Lisa brought out several laundry baskets and taught them to sled down the hill. Michael took turns pushing his siblings down the hill and watching as they flew to the bottom. Maddie never realized how steep the backside of Aunt Lisa's property was, but it appeared that being on a mountain made for an exhilarating sledding experience.

Before long, Michael and Aunt Lisa's husband, Uncle Richie, decided that a race would be a good idea.

So, Uncle Richie pushed Matthew while Michael pushed Maddie to see who would win. Of course, Max wasn't one to be left out as he chased them down the hill while cheering them on with his thunderous bark.

Holding on to the sides of the basket for dear life, Maddie squealed as the wind took her breath away. While she was trying to stay upright, Matthew figured out how to maneuver the basket to his advantage so that he won every time. After a precarious run that left Maddie tumbling down the hill, she decided to teach her brother a lesson. Grabbing a handful of snow, she packed it solid and ran up the hill, throwing it smack dab into her brother's face. *This is war!*

The next few hours were a joy. Even Eva Mae got involved in the play by grabbing a little hand of powder and throwing it on Matthew.

"Alright, you'ns, come in an get warshed up fer supper! It'll be black dark soon." Grammy yelled.

"Ugh, do we have to?" Matthew whined.

"You heard your Grammy," Dad said.

"Take the baskets over to Aunt Lisa's," Mom added.

They each grabbed a basket and followed Aunt Lisa over to her house. Winking at Matthew, she said, "If the snow's still 'round, we'll do it again tomorra."

You could have told Matthew he had won the lottery, and he wouldn't have been happier. He sang a little ditty as he skipped all the way to Grammy's.

After dinner, Maddie joined Grammy as she sat on the front porch, covered in a blanket.

Pulling a chair beside her gram, Maddie grabbed a corner of her blanket to cover her feet. "Grammy, I had another weird dream last night."

"Now, tell me 'bout it."

She proceeded to tell her Grammy about the dream. Afterward, she asked, "What do you think it means?"

"Well, I don't rightly know; what did God say 'bout it?"

Laughing, she answered, "How did I know you would ask that?"

"Girl, yer gonna hear that fer the rest 'a ma days, cause all yer answers need ta come from him. He may choose ta use me, but he's the one ta inform ya."

"Well, I did ask, but I haven't heard anything yet."

"Alrighty then, I got a challenge fer ya. How 'bout we spend some time in his word learning 'bout ships. We'll do a little study fer the next couple days 'til ya have ta go home."

Over the next week, she and Grammy spent every morning studying a different passage on ships and boats, *"Don't jes get in the word,"* Grammy would say, *"ya gotta let the word get into you."* After they read a passage, Grammy would ask, *"Now what did ya read?"* After discussing it, she'd ask, *"What did ya learn about God?"* At first, Maddie wasn't sure how to answer. She knew God was the Author of the Bible but couldn't quite describe how he spoke to her through it. But Grammy said something that opened her eyes to reading God's Word. *"Maddie Ruth, close yer eyes and see Jesus sittin' next to ya. See him readin' to ya. Jes' like I'm sittin' here, see him. Ask him questions, write 'em down, and then write down yer thoughts. What I've learned 'bout God in ma meager lifetime is that he wants us ta know him more; and getting' his word into ya, well that's one way a doin' it, don'tcha think?"* After they discussed how they saw God in the passage, Grammy would challenge Maddie to figure out how to apply the passage to her own life.

On the third day of study, they read in Luke eight about Jesus and his disciples being caught in a storm. Reminded of her dream, she wondered if the disciples were afraid.

"Girl, where'd ya go?" Grammy asked after waving in front of her granddaughter's face.

Maddie snapped out of her thoughts as she looked at the curious gaze on Grammy's face. "Sorry. What was that?"

"Where'd ya go?" Grammy repeated.

"I was thinking about my dream. Everyone was scared, just like the disciples. And like, in their fear, they were jumping overboard. But the man at the front wasn't afraid. He had this expectant look on his face. I knew that he was taking us to safety. This story is kinda like that, Grammy. I don't know what to do with that."

"Well, ya do the only thing ya can, ya pray. Let's do that right now."

Grammy thanked Jehovah Nissi for leading her granddaughter and instructing her through dreams while Maddie asked for wisdom to know what to do with them.

After they said amen, Maddie asked, "Grammy, who's

Jehovah Nissi?"

"Jehovah Nissi means the Lord is our Banner, the One who goes a'fore. He's yer mighty Warrior, and he declares vict'ry on yer behalf. God has names that speak to specific attributes a his char'cter. Jehovah Nissi is jes' one. I challenge ya ta learn all of 'em.

Remembering the man at the ship's helm, Maddie wondered if he was this Jehovah Nissi. She would have to ask Rachel what she knew about God's attributes.

Fireworks spiraled in the clear night sky to celebrate another new year. Shimmers of color exploded into a beautiful array of blossoms, umbrellas, and stars. While Maddie and Matthew oohed and aahed over the display set off by Michael and Uncle Richie, Grammy about had a conniption when a firework backfired into the trees. But Maddie wasn't too concerned, considering Dad and Mom were with them.

The night began with pizza and a board game. Being the house champion at Scrabble, it was Mom's turn to win the night. She just had a way of spinning up four-letter words that nobody could beat. At five minutes to midnight, they prepared their sparkling grape juice for the yearly toast.

"What are you wishing for this year?" Matthew asked his sister.

"I'd love for it to snow again," she answered. "How about you?"

Matthew cocked his head and looked solemnly up at the sky. "Hmm, I've been thinking about that a lot. I'm praying that nothing bad will happen to you this year."

She loved her brother. Tousling his hair, she said, "Thank you, Bro, I'll join you in that prayer."

Reclining in her chair, she shivered and tightened her blanket as she pondered her brother's heart. Once upon a time, his sweet and innocent prayer would have caused her to worry. But something had changed. In her time with her gram, she was learning how to seek the voice of God. Where she had been waiting for him to speak, Grammy taught her how he had already spoken; she only needed to listen. She was grateful for the time her gram took to help her grow closer to God. She was finally beginning to understand what running to the Tower looked like. Perhaps that's what the man in her dream was also showing her. She had to keep her eyes on the One building her faith. She had to keep her eyes on Jesus.

As he drove over the Tennessee-Georgia line, David looked in the rearview mirror at his sleeping family. His heart was filled with gratitude. He couldn't even be mad over the delay they experienced as they hovered over the Appalachian goodbye. Outside of Wild Rock, everyone was in a hurry. But not here. You would think when it was time to leave, that they left. A handshake or a quick hug was the best you could hope for in the city, but in Wild Rock, saying goodbye was a process. There was a hug, a "see-ya-later," another hug, a "y'all come back now," another hug, then, of course, they had to give you four slices of pie for the road. When the family was finally packed up in the SUV, everyone had to roll their window down to blow kisses. An hour later, they were waving goodbye. David shook his head as he smiled; he wouldn't have it any other way.

He calculated the miles that separated him from his slumber to keep from falling into road stare. When this distraction was no longer enough, he began to think about the case awaiting Daniel Reese and Ambassador Cohen. The overwhelming dread he struggled with before arriving at his mom's house had finally lifted after Christmas, and he felt it was time to contend with the two who appeared to be on the front lines of his forced resignation. He thought they were the only ones who could help him understand what was happening at BALDR Industries.

He had a bad feeling about Lucien Baldur and this Kindness

Tax. Mordy thought the man wanted to use David to get what he wanted out of Israel, but he still didn't understand what he felt he could contribute to his wild scheme.

One thing that he knew was true: something was afoot. David wondered if he should have played into his hand, even for a little while, to see what was rattling around in the man's head, but he couldn't. His mom was right; there was no way he could be even a tiny part of what he knew Lucien Baldur had his hands in. But David wasn't one to back down from a challenge. He was going to find out what this man was up to, one way or another, and it would begin with Reese and Cohen.

If Lucien Baldur thought he could pick a fight to get David out of his way, he was wrong. No, this is war. He thought to himself.

Catching another glimpse of his daughter sleeping quietly in the back seat, he whispered, "Kaitlyn will not have died in vain, my daughter. I promise you this."

CHAPTER 30

A United Front

The annoying buzz would not quit. Maddie hit the snooze button for the second time and rolled over. She couldn't believe Christmas break was over. She wanted nothing more than to be back at Grammy's wrapped in covers as she dreamt of sledding in the snow. Sighing, she rolled on her back and looked up at the ceiling. Well, at least I'll see the Fam today. She thought. As she grudgingly crawled out of bed, her phone buzzed on the bedside table.

Jade: "So, what's the fit today?"

Emma: "Pink sweater and jeans."

Rachel: "Mom got me a cute purple romper for Christmas, so I'm in that with a jean jacket. Hey, do you think I should go with boots or Converse?"

Jade: "Most def the Converse! You'll slay, Rach! Hey, what about you, Maddie?"

Grabbing her towel, she picked up her phone and typed a few words.

Maddie: "Shower. Give me a few."

Once upon a time, she would be anxious about responding right away. Jade, on the other hand, refused to leave a convo hanging. Everyone had to respond, especially after they lost Kaitlyn. Waiting for the water to heat up, she leaned against the wall and closed her eyes. She missed her friend. She would be lying if she said that she was over the trauma of her loss. Grief would hit her like a wave, and then anger and sadness would invite her into dark places. Maddie could hear Sonya's voice, *"Give yourself permission to feel the anger and sadness, then surrender them at the Lord's feet. God blesses us with feelings that serve as flags that signal the depths of our joy and pain. Sweet Girl, he meets you right in that pain and lifts you out of the muck into his healing light."*

As Maddie stepped into the shower, she thought about the painting on Ms. Lorna's piano. The painting of a girl looking up as a hand leaned down. A year ago, the peace displayed in the painting was overwhelming for Maddie—seemingly beyond her reach. Whispering "thank you" under her breath, gratitude filled her as she realized that not only was peace within her reach, but it surrounded her. Before Grammy took her to Wild Rock to pray, she had only experienced fleeting moments of peace, but through the action of breathing in the cool mountain air and feeling the vibration of the words from Psalm 23 fill her soul, it was clear. She had to be intentional about taking time to be still before God. She would have to lay down the distractions that kept her from reaching out to him and seek him first to walk in his peace. Looking up, she followed her gram's model of prayer and praised God for his holiness and faithfulness. She then asked him to walk with her throughout the day and help her stay strong. Finally, she laid down the wave of grief she felt at that moment. Tears welled up and began to flow in sync with the water cascading over her face. "Father, please allow me to walk in your peace today." Suddenly, Maddie felt lighter; almost like a blanket of comfort was wrapped around her. Whispering another "thank you," she stepped out of the shower to dry off.

Wrapped in her bathrobe, she walked to her closet to find something to wear. As her fingers lightly touched each garment, she wondered what Kate would wear on the first day back to school. Kaitlyn's colorful, grungy style contrasted sharply with Maddie's white T-shirt and jeans. After deciding on a purple long-sleeve t-shirt paired with a lace camisole and blue jeans, she pulled her hair into two little buns and added a pair of cute earrings to finish the look. *Perfect,* she thought. Grabbing her phone, she took a selfie and sent it to the Fam.

Jade: "Girl!"

Rachel: "Love the Princess Leia look!"

Emma: "Awe, Maddie, you look like Kate."

Grabbing her book bag, she ran downstairs and grabbed a banana before heading out the door.

"Maddie!"

"Gonna be late, Mom; I'll see you this afternoon." Rushing out the door, she reached the bottom of the stairs before her mom called after her again.

Turning to see her mom standing in the doorway, she said, "Sorry, Mom, I don't want to be late."

Closing the door behind her, she walked toward her daughter and said, "I'll just be a moment. Olivia is picking you up after school. I have a client meeting."

"Yes, ma'am, good luck on your meeting." As she turned toward the bus stop, she stopped in her tracks as she heard her mom's soft reply.

"I love you, Maddie."

She had not heard her mom say those words in a long time. Turning, she smiled and blew her a kiss. "I love you too, Mom." She watched as her mom, smiling, caught the kiss and placed it in her pocket, just as she used to do when she was a little girl. Seeing the bus off in the distance, she began to run so she wouldn't miss it.

With seconds to spare, Maddie happily greeted her best friend while trying to catch her breath.

"I need a hug," Rachel blurted out.

"What's wrong?" Maddie asked.

"Emma was right, you look like Kaitlyn. Was it on purpose?"

Shrugging her shoulders, she said, "Maybe."

"I guess you need a hug, too," Rachel said as she hugged her again.

The girls stood at the bus stop arm in arm as the bus pulled up to the curb. As they giggled and cut up, everyone around them was absorbed in their phones. This was the awkward silence Maddie had grown accustomed to. People didn't know what to say. She wanted to scream at them that sometimes it's okay not to know what to say but to say something. Life is too short to walk in a bubble of insecurity. Unfortunately, she learned this life lesson the hard way.

At the end of the school day, Rachel's mom dropped the girls off at The Coffee Bar. Frothy drinks made for great table talk as they found their spot in the back. It was good to catch up. Maddie shared about Amy Jayne's dad and her brother's decision to follow Jesus. Jade shared about serving with her mom over Christmas. Emma made everyone jealous when she shared about her family's trip to the beach in Florida.

"How about you, Rachel?" Emma asked.

Hesitating for a moment, Rachel looked at Maddie and said, "I have a confession to make, ya'll."

"Oh, is it juicy?" Jade whispered.

Rachel snickered and gave her friend a light push. "Why, just why?"

Jade winked at her friend as she said, "You know you love me."

Shaking her head at her friend's signature primp, Rachel answered, "Yes, I do." Her smile turned serious as she added, "I shared a little with Maddie before the holidays, but I'm struggling. I had a lot of time to sit with God over Christmas, and I think I blame him for what happened."

The girls sat and just allowed Rachel to talk. As Maddie listened to her friend, she knew that out of all the things God was teaching her in this season, this was perhaps her favorite thing. She couldn't explain it, but she could feel God when she shared in the pain of others: Rachel, Amy Jayne, and even her mom. It scared her at first, but there seemed to be a bond created when she truly listened.

"So, what can we do for you, Rach?" Emma asked.

"Can you pray? Pray that I will finally let go of this doubt and anger. I want to know my Father again, like before."

"But what if you're not meant to know him like before?" Maddie asked. "What if he wants you to know him more? Remember when you told me how a seed must die before it can live? Maybe your expectations have to die, too.

"Rachel looked at her friend, "I think that's the most profound thing I've ever heard you say. Tell me what you mean by expectations?"

Truthfully, Maddie wasn't sure where that word came from; it just slipped out, but she had an idea. "Remember when you prayed for Kaitlyn to find Jesus?"

"Yeah."

Slightly uncomfortable with what she was about to say, Maddie just spit it out. "What did that look like for you?"

With a sad smile, Rachel took a deep breath and said, "I had visions of leading her to Christ, of hearing her say the words, 'Thank you Rachel, for saving me.'" Tears began to fall as she shook her head. "But I could never save her, could I? Obviously."

Jade placed her hand on her friend's knee, saying, "No, you couldn't, but Jesus could, you know that. How often has Sonya told us that it ain't gonna be our way, but his?"

"My head knows it, but my heart is broken." Rachel jumped out of her chair and paced behind the table.

"Hey, Rach, come here," Emma said as she grabbed her friend's hand. "It's okay, we're all with you. See that," Emma pointed to the ground, "all those broken pieces are just waiting for God to put them back together. Didn't Sonya say that God turns broken pieces into masterpieces?"

Shaking her head in surprise, Rachel asked, "Do you know what I just realized?"

Intrigued, the girls focused on their excited friend.

"I treated Kaitlyn like a project. Like somebody I had to fix."

"Girl don't go there," Jade said.

"No, hear me out. I was desperate. I would've done anything. Do you know how many times I've yelled at God and asked him why he didn't take me instead? I just wanted her to know him!"

Emma encouraged her friend to sit down. "Rachel, I need to tell you something. You are the kindest, smartest person I know. You weren't desperate; you had God's heart. What was it, Pastor Derrik said? God doesn't want anyone to die, so he's patient to wait for them to come to him. You wanted what he did. But have you ever thought that maybe, in the end, she did say yes to him?"

"But wouldn't she have told us?" Rachel asked emphatically.

"Okay, this is gonna sound really weird," Jade said as she leaned in and looked at each of them. "But I've been reading these stories of evangelists who share the Gospel around the world. You wouldn't believe some of the things they see! Anyway, one of them told the writer about this family shot by mercenaries. The man was in mourning for this family because he had been trying for months to get the dad to follow Jesus. But the weirdest thing happened. He had this dream where he saw the family facing the bad guys, and they were completely at peace. He couldn't understand it. And then he saw it."

"Saw what?" Emma asked curiously.

"Angels surrounded them. Almost like the bullets went into them, but they didn't. Then their spirits just left their body and went up."

"He saw this in a dream?" Rachel asked.

"Yeah. Crazy, right? But he said God's kindness gave him

hope for the dad at that moment. He said sometimes it happens in our last breath."

Maddie smiled. *In our last breath, that was it, wasn't it, God?* She prayed silently.

"Thank you, Jade. I need some of that hope." Looking at Maddie, she asked, "Will you pray for me?"

"Yes, of course," she said as she nodded her head. Grabbing the hands of her friends, they all bowed their heads as Maddie prayed for God to provide the answers their friend was looking for while surrounding her with his peace. After saying amen, she caught a glance of her friend sighing. *She'll be okay, God, won't she?*

A bright red box caught Jade's attention as she stood up to stretch. "It's getting a bit heavy here. Hey, I know, let's play a game!" Grabbing the box, she laid out the cards to play.

Apples-to-Apples happened to be one of Maddie's favorite games. She was always curious at how each of her friends played it so differently. She took each question literally, whereas Jade always made a joke out of the questions on the green apple card. The object wasn't to pick the correct answer but to know the answer the judge would decide. Maddie wasn't very discerning, so she found it hard to get into the heads of her friends, but Rachel, being the most discerning of the four, seemed to know what each of them was thinking. It made for interesting gameplay.

When Jade pulled the green card "trustworthy," Maddie couldn't understand why she chose Emma's red card- "spit" from the pile. "I don't get it," she said.

Hocking a big loogie into her hand, Jade showed it to her Fam and said, "You can always trust that you'll have to spit."

Maddie was relieved to finally feel some of the tension they had all been carrying release as they laughed at Jade's disgusting visual. Mr. C would be proud of them. He encouraged them to have more moments of laughter like this.

As they wrapped up their game, Jade grabbed their attention again. "Girls, we need to return to The Refuge."

Three pairs of eyes glared at her in shock as the tension

returned.

An anxious look on her face, Emma asked, "What do you mean?"

"Before you cancel the idea, hear me out. Mom and I spent a lot of time down there over Christmas. Oh, and Hazel says hello," she said as she winked at Maddie and Rachel.

Maddie immediately softened at the reminder of the woman at the shelter.

Placing cards back into the box, she continued. "We have to go back, otherwise, we'll live afraid. Maddie, didn't you say you had to face your fear with faith after what we went through last spring? Well, I refuse to live in fear."

Quietly, Rachel mumbled, "She's right, we can't hide forever. Kate wouldn't have wanted that."

Maddie looked at her friend and said, "You know our dads will not like this."

"I know." Rachel's eyes narrowed as sighed. "That's why we need to ask and be united in our reason. How many times have they told us they want us to live unafraid? Well, maybe they need to be reminded."

While she knew her friends were right, that old familiar burning sensation arose in her gut. Closing her eyes, Maddie whispered a quick prayer and felt a calm in her spirit. I trust you, God. "Okay, let's do it," she said.

After picking up their things, the girls worked through the details and walked out to Rachel's waiting mom.

As they finished dinner, David's phone began to ring. Ignoring his wife's look of disapproval, he left the table and walked into his office, wondering who would be calling at this hour. "David Bennett," he answered.

"David, this is Gabriel Hawke."

Surprised, David said, "Hello, Senator, this is a surprise."

"Did I catch you at a bad time?"

"No, just finishing dinner. How can I help you?"

"I was wondering if you would be willing to meet me at The Lunch Spot tomorrow. I have some news for you."

Intrigued by the excitement in his voice, David asked, "Of course, what time?"

"Can you meet at eleven?"

"Yes, I can do that."

"Great, see you then." The phone clicked as the line went dead.

At eleven sharp, David was greeted by Mrs. Hawke as he opened the door to The Lunch Spot.

Looking up, she gave him a warm smile as she said, "Commander Bennett, it's good to see you again."

"That's Mr. Bennett," he said, "but you can call me David."

"Why, thank ya, David. But you earned your rank, Sir." Peering at him intently, she added, "Nobody can take that from you."

"You sound just like my Momma."

"Well, your mom must be a wonderful woman." The male voice from the back of the restaurant revealed the Senator as he walked into the room and kissed his mom on the cheek.

Holding out his hand, David said, "Senator Hawke."

A broad smile reached the Senator's eyes, matching the firm handshake he extended. "We've officially had lunch twice; you can call me Gabe." He pointed to a booth in the back and said, "Have a seat."

Mrs. Hawke locked the door and walked to the back to grab their sandwiches.

"Did you and your family have a good Christmas?" Gabe asked.

Impatient to get to the point, David asked, "Yes, but you didn't call me over to make small talk, did you?"

Sitting back in the booth, Gabe nodded toward the door and snickered. "You are just like your dad; he always did like to shoot 'em straight. But I'm a politician, so small talk is my bread and butter."

"Next to kissing babies?"

"Something like that." Smiling as his mom brought their plates, he said, "My Mom makes the best chicken salad. World famous, it is."

"Oh, Gabe, go on now." Turning her head, Mrs. Hawke couldn't hide the bright blush that graced her features. "Y'all enjoy that chicken salad now; I'll check on you in a bit."

As David took a bite, he had to agree with the senator's praise; the chicken salad had a fantastic crunch and a flavor he couldn't quite decipher.

Peering intently at his lunch companion, Gabe said, "I know, right? To die for."

"What is that?" David asked.

"Oh, you mean the apples or the dill?"

Surprised, David looked at the bulging croissant and said, "Hm, that's the crunch. I never would have thought of apples." Placing his hand next to his face, he leaned over and whispered, "I may need the recipe for Momma."

Gabe laughed, "This is why The Lunch Spot is world famous. So, let's get to it, shall we? I assume you have heard about the investigation surrounding Ambassador Cohen and Deputy Director Daniel Reese?"

He lowered his fork and answered, "I heard something about it."

"Do you know what they were after?"

Raising a brow, David repeated, "Do *you* know what they were after?"

"The more I talk to you, the more I hear George Bennett. You know, he would never show his cards to anyone. Not even a poor city councilman."

David could feel the impatience rising again as he retorted, "No disrespect, Senator, but if you think you can soften me with sentimental chatter, it won't work. What were they after?"

"Israel is working on a project called Project Manna. This digitized financial system is much more than just a digital dollar; it is a global banking system that will overhaul our financial system and streamline financial transactions in a way Wall Street never could. And Israel is on the front lines to release this globally."

"So, what would the Ambassador and Deputy Director want with it?" David knew the answer, but he wanted to hear Gabe's take.

"That's what we want to know, but unfortunately, they aren't talking. I was hoping you might shed some light on who they might be working for. We pulled all the emails, and they didn't divulge anyone."

"Last we met, Lucien Baldur's name came up."

The Senator bristled at the mention of the name.

David thought he would circle around from a different angle. "When we met last, you mentioned working covertly to investigate Cohen and Reese; how did that go?"

"Honestly, it was the easiest thing I've ever uncovered. I couldn't believe the audacity of the two using government property in their communications."

David nodded, "Sounds familiar. Everything about the PeaceKeeper mission was like child's play. Nothing was encrypted. It was as if the bad actors wanted to get caught. A bit too coincidental, don't you think?"

"So, is it your opinion that Lucien Baldur was behind the PeaceKeeper mission and the coup to obtain information regarding Project Manna?" Gabe asked.

David leaned forward and looked the Senator straight in the eye, "You said my dad always shot straight; well so do I. I have a question for you, Senator: if you wanted to take over the global financial system while subtly obtaining the world's approval and submission, how would you do it?"

The silence was deafening as the Senator fixated on the far wall. Following his gaze, David read the quote he had seen so many times before, "For I know the plans I have for you, plans to prosper you and not to harm you, plans to give you hope and a future."

"I would devise a plan to lead the world into believing I was here to save them."

A shiver ran up David's spine as he sat back against the cushion. Dread filled him as Gabe communicated what he most feared. He could see Lucien Baldur declaring himself as a savior, but for the world to believe and affirm his declaration was terrifying. The future "plans" David had made to protect his family suddenly took on a whole new meaning. It was time to put them into motion.

CHAPTER 31

True Courage

"No, absolutely not!"

Maddie watched as her dad paced the living room floor. *Deep breath, Maddie,* she thought to herself as she clenched her trembling hands. She had a hundred things she wanted to say but wasn't sure how to begin. Thankfully, she didn't have a chance, as Rachel's dad interjected.

"Rachel, I know you and Maddie have good intentions." Mr. Tom said calmly. "You both served The Refuge well, but you must know that this is a difficult request to consider."

"I know, Dad, and we wouldn't ask if we didn't think this was the right thing to do. Mr. Bennett, that day was the hardest day of my life. And watching you," Rachel closed her eyes as she focused on keeping her breathing steady, "watching you do everything you could to save Kaitlyn; well, that was the most courageous thing I've ever seen. Maddie and I, we just, like. . . You and Dad have always told us to do hard things and to be brave. We can't hide forever."

David clutched the fireplace hearth and pressed his forehead against the cool, dark wood, thinking, *get it together, David.*

The quiet was deafening; Maddie had to show her dad she wasn't afraid. Attempting to swallow the lump in her throat, she sat up perfectly straight and said, "Dad, you are the bravest man I've ever known. You've served your country and this family so well. I know I haven't been the bravest daughter, but

329

in the last year, I've learned so much about what true courage is. And Dad," pushing through her anxious thoughts, she walked over to place a hand on his shoulder and said, "Dad, true courage is trusting that God has me and all of us in his hand, right? If there's one thing I've learned this past year, I can't control what happens in this world, but God can—and knowing that he is in control, I CAN DO hard things. I can be brave. I want to be brave."

David shuddered when Maddie touched his shoulder. *I will not lose my daughter!* He thought to himself, and directly behind that thought came another. *"She's his first, David Allen Bennett."* His momma knew precisely when to rebuke him, even when she wasn't in his presence.

As Maddie lowered her hand, David turned and pulled her into a bear hug. Clasping her tightly, he imagined her as five-year-old Ruthie. Images of Band-Aids and baby tears made him want to weep in her long hair. His daughter wasn't a little girl anymore, and he would have to let her go, but it was the last thing he wanted to do.

As her dad towered over her, Maddie closed her eyes. She didn't want to upset him but wanted to show that she could be strong. Memories of her dad patting her back when she needed comfort led her to reciprocate. As she tapped his trembling back, she said the words, "It'll be okay, Daddy, I promise."

With a chuckle, David looked her intently, and said, "And now you comfort me. Is that how it is?"

Relieved that he wasn't mad anymore, Maddie gave a comforting smile as she said, "You taught me well, Dad."

As the two sat back down, Tom looked at David knowingly and said, "They're right, David. We can't shield them from the world, but we can teach them how to live in it."

Leaning back into the chair, David placed his arms above his head and closed his eyes as he thought reluctantly. *I can't believe this.* Opening his eyes, he looked at the ceiling and took a deep breath. "If I agree to this, it's under my terms, got me?" Turning to Maddie, he looked at her sternly and repeated, "My terms."

Surprised at his quick response, she nodded and said, "Yes, Sir." With eyebrows raised, she looked at Rachel, who smiled slightly and nodded.

The tension in the SUV was thicker than butter.

Since Maddie talked her dad into going to the Refuge two weeks ago, she had been on pins and needles. Her dad had not said a complete sentence to her since that day. She wasn't sure if he was angry with her or just concerned about going.

Looking around the cabin, Maddie could sense that each person was struggling. Wanting to lighten the mood, she asked her dad, "Can we listen to music?"

Taking one of his clenched hands off the steering wheel, her dad looked into the rearview mirror and said, "Oh, yeah, sure."

"Dad, are you okay?"

Looking back to the road, he answered, "Fine."

Maddie turned to look at the non-descript black car following behind them. Dad insisted on having guards as protection.

When the men showed up at their house, Jade gasped as two men six inches taller than her and probably twice as wide stood before her. "I feel safe," she said as she looked at her friends in awe.

Please, God, don't let this be awkward. Maddie prayed silently. Dad's terms were beginning to feel a bit claustrophobic. Today was important for all of them. *How can we serve well with armed guards standing over us?* She wondered.

The song on the radio inspired Maddie to hum under her breath. Suddenly, she could hear Emma harmonizing, after which Jade and Rachel piped in. As the tempo increased, their voices merged into a symphony that ended in laughter as Jade snorted over the closing lyric.

"Why, just why?" Rachel asked as she shook her head.

"You know you love me." Jade responded as she drew her

hands together into a heart.

You could hear a pin drop in the quiet cabin as they drove up to the guardhouse. Maddie's dad spoke quietly to the guard, who looked at the car behind them and waved them both through.

Maddie and her friends walked up the ramp and said good morning to their host, Bob, who was waiting for them.

"I am so glad you ladies decided to come back. We have quite a morning planned. Are you ready?"

"What are we doing?" Jade asked.

Looking at Jade, Mr. Bob asked, "Your mom didn't tell you?"

The girls shrugged as they looked at each other and then back at him.

"Today, we have a special guest who has come to lead the women in Bible Study, and a craft afterward. I want you girls to find a woman to sit with for the morning. Eat breakfast, ask her name, and share life with her today."

"Awesome!" Rachel transformed into her bubbly self as she opened the door to go in.

Never had Maddie experienced a morning such as this. She and Rachel sat with Hazel and a new resident named Gina. Jade and Emma sat with two women—Lila and Beth. After they ate breakfast, they went into a room with round tables covered in craft supplies.

Emma's eyes widened in astonishment when she saw the array of paints and glitter surrounding stacks of paper plates and laminate sheets. Bowls of dried flowers adorned each table with twine and cotton string on either side.

Maddie listened to Hazel tell stories about her daughter as they created their crafts. Looking around at all the women in the room, she couldn't believe they were sitting in a homeless shelter. It felt like a community—a family even. The women knew each other and weren't afraid to call each other out, even as they encouraged each other, but they held each other to a higher standard. It took a lot of courage to live in a place like this. Mr. Bob shared with them that this was their temporary home, and no one took it for granted. Each woman had to respect the other, and for the most part, they did. Thinking back to the PKO, she could see the stark differences. Where the PKO was orderly, quiet, cold, and terrifying. The Refuge was a home filled with hope, life, and encouragement. Both provided for physical needs and helped the residents for their future, but at the PKO, there was no love. God, that's the difference, isn't it? Love. A community is held together with love. Smiling with the realization, Maddie looked at Hazel, who was quizzically peering at her.

"Ya shore did look like you were thinkin' hard right then," Hazel said.

A flash of color brightened Maddie's cheeks when she realized she wasn't listening to her table-mate. "Oh, sorry."

"What'cha thinkin' 'bout?" She asked.

Not wanting to ruin this perfect moment, she remarked, "I'm so happy we got to come today."

Placing her hand on Maddie's, Hazel looked straight into her eyes and said, "Me too, Dear, me too."

It was the perfect day. At the end, Mr. Bob took a picture of the group holding their sun catchers.

As they prepared to leave, Hazel hobbled over to the four girls and grabbed Rachel and Maddie's hands. Without skipping a beat, she bowed and prayed for protection over the girls. Maddie would never forget the words she ended with, "Lord, may ya bless 'em and keep 'em, may ya make yer face to shine upon 'em, may ya turn yer face to 'em and give 'em yer perfect peace."

"What was that prayer, Ms. Hazel?" Maddie asked after she said amen.

"Why that'd a blessin' Ms. Maddie. All the way back to the Book a' Numbers. Ma Lord gave Moses a command fer Aaron, the priest, to bless the Israelites. This blessin' signified the Lord puttin' his name on 'em. A seal ya might say, a seal that tole ever'body who knew 'em that they were the Lord's. And so, you girls are the Lord's. He'll watch over and protect ya, never ya doubt. An' r'member the Good Book says that the Lord'll fight fer ya, ya need only ta be still." With that, Ms. Hazel said her goodbyes and the girls left.

"Why do I feel this is the last we will see of Hazel?" Rachel asked sadly as they walked to the SUV.

Ruminating on her friend's question, Maddie sure hoped she was wrong. Hazel reminded her so much of Grammy. She knew they would be fast friends if they met.

As they pulled into her driveway, the tension that filled the SUV seemed to dissipate immediately. There was a stark contrast between the tension in the car and the peace while serving at The Refuge. It was almost as if a protective bubble surrounded them while they served. She could hear her Grammy encouraging her with, *"Well that'd jes' be how the Lord works, Maddie Ruth. But ya know, ya can have that all day ever' day, jes' seek him first."*

She was learning how to seek him. As they walked up to the house, she remembered Hazel saying something similar, "Ya gotta keep yer eyes on Jesus, Girls, no matter what happens. He will give ya the strength ta get through ever' day of yer life."

That night, Maddie sat with her Bible and journal and drew pictures of the flowers that adorned her sun catcher. She was so excited to hang it in her window, but first, she wanted to draw them next to the blessing Hazel prayed over them. Finding the passage in Numbers Six, she copied it word for word and then colored it with her pencils.

There were several scriptures she had been challenged to memorize. This was one she *wanted* to memorize. Being blessed inspired her to want to do the same for someone else.

January 28
Father,
Thank you for today. Thank you for protecting and allowing us to be with Hazel and the other residents. I don't know what the future will bring, but I'm grateful you are in

it. Help me to trust you in all things. I'm not very good at it, but I want to try. Grammy says that you promised to hear us if we ask anything according to your will. And if we know that you listen to us, that whatever we ask, we will have it. Please protect my family and friends and keep us safe. And Lord, will you help my daddy see you? I want him to know you, too. In Jesus' Name, I pray, Amen."

David closed the door and breathed a sigh of relief. The day was over, and everyone arrived home safely. After grabbing a glass of water, he sat in his high-back chair and closed his eyes.

He had been on more missions than he cared to count; but for some reason, this one was excruciating. While the girls sat with the ladies of the Refuge, he, Tom, and the guards stood watch. By the end of the day, he was as tight as a taut rubber band ready to break.

The retired Navy Seals made a great security team. Tom was a retired Navy Seal himself with many connections. Like David, he was called out of retirement to assist in training the Navy's seal teams. As he traveled the country, he trained the young men who served. His work earned him the respect of many men, who, after retiring, would offer to do side work as needed, such as rescuing David's oldest son from the PKO in California and standing guard for his daughter and her friends. David was grateful for his friend and his Mighty Men.

Massaging his temple, he thought, we can't keep living like this. High stress on a mission was a given, but missions ended, and he couldn't see an end in sight this time. The circumstances swirling around them were getting more and more strange. A psychotic narcissist was running a cult that staged peaceful protests—turned riots, kidnapped innocent people, and expected the world to foot the bill. A righteous chaos all in the name of defeating world hunger. Flash fires were popping up nationwide, while manufacturing and food distribution facilities had to step up security due to daily attacks. The Ambassador and Deputy Director to Israel were staging coups to draw in trusting hackers to obtain intel on a secret financial system. According to Mordy, Israel was planning to roll out said financial system globally that would lead the unsuspecting world into a one-world system. Contemplating the chaos that surrounded them, David wondered, *where does that leave us?*

Before leaving Wild Rock, he and his mom discussed a safety-plan in case things escalated in Atlanta. It looked like it was time to put those plans into action.

CHAPTER 32

An Abomination

Spring had sprung, and Maddie was for it! Two months after their trip to the Refuge, Maddie had a skip in her step as she walked toward the gym to meet the girls. The cherry blossoms were blooming, and the daffodils were showing off. Mom had bought her a new Spring fit and she was pumped! She loved spring, even if there was rain in the forecast.

"Hey, Girl!" Jade hopped onto the half-wall and laid her books down. Whistling, she pulled her shoe up to tie a loose shoelace.

"How'd you do on the math test?" Maddie asked.

Lowering her head, she stuck out her lower lip in jest and said, "Abominably."

Confused, Maddie asked, "And that would mean. . ."

"Unfair, of course." Jade was taking a public speaking course, and she was learning a word a day. Unfortunately, the rest of her squad couldn't make sense of the words she was using half the time, except for Rachel.

"Aah. . ."

"Hey y'all! Guess what?" Running up to meet them, Emma had a white box in her hand.

"What's that?" Jade asked.

"That, my beautiful friend, is an invitation."

"A boxed invitation? To what?"

"You will never guess!" Emma exclaimed giddily. Opening the box, she tilted it so they could see inside. A single pink rose sat inside white tissue paper with a note.

"Is that what I think it is?" Maddie asked.

"Yes! He asked me to prom!" Emma jumped up and down with glee.

"You don't mean Marvin, do you?" Jade asked with skepticism.

"Yes!!!"

Jade crossed her arms and said, "I can't believe that boy said two words to you, much less a whole sentence."

"Oh, he talks more than you think. He just chooses to do so when he has something important to say." Emma looked toward the football field with stars in her eyes.

Rachel walked up behind Emma and hopped up beside Jade. "So, what's the scoop?" She asked.

"Emma's going to prom. . . with Marvin."

"Marvin Steele? He's so sweet. Congratulations, Em!" Rachel smiled at her friend.

"Thanks! Has Jackson asked you yet?"

"Uh, not yet. We're not sure if he'll be here. He's starting workups for boot camp."

"Oh yeah, I forgot he's leaving for the military this summer."

With a frown, Rachel said, "Yeah."

Noticing her friend's countenance change, Maddie cautiously asked, "Are y'all going to continue to talk after he leaves?"

Rachel shrugged. "I don't know. Long-distance relationships are so, you know. Besides, I'll be a senior next year, and I really need to concentrate on preparing for college."

Maddie was trying not to think about her best friend leaving them for college. "You can always go to Kennesaw and live at home. I hear you save a bunch of money that way." Wiggling her eyebrows, she hoped to coerce her friend into staying.

Placing a fallen strand of hair behind Maddie's ear, Rachel said, "I love you, Girl, but you know I want to go to a Christian College."

"Isn't there a Christian College local?" Emma asked.

"Truett-McConnell or Toccoa Falls, but I really want to go to a big campus. So, I'm looking at Liberty, IWU, or SWU."

"SWU-Who?" Jade asked.

Rachel shook her head as she said, "SWU—Southern Wesleyan."

"Now, how was I supposed to know?" Jade asked.

"Well, you knew abominably." Maddie countered with a giggle.

"Abominably? Really, Jade? Use it in a sentence," Rachel countered with her hands on her hips.

Jade placed her hands on her chest and looked in distress toward their friend, saying, "We will suffer abominably if you dare leave us and go to college." After batting her eyelashes, she bowed to Maddie and Emma's roars of laughter and applause.

Rachel laughed as she shook her head, joined the others in a little clap, and said, "Touché."

Later that night, Maddie told her family about Emma's invitation from Marvin. Her mom was ecstatic, while her dad just seemed angry.

"Maddie, will anybody ask you?" Matthew asked.

Frowning, she said, "I doubt it. The only boy who gives me the time of day is three hours away."

Scooping up a spoonful of macaroni, her dad said, "You're too young, anyway."

Worried that her dad wouldn't let her go even if she were asked, she blurted out, "Dad! I'm not too young. I'm sixteen!"

"Well, if you're asked, we'll discuss it." He stated firmly.

Maddie knew her dad's "end of discussion" look. Worried, she looked at him as he focused on his food. He sure was working hard to keep from looking at her. Deciding she would drop the matter and talk to him later, she sat quietly and finished eating dinner.

After dinner, David sat alone in his office. Taking a break from writing, he got up and looked out the window. He sat back in his chair with his eyes closed, listening to the storm raging outside. Deciding he needed to take a break, he wandered to the window, watching as rain angrily pelted the glass and lighting flashed across the sky. The stormy night mirrored his heart's distress.

His family would not like what he had planned, but if it meant his family was safe, he could live with that. His gut told him it was time to act, and it hadn't steered him wrong yet. Things were only going to get worse.

The buzzing on his desk broke into his distracted thoughts. "David Bennett."

"David, this is Gabriel Hawke. Do you have a moment?"

"Yes, Senator, is everything alright?"

"I'm not sure. Things are moving much quicker than I expected. Chaos has taken over the Senate floor, and my sources tell me that an announcement will be made on Monday about Project Manna. Can you meet tomorrow to speak to the Ambassador and Deputy Director Reese?"

"Where are they?"

"They are in Washington. Can you break loose and fly out tomorrow morning?"

Looking at his watch, he wondered if it was even possible. "I don't know if I can get a flight, but if I can. . ."

"No need, meet me at Hartsfield, and you can fly with me."

Surprised at the resources the Senator had at his disposal, he said, "What time?"

"Nine a.m."

"I guess I will see you then." As David hung up the phone, he wondered what he had gotten himself into.

David perused the small C-20A as the private jet left the runway. The jet was designed for comfort, with leather captain's chairs, full-width tables, and a leather couch.

"What do you think?" Gabe asked as he caught David's examination of the cabin.

"I've seen better."

Gabe chuckled, "I'm sure you have."

Waiting for his laptop to boot up, he asked the Senator, "So what is the itinerary?"

"When we land, a car will be waiting to take us to an undisclosed location."

"Do Ambassador Cohen and Deputy Director Reese know we are coming?"

"No. I want to surprise them."

Nodding in half-hearted agreement, David peered out of the tiny window at the disappearing tarmac. An uneasiness filled him as he considered the outcome of this conversation. *What am I being drawn into?* Making a few notes, he glanced at the Senator, who was reading a message on his phone, and then covertly hopped into another application to send a secure message to Mordecai Oronoff.

> *David: Mordy, on my way to DC. It's a sensitive meeting; I need to debrief later if you're available.*

In seconds, he received his response.

> *Mordecai: I've been waiting. I'll be available tomorrow. Let me know.*

What does that mean? He thought as he shook his head. *For someone in the cloak and dagger business, I sure am surrounded by a pile of secrets.*

"David, this could get precarious. I want you to know that we will be completely protected today, but I cannot promise what will happen after this meeting transpires."

And the other shoe drops. "You could've told me that last night before I agreed to come," David said sarcastically.

Gabe lifted a brow and asked, "Would it have changed your answer?"

"Probably not."

The men sat quietly for the rest of the trip. David read through the FBI debrief he gave the Ambassador along with his notes from the mission. He was honest when he said he probably would have come anyway. He wanted answers and felt that the Deputy Director might be in just the right place to give them, or so he hoped.

As the plane landed at Dulles Airport, David could see the black car just as the Senator promised. Not far behind was another with four men in plain clothes built similarly to Tom's Navy Seals standing at attention. He wondered if they knew each other. "Protection, eh?" He asked Gabe.

"Only the best." Nodding, he stepped out and motioned for David to go first.

Paying close attention to their route, he knew immediately that DC was their destination as the car pulled onto I-66. The Senator seemed preoccupied with his phone, so David also decided to pull his out.

The news article on his home screen caught his attention immediately:

Groundbreaking day in Israel.

Clicking into the article, he began to read about a scheduled Passover ceremony to be held on the Mount of Olives in East Jerusalem. The article mentioned something about red cows and the rebuilding of a temple. Copying the link to read later, he placed his phone in his pocket and looked out the window. As they passed the White House, alarm bells went off, and he noticed protestors holding up signs—NO ORDER, NO PEACE.

"What do you know about them?" Gabe asked as he leaned toward David's side of the car.

Hesitating, David gave his carmate a side glance, wondering how much he should share. He believed he could trust the Senator, but he was a politician. His experience with politicians was to share the facts as they revealed themselves but to keep everything else close to the chest. "Well, Senator, it has been my experience that these peaceful protests often precede riots. When I see these signs, I know something is about to go down."

"That's what I thought," Gabe said as he sat back against his seat and proceeded to send a text message.

Early Monday morning, David picked up his phone to dial Mordecai Oronoff.

Suddenly, his office door opened, and his daughter's head peeked in, "Hey, Dad?"

"Not now, Ruthie. I have an important phone call to take."

"But I need. . ."

Covering his phone, David said, "Not now, Sweetie, ask your mom, and we'll catch up this afternoon."

"Okay, love you, Dad," Maddie said.

David fought the guilt that immediately set in as he watched his daughter forlornly close the door.

"Shalom, David!"

Moving his focus back to his phone, he greeted his friend. "Mordy, how are you?"

"Very good, my friend. You should see this view! The night sky over the Aegean is magnificent. We were telling the boys about the myth behind Zeus, Callisto, and her baby bear as we enjoy the beauty of Ursa Major and Minor."

"Where are you anchored?" David asked.

"The Kythnos in Greece. David, when can you join us? We have room for your whole family; just say the word. Benji and Eli talk all the time about meeting your Matthew."

Pushing aside the growing desire to take his friend up on his offer, he wondered where to start. "Thank you for the offer; I might just take you up on it one day."

"Please, do! Hannah is dying to meet your beautiful wife. She claims to have never seen a redhead in person."

Chuckling under his breath, David said, "Nor their temper, I am sure."

He had to pull his phone away from his ear at the sound of his friend's belly laugh.

"So, my friend, how can I help?"

Itching to know what Mordy knew, David asked, "Well, first, I was wondering why you were awaiting my call?"

"I knew it was only a matter of time. Did you know that Project Manna is being unveiled today?"

"I heard as much, yes."

"Well, I expect many of your answers have come to roost."

David laughed at his friend's faux pas. "Do you mean my chickens?"

"Oh, yes, of course. Chickens, why chickens?" He asked curiously.

"I think the saying goes, 'Be careful what you hope for, curses, like chickens come home to roost.'"

"Well, I didn't mean to curse you, David! I will never understand your English expressions. I meant that you must have more answers today than when you started this journey?"

Remembering his conversation the day prior, David couldn't agree more. "Yes, I spoke to Ambassador Cohen and Deputy Director Daniel Reese yesterday."

"You don't say! And how did that go?"

"It was enlightening." Frowning, he continued, "They came just short of naming Lucien Baldur, however."

"David, they will not divulge the evil one. Once they do, they know they are dead men."

"What do you know that I don't?" David asked.

"We've had this conversation before, my friend. And I think this week, everything will be revealed."

Not liking where this was going, he asked, "Besides the unveiling of Project Manna, what happens this week?"

"David, do you remember we discussed the man of

lawlessness?"

"I do. Didn't you say that he was some anti-christ?"

"That is correct. Keep your eyes open this week. I could be wrong, but I believe that prophecy is being fulfilled as we speak."

"What prophecy?" David asked impatiently.

"Just remember, signs, wonders and abominations."

"Mordy, I appreciate your honesty, but you're talking in riddles. What exactly are you telling me?"

"The Bible speaks to the abomination that causes desolation in the book of Daniel. This was a two-part prophecy, the first of which occurred in 70 A.D. when Rome destroyed the temple in Jerusalem. It is possible that we will witness the second half of the prophecy take place this week."

"Are you going to make me read a book of the Bible to find the answer to your riddle?" David asked.

With a scratch of his beard, Mordecai answered, "Hm, that's not a bad idea."

His temple throbbed as he said, "Okay, I was kidding, Mordecai. Please tell me what you are referring to?"

"Today, an announcement will be made about Project Manna. I believe the beast system will be revealed, and on Friday, an abomination will occur on the Mount of Olives."

"Wait, I read something about the Mount of Olives. Do you mean in Jerusalem?" Pulling up the marked article on his phone, he began to read through the text. "Are you talking about the red cows?"

"They are heifers, David, or female cows. In Hebrew, they are called Para Aduma. The parah adumah mitzvah, or law, in the Torah, commands that a red heifer be sacrificed for ritual purification. According to the Mishnah, nine such heifers have been sacrificed; the tenth will be brought by the king Mashiach or the Messiah."

"But I thought Jesus was your Messiah?" David asked.

"Yes, Yeshua, Jesus, is the Messiah; but the High Priests of Jesus' day rejected him and so their descendants do not believe that he is the son of God prophesied by the prophet Isaiah."

"And so, they believe that another will come?"

"Exactly."

"Do you believe that Lucien Baldur is the man of lawlessness?"

"What did the Ambassador and Deputy Director reveal to you, David?"

"They confirmed that the coup was a cover-up, and everything was about to change."

"Hmm, just as we suspected, and?"

"They would be vindicated."

"So, they believe that their accomplice will set them free?"

"Pretty much."

"If you were in their shoes, David, who would have the power to do such a thing?"

Closing his eyes, he rested his head back on the soft leather. *Why do we keep coming back to this?* "Some kind of savior?"

"Hmm, how do you Americans say it? Bingo!"

CHAPTER 33

A Sheltered Fortress

"Ms. Bennett, earth to Maddie Bennett."

The cherry blossom outside the classroom window held Maddie's attention even as her thoughts spiraled. What is wrong with Dad? Suddenly, a shove from behind broke her concentration and knocked her chin off the shelf of her hand.

She turned to glare at the person who had shoved her, her heart pounding as she was directed to the front of the classroom.

"Yes?" She asked, embarrassed.

"Spring break is coming, Ms. Bennett, but can we please focus on math for now?"

"Yes, ma'am." Looking down at her book, she picked up her pencil and began to write on a blank piece of paper. She didn't know what she was writing but wanted to appear busy. Thankfully, Ms. Truett chose not to pick on her anymore after that.

Maddie grabbed her things when class was over and made a beeline for the door.

"Ms. Bennett."

Stopped in her tracks, she turned around and said weakly, "Yes, Ms. Truett?"

"Is everything okay?" She asked.

"Yes, ma'am, why?"

Ms. Truett made eye contact and hesitated. It was clear she wanted to say something but was holding back. "I'm so sorry

347

for what happened to Kaitlyn. I want you to know I am here if you need to talk."

Tears threatened as Maddie saw the empathy in her teacher's expression. Accustomed to stern looks and critical comments, she didn't know what to do with this empathetic Ms. Truett. "I'm okay, but thank you, though."

Looking as if she would say something further, her teacher must've thought better of it as she said, "Okay, I'll see you tomorrow."

Maddie felt a little guilty as she turned to leave, but she knew that if she stayed another moment, she would cry all over her teacher's desk.

Walking up the hallway, she ran into Emma, who looked lost. "Hey Girl, are you alright?" She asked.

"Yeah, I'm good. Having trouble in science." Leaning against a locker, she closed her eyes and said, "I wish Kaitlyn were here," she said.

"Me too," Maddie said, holding her books tighter.

"Hey, Emma." A boy said from behind them.

Opening her eyes, Emma immediately softened as she saw Marvin walk by.

Maddie smiled as her friend melted into a puddle. "Have you thought about what you'll wear to prom?"

"I was thinking something in coral." Emma showed her friend a picture of the dress she wanted. "What do you think about this? Mom and I are going shopping this weekend."

Maddie looked at her friend with stars in her eyes. The dress had spaghetti straps, a fitted bodice, and a full skirt that flowed to the ground. Covered with lace tulle, it was perfect. "You'll look like a princess," she said.

Emma beamed as they left her locker and walked to their next class.

After school, Maddie and Rachel walked to Rachel's house to study. Maddie needed help if she would pass her math test on Tuesday.

Surprised to see Mr. Tom's truck in the driveway, they hurried through the garage to find him in the house.

"Hey, Dad, why are you home so early?" Rachel asked as they stepped into the kitchen.

He hugged his daughter, saying, "Hi Angel, how was school today?'

Giving him a look, she answered, "Fine. What's wrong, Dad?"

Turning away, he answered, "Why would you think something is the matter?"

"Because you typically aren't home this early, and you're not answering my question. Sooo, what's up?"

Rachel's mom walked into the kitchen with her little sister just as he was beginning to answer.

"Hi, Girls, how was school today?"

"It was fine, but Dad was just about ready to tell us something." Looking back at her dad with her hands on her hips, she waited expectantly for his answer.

Maddie watched as Mr. Tom looked at Ms. Olivia with concern. Butterflies began moving in her stomach as she wondered what was happening. Looking at her friend, she could tell that similar thoughts were going through her mind.

Just then, Maddie noticed the television in the corner tuned into the late afternoon news.

> "Susan, thank you for covering this news conference in Israel. Fill us in on the latest developments."
>
> "Bob, the waiting is over. Lucien Baldur has unveiled how he and the world nations will enact The Kindness Tax and end poverty as we know it. He and his business partner have revealed a digital financial transfer system called Project Manna. Let's listen in."

The camera focused on two men dressed in three-piece blue suits with slicked-back hair and a group of men and women surrounding them. Maddie shivered as she looked into the eyes of the two men.

"Thank you to the nations who have wisely aligned to end world hunger. I want to introduce my business partner, Helel, who has brought the parties to the table to bring this monumental plan to fruition."

The man, Helel, stepped up to the podium and spoke with a hefty accent.

"Thank you, Lucien. Yes, with each nation's compliance, I will end poverty as we know it. The plan I have procured from Israel will make participation in this program convenient and transparent. Project Manna will provide a hassle-free means to transfer the obligatory funds required by the PKO without complication."

The camera panned from the conference back to Susan.

"There you have it, Bob. Project Manna will be the vehicle the nations will use to facilitate The Kindness Tax. Can you imagine the time and money saved by enacting a financial transfer of funds that goes directly to the PKO?

"This sounds great, Susan, but is there an option to opt out of this program?"

"I asked this question, Bob, and the answer is no. Lucien clarified that we must provide for the physical needs of those in need."

Mr. Tom and Ms. Olivia looked at each other and then at their daughters. Maddie could tell that something was off, but it didn't look like they were willing to divulge their thoughts.

"Girls, can you go upstairs while your mom and I talk?"

Placing her hands on her sister's shoulders, Rachel led her out of the kitchen as she nodded for her friend to follow. As they walked up the stairs, they could hear the muted sounds of their parents talking.

"What did all that mean, Rach?"

"Honestly, I don't know."

The rest of the week leading up to Easter was chaotic for Maddie and her friends. Buzz around this Kindness Tax and Project Manna had everyone in an uproar. Maddie didn't understand it all but knew it wasn't good when her peers at school were fighting about it. Some said it was good to give to the homeless, while others claimed that it was a denial of their rights. She didn't understand how giving to others denied the rights of another. *I mean, we're supposed to help other people, right?* She mused.

At Church on Wednesday night, Pastor Derrik taught about three men named Shadrach, Meshach, and Abednego, who were forced into a fiery furnace for their faith. The men walked in alone, yet a fourth walked among them. Pastor Derrik taught us that when we walk through our fiery furnace, Jesus walks with us. Our sheltered Fortress, Jesus, protects us while giving us strength so that we, too, will emerge from our challenge unsinged. As Maddie took notes, she drew a picture of the tower she had dreamed of so many times. She named it the Tower of Trust. As she pondered the tower and what it meant, she wrote a prayer:

> *Father,*
>
> *If I ever walk through a fiery furnace, I pray that you will go with me, just as you did for Shadrach, Meshach, and Abednego. I trust you, God, to give me strength, and I pray that you will protect my family and me as a sheltered Fortress, just like Pastor Derrik taught. Help me to keep my*

eyes on Jesus no matter what happens. In Jesus' Name, I pray, Amen.

The girls were out of school on Friday. They decided to have a sleepover at Maddie's to celebrate Spring Break. Rachel brought supplies for mini facials, while Jade brought her favorite movie. Everyone wore their favorite onesie and watched the movie in the living room. Her attention was distracted toward the kitchen, where Maddie watched as her dad frowned at her mom and pushed his hair back from his forehead. She wished she could hear what they were saying.

After the movie, the girls went up to Maddie's room. As Rachel was applying a mud mask on Maddie's face, Maddie asked, "Rachel, have your parents told you what's going on?"

"No. Every time my parents see me, they stop talking."

"Mom's been acting weird, too," Jade said.

"Really?"

"Yeah, we were having dinner the other night, and she was quiet. When I asked her what was up, she shrugged and returned to eating. It was strange. She always tells me what's on her mind."

As Emma applied astringent to her face, she looked into the mirror at her friend's reflection, "Maybe it's time that we confront them and ask."

In agreement with Emma's suggestion, the girls crafted a plan to confront the parents by the end of the weekend. Once the moment's heaviness was over, Emma encouraged a joy break. Maddie pulled up her favorite worship playlist and they spent the rest of the night singing and eating way too much junk food.

In the early hours of Saturday morning, Maddie was suddenly awakened by her dad. "Maddie, I want you to listen to me very carefully."

After rubbing her eyes, she sat up and asked, "What's

wrong, Dad?"

"Just listen to me, okay? Please wake up your friends and have them grab their bags. I want you to grab your book bag, a duffel bag, and a change of clothes."

Alarmed, Maddie said, "Dad, you're scaring me."

"Ruthie, do you remember when you told me you wanted to be brave? Well, this is the time that I need you to be brave. This is not the time to be afraid. Some bad people are planning very bad things in the city, and we must get out of town now. So, I need you to pack a minimal bag. Do you hear me? Grab the necessities only and meet me downstairs."

"Oh, okay, Dad. Do you want me to help Matthew?"

"No, I will help your brother. I need you girls to hurry."

Maddie proceeded to awaken her friends. Everyone hurriedly packed their bags and met Maddie's parents' downstairs.

As they reached the bottom of the stairs, they were surprised to see Rachel's parents, Emma's parents, and Jade's mom standing in the living room. Everyone looked somber and quiet, and nobody knew what to say.

Jade ran to her mom, Alisha, and hugged her. Emma grabbed her mom's hand while her dad, Isaiah, placed his hands on both shoulders. Rachel went to her dad, who put both hands on either side of her face and whispered something just for her.

Maddie didn't know what to say. She wished somebody would say something about what was happening. So many thoughts overwhelmed as she waited quietly for her dad to give instructions.

"Thank you for all for coming. Girls, Matthew, we know this is scary, but downtown Atlanta is on fire, and the word is that the demonstrators are working their way here. I know you have questions, but now is not the time. We must concentrate on getting out of town quickly. Others are making their way out of town, so we will go back roads so as not to get stuck in the traffic."

"We trust you, David," Tom said.

Remembering her prayer from just a few days ago, Maddie whispered it again as she listened to her dad. Everyone would get in their vehicles and travel north to Wild Rock, Tennessee. They were to move quickly since they didn't know how long it would take for the rioters to make it to Marietta. They were not to stop for anyone but to drive straight there. Her dad laid out a map and gave directions, and then everyone got into their cars and made their way.

Driving on dark two-lane back roads was nothing like riding down the lit freeway, but Dad seemed to know where he was going. Maddie laid her forehead against the cool glass. Looking up at the full moon in the night sky, she couldn't help but think about everything that had happened over the last year. *God, please go with us.* She could feel his perfect peace, and she knew without a shadow of a doubt that he was with them.

When she was a child, long road trips would require unique ways to fight boredom. Much to her dad's chagrin, she would draw pictures on the glass. It was well worth the time it took to clean the glass when they arrived at their destination. Since she couldn't sleep, she figured this would be an excellent way to pass the time.

Blowing on the glass, she drew the straight lines of a tower on the glass, with rays of light emanating from the top. She knew that *no matter where they went, she could trust the Lord, her God, to be with her, for the name of the Lord is a fortified Tower; the righteous run to it and are safe.* And with that thought, she closed her eyes and found the slumber she desperately needed.

Epilogue

Sometime in May
Wild Rock, Tennessee

A month after everything changed, Maddie, Emma, and Rachel picked peas, strawberries, and asparagus in Grammy's garden. Taking a bite out of a strawberry, Maddie closed her eyes as she enjoyed the flavor explosion.

"Girls, come on in fer Supper," Grammy called from the back deck.

"Coming, Grammy!" Maddie replied.

"Check out these peas." Emma brought a basket full of plump green and purple pea pods ready to snap. "Momma will be so excited!" She exclaimed as she ran toward the house.

Since everyone had migrated to Wild Rock, Grammy made a point of planting a rainbow of colors for them to enjoy. Giddy, Emma would talk about it whenever she found a new color as if it were a brand-new find.

Maddie and Rachel turned to each other and laughed as they watched their friend. It was the same every day with her. You would've thought Emma would be depressed considering the events of the last month, missing prom, and all, but she loved gardening so much that everything else took a back seat.

Rachel finally had a breakthrough the day after reaching Wild Rock. Maddie could see the change in her friend immediately when her dad and Mr. Tom sat them down and explained how the chaos of the previous year boiled down to harassment. It was weird to think that one man singled out the

Bennett family to coerce Maddie's dad into stealing Project Manna. The mission to Israel, Kaitlyn's social media grooming and abduction, the subsequent kidnapping of Maddie, Rachel, and Jade, Michael's captivity, all roads led back to this Lucien Baldur. Tragically, this man's harassment of their families led to Kaitlyn's death, which was so hard for them to process. Still, through Grammy's coaching, Rachel concluded that God wasn't punishing them after all but was guiding them through.

Project Manna had thrown their lives into a tailspin. No longer could they go to the store and buy anything they wanted. Instead, they had to grow vegetables and eat meat from locally raised animals. Grammy took on chickens and goats to provide eggs and milk while they traded for other foods they didn't specifically grow. It was cool to see how the community came together. There was a pig farmer, a cattle ranch, and even a family of sheep herders in Wild Rock. They only struggled with maintaining a water supply, but Mr. Tom was working on a means to collect rainwater in the water tanks they secured. This would eliminate their need for municipal utilities, which Pastor Ron said could be disconnected any day now.

Dad collected everyone's phones to keep them safe. He said something about getting off the grid or something like that, and Maddie guessed this was what he meant by keeping them safe. She didn't quite understand it, but she trusted that he knew what he was doing. Strangely, they found peace in the chaos, even if life was hard.

While Emma was, in the words of Grammy, in hog Heaven, Jade wasn't so much. She loved the chickens and the goats, but that was about it. When it was time to pick from the garden, she mumbled something about having her feel of gardening at the PKO and made her way to play with the goats instead. Jade made it clear that she wasn't an animal to be caged, and with her mom returning to Atlanta as an essential worker, she felt the itch to follow. Maddie, Rachel, and Emma tried to talk her out of it, but they knew her rebellious heart would not let her stay put.

Maddie's brother, Michael, surprised them all with his

transformation. As he worked with Uncle Tom in his woodworking business, he realized he loved working with his hands. They had cut down trees and made small furniture and tools for the community. Even though he came home every night dirty and exhausted, he loved what he was doing. He loved it so much that he saved all his money and asked Melissa to marry him. Grammy and Aunt Lisa were thrilled!

Grammy took the girls to Wild Rock Overlook to pray each day. She would pray a Psalm 91 prayer of protection over everyone as she taught the girls about intercession. One day, she called each of them Watchmen and led them to a passage in Isaiah sixty-two, giving them the charge to watch and pray in the Lord.

The craziest thing about this season was watching the prophecy Grammy spoke over Maddie come to fruition. Every week, it seemed, another friend from Church would find their way up to Wild Rock. Before her dad took their phones, the girls texted Sonya with Grammy's address. They permitted her to share with people from the Church as necessary. Sonya was an essential worker, like Jade's mom, so she and her family stayed behind in an underground shelter. Still, Maddie and Rachel prayed that they, too, would make their way up eventually.

About a week after Easter, Maddie and Rachel's dads returned to Atlanta. The fires leveled everything to the ground. Maddie couldn't believe it, but the home she had grown up in was gone. Even the police and fire departments were destroyed. The PKO taught her about evil, but this was on another level. *What happened to order?* She wondered.

The night after her dad's revelation, Maddie had another dream. As she walked over the bridge to the tower, a door opened, and a bright light welcomed her inside. Maddie felt a love, unlike anything she had ever felt before.

Grammy told the girls not to focus on all the bad things going on around them but instead to stand on the Name of Jesus and to keep their eyes on him. As she took off her shoes and opened the back door, she had a revelation as she remembered the door to the tower in her dream. It was safe. She felt that same safety as she stepped into the kitchen and smelled all of Grammy's yummy smells. As she watched Rachel and Emma's mom chop up veggies with Grammy and her own mom, she realized that even though the world was burning down around them, God was providing for all their needs, just as he promised. He was trustworthy. *That's why the righteous run to you, isn't it God? They run to you for safety, but more so because you can be trusted with everything.*

In the next month, Maddie would turn seventeen. Her mom asked what she wanted to do for her birthday. Her heart wanted something low-key with her friends and family.

Sitting down at the table her grandfather built with his hands, she was grateful to be surrounded by love. She couldn't think of anything else that she needed except for one.

Bowing her head to pray, she listened to Grammy's prayer of thanks and agreed with an amen. She then followed it with her silent prayer:

> *Father,*
>
> *Thank you for drawing me near to you. Thank you for teaching me to be still. Lord, please go before me, prepare me for what you have for me to do, and grant me the courage to face whatever comes my way. I trust you, God. In Jesus' Name Amen.*

And don't you know that he will?

APPENDIX

Appalachian Dictionary

Grammy was born in Appalachia. The Appalachian vocabulary is very colorful. While this isn't a comprehensive list, you may find several of these colorful sayings sprinkled through the book.

'bout = about	
'Cause = because	
'Cept = except	
'em = Them	
'er = her	
'ere = here	
'fraid = afraid	
'im = him	
'Magine = imagine	
'Mater = tomato	
'maters = tomatoes	
'Nother = another	
'Nough = enough	
'Spect = expect	
'Splain = explain	
S'posed = supposed	
'Tater = potato	
A' = of	
A'course = of course	
Acrost = across	
Acrost the waters = from overseas	
Afeared = afraid	
A'fore = before	
Aggin = against	
A'growin' = growing	
Aimin' = have been going to	
Ain't = is not	

Ain't got a dog in that fight = It's none of my business
Ain't no hill fer a climber = Not a big deal for someone with experience
Anxi'ty = anxiety also Jim Jams = Anxiety (Appalachian)
Any word with "g" on the end is abbreviated with an apostrophe at the end
App-a-LATCH-un = Appalachian
Appa-latch-uh = Appalachia
As the twig is bent so shall the tree grow = The direction you point something/someone in is the direction it/they will go
Back in the day = years ago
Bad off = very sick
Bad turn = someone ill-tempered
Barking up the wrong tree = you're wrong
Bat = quick blink of the eye
Be a-waitin' on 'em at the house = I'll be waiting for them at the house
Beauty never made the kettle sing
Bein' ugly = being hateful, rude, cross, cruel
Beside Oneself = confused or worried
Better git on = need to leave
A bird in the hand is worth two in the bush = It's better to have the certainty of what you do have that the possibility of what you might have
Bite yer tongue = be quiet, don't say it
Black dark = night time
Blackberry winter = time when there is cool weather at the same time as the blooming of wild blackberry shrubs in May
Bless yer pea-pickin' lil heart = you poor, unfortunate soul
Blind house = windowless cabin
Blinked milk = sour milk

Bobble = mistake
Britches = pants
Brung up = raised, as in from childhood
Bugger = frightful (wooly bugger = anyone who is frightful looking)
Buggy = shopping cart
Bumfuzzle = confused or puzzled
C'mon = come on
Cain't = Can't
Cain't tell nobody nothin' that ain't ever been nowhere! = They think they know more than they do
Cain't think of nothin' right off = Can't think of anything at the moment
Cake a' soap = bar of soap
Call on = to visit someone
Care = will do something, don't mind to do something
Carry on = to misbehave
Catawampus = askew, awry
Cause = because
Cheer = chair
Chewed up and spit out = feeling poorly
Chil'ens = children
Chock Full = full to running over
Clean fergot = I forgot
Commode = toilet
Conniption = a mad fit
Could'na = could not
Courtin' = dating
Crayun = crayon
Crick = creek
Crooked as a dog's hind leg = a person who is crooked or deceitful
Cut on the light = turn on the light
Cuttin' up = acting a fool
D'ya = Do you

Dab = cooking measurement – small amount
Dahlin' = darling
Dawg = dog
Did'na = did not
Differ'nt = different
Diggin' his own grave = messing up
Do what? = What did you just say?
Dodge = to avoid
Don't go gittin' yer gussie up = don't get upset
Done = finished
Don't you blare yer eyes at me = don't give me a dirty look
Dope = soda water - coca-cola
Dorter = daughter
Drawers = underwear
Dreckly = directly
Druthers = things one would rather do over anything else
Duns = bills
Ears are burnin' = someone is saying bad things behind your back.
Eat up = consumed. "I'm eat up with love."
Eh law = Oh well
Ever'body = everyone
Ever'time = every time
Ever'where = everywhere
Ever'thin'll be fine, good Lord willin' and the creek don't rise = something should happen unless
Fair to midlin' = I'm okay
Fair up = when rainy weather clears up
Far = fire
Farboard = fire place mantle
Faster thcn a hot knife through butter – fast and easy
Fatback = fatty meat from the back of a hog that is salt cured

Favor = to resemble
Feisty = spunky, lively
Fer = for
Ferget = Forget
Fetch = to get or bring
Finer 'n frog hair = Things are going well.
Fisticuff = a fist fight
Fit = suitable, ready to use
Fit as a fiddle = fine
Fit ta be tied = angry
Fitified = frozen with fear
Fixin' = fixing to or a side dish
Flatter'n a flitter = something is pretty flat
Fler = flour
Flares = flowers (I chose to substitute flow'rs instead)
Foller = follow
Foller = follow
Follerin' = follow
Foretole = foretold
Fotch = fetch
Frail = old, feeble, sickly
Fret = to worry
Friz = frozen
Fuss at = to scold
Gall = nerve
Galoot = an older man who acts like a fool
Gander = look, stare
Garden sass = greens-turnip, mustard, lettuce
Garntee = guarantee
Father up = to assemble; to collect
Gimme some sugar = Give me a kiss
Gittin' = leaving
Gob = a large amount of something
Gom = make a mess or stop up something
Gonna = going to

Go on = talk at length
Good turn = someone with a pleasant personality
Got that straight = You are correct
Gotta = Have to
Gotta = must or got to
Grinnin' like a possum eatin' a sweet tater = someone who is a mite too pleased with themselves.
Hand = worker or hired hand
Hanker = want or crave
Hard feeling = animosity between people
Harder'n a one-eyed man doin' push-ups = Doing something really hard- with all your strength.
Haul off = to take action
He 'bout skeered me outta my house shoes = he scared me.
He ain't got no sense a-tall = He doesn't make any sense
He ain't no count a-tall = of any account
He gets my goose = irritated
He's as crooked as a dog's hind leg = he's a thief
He's as happy as if he had good sense = Happy and that's a good thing
He's crooked as a jay bird = a thief
He's lower 'n a snake's belly in a wagon rut = bad character
He's mad as a mule chewin' on bumblebees! = He's really angry
He's probably just laying off drunk somewheres = drunk and passed out
Heap o' = a lot of
Hear tell = to be informed or learn of
Heared = heard
Hep = help
Hesh up = be quiet
Hissy fit = tantrum

Hold yer horses = wait
Holler = valley
A holler is a place where ya can let yer young'uns run loose cause ya know ya got plenty a time a'fore it gets dark.
Holp = help
Hootenanny = a part with fold music and dancing
Hotter 'n blue blazes = really hot
Hunker = to work in a determined manner
I better git on = I have to leave
I don't chew my cabbage twice = I'm not going to repeat myself
I feel like I've been chewed up and spit out = Yelled at and criticized
I knowed = I knew
I reckon = I guess
I'm just loaferin' today = I'm just hanging out
Ideal = idea
Iffen = if and
Ill = hateful, angry, combative, always ill-tempered.
If I had my druthers = If I had my way
Infare = wedding
In a great while = a long period of time
In under = beneath, underneath or below
Is all = that's all
It's blowin' up a storm = really windy
It's rainin' cats and dogs = it's raining hard
It's never to late to mend = It's never too late to forgive
It's ver' airish = a little bit chilly outside
I've a mind to = of a particular inclination
It doesn't amount to a hill of beans = something that has little of no value
Jack = bust, tear, steal
Jasper = a bad person, a dishonest person

Jaw = talk	
Jerk = pulled	
Jim jams = to be restless or feel anxiety; nervous	
Jes' = Just	
Jist =Just	
Job = poke	
Jump the broom = get married	
Jumped out of the fryin' pan an' into the fire = someone went from one bad situation right into another	
Keer = care	
Kilt = past tense of killed	
Kin = family	
Kinda = kind of	
Kindly = kind of, somewhat, rather	
Knee-high to a grasshopper = someone or something is short	
Knee-deep = a bull frog	
Knock a tater in the head = Let's go eat	
Knows'll = knows will	
Knowed = past tense of know	
Laid up = sick, hurt, bedridden	
Latch = lock, close	
Lay down = to give up or surrender	
Leastways = at least, at any rate	
Leave things in the floor = leave things on the floor	
Lemme' = let me	
Lessen = unless	
Let on = pretend	
Lie down with dogs and you'll get up with fleas = bad pals will rub off on you	
Like it or lump it = deal with it	
Lil' = little	
Lipping full = filled to capacity	
A little birdie tole me = Juicy gossip that you don't	

want to share who told
Lookie = look
Lookie here = Look here
Lookin' like the hind wheels o' destruction = You look terrible
Looks to me like = I agree
Lotta = lot of
Ma = my
Makin' a mountain outta molehill = exaggerating
Mayhap = perhaps and maybe
Meaner 'n a wet hen = making someone really mean or meaner.
On the Mend = to improve in health
Mess = enough food for your family
Might could = it's a possibility
Mighty = very, especially, exceedingly
Mill over = to study or ponder
Mind = to watch or attend
Mite = little
Mizzle = fine misty rain
Mock = imitate
More'n = more than
Mushmelon = cantaloupe
N'er = never
Nary = none, not one
Naw = no
Near about = nearly
Never get yer horse in a place where ya cain't turn 'round = don't do something you'll regret later
Never mind = makes no difference
No bigger 'n a minnow in a fishin' pond = not very important.
No count = of little value
No how = in any case
Not shore = not sure or Shore = sure

Notion = inclination
Now that's the pot callin' the kettle black = don't criticize someone for something you do
Now y'all don't be bad-mouthin' her = Don't talk about her in a mean way.
Of a mind to = to decide to do something
Offer = To try
Offish = quiet, unfriendly, hard to get to know
Ole = familiar with somethin', an attachment.
Oh, my country alive = an expression of unbelief
Old as methusaleh's housecat = pretty old
Oodlins = a large amount
Ornery = hard to deal with or get along with
Outlander = a stranger; outsider
Paper Poke = a bag to carry groceries
Pick = to play a stringed instrument
Pick'n' grin'n = A party with stringed instruments
Piddlin' = dawdling, wasting time doing something
Pig in a poke = not having all the information about what's about to happen
Pinch = small amount in cooking
Pitch a fit = to become uncontrollably upset
Plumb foolish = stupid (Plumb added to a word = completely)
Plumb give out = exhausted
Plumb tickled = pleased to hear
Plumb wore out = tired
Point blank = exact; precise
Pot callin' the kettle black = accusing someone of something you're guilt of
Pole cat = skunk
Pray'r = prayer
Prouda = proud
Puny = sick or sickly feeling
Quit piddlin' around and get ta work

R'call = recall
R'member = remember (In a command, you always say r'member)
Racket = a noisy fight, a sudden loud occurrence
Ragler = regular
Rare up = to raise up
Reach me a = hand me a
Recollect = remember to do something
Reckon = suppose
Rern = ruin. Past tense: rernt
Resternt = restaurant
Right quick = quickly
Right smart = pretty good amount
Righter'n rain = You did that correctly
Rightly = correctly
Riled up = angry
Ruckus = a commotion
Ruination = total destruction
Run together = spend time together
Salat = salad
Ser'ous = serious
Settin's cheaper'n standin' = sit down and rest yourself
She's as pretty as a peach = she's pretty and sweet
Shine = to like
Shiny britches = dress pants
Shivaree = a loud noisy celebration occurring after a wedding
Sight = a large amount
Sigogglin = not built correctly, skewed or out of balance
Silly ole' me = I should have known better
Sit with me a spell = sit with another typically for conversation
Skedaddle = leave immediately

Skeered = scared
Skift = A dusting of snow
Sleep tight, don't let the bed bug's bite = can lids filled with oil were placed under each bed post to discourage "bed bugs" – this was a hint that it was time to leave.
Slew = a large amount
Slip off = ran away and got married
Slower than a Sunday afternoon = slow
Smack = to chew loudly on food
Smidgen = small amount in cooking
Sorry = worthless
Stout = physical strong
Stove up = hurt, arthritis
Sweet milk = regular milk (as opposed to buttermilk)
Sweet on = you like someone
Swipe off = to wipe off
T'know = to know
Ta = to
Take after = to inherit qualities from someone
Talkingest = talkative
Tell a man what fer = tell him off
Thar' = there
Thar's a fox in the hen house = someone is somewhere they don't need to be
That dog don't hunt = the story doesn't add up
That possum's on the stump = that's as good as it gets
Thataway = that way
Them polecats are from my neck of the woods =
Thick = dense, numerous, plentiful
Thick as fleas on a dog's back = Where there is a lot of something- such as a crowd
Til the cows come home
Toboggar = snug wool cap- like a beanie

Tole' = told
Too big fer his britches = conceited, self-important
Tore up about it = upset
Torn up = something is broken
Tote it in the house = carry it in the house
Upscuddle = A quarrel
Ustocould = past tense of could
Varmint = a wild animal
Ver' = very
Wanna = Want to
Want'cha = want you
Warsh = wash
Warshed = washed
Was you born in a barn? = shut the door or you don't have manners.
Ways = a distance
Worter = water
We just live right 'round the bend = we live around the corner
Weddin' without courtin' is like vittles without salt = salt seasons food just as courting prepares for and seasons a marriage.
Well, I'll be = surprise or astonishment
Well, it's six of one, half dozen of the other = no difference between two choices
Whaddya' = What do you.
What can't be cured must be endured = Be patient and endure
Give someone what fer = Going to tell them just what you think
What's got yer bee in a bonnet = someone who is agitated about something
Whatch'all = what are y'all
Whatcha' = What are you
Where thar's bees thar's honey = something

attractive to a person or group
Whoo-wee = astonished
Whoo-wee doggee = astonished
Whoop and a holler = a short distance
Winder = window
Windshaken = a crack or twisted grain in timber, produced by high wind
Woulda = would have
Ya = You
Y'all = You all
Y'all come back now, ya hear? = Come back soon
Yassir = yes sir
Yer = Your
Yer not from 'round these parts are ya? = You're not from around here, are you?
Yer slower than molasses = slow
Yonder = Over there
You favor yer Momma = You look like your mom
You'ns = You all
You'ns ain't seen me in a coon's age = You haven't seen me in a long while
Young'un(s) = One or Multiple young people
Younger'n = younger than

Many thanks to:

Backroads Living
Blind Pig & the Acorn
Directory of Smoky Mountain English
Dancing on Mountaintops
These Storied Mountains – John Parris
Three Ladies and their Babies
And many more who lovingly share the beautiful Appalachian culture.

Acknowledgments

Thank you to my Heavenly Father for pouring Your Word into me and giving me a deep desire to serve you. May You be glorified by this work.

To my amazing husband, Tony. When the Lord laid this daunting task on my heart, I had no idea where to begin. You encouraged me through your excitement. You led me to people and places that would help me on my journey. I am so grateful for your support my Love!

Mom, thank you for loving us always. I am eternally grateful for the life you gave and the love you taught. Thank you for sharing with us your love of reading.

To my Grandmomma and Granny, thank you both for being my Grammy! Your love and consistent faith have helped me on my journey. I am forever grateful for your prayers over my life.

To my sisters, Jennifer, Patricia, Amanda, and Beth, thank you for helping me to become a better sister.

Thank you, Lauren, for helping me to sort out my jumbled thoughts and make them legible. Thank you for being a prayer warrior and an encouragement master. You never let me quit and for that, I am eternally grateful. Now go write that story!

Thank you, Natalie, for dotting my I's and crossing my T's. You make me better.

Derik, you unlocked the zeal for God's Word within me that I never knew I had. You had no idea that as you taught my girls, you were teaching me. God has changed my life through His word. I thank you for allowing Him to work through you.

Dave, thank you for leading students so well. Your intentionality makes *others feel seen. We are eternally blessed through your shepherding heart.*

To my Flourish girls, thank you for saying yes. You have forever marked me with your love for the Lord. Thank you for allowing me to be part of your journey.

To every young woman who has allowed me the honor of walking alongside you, thank you. You have blessed me in your journey. Keep the faith, Beautiful, and run your race knowing that God is with you always.

Nelum, thank you for your yes to Jesus! I am so thankful for your servant's heart and for all that God does through you. It is an honor to serve alongside you, my sister!

Olha, thank you for your beautiful photography! You have a beautiful eye for God's creation- may the Lord bless you and keep you always. You can find Olha and her journey at life.by.olia on Instagram and YouTube.

Rachel, you are a world changer, my friend! Thank you for shining the light of Jesus everywhere you go.

Thank you to my launch team! You have inspired me more than you know.

Thank you to the many who publicly share the life and speech of our Appalachian neighbors. And a special thank you to @CelebratingAppalachia for sharing the love of your culture so well. Your heritage is rich and beautiful my friends!

Thank you to the Spy Museum for your intriguing language of espionage.

Thank you to the courageous warriors who gave God their yes and embarked on the voyage of a lifetime to this new world. Thank you to those who share the covenant made when a group of settlers touched the shores on this nation in 1607. You can find the covenant prayer and petition here: http://1607covenant.com.

Thank you to every reader who joined me on this journey. I hope you loved it as much as I did. If so, please take a moment to post a review and tell a friend.

Thank you to Creative Fabrica and designer genesislabstudio for the beautiful Malibu Script Font used under license for the book and chapter titles.

I love feedback! You can submit feedback and suggestions directly to me on my website at https://adaughtersjourney.net.

<u>**Additional works from Eve M. Harrell**</u>

Confessions:
A Mom's Journey from Hovering to Hope

Hello Beautiful:
See Yourself Through the Father's Eyes

Hello Beautiful:
Companion Journal

Running with Zebras:
A Daughter's Journey Through the Fire

Revealed Book Series™
Book 1 – Revealed Truth: A Journey from Fear to Faith
Book 2 – Revealed Mercy: A Journey to the Tower of Trust
Book 3 – Revealed Courage: A Journey Forged Through Fire
Book 4 – Revealed Hope Coming 2026!

Revealed: A Journey Through Prayer Journal
Revealed Pocket Journal
Living Revealed: A Discipleship Journey

THE NAME OF THE LORD IS A STRONG TOWER;
THE RIGHTEOUS RUNS INTO IT AND IS SAFE.
PROVERBS 18:10

About The Author

Eve Harrell and her husband, Tony serve their local church as Small Group Leaders to some amazing future leaders. In addition to serving students and their leaders, Eve encourages women of all ages to rest in the love of their Heavenly Father.

Singing, blogging, speaking, writing, spending time in nature, and watching others find freedom in Christ are some of Eve's favorite things.

Eve's passion includes encouraging the next generation to recognize the great value, purpose, and strength they have been given while finding the Father's little gifts along the way.

You can connect with her at https://evemharrell.com.